HINDSIGHT

IRIS JOHANSEN

ROY JOHANSEN

GRAND CENTRAL
PUBLISHING

LARGE PRINT

Copyright © 2020 by IJ Development, Inc., and Roy Johansen

Cover design by Flag. Cover copyright © 2020 by Hachette Book Group, Inc.

Grand Central Publishing

Hachette Book Group

1290 Avenue of the Americas, New York, NY 10104

grandcentralpublishing.com

twitter.com/grandcentralpub

First Edition: January 2020

Grand Central Publishing is a division of Hachette Book Group, Inc. The Grand Central Publishing name and logo is a trademark of Hachette Book Group, Inc.

The publisher is not responsible for websites (or their content) that are not owned by the publisher.

The Hachette Speakers Bureau provides a wide range of authors for speaking events. To find out more, go to www.hachettespeakersbureau.com or call (866) 376-6591.

Library of Congress Control Number: 2019948240

ISBNs: 978-1-5387-6292-9 (hardcover), 978-1-5387-3405-6 (large print), 978-1-5387-6291-2 (ebook)

Printed in the United States of America

LSC-C

10 9 8 7 6 5 4 3 2 1

HINDSIGHT

CHAPTER

1

BAGRAM AIRFIELD
AFGHANISTAN

I'm going to murder him!" Kendra Michaels jumped out of the open jeep and stalked across the tarmac toward Jessie Mercado, who was standing in front of the waiting C-130 transport plane. Her eyes were glittering with rage as she hissed through bared teeth: "You're not going to talk me out of it, Jessie. I'm going to kill Adam Lynch."

"I wouldn't presume to interfere," Jessie said soothingly. "I'm sure he deserves it. But might I point out that you're the one under arrest and he seems to have all these military types at his beck and call? It might be a bit awkward." She glanced at the name tag of the army private, who couldn't have been more than twenty, scurrying desperately after Kendra. "Isn't that right, Private Dalrymple?

I'm sure your superior has told you that she's not allowed to kill Adam Lynch."

The soldier was having to catch his breath as he reached them. "I don't know anything about Adam Lynch, ma'am. I take my orders from the general." He gazed reproachfully at Kendra. "You shouldn't have tried to run away from me, Dr. Michaels. No one is trying to hurt you."

"Only trying to toss me out of this country," Kendra said coldly. "And I didn't *try* to run away, I succeeded." She glared at Jessie. "If you'd had your motorcycle, I would have been able to get away from my jailer here and gotten back to those poppy fields where I might be able to do some good."

"After you kill Lynch," Jessie murmured. "Sorry, the MPs made me leave my Yamaha at the hangar."

"I'm not your jailer, Dr. Michaels." Private Dalrymple looked pained. "I'm your official escort. And I was ordered to show you every courtesy until I could turn you over to General Kotcheff here at the base."

"So that he could 'courteously' kick me out of Afghanistan?" She was still steaming as her gaze shifted back to Jessie. "This kid showed up at my hotel room an hour ago to tell me that my visa had been revoked and that I was being put on the next transport back to the U.S. Can you believe that?" Her eyes suddenly narrowed on Jessie's face. "Oh, yes, you can believe it. I don't see any signs that you had your very own jailer toss all your belongings into a suitcase to put on this transport. That means they're not kicking *you* out, even though we came here on the same mission. That's why you're here. I *knew* that Lynch was responsible. He was pissed off at me. And he was the only one who had the kind of influence and contacts to get this done. Lynch sent you, didn't he?"

Jessie nodded. "He said that you were angry and you'd run out of his hotel room before he could look at that wound in your arm. He asked me to check it out."

"He was the one who was angry. I was trying to reason with him. He was yelling at me." But she hadn't dreamed he'd been this pissed off. "And it's only a flesh wound."

"Then you won't mind if I take a look?" Jessie was suddenly standing next to Kendra and pushing up the sleeve of her cotton shirt, carefully lifting the bandage to examine the small wound. "You're right, this is practically a nonissue. He was worried for nothing."

"That's what I told him. It hardly bled at all. You can see that." She threw out a hand to indicate Private Dalrymple. "That's all, so will you tell this . . . this . . . escort to take me back to my hotel."

"Not quite all. I'm afraid I can't tell anyone to do

anything." Jessie made a face. "They wouldn't even let me keep my motorcycle, remember? You're stuck. You're right, Lynch did do this, and I have no idea why. It probably had something to do with that wound. I'll try to get it out of him later. I only came because you're my friend and I didn't want you to face this alone." She added dryly, "Though Lynch also mentioned he needed someone to keep you from causing a major uproar that would draw more attention to you."

"And he thought you'd do it?" she asked silkily. "He was right not to come himself, I'm feeling lethal. But I'm not pleased that you decided to let him get away with this."

"'*Let* him'?" she repeated ruefully. "You know better than that, Kendra. Adam Lynch is the black ops specialist everyone calls when they want to bring down a regime. He has more influence than half the governments and mega-corporations that hire him. What made you think I could stop him?"

Kendra knew that was true, but it didn't make her less irritated. "It would be nice if you'd made the attempt. The three of us came here to get a job done. I was so damn close last night, Jessie."

She soberly shook her head. "I didn't have the right to make the call. Lynch doesn't usually go off half-cocked, and when he phoned me this morn-ing, he was close to exploding. He didn't tell me what happened in that poppy field last night, but you scared the shit out of him."

"I only did what I was supposed to do, what I'm fully capable of doing. He had no right to step in and stop me." Kendra was growing more angry. "Would he have stopped you? Hell no, he would have treated you with the respect you deserve. Because you had two tours here in Afghanistan and a background as a private investigator—I couldn't agree more that you're super qualified. But that doesn't mean that it's fair to ignore the fact that I might have my own capabilities."

"Bullshit." Jessie grinned. "You know damn well Lynch respects your 'capabilities.' His problem is that he's a good deal too involved with certain other qualifications you display that have absolutely nothing to do with what's going on in your head."

She didn't want to hear that right now. "Then he should concentrate on what's important. The truth is that he never wanted me to come here anyway and he's using this as an excuse. And you should never have agreed to carry his water for him. This has put me in an intolerable position, and I won't—"

"Intolerable?" A booming voice behind Kendra caused her to whirl to face a tall officer with iron-gray hair who was getting out of his jeep. Both his stripes and the fact that the young private was at full attention indicated that this was the Brigadier General Kotcheff for whom he'd been waiting. He was gazing sternly at Kendra. "That's a very harsh word when we're trying to make this departure as comfortable and easy for you as possible, Dr. Michaels." He turned to Jessie. "You're Ms. Mercado? When I spoke to Adam Lynch, he told me that you'd make our task easier. I don't see any signs of that."

"Then you'll have to take it up with him," Jessie said. "I'm sure you won't have any objection to doing that. He's so easy to deal with."

Kotcheff's stare became even cooler. "That's not been my experience. But we're always willing to work with him when he requests a favor. It usually pays dividends."

"Does it?" Kendra took a step toward him. "And interfering with my rights as an American citizen is worth that payoff? What the hell happened? Look, together with Adam Lynch and Jessie Mercado, I've been investigating Brock Limited, a government contractor that's been sharing space on your base. That investigation has led us from San Diego to Kabul in search of evidence that would reveal the corruption Brock has been spreading throughout the world. You can't do this. I'm not finished with my job here yet."

"You are as far as we're concerned. I'm afraid you've been a disruptive influence."

She gazed at him, stunned. "I've only been here for three weeks. Even I couldn't disrupt much in that time."

"You underestimate yourself," Kotcheff said sourly. "It appears that you caused something of an upset last night in Nurestan Province. In a war-torn country like Afghanistan, that sort of behavior can't be permitted. You'll have to leave."

"What? Nurestan? There's no way you could possibly know what happened there last night." She paused. "Unless you were told." She took a step even closer to him. "Perhaps by our friend Adam Lynch?" Her hands knotted into fists at her sides. "Dammit, you can't *do* this to me."

"On the contrary, I can do anything I please on this base. You're the one who has no business here." His lips twisted. "From your dossier, it seems you're only a music teacher without even the credentials that Ms. Mercado possesses." He yanked his thumb at young Private Dalrymple standing beside him. "Even this private has far better skills and qualifications than you. I find it incredible that you were even given a visa in the first place."

Lord, he was arrogant. "Music *therapist*. I'm very proud of working with those children. But I do also have an affiliation with the FBI." She was trying to hold on to her temper, but she was afraid it was a lost cause. "And I'm beginning to find it fairly incredible that someone actually thought you could command this base."

"Oops! Easy, Kendra." Jessie turned toward the general and said quickly, "It's true that Kendra works closely with the FBI and definitely has qualifications they find irreplaceable. I imagine even you might have found that out if you'd done more than just scan her paperwork. She deserves your respect. It would be smart of you to show it."

"You're giving me orders?" A faint flush stained the general's cheeks. "You'll be lucky if I don't send you out on this plane with her. I'm done with this discussion. The FBI has no jurisdiction outside the U.S. You and your colleagues were only here because someone in the Justice Department pulled strings for you." He added, "And you're going home for the same reason."

Kendra stared at him. "And isn't it odd that Lynch has so many dealings with the Justice Department?"

"I don't find it at all unusual. I hear he has influence in a number of quarters."

"Give it up, Kendra," Jessie murmured.

"The hell I will." She had to make one more try. "Give me time to figure this out, General. I just need another few days. There must be a mistake."

"Figure it out stateside. Our planes run back and forth every day, Dr. Michaels."

Kendra glanced up to the plane's forward door, where a young soldier was looking expectantly at her. She shook her head and muttered a curse beneath her breath. "I can't *believe* this is really happening."

"Believe it," the general said. "And accept the United States Army's wishes for a safe flight home." His smile was both snide and dismissive.

Kendra wanted to turn and run, but she knew that would only result in a pair of handcuffs and a trip to the stockade.

Shit.

General Kotcheff impatiently motioned toward the plane. "Dr. Michaels, you can get on this aircraft under your own power, or four MPs will pick you up and place you aboard."

Jessie instinctively took a protective step closer to Kendra. "They're not fooling around. I know you're pissed off, but try to hold it together."

"I am." She watched as her duffel was loaded into the plane's cargo hold. "Not easy."

Jessie shook her head. "I'm sorry, Kendra."

"It's not your fault. It's Lynch's. Even if we'd come up with nothing, I wanted to see this through to the end. I hate it that I almost had them." She added fiercely, "But don't you give up on it, Jessie. I gave Lynch the key to finding those documents. You get it from him and go after those bastards."

"You know I will."

Yes, Kendra knew that Jessie was as dedicated and passionate as she was about arresting the crooks who had not only cheated soldiers who'd given their lives and service here in Afghanistan but had actually condoned murder. The knowledge didn't help; Kendra still wanted to be here with Jessie when she brought them down. "Yeah, just do it soon. Tell Lynch that I didn't go through what I did last night to have him take his own sweet time about doing a search."

"I'll tell him. Do you have any other message for him?"

"Flip him off for me. Both hands."

Jessie chuckled. "I can do that."

"On second thought, no. No message. Tell him to not try and get in touch with me."

Jessie's smile faded. "Kendra…" She shook her head. "That's not going to fly. We both know it."

"I'm serious. I'll reach out when and if I'm ready. Until then, I don't want to hear from him."

"Yeah, sure."

"Dr. Michaels." General Kotcheff gestured to the plane, a self-satisfied smirk on his face.

"I'm going, dammit." Kendra threw her arms around Jessie. "Stay safe, okay?"

"Absolutely."

Kendra pulled away, turned, and gave a curt nod

to General Kotcheff. She started toward the plane. But he was still smirking. It was just too much to bear. She suddenly whirled back to face him. "What an asshole bully you are. I can tell you're enjoying this. Do you know how much I hate bullies? I've known so many people like you."

"You know nothing about me, Dr. Michaels," he said coldly.

"Don't I?" She slowly stepped back toward the general and looked him up and down. "I know you've been spending a lot of time at Kolula Pushta Road lately."

Kotcheff blinked. "Who told you that?"

"No one. I'm only going by what I see despite the fact that I'm just a lowly music therapist. You don't wear your uniform there, which is probably a good idea. I think it's good you go there, relax, and blow off steam. What's your average?"

He was staring at her indignantly. "Excuse me?"

"You enjoy bowling." She let the words rattle out swiftly, accurately. "And fishing. I think you probably have your own boat back home, maybe on Lake Huron? You fish, but you also do some diving."

Kotcheff's jaw dropped.

"You grew up in the South but later moved to Michigan. Your family is still there. You saw them recently, in the past few weeks. They must miss you. It's lucky they don't realize what an asshole you are when it suits you. They'd be shocked and disappointed. But you're also diabetic, so I hope you're taking good care of yourself here."

Kotcheff was now glaring at her in horror, struggling to speak.

Should Kendra go for it? Hell, yes. "Oh, and one more thing." She was smiling recklessly as she took another step closer to him. "You're a by-the-book kind of guy, so I'm surprised and impressed you're rebellious in one aspect of your miserable, boring existence: You're wearing bright red underwear."

Kotcheff immediately looked down at his crotch in alarm.

"Don't worry, General. Your fly isn't open."

Kendra bounded up the stairs to the plane's forward door, which immediately closed behind her.

◆———◆

"What the hell?" The general was staring after her, stunned. "How could she know all that?" He turned indignantly to Jessie, who was bent double, tears of laughter running down her cheeks. "Stop laughing, damn you."

"I tried to tell you. I could see it coming." Jessie was trying to stop laughing, but she couldn't do it. "But you deserved it. Good for you, Kendra." She caught another glimpse of the general's baffled expression and broke down again. "Dear God, your face . . ." She took a deep breath. "How could she know it? Kendra was blind until she was twenty, and by then, like all blind people, she'd trained her other senses to be ultrasharp to compensate. When she underwent a stem cell operation that gave her sight, she became the complete package. She takes nothing she sees for granted. She notices *everything*. Do you wonder why the FBI considers her irreplaceable?" She started to laugh helplessly again. "And do you still think your Private Dalrymple here is more qualified than her? I really must get his input on that bright red underwear!"

———◆———

She shouldn't have mentioned the red underwear, Kendra thought as the C-130 took off. It had probably been the crowning blow as far as Kotcheff was concerned. She'd held on as long as she could, but he'd been so damn obnoxious. She'd be lucky if that pompous asshole didn't scramble some F-18s to shoot down the plane. Yet she hadn't been able to resist that last parting shot. She had been so angry and frustrated . . . and hurt.

Face it: Not about the smirking general, about what Lynch had done to her.

Yes, she had tried to smother it, but there had

also been hurt mixed up in all those other emotions she had felt toward Adam Lynch today. How could there not be after these years when they had been friends and partners, solved cases, laughed, gone through terror, watched each other's backs, while constantly growing closer and closer?

Until only recently when that inevitable sexual explosion had almost torn her apart.

Don't think about it. She had been right to try to take an immediate step back after that mistake. She had a career, friends, and a mother, all of which filled and enriched her life. She had no need of Lynch and he clearly had no need of her if he could betray her as he'd done today.

Her satellite phone was ringing. She glanced down at the ID.

Adam Lynch.

She let her voicemail pick it up.

Four minutes later her phone rang again.

Lynch.

Screw him.

She turned her phone off.

She leaned back and closed her eyes. Concentrate. She couldn't let Lynch do this to her. Try to think of a way to pull enough strings to get her visa reinstated so that she could go back to Kabul...

"Dr. Michaels, you have a telephone call." She opened her eyes fifteen minutes later to see a very irate copilot glaring down at her. He thrust his phone at her. "I have orders from General Kotcheff that you're to take this call. I'd appreciate you doing it immediately so that I can have my phone back." He added sarcastically, "There just might be an emergency."

He turned on his heel and strode back to the cockpit.

Kotcheff? He must have been even more pissed off than Kendra had thought.

She lifted the phone to her ear. "You're not going to get an apology, Kotcheff."

"I don't believe he expects one," Adam Lynch said. "He's too busy gathering the shards of his dignity around him at present. Bright red underwear, Kendra? Seriously? Now, I can wait for you to tell me how you knew the rest of it, but I really have to know about the red underwear."

She stiffened. "I'm hanging up, Lynch."

"I don't think so. That copilot would only get another call from Kotcheff, and that would further indicate what a disruptive influence you can be. You might never get your visa reinstated. Wouldn't it be simpler to just talk to me and get it over with?"

"No." But she had to consider her options. It wasn't smart to let stubbornness get in the way of long-term goals. "Nothing is ever simple with you, Lynch. Particularly the outrage you've managed to concoct this time." She paused. "You talk, I'll listen. Then I get to hang up and forget about you. I only have one question I want you to answer: How the hell did you have the nerve to go to these extreme lengths just to get me thrown out of Afghanistan?"

"With equally extreme trepidation. You can see how terrified I was if I had to send Jessie to keep you from blowing up the base."

"I noticed you decided to cower at a safe distance and let her take the flak. You didn't even tell her what happened last night. Were you afraid she'd agree that I was right and not let you get away with this?"

"There was always that possibility. Jessie is super sharp and she wants to bring down Brock Limited as much as you and I do. She might have thought that I was wrong." He chuckled. "Ouch. That hurt. Naturally, she'd be wrong, but there's still a sting to my ego."

"*Gigantic* ego," she amplified. He was taking this too casually. She could almost see him sitting there, those movie-star good looks, the blue eyes dancing with mischief. "But you went too far this time, Lynch."

He was silent. "I don't agree. I only hope I went far enough." He paused. "And the reason I sent Jessie was that I was too busy trying to pull this situation out of the toilet to come myself. I had to work fast to get you safely out of the country."

"Which should never have happened."

"The hell it shouldn't." His voice was suddenly rough. "There was no way I was going to let you be a target for those sons of bitches. The Taliban were probably already sharpening up their scimitars by the time you left my apartment."

"You don't *know* that. I got the first clue we'd found since we arrived here in Afghanistan that Brock Limited was actually making deals with the Taliban for weapons. All you had to do was follow up on it." She added fiercely, "And I should have gone with you. I had the right."

"Yes, you did." He didn't speak for a moment. "You've done a great job since we got here, and under normal circumstances I'd have let you go for it."

"*Let* me?"

"Wrong word. Just calm down and let me go over my side of what happened last night so that you might see why I did what I did."

"Not likely," she said bitterly.

He ignored the comment. "Look, from the moment we arrived in Kabul, you were on fire. You were doing everything you could to find evidence that Brock Limited had been involved in corruption since they opened their headquarters here. Not only that, but you were looking for documents that Brock's main headquarters in the U.S. stashed away here."

"So were we all," she said defensively. "Why are you acting as if I was the only one?"

"Because you were the only one on fire," he said quietly. "You couldn't help it. That's the way you operate. And you were smart, you were careful, but you had a skill that Jessie and I didn't have. It was natural that you were driven to use it." His voice hardened. "But why the *hell* couldn't you wait for us before you went after them?"

"Because I wasn't sure I was right. I thought I smelled that same damn cinnamon scent at the Brock headquarters as I did in the Tangi Valley, where the Taliban has a strong presence. I had to check it out to make sure I wasn't mistaken."

"And got yourself shot by a sentry."

"It was only a scratch. And I got away without anyone getting a glimpse of me. Anyway, I got the verification we needed. And we might be able to nail them." She added hotly, "I was careful. I did everything right. So why the hell am I on this damn plane?"

"You got shot. I'd hardly call that doing everything right. I'm not giving them another chance at you."

"I told you, they couldn't have known it was me."

"They'll know *someone* is investigating the conspiracy that they desperately want to keep secret. The first thing Brock and the Taliban will do is scatter and dissolve any sign of collusion. It's probably being done already. The second thing they'll do is start an investigation of their own. They'll move very fast, Kendra."

"Then we should move faster. We can find the evidence we need." She was frantically trying to salvage an opportunity that seemed to offer so much hope. "Bring me back there, and I'll start to—"

"It's not going to happen, Kendra. No way on Earth I'm going to yank you back here and make you a target." He paused. "We're going to shut down the operation for the time being."

"What? No!"

"Yes," he stated firmly. "Right now there's no actual proof we got that close to any cozy arrangement existing between Brock and the Taliban. As I said, they'll probably scatter and be cautious for a while. We need them to feel safe enough that they'll come back and let us get that proof. Temporarily, I'll turn our mission over to the CIA to see what they can dig up. Jessie and I will stay here for a little while and continue to look as if we're still searching for clues, before we supposedly throw in the towel in disgust. You will have already officially given up the search, and Kotcheff's records will show that you left Kabul three days ago."

He was rattling off plans with his typical efficiency, but she wasn't happy with any of it.

"I don't like it. It's giving up. There has to be some other way to do it."

"And I don't like the idea of anyone thinking that you know too much and they have to put you out of commission," he said grimly. "That was a flesh wound, but you left blood at the scene. The Taliban might not be up to tracing your DNA through that blood, but the Brock medics would have no problem." Lynch continued crisply, "Listen to me, here's how it goes. You left Kabul three days ago and promptly forgot the place ever existed. In fact, you were immediately involved in an FBI case that had absolutely nothing to do with Brock Limited or Afghanistan."

She tensed. "Is that an order?"

"I wish it could be," he said wryly. "I'll have to settle for calling Griffin with the FBI and begging him to find some way to cover for you."

"Ridiculous. You never beg Griffin for anything."

"Until now," he said softly. "I'd beg him to keep you safe."

"Is that supposed to make me feel all warm and fuzzy?" she asked coldly. "It's not working. I've no intention of forgiving you. Getting me thrown out of Afghanistan was completely unnecessary. You could have found a way to handle the situation that left me with dignity intact."

"I admit I wasn't overly concerned with your dignity at the time. I was more worried about Brock or the Taliban finding out that it was you who'd made that connection and coming to look for you." He paused. "And to be honest, I'd do it all again if it meant that it had the same result. Afghanistan can't exist for you any longer. It's not safe. Forget about it." He suddenly chuckled. "Saying that, I'd judge it would be very wise to make my exit quickly before you verbally strike me down. I'll be in touch. Have a good flight, Kendra." He cut the connection.

Always the last word, Kendra thought as she looked down at the phone with frustration. Even as furious and upset as she was with him, he'd still managed to do it.

As well as disturbed her and turned her life upside down with his orders and this latest outrageous action. He always thought he knew best because all those corporations and governments believed he walked on water. Yes, he was brilliant and able to pull strings that no one else even knew were there, but he wasn't always right. He was sending her home where she was presumably safe, but what about Jessie Mercado and him? They could still both be in danger. They had started this mission together, and they should finish it together. But now he was arbitrarily putting it on hold and sending her off to pretend she was working with Griffin and the FBI again?

No way. He might have been able to ban her from Afghanistan, but he had no control of her once she was back on U.S. soil. She worked with the FBI only at her own discretion, not Lynch's. She'd go back to teaching her students until she decided what she wanted to do next.

The phone was ringing.

A text.

DON'T THINK I'VE FORGOTTEN ABOUT THE RED UNDERWEAR. IT'S STILL INTRIGUING ME. BUT I'LL LET YOU EXPLAIN THAT THE NEXT TIME I SEE YOU. CONTACTED GRIFFIN. HE'LL BE WAITING EAGERLY FOR YOU THE MINUTE THAT C-130 LANDS.

   LYNCH

Damn him!

———◆———

NAVAL AIR STATION
NORTH ISLAND
CORONADO, CALIFORNIA

The first person Kendra saw when she climbed down the steps of the C-130 was FBI Special Agent in Charge Michael Griffin, who was standing beside a black SUV several yards from the aircraft.

"Hello, Kendra. You don't look too happy. I

wonder why." He smiled sourly as he took her elbow and nudged her toward the SUV. "Could it be that you've gotten your fill of Adam Lynch this time? Join the club. Now you know how I feel when I have to deal with him."

"But I notice that you still come when he calls you. You're a busy man. There's no way you have time to show up yourself to pick me up." She looked at the troops being processed out of the transport plane. "Nor go through all the hassle of dealing with the military and the Justice Department to slip me out of here with no problem when my documents are, shall we say, questionable."

"Lynch has been pulling in favors since you left Afghanistan to make you fade into the landscape as soon as you hit the tarmac." His lips twisted. "I'm just one of the primary pieces in the main puzzle. He had to offer me a mega-favor to get me to take you under my wing."

"Well, I won't bother you for very long," she said coolly as she stopped in front of the SUV. "You can drop me off at my condo and I'll handle my own repatriation from here on. But by all means take advantage of whatever favor he offered you. Stick it to him. He deserves it."

Griffin looked at her in surprise and then chuckled. "He really did piss you off," he said as he opened the car door for her. "Would you care to elaborate?"

"Isn't getting me thrown out of Afghanistan enough? He thinks he owns the world. Let him pay for it." She climbed into the car. "Just get me off this base and let me go back to running my own life. Your work is officially done."

"Well, not exactly," Griffin said. "Lynch always strikes a hard bargain. In order to get my particular payoff, I have to produce results that will make him content." He gestured to the bustling military hubbub going on around them. "This was only the beginning."

She tensed. "What are you talking about?"

"It appears that he's apprehensive about your well-being and wants me to take the heat off you until he can do it himself. I believe you discussed it?"

"He discussed it. I didn't agree to anything." She gazed directly into his eyes. "Drop me off at my condo."

"You're being very difficult." He sighed. "I can assign you surveillance but apparently that won't be enough. Lynch wants to make sure that whatever you did in Afghanistan won't be traced back to you." His brows rose as he asked curiously, "What *did* you do?"

"Nothing that should have put me in this position. I'm surprised Lynch didn't share it with you since you seem to be such friends."

"You shouldn't be. Lynch doesn't share anything with anyone, except maybe you. He told me what he needed and that you probably wouldn't want to give it to him. He told me to get it for him." He grimaced. "He made me feel like a pimp. I reminded him that I was head of this office and I'd do what I damn well pleased."

"Yet here you are."

He shrugged. "He made me an offer I couldn't refuse. So my team spent the last eighteen hours focused on getting him what he needed. He made it clear that this meant making it look like you've been working on an FBI case during the past week . . . a project you'll continue for the foreseeable future. Now, what would make you want to do that?" He chuckled. "I guarantee you've never been this carefully researched before." He started the car. "It became almost a game to my agents."

"Which I regard as the ultimate violation of my privacy."

"It was done very respectfully. You have an awesome reputation."

"Yeah, sure."

"Well, you're not always polite, but they do respect you. And your friend Agent Metcalf likes *and* respects you." He darted a glance at her face. "And he's known you long enough that he's able to see things other agents might ignore. He knew what would push your buttons. Yes, I think Metcalf might have won the grand prize."

"I like Metcalf. But I have no intention of joining your happy little group. I'll go back to teaching my music students until I find a way to get back to Kabul. And there's no way you can convince me to do anything. Give it up, Griffin."

"I haven't begun to fight yet," he murmured. "Let's play our own game, Kendra. You want me to take you to your condo? No problem. There's a manila folder on the floor at your feet. Pick it up and open it. It's the case that Metcalf thought might tip you over the edge. Read it. Study it. Then tell me whether you want me to drive you home. Or whether you want me to take you to the regional office so that you can talk to Metcalf."

Kendra hesitated, then slowly picked up the folder. It was probably a mistake. She should probably just refuse to open it and ask to be taken home. Griffin was brilliant and had no compunction about manipulating people to suit himself. If he thought he had something that might intrigue her, then he probably did.

But she was curious, dammit. She wanted to know why Metcalf had thought this case would interest her.

She slowly opened the folder.

She inhaled sharply as she looked down at the photo on the first page.

"Kendra?" Griffin said softly.

She couldn't take her gaze from that photo.

Griffin tilted his head, his eyes narrowed on her face. "Your condo or the regional office?"

The bastard knew he had her.

"Neither."

"You have someplace else in mind?"

She held up the photo. "Take me here."

"It's late. It's already getting dark."

"I don't care."

"Your time will be better spent at the office, getting brought up to speed. Tomorrow we can go out there, and—"

"Now." Kendra flipped the pages of the file. "Or you can drop me off at my condo and I'll drive myself. But one way or another, I'm going there tonight."

Griffin sighed. "Okay. Fine. I'll have Metcalf meet us there."

"That'll work," she said jerkily, her eyes already devouring the text. "I'll read the report on the way."

CHAPTER

2

WOODWARD ACADEMY FOR THE PHYSICALLY
DISABLED
OCEANSIDE, CALIFORNIA

Kendra looked up as Griffin negotiated the long driveway that rose to the Woodward Academy's main entrance. Darkness had already fallen, but even at night the main building was astonishing. Situated on the top of a tall hill thirty-eight miles north of San Diego, the three-story structure looked like it belonged on a Northeastern Ivy League campus instead of the beach town where it had existed for over seventy years. The building had been constructed as the fourth home for one of California's wealthiest oil families—the Woodwards, who had lived here in splendor before finally deeding the mansion and grounds to create Woodward Academy in the late 1940s. The extensive grounds upon which it was built were equally impressive. Rolling hills, meadows, and cliffs towered over the crashing Pacific Ocean, and the many out-buildings and lovely chapel in the garden were also magnificent. The school was world-renowned for its work with the physically challenged, and many of its alumni went on to great success in a variety of fields.

"How long were you here?" Griffin asked.

"I left after the eighth grade. I could have stayed through twelfth, but I wanted to go to a regular public high school."

"Did you regret leaving when you did?"

She shook her head. "Never. I was ready. But I had some good times here. It felt like home to me. The teachers are the best anywhere."

"So I've heard. I once thought this was just a school for the blind, but it's more than that, isn't it?"

"Much more. It's for the hearing impaired, kids confined to wheelchairs... This school helps a lot of people. I still keep in touch with some of the teachers."

"So you've come back to visit?"

"Occasionally." Kendra looked at the file in her lap. She had to clear her throat. "But I never thought I'd come back under these circumstances."

She was staring at photos of Elaine Wessler and Ronald Kim, two staff members she'd known since she was five years old. Dear God, she had hundreds of memories of them from the years after her mother had brought her here as a nervous little girl. She remembered how tightly she'd held her mother's hand as she'd been driven up this driveway to the front door. But more with excitement than fear, because her mother had prepared her for that first venture into the world outside the safety of the only home Kendra had ever known. She had been sure that she would be greeted with only kindness by everyone here at Oceanside.

But neither of the people in these photos had been met with kindness. Kendra was looking at crime scene photos of their bloody corpses.

They had been murdered.

Their bodies had been found on opposite sides of the campus within a day of each other. Elaine Wessler, who specialized in real-world survival skills for the visually impaired, had been stabbed on the flat rocks of the school's west side, a boulder-laden area that offered a spectacular view of the Pacific Ocean. Groundskeeper Ronald Kim, wearing the same blue overalls Kendra remembered from her campus visits, had been killed by a single gunshot behind his left ear. He'd been found on the far side of the great lawn adjacent to the campus's main building.

"Did you know them?" Griffin asked.

Kendra nodded. "Almost for my entire life." Her lips tightened. "They didn't deserve this."

"No one does."

"Why are you even handling this investigation? Shouldn't it be an SDPD case?"

"The director asked us to offer our services. Several of the resident students are the children of very powerful foreign diplomats." He grimaced. "And the fact that the entire student body is made up of special-needs kids has already started generating a lot of public pressure. We have to close this case very quickly."

"Yes, we do. And I didn't see anything in the file about suspects."

"That's because there aren't any."

"None?"

"Not yet. At least none we've been able to identify. Neither of the victims had enemies anyone knows about, and they didn't have criminal associations. They weren't drug users, had no criminal records."

"Robbery?"

"No. Elaine Wessler was wearing a fairly expensive Movado watch, and it was still on her wrist when her body was found. Ronald Kim was found with a wallet full of cash, which was normal for him. He didn't use credit cards. We've ruled out robbery as a motive."

Kendra looked out her window at the Latin phrase chiseled in stone over the main entrance: AD ASTRA PER ASPERA.

Griffin squinted at it.

"It means 'To the stars in spite of difficulties,'" she said.

Griffin nodded. "I know, Kendra. Despite what you may think, my education didn't begin and end at Quantico. Good motto."

"Sorry for underestimating you."

He shrugged. "*Non forsit.*"

"Now you're just showing off." She looked ahead at a Ford Explorer parked on the stone driveway. "Looks like Metcalf beat us here."

They pulled up behind the Explorer just in time to see FBI Special Agent Roland Metcalf climb out. He was a tall, handsome man with a fit, muscular body and floppy brown hair.

"I had an *amazing* presentation prepared for you at the office, Kendra." Metcalf shook his head. "A PowerPoint extravaganza. Photographs, crime scene video, pithy yet informative bullet points..."

"Sorry, Metcalf. Tonight I needed to be here." She held up the file folder. "This helped catch me up."

"A poor substitute."

"Maybe you'll run your extravaganza for me later."

"Perhaps, if you're *extremely* lucky." He smiled. "Good to have you home. Sorry it's under these circumstances." He grimaced. "And I don't mean Lynch getting you kicked out of Afghanistan. I know this case is going to be difficult for you."

"Obviously. Or you wouldn't have been the one to win the office prize on how to draw me into the game Griffin set up." She saw him flinch and felt a moment of regret. He was clearly sincere. Lynch, her best friend Olivia, and even her mother insisted that Metcalf had a crush on her, and she'd only recently admitted that it was probably true. "He's right, you do know me well enough to know I'd want to be here and work this case. That's all that's important now."

Griffin glanced around. "Seen anybody here yet?"

"I called on my way down," Metcalf said. "I talked to a night supervisor, Dr. Madeline Turman, and told her we were coming. She didn't seem thrilled about it."

"That's because she's responsible for a hundred and fifty resident students who are trying to sleep in that building over there." Kendra motioned toward the dormitory, a four-story building with a sloping bonnet-style roof. "Maddie doesn't like anything to come between her and her kids."

"Did you stay there when you were a student?" Metcalf asked.

"No, I was a local. More than half of the students live in the San Diego area with their families. This school was the main reason my mom moved us here. It's a special place."

"So I gather," Griffin said. "But a great many

parents have taken their students home in the past day or so, and more are coming tomorrow."

"Can't say I blame them," Kendra said. "Parents of special kids are very protective of them. It's ingrained the instant they realize their child has a problem. This would set off more alarms than an EF-5 tornado warning. I'm surprised they haven't closed the place down."

A woman's sharp voice came from behind them. "It could still happen."

They turned to see a tall, slender woman in her late sixties. Kendra instinctively tensed. It was Dr. Allison Walker. The school's head administrator had lost none of her power to cast an imposing figure. Her long, straight hair was now gray, but her slender physique appeared more toned than ever. Kendra had once assumed it was the result of some serious gym time, but a colleague told her Allison never exercised or even watched her calories. Lucky woman.

"Good to see you, Kendra," Allison said quietly. "I hoped you would come."

"You couldn't keep me away."

Allison raised an electronic cigarette to her lips and took a puff. "Please excuse this. It's not allowed here, but it's been that kind of week."

Kendra nodded. "I understand. I take it you've met FBI Agents Griffin and Metcalf?"

Allison nodded. "Yes. Yesterday morning, after

Elaine Wessler's death. Good evening, gentlemen. I didn't expect to see you again so soon."

"Didn't expect it, either," Griffin said as he cast a sour glance at Kendra. "Plans change."

"I'm only just now getting brought up to speed," Kendra said. "I'm sorry, Allison." The name caught in Kendra's throat. After all these years, it still felt strange not to call her Dr. Walker. "Elaine Wessler and Ron Kim were good people."

Allison nodded. "You'd realize that more than most. They were part of the heart and soul of this place. Each of them in their own way."

"I know."

Allison said fiercely, "It's just...senseless."

Evidently Allison was feeling a bit raw. Kendra instinctively stepped closer to her. "Did they have any connection to each other?"

"Elaine and Ronald? Not at all. Ronald was always around, tending to the lawns, his flowers and shrubs. The teachers might give him a smile or a quick hello as they walked past, but mostly he was just...*there*. We've all been racking our brains for a common thread between them, but we haven't come up with anything."

"Enemies? Volatile personal relationships?"

"No. Nothing like that. Ronald's wife died of cancer a few years ago. Elaine's divorced and she hasn't been seeing anyone we know of."

"We've been digging into their friends and associates," Metcalf said. "I'll give you a rundown, but so far there isn't anything promising."

"Okay." Kendra glanced around them. "Allison, I'd appreciate it if you could walk with us. Would you mind?"

"Where?"

"I want to see where each body was found."

"It will be difficult to see at night, especially where we found Elaine."

"I know. I'll come back tomorrow, but I need to see these places now."

Allison turned toward Griffin and Metcalf. "I take it you've already tried to talk her out of coming here tonight?"

"We have," Griffin said with a sigh.

Allison took another puff from her electronic cigarette. "I sympathize. Even when Kendra was here as a little girl, it was difficult trying to talk her out of anything she'd set her mind on."

"Sorry," Kendra said.

"No, you're not. I know you better than that, Kendra." Allison motioned toward the great lawn that extended to the south of the main building. "I hope you brought flashlights, otherwise it's entirely possible one of us will end our evening tumbling headfirst into the Pacific Ocean."

"We'll try to avoid that." Griffin and Metcalf fired

up their flashlights and shone the way across the lawn as they walked.

"Ronald Kim's car was in the parking lot overnight Monday," Allison said. "It was logged by the security officer on duty."

"Didn't anyone think that was unusual?" Kendra said.

Allison shrugged. "It was an older car. The officer thought it probably had engine trouble and Ronald just caught another ride home."

Kendra sniffed the air as they walked. Gardenias. Mr. Kim based his planting on scents as much as visual aesthetics, so the sightless students always knew where they were on campus. Even after all these years, Kendra knew she'd soon be smelling roses, followed by a wisp of honeysuckle.

"The security officers' shift change came at seven A.M.," Allison said as they approached the rose garden. "That's when Ronald's body was dis-covered, when the daytime officer made his first patrol around campus."

Metcalf shone his flashlight toward a large stone wall at the far end of the lawn. "His body was found there, on the ground at the base of the trellis."

Kendra slowed as they approached the scene. The grass had been matted by the dress shoes of more than a dozen cops, FBI agents, and evidence teams, along with the thin wheel marks of the gurney used to cart away Ronald Kim's body.

Griffin directed his flashlight beam along the ground in front of them. "He was here, mostly covered by these trellis vines down to almost his knees. He was killed by a single nine-millimeter shot to the back of the head."

Kendra pulled out her phone, activated its flashlight, and studied the scene. "Were these drag marks here or did the M.E. make these removing the body?"

"They were there already," Metcalf said. "He was moved just a few feet, enough to hide the body. He appears to have been murdered here at close range. A silencer was used to muffle the sound."

"So no one heard the shot?"

"No one," Allison said. "And in the dormitory, we have dozens of children with highly developed senses of hearing, as I'm sure you can imagine. Stray cats a hundred yards away are known to cause a disturbance around here."

Holding her phone flashlight in front of her, Kendra walked down the length of the stone wall.

"What are you looking for?" Griffin said. "We searched this entire area."

"I'm sure you did." Kendra didn't look up as she continued her scan of the area. She had no idea what she was looking for, but a lawn and garden this pristine would make it easier for her to spot something, *anything*, that could give them a lead.

Or it could give them nothing.

She'd definitely have to come back the next day when the sun would light up the area far better than her phone. In this respect, Allison and the agents had been right to question her wisdom in visiting the scene in the dead of—

She stopped.

She turned her head and took half a step back.

"See something?" Metcalf called out.

"No."

Metcalf, Griffin, and Allison joined her next to a clump of tall bushes. "What is it?"

"Ronald Kim stood here." She looked over the wall, which was about four feet tall at this point. "He was here for quite a while, probably looking at the access road leading to the Pacific Coast Highway."

Griffin squinted at the ground. "I don't see how you can tell that."

"I couldn't if I was only using my sight." She grabbed a branch from the nearest bush, leaned in, and took a deep whiff. "Try it."

Only Metcalf moved closer and sniffed the bush.

"Smell that?" she asked.

"I'm . . . not sure."

"You'd probably be surer if you'd been paying attention to what the others smelled like."

"How is this one different?" Griffin said.

"It's been bathed in cigarette smoke. And not just a few puffs. Probably several entire cigarettes. The smell wouldn't linger this long otherwise. Which means he was standing here for quite a while."

"How do you know it was Ronald Kim and not someone else?"

"The scent of this tobacco is sharp, very distinctive. It's a Korean-made cigarette brand, Raison. The odor was always on Mr. Kim's clothes. A young woman in your office also smokes this brand, by the way."

"What woman?" Griffin asked.

"The forensic accounting specialist two cubicles down from Metcalf. Special Agent Park."

"Huh." Griffin's forehead creased in surprise. "I didn't even know she smoked."

"Me neither," Metcalf said.

Kendra turned back toward the wall. "Something here interested him. He stood here for a reason."

"Maybe he just came here for his smoke breaks."

"No," Allison said. "No staff member is allowed to smoke anywhere a student may see them. There's only one smoking area, and it's near the garbage dumpsters behind the dining hall."

"He only would have smoked out here late at night, when no one could have seen him," Kendra said.

"Interesting," Metcalf said. "You would have known this if you had attended my scintillating presentation, but crime scene techs found six cigarette butts in the left pocket of the coveralls."

Kendra nodded. "Of course. He wouldn't have littered in his garden. So it was that night. He was waiting out here for a reason."

"Maybe to meet someone," Metcalf offered.

Kendra glanced around. "Kind of an out-of-the-way place. It seems more like a spot where he could look down to that area below without being seen."

Griffin stood between the tall bushes and looked down toward the access road. "Yes, it does."

Kendra turned and continued her scan of the area, but nothing else caught her attention. "Okay." She braced herself. "Now I'd like to see where Elaine Wessler was found."

Allison motioned toward the far side of the campus. "It was on the hillside, on the other side of the athletic building."

"On the Slide?"

Allison wore a pained expression. "I strongly discourage that name."

Kendra smiled. "Still?"

"Yes."

Kendra turned toward Metcalf and Griffin. "For years, students have grabbed flattened boxes to slide down the hill over there."

"Even the blind kids?" Metcalf said.

"Of course. Some of the best times I had here were over on the Slide."

"Dodging any teacher who might try to stop you," Allison said sarcastically. "And you and your friend Olivia always led the pack. Fun times. Until someone inevitably gets hurt. The area should have been cleared and leveled to take away the temptation."

"But that would have broken our hearts."

"Better your hearts than your heads. You students had enough problems to worry about."

"But Elaine Wessler wasn't sliding on boxes," Griffin said grimly.

Allison shook her head. "No. This way. I'll show you the best way to get there without hurtling into the ocean."

They followed Allison past the main building and around the athletic complex and swimming pool. A paved stairway took them down a long slope that appeared to end at the ocean. Kendra knew, however, that it was merely an illusion, since a fence and service road separated the base of the hill from the water. The school did have a private beach on the coast, but it was closer to the cliffs.

There were no lights on that part of campus, but

the moon cast a blue glow over the hillside. Several boulders jutted from the earth, appearing smaller than how Kendra remembered them.

Allison walked toward the largest boulder. "Elaine was found here less than twenty-four hours after Ronald Kim's body was discovered."

"Who found her?"

Metcalf shrugged. "San Diego's News Copter 7, believe it or not."

"A news helicopter?"

Allison extinguished her electronic cigarette and placed it into her pocket. "Yes. They were covering the morning rush hour and happened to see Elaine's body here. They notified the police and we found out from them."

"She was stabbed twice," Griffin said. "Once in the chest, once in the throat. Time of death probably before midnight."

"Did she have a reason to be here on campus at that time of night?" Kendra asked.

"None," Allison said. "She should have left about four the previous afternoon."

"But she didn't," Metcalf said. "At least not according to the entrance and exit camera feeds. It looks like she arrived for work that morning, but never left."

Kendra was gazing at the much-trampled area ahead that they were approaching. So many memories...

Big Rock, the huge flat boulder where she and other generations of children sat, ate lunch, and listened to stories and waves crashing in the distance. They had all considered this place peculiarly their own. There were now hundreds of carvings on the rock, some etched there in the decades before her time, many in the years since. She remembered constantly tracing an odd design with her finger that only later, after she'd gained her sight, had she realized was a four-leaf clover. She recalled a star, a heart, and a pyramid with wavy lines...There were even hundreds of students' initials carved through the decades on the underside of the rim of the rock. Kendra knew exactly the place where she and Olivia had carved their own initials to join them. They had crept out early one morning, and she could remember the excitement, the sound of the sea, and the scent of the earth as they'd knelt down there beside the rock. Sounds...scents...tastes...friends.

"This is where Olivia and I first met." Kendra cleared her throat and then turned toward Allison. "We're still best friends. She has her own condo on the floor below mine in a building on Fifth Street."

"I know. She still visits here from time to time. Did she mention to you that she's given motivational speeches to our classes at least two or three times a year since she left here?"

Kendra nodded. "You couldn't have chosen any-one better. She's an exceptional person."

More than exceptional, she thought. Olivia was beautiful, brilliant, innovative, and had never let her blindness keep her from accomplishing any goal she set herself. She had developed a website, *Outasite*, which had recently become a major online destina-tion for the blind, who browsed its pages with one of several screen-reading applications. The site fea-tured product reviews, interviews, and news stories mostly written by Olivia herself. In just a few years, what had been a spare-time hobby now afforded her a comfortable living with a potential in the seven figures.

"Oh, I realized that," Allison said bluntly. "You've been very generous with your time when I've asked you to come and speak, but Olivia is really of far more value to us." Then she sighed and ruefully shook her head. "I shouldn't have said that, diplo-macy isn't my strong suit. It's been a very bad day and I tend to just say what I'm thinking when I'm hurting."

"So do I," Kendra said quietly. "Do you suppose I learned it from your example? I always admired you...when you didn't intimidate me."

"Lord, I hope not. These kids have to learn to cope, not antagonize." She paused. "Your visits here did have value. I'm not saying they didn't. But you're a superstar. You do it all. The kids hear about your work with the FBI on the Net. Very exciting. Crime-fighter deluxe. And they know that you're respected for your academic accomplishments with special kids in the classroom. They admire all that about you. But they can't connect with you as they do with Olivia." She added simply, "Because you received a miracle that might never happen to them."

"And Olivia is still blind, yet she's making a success of her life at every opportunity that comes her way," Kendra said. "She's out there in the trenches and showing the kids what's possible. Of course she's a better motivational inspiration than I am. That's why my speeches to the students weigh in heaviest on what I learned in the twenty years I was blind that I can apply to what I do now."

"I've noticed," Allison said gruffly. "That's really the only reason I invited you to speak." She shrugged. "Though the kids do get excited when you show up. Everyone likes a superstar to shine down on them." She added dryly, "Well, have I hurled enough insults at you for one evening?"

"I actually feel complimented that you'd be this honest with me." Kendra couldn't help but be amused. "It makes me believe I might have at last reached your august level. Even though Olivia is far ahead of me."

"You might get there yet. As long as you make

sure Olivia stays around to keep you balanced. I admit it didn't surprise me about the condo. You never could let go of anyone you cared about."

"Can anyone? Friendship is very precious."

She nodded slowly. "To some more than others."

"I assure you that we never get in each other's way. You taught us that we had to be totally independent." She paused as a thought occurred to her. "Does she know about the murders?"

"Maybe not." She shrugged. "I asked your FBI friends to try to keep their identities confidential until I could talk to the parents of our students. They did a good job of stalling the media. I think she would have contacted us if she'd known."

"You're probably right. Or called to tell me. She might have been out of town. Once a month she flies to Dallas to give seminars on computer technique for the blind at a VA hospital. I'll phone her on my way home and tell her what happened." She grimaced. "I'm not looking forward to it." They had reached the rock, and Kendra lit up her phone and scanned the area. "The ground is soft. There should have been footprints here."

"There were," Metcalf said. "Hers."

She turned to look at him. "No one else's?"

"Nothing I would call a print. More like...vague impressions. It looks like the killer wore padded booties of some kind."

"Do we at least have a shoe size?"

"Forensics gave us a man's shoe size estimate of between ten and twelve."

Kendra crouched next to the boulder. "Great. That narrows it to what, fifty percent of the population?"

"Close," Metcalf said. "Forty-four point five percent."

"Tell me you didn't know that off the top of your head."

"Would it impress you if I did?"

"Not sure. I'd have to decide if you were a genius or some kind of freak."

"Now you know how we feel about you when you help out on our cases."

"Point taken."

Metcalf smiled. "I looked up the stat after the Evidence Response Team gave me the shoe size range. Guess I'm not such a freak after all."

"I wouldn't say *that*." Kendra stood up. "I saw the crime scene pics of Elaine's body...Her hands had wounds, didn't they?"

"Yes," Griffin said. "They appeared to be defensive wounds, but the M.E. isn't sure about that. The wounds weren't from the same blade that killed her. And if they were truly defensive wounds, they most likely would also be on her lower arms, but those were untouched."

She turned to Metcalf. "Mind if I use your flashlight? My phone battery is almost dead."

"Sure."

She took his high-wattage xenon-bulb flashlight and walked around the area just as she had at Ronald Kim's murder scene. The close-cropped grass yielded nothing, and the nearby boulders seemed undisturbed. She studied the railing that bordered the path down the hill. It consisted of a series of wooden posts connected by six-foot lengths of nylon mesh.

Kendra turned back to the others. "Was this railing moved or in any way disturbed by investigators on the scene?"

"I don't believe so," Metcalf said. "Why?"

Kendra stepped back and looked at it from another angle. "So this is how it looked when Elaine's body was found?"

Allison moved closer to her. "This is how it's *always* looked. At least since it was put up about ten years ago."

"I'm not so sure about that."

Griffin stared at the railing. "What are you seeing that we aren't? Or is it *smelling*?"

"Seeing." Kendra moved the flashlight around the surrounding area. "The position of every garden stake, fence, and gatepost matches the others perfectly."

"Our grounds staff possesses an impressive atten-tion to detail," Allison said. "Nothing unusual there."

Kendra ran the beam of her flashlight across the railing posts. "Look at these. Each post is stuck into the ground up to a small globe at the bottom." She used her flashlight to point out each one. "Globe, globe, globe, globe..."

"No globe," Griffin said as her flashlight came to rest at the base of a post just a few feet away from them.

Kendra moved closer to it. "This post is slightly shorter than the others. Because it's been jammed farther into the ground. If you look, you'll see that the ground has been freshly disturbed around the base. It looks as if it was pulled from the ground, then thrust back in without the time or care of the other posts. See?" She moved the flashlight up the post. "And higher up, look at the rough patterned cuts in the wood. If you look closer, you'll see they're not completely clean. That could be dirt in the ridges, but I'm thinking it might be..."

"Blood," Metcalf finished for her. "That would explain the cuts we saw on the victim's hands. You think she tried to use this as a weapon?"

"Maybe. Give me a pair of evidence gloves. I want to see how hard it is for a person my size to pull this out of the ground."

Metcalf pulled a pair of nitrile evidence gloves

from his jacket pocket and handed them to her. Kendra smiled as she handed him his flashlight and pulled the gloves on. "You brought them in my size. Thanks, Metcalf."

"Figured it was time. You've earned it."

"You're spoiling me," she said mockingly.

Kendra gripped the post midway up and pulled. It rose easily from the soft ground, and with a slight twist it was free from the mesh that still joined the other posts. She held it in front of her, as if fending off an attacker. "It's awkward, but this might have been the closest thing to a weapon Elaine could get her hands on."

Griffin looked doubtful. "But why would the perp bother planting it back into the ground after he killed her?"

"We've all seen serial killers who tidy up their scenes." Kendra lowered the post. "It could be that he..."

She stopped and squinted, then slowly raised the post again. Could that be...?

"Guys, aim your flashlights at the very bottom of this thing."

Griffin was the first to react, but after a moment both agents had trained their beams on the post's pointed end.

It was dirty from the soft earth, but there was something else there.

"Blood," Kendra said. "More blood. But this time I don't think it's Elaine's."

Metcalf inspected it more closely. "If this belongs to the killer, then we have his DNA." He looked back to Griffin. "We need to take this thing back to the lab."

Griffin was already entering a number into his phone. "I'm calling the Evidence Response Team now. I'll have them come out here and take it themselves."

"Now?" Metcalf said.

"Yes. It'll serve them right for not catching this themselves."

Kendra carefully leaned the post against the boulder bottom-side up.

Allison shook her head. "Impressive. I have to admit that I haven't paid much attention to this sideline of yours, Kendra, but it's amusing to finally see you in action."

"Don't be too impressed," Kendra said. "I have no idea if any of this will help find the killer."

Metcalf raised his phone and snapped several photos of the post. "We're a hell of a lot closer than we were twenty minutes ago." He turned to Griffin. "Don't you think?"

Griffin shrugged. "Possibly."

A dog howled in the distance.

Kendra frowned, her gaze searching the campus.

The howl came again. It appeared to be coming from somewhere in the vicinity of the main building.

Kendra turned to Allison. "Hound of the Baskervilles?"

"Hardly. Harley of Oceanside."

Kendra wrinkled her brow.

"You may remember that Elaine fostered and trained Seeing Eye dogs," Allison said. "She was seldom without one in her home. The day after her murder, we remembered she had one there. So we brought him here until other arrangements could be made. Our dorm supervisor, Maddie Turman, keeps him in her room overnight. Unfortunately, the dog isn't exactly quiet."

"He's probably just missing Elaine," Kendra said. "His name is Harley?"

Allison nodded. "That's what Elaine told me. Though she didn't name him. She got him from one of the local vets who knew she had a way with dogs. I'm not sure if Harley is going to cut it without her around."

"Why not?"

"He's . . . unusual."

Kendra cocked her head. "Unusual how?"

Another howl wafted across the campus.

"I'd better go tend to this," Allison said. "He's

probably woken up everyone in the dorm by now. If you'll excuse me ... "

"May I go with you?" Kendra asked.

Allison nodded. "Certainly, but trust me, that dog isn't going to help you solve this or any other case."

Kendra turned back to Griffin and Metcalf. "I'll be back in a few minutes. You'll be here?"

"Metcalf will," Griffin replied. "He'll wait here for the Evidence Response Team. I'm heading home and going to bed."

Metcalf sighed. "Rank has its privileges."

The dog wailed again.

"This way," Allison said.

Kendra followed her up the path and across the lawn to the dormitory. A single window was illuminated on the first floor. Allison swiped her key card across a reader at the main entrance, and she and Kendra made their way down a long hallway.

The dog's wail echoed eerily down the dim corridor. In there, it sounded less pathetic and more creepy, Kendra thought.

They made their way toward the one door where a sliver of light cut underneath. Allison rapped sharply on the door and it was answered by Maddie Turman, who looked totally exhausted, with dark circles under her eyes.

"Dr. Walker, I'm so sorry," Maddie Turman said quickly. "I've been trying to keep him quiet."

"I know, Maddie," Allison said. "But this can't continue. The students are already upset and on edge."

"Tell me about it," Maddie said wearily. "And the kids could take that wailing, it's the other stuff that keeps scaring them. He's definitely an acquired taste. Even Elaine was at her wit's end trying to find a home for him. That's why she still had him four months after he was rescued."

"Home?" Kendra repeated. "She wasn't training him to be a Seeing Eye dog like the others?"

"Not Harley," Allison said dryly. "He'd already had his initial training but something happened and Dr. Napier, the local vet, asked Elaine if she could take him. You know Elaine, she's always been a sucker for a lost cause."

"He flunked out as a Seeing Eye dog?" Kendra asked. "Not smart enough?"

"Elaine said he's the smartest dog she'd ever seen. He's just...different." She saw Kendra frown and then said impatiently, "Oh, see for yourself. I'll wait for you here." She dropped down on the couch. "Take her to see him, Maddie."

Maddie shrugged. "Why not? At least he'll stop howling." She led her down the hall to the bed-room from which the howling was issuing. "Don't be scared, okay? He won't hurt you. You shouldn't be afraid."

"I'm not afraid. I like dogs. And Elaine would never accept a dog that would be a danger to anyone. He probably just needs some additional training."

The dog broke off in mid-howl as Maddie started to open the bedroom door. He whirled on Kendra and then bounded toward her. She had a lightning glance of a large, golden-tan dog, either a German shepherd or a retriever or...something, and braced herself for the leap. But before he reached her, he fell to the floor and made a sound deep in his throat.

Chills ran down her back. He sounded like a hungry lion snarling. "He's going to attack." She instinctively backed away as the dog snarled at her again. "I've never heard anything like that."

"None of us have," Maddie said. "But he's not growling, Kendra. Elaine said that he's barking. He's not threatening you. She thought it was his attempt to make friends."

"He's growling," Kendra said positively. And it was the deepest, roughest, fiercest growl she'd ever heard. "And forget the bit where I told you I wasn't afraid of dogs." She tried to get a grip on herself. "You're sure he's not on the attack?"

"I'm sure. You saw how he dropped and lay at attention before he reached you. That was part of his training as a service dog. Harley was probably the most affectionate dog you've ever met until he was injured. Elaine said she believed that's part of his problem now. Just ignore that blasted sound he's making and *look* at him. You'll see it."

Kendra was already looking at him. His tail was wagging and his large, dark eyes were shining at her from that big, square retriever face. No, one dark eye, she realized. The other was a crystal light blue, but it was shining at her with just as much eagerness as its darker mate. It was as if he was trying to tell her something. His golden fur clung tightly to his lean, powerful shepherd body, and his ears were long and floppy. He looked unusual, funny, and maybe even almost huggable...as long as he didn't open his mouth. "What breed is he?"

"Mutt," Maddie said flatly. "He was donated to the Seeing Eye program by a breeder of German shepherds. But evidently some other dog of dubious ancestry saw fit to pay his mother a clandestine visit. He appeared healthy and had a wonderful temperament so he was accepted in the program."

Kendra took a step forward and then she knelt, tentatively reaching out and gently stroking Harley's ears. He lifted his head and gazed at her intently...and she was aware once more of that feeling that he was trying to tell her something...

And then he growled.

Kendra shuddered. "Oh, shit." She glanced at Maddie. "That snarl sounds like a cross between a panther and a lion and totally deadly. No way would anyone see that 'wonderful temperament' if they heard that. It doesn't make sense."

"And everything has to make sense to you, it all has to fit together. You haven't changed." Maddie shrugged. "I can see it. It was hard for me to understand what Elaine was talking about. I still have trouble. I don't have her empathy for animals. But when Elaine first brought Harley home from the vet, she knew he was going to be a headache. He was very depressed and so quiet it was almost a relief when he'd give that lion roar."

"Difficult to imagine." But now that Kendra was up close and personal with Harley, she could see what Maddie meant. In the dog's silence, she could sense the intensity, the aloneness, even...desperation. "You said she brought him home from the vet? What was wrong with him?"

"Elaine said he'd had a battle with a fire caused by an exploding gas pipe." She shrugged. "And I don't want to sound schmaltzy, but she really thought he had a broken heart. That's a little harder to fix."

"If anyone could do it, Elaine could." Kendra was looking into those strange eyes, trying to read what Elaine had seen. *Did she heal you, boy? She healed a lot of us over the years. But no one can heal her now.*

"You're right." Maddie had to clear her throat. "But she didn't have much time to do it, though I believe she was making progress. The dog was responding to Elaine, and she was even bringing him here to stay in her office during the day so that she could work with him on her breaks. And I wasn't lying to you. Harley didn't sound like that during the first year of his training. He couldn't have been a more perfect service dog. In fact he was so extraordinary, he'd been assigned earlier than expected because an eight-year-old boy, Terry Calder, needed a dog and his trainer thought Harley could handle his needs. It worked out beautifully and they were both ecstatic at being together. But a gas main blew up in his neighborhood and Terry was killed." She grimaced. "It's likely he was killed instantly by the explosion itself, as his parents were, but Harley wouldn't believe it. He dragged the boy through that burning house to the front door and stayed there barking until the firemen heard him and managed to break down the door to get to them. But it was definitely too late by then." She reached down and patted Harley. "This one almost died, too. Severe smoke inhalation, they had to operate twice on him. But he's well now except the damage done to his vocal cords. Needless to say, when the Guide Dog Foundation directors heard what he sounded like after he recovered, they no longer wanted him as a Seeing Eye dog. Service dogs have to be almost perfect in every way so that they can interact with the public." She made a face. "Though they did give him a medal for his service at the fire. But he wouldn't eat, he was almost catatonic, after he lost the boy. Dr. Napier did his best, but he was finally considering sending him to a shelter as a solution when he thought about Elaine. Naturally Elaine took him, but she really didn't know what to do with him, either. She was just edging along trying to use Harley's instinctive love of people, particularly kids, to bring him back. But they're all afraid of him now." She looked Kendra in the eye. "Admit it, even you were scared."

"I won't deny it. How can I?" But she wasn't afraid now. Elaine had tried to understand and save this dog. She had seen his pain and tried to soothe it. "So what are you planning on doing with him, Maddie? You volunteered to take him in after Elaine died. You must have some feeling for him."

"You want me to take him? I'm not that noble. He doesn't really like me. He didn't like anyone but Elaine after his Terry died. And I wouldn't have volunteered to take care of him except I heard him howl."

"What?"

"The day that Elaine died, I heard him howl. He'd never done that before. I'd heard that scary bark, but not that horrible, mournful howl. The vet told Elaine that he howled for Terry for weeks after he died and then just gave up and went into depression." Her eyes were tearing. "Harley knew Elaine was dead. He knew he'd lost someone else. Just as we'd lost her. I couldn't help her, so I thought I'd do what I could for him. I offered to keep him for at least a couple of weeks. After that, I'll try to find him a home, but it probably won't work out. He has a handicap that's hard to take." She swallowed hard. "So there you are. Another tragedy added to the one that happened to Elaine and Mr. Kim."

"Bullshit. There has to be something we can do. Saving this dog was one of the last things that Elaine tried to make happen before she was killed. We can't cheat her of it." Kendra rubbed Harley's broad nose, velvet soft, so different from that harsh, fierce snarl that was meant to be a bark. She had been terribly touched by the story of the sacrifice that had caused his hideous hoarseness. What must it be like to reach out in love and have it be mistaken for violence? And she had an idea that beneath the intense, searching emotion she could see in the dog's eyes, there might be pure love. "I'd take him, but I'm never at home. If he needs people contact as much as Elaine said, my neighbors would be calling the police at the first howl."

"Absolutely," Maddie said. "I guarantee they'd be

knocking on your door. But you're working with the FBI these days as well as your music therapy groups. You can figure it out, Kendra. Because I don't know how long I can fight off Allison. She has a good heart but this school is everything to her. She's not going to let Harley get in the way of helping the kids."

"And she shouldn't." She was frowning. "That doesn't mean we have to sacrifice one for the other. We just have to make the best choice and then go with it."

"Choice? Harley's more like a challenge. I'm not much into challenges these days, Kendra."

"Challenge?" Kendra went still. Something had just occurred to her. "Yes, you're right, he *is* a challenge. Let me think for a minute..."

CHAPTER
3

KENDRA'S CONDO
FIFTH STREET

I'm coming down to your place," Kendra said when Olivia picked up her call two hours later. "I just dropped off my luggage at my condo and I don't care if you want to cry yourself to sleep. She's *dead*, Olivia. I've been keeping a stiff upper lip and being professional and all that crap for the last few hours." She didn't bother to wait for the elevator but was running down the steps. "Now I deserve to have a drink with my friend who loved her as much as I did. So suck it up, Olivia."

"Just shut up." Olivia's voice was as husky as Kendra's. "You only called me on your way home because you knew we'd both be a mess if you hit me with it face-to-face. I'm over the worst of the shock now and I'm not going to bury my head under the covers." She threw open her front door as Kendra reached it. Her eyes were red from crying and she pulled Kendra forward into her arms. "But it should never have happened." She hugged her close and whispered, "She was so *good*, Kendra. Why?"

"We don't know. That why I went there to try to find out." She wiped her wet cheeks. "Mr. Kim's death must have had something to do with it. It will just take time to figure it out." She went over to Olivia's bar and poured them both a glass of wine. She brought them back and handed one to her. "But I don't want to wait," she said wearily. "She was family, Olivia. It wasn't only what she taught me, but what she made me teach myself. I'd ask her a question and she'd tell me to look inside myself and if I couldn't figure it out then she'd tell me." She dropped down on the couch and patted the cushion next to her. "Come and sit and talk with me. I need to remember everything about her. You were already at Oceanside when I came, and you were closer to her than I was. It's you who would take me to her whenever I had a problem. I'd been born without sight and you didn't lose yours until you had that automobile accident. So you were able to kind of bridge the gap between us."

"Yes, I was closer to her than you were." Olivia sat down and took another drink of wine. "I could talk to her." She paused. "Do you know I went to see her on the night I heard that the stem cell operation to give you your vision was a success? I was so happy for you." She finished her wine. "And so damn jealous that it was killing me."

Kendra went still. "You never showed it."

"Because I'm smart, and a great actress, and I love you like a sister. I'd never let how I felt spoil the gift you'd been given." She stood up, got the wine bottle from the bar, and brought it back to the couch. "It would have poisoned both of us. But it was a pretty hard blow to take." She refilled their glasses. "Not only were you leaving me in the dark alone, but it might be forever. And I wasn't sure as you moved forward in your new world if we'd be able to keep what we had. So I lied until I learned to deal with it. And I *did* learn that, Kendra." She nestled close to her. "No poison. No jealousy. All gone. But I needed someone to talk to that night."

"And you went to Elaine."

"She let me talk. She let me rejoice for you. She let me cry for myself. It was the start of the healing. By dawn I was a little drunk, but I was on my way back." She smiled. "And we toasted my friend Kendra, and the miracle that had come into all our lives that day."

"I wish I'd known." She had to swallow to ease the tightness of her throat. "Yes, there was a miracle, but you both gave me a very special gift that night."

"No, not me, that was courtesy of Elaine."

"I don't agree." Kendra raised her glass in a toast. "But here's to Elaine, the giver of many gifts."

"Elaine." Olivia drained her glass. She filled their glasses again. "I'm getting a little woozy. Did I mention I started before you got here?"

"Doesn't matter. It numbs it a little." She sipped the wine. "I had to go to the Big Rock tonight, and I was thinking how she'd have story time there for all of us once a week. They were usually about the sea, or mermaids, or wonderful mysterious creatures from the depths. How we loved those stories. All those kids she helped over the years were—"

"Why are you here?" Olivia suddenly interrupted to ask. "You were in Afghanistan and suddenly you're here investigating those murders? Where's Lynch?"

"Later. I don't want to talk about Afghanistan. And I certainly don't want to talk about Lynch." She filled Olivia's glass again. "It's time to remember Elaine..."

✦

4:40 A.M.

"Your phone is ringing," Olivia said drowsily. She lifted her head from the arm of the couch where she'd curled up and fallen asleep sometime in the past few hours. Then she was digging through Kendra's handbag on the coffee table. "Whoever it is keeps calling back." She threw the phone on Kendra's lap. "Answer it or turn it off." She suddenly straightened. "Unless it's Griffin with some word about Elaine."

"I doubt it." Kendra gazed blearily down at the phone. "Too early in the game to get any—" She inhaled sharply as she looked down at the ID. "Oh, shit. I forgot him."

Olivia frowned. "Lynch?"

"Of course not. Metcalf." She jumped to her feet. "I'll be right back. Will you make coffee? We might need the caffeine." Then she was running out of Olivia's condo and up the steps to her own floor.

She heard the howling as she reached the second landing.

She heard the cursing as she threw open her front door. "I'm sorry. I got distracted and then I fell asleep."

Metcalf glared at her. "Tell that to your super. He's been up here twice because your neighbors are complaining you're keeping a lion in your condo." He looked balefully down at Harley, who had backed him against the far wall of the foyer. "And that dog doesn't like me. I don't care what your friend Elaine said about him having such a wonderful disposition. He's been at that front door waiting for you since you went down to see Olivia. Between the growling and the howling, he had to have been heard by everyone on this floor."

But Harley had suddenly noticed Kendra. He tore across the room and skidded to a stop in front of her, his tail wagging excitedly. He lifted his head and opened his mouth to—

She quickly put her hand on his muzzle to change the greeting from a roar to a whimper of questioning alertness. "Nonsense. You should have just given him a little attention."

"He didn't want it. All he wanted was *House Hunters*."

"What?"

"When I realized you weren't coming back anytime soon, I flipped on the TV. I tried to watch *SportsCenter*, but—"

"*SportsCenter*? You disappoint me, Metcalf. I thought you'd be watching the Syfy channel."

He shrugged. "I tried. They were showing a *Battlestar Galactica* episode I'd already seen a hundred times."

"Oh, good. For a minute there, I thought I was going to have to take away your geek card."

"Not necessary. Anyway, the dog's howling suddenly got unbearable. So I flipped the channel. And I kept flipping it. He only stopped howling when I put on HGTV."

"Seriously?"

"Yes. Specifically, a show called *House Hunters*. They were having some kind of marathon. Do you realize all they do on that show is look at homes?"

"Yes. It's very popular."

He shook his head. "I don't get it. Anyway, it kept Harley quiet for a while. I actually fell asleep on your sofa. But when they started showing infomercials, everything changed. That's when he started stalking me around the living room."

"Stalking," she repeated skeptically. "He's a service dog. They don't stalk."

"Don't tell me that. I did my best, but he's very selective." He said flatly, "He's Jekyll and Hyde. With me he's Mr. Hyde. He showed me in no uncertain terms that he'd had enough and wanted to follow you. And after a while he got impatient and started stalking me around the living room until I started phoning you for help. Then he stopped and sat down as if he was waiting."

"Really?" She tilted her head, gazing speculatively at the dog. "Do you suppose he's that intelligent? Instigate a call and then wait for a response? Maddie said that he was one of the smartest dogs Elaine had ever seen. But that would take an amazing degree of—"

"I don't care," Metcalf interrupted. "I just want to get out of here and finish the night in my own bed without having to dog-sit your lion wannabe for one more minute." He stalked past her, carefully avoiding brushing against Harley. "You owe me, Kendra."

"Yes, I do." She was stroking Harley's throat, and the lion-growl was almost like a purr. "And I'm grateful. I needed that time alone with Olivia before I brought Harley into the mix. Thank you, Metcalf."

His scowl turned to a grudging smile. "You're welcome. Just don't ask me again." He paused as he opened the door. "I take it you have plans to pawn off this mutt on Olivia? She *is* blind, so I guess that makes some kind of sense. Does she think she needs a Seeing Eye dog?"

"Absolutely not."

He gave a low whistle. "Are you in trouble..."

The door closed behind him.

He was probably right, she thought wryly. She gave Harley a quick hug before grabbing the leash she'd put on the foyer table. She clipped it to his collar and got to her feet. "Come on. It's time we got to work. Elaine thought you were worth the effort and we've got to convince Olivia that you'll make a good team. Who knows? Elaine might even have planned on doing this herself." She wrinkled her nose as he gave a lion-bark. "Or not."

But Harley was staring at her alertly and took an eager step toward the door.

"Okay, I'll follow your lead. I guess we're in

this together." She opened the door. "Elevator or stairs?" But Harley was already pulling her toward the staircase, and she had to run to keep up. "Whatever..."

Two minutes later Harley was jumping on Olivia's door with his full weight. When Olivia opened it, he whirled into the living room of the condo like a golden tornado. He turned round and round in a dizzying circle and then lifted his head and roared.

Olivia's jaw dropped. "What the *hell* is that?"

"Harley. I think he's excited to meet you. I haven't seen him act like this before." Kendra entered the condo and slammed the door. "He's Elaine's latest project. He has a few problems but nothing we can't work out." She ran over and put her hand on Harley's head to stop him from bark-roaring. "If we can keep the super from kicking him out. Metcalf said he was causing a disturbance when I left them alone together."

"Imagine that," Olivia said dryly. "Does he look as fierce as he sounds?"

"No, he looks like a big, adorable mutt who needs a home...and a job." She paused. "He's a Seeing Eye dog, Olivia."

She stiffened. "Oh, no," she said fiercely, "Don't you dare try to do that to me, Kendra. You know I don't want a service dog. I can take care of myself."

"I know you can. You're the most independent

woman I know. Heaven forbid you get a little help from man, woman, or child."

"Or dog," Olivia said through set teeth. "I realize that the Seeing Eye program is a valuable service and it's fine for those who need it. I don't need it. I refuse to let myself need it. I've gotten along just great on my own all these years. Now take this animal out of here."

"I'll do that after I've told you everything Maddie told me about Harley. Just *listen* to me," she pleaded. "Elaine deserves that you at least know what you're refusing." She quickly recounted all that Maddie had told her about Harley; she ended urgently, "He reminds me a little of us when we were kids. We were both a little broken and having to make the best of everything we were to survive. That's what Harley is doing, but he doesn't know how. But maybe he could learn. Because besides being brave enough to risk his life trying to save that little boy, he's very smart." No response from Olivia. Kendra desperately tried something else. "And he *likes* you. I can tell. He seemed to know exactly where he was going when I brought him here. And you saw how happy he was when you let him come in."

"Stop trying to con me. I'm not buying it."

"It's not a con. I know my chances are zilch of getting you to let him stay. Though you'd be perfect.

He needs people, and you work here from your home. Every single thing I said, I believe." *Okay, tell her the entire truth.* "Besides, he'd be a security asset. You live alone and everyone knows that a home with a dog is much less likely to be robbed or vandalized. It's a statistic." Then she burst out, "It wasn't even a month ago that you were almost killed by that psycho who attacked you right here in this condo. And it was *my* fault, dammit. Because you're my friend, that serial killer I was hunting decided to go after you to hurt me. You should have all the protection I can give you."

"I was wondering when you'd get around to that." Olivia crossed her arms over her chest. "Nice point. I can't deny that being your friend has its hazards. But it's my choice if I want to accept those hazards. Are you finished?"

"No, not quite. Elaine wanted this dog to be healthy and happy. She thought he was worth the trouble. If she'd lived, she'd have tried to make sure of it." She added wearily, "I think that it's not too much trouble for us to find a way to give her what she wanted."

Olivia was silent. "Oh, that struck deep. But not deep enough. You have all the answers except how to make me accept a dog I don't want or need." She paused. "But you used a lot of *we* and *I* in your little presentation. That might get you somewhere." She held up her hand. "But not where you want to go. I'm not going to let this dog with his sad story and all his problems rule my life. Forget it." She moved toward the kitchenette. "But I'm willing to spend a little time searching for a home for him that even Elaine would approve of. As long as you remain involved and we do it together." She sat down at the table and poured herself a cup of coffee. "But *share* is the key word. Understood?"

Kendra drew a deep breath of relief as she dropped down opposite her. "Understood. Share."

"I'm glad that you—Oh, for Pete's sake." Her teeth clenched as she faced Kendra across the table. "Am I to assume that's your Harley's head on my lap? You didn't leave out any details about him, I hope. He doesn't drool as well as roar like a lion?"

"Not to my knowledge. But he's never put his head on my lap." She poured herself a cup of coffee. "I told you he liked you."

"Bullshit." But one of her hands was exploring Harley's big head beneath the table, learning him, as she did every new element in her life. "Coarse, rough hair, he obviously needs the services of a barber. Huge ears . . . What color are his eyes?"

"Brown." She took a sip of coffee. "And blue."

"Of course," Olivia said. "Why not? Nothing conventional that would please an ordinary family looking for a dog. He probably resembles a creature from outer space. But don't think that will keep me from finding a home for him. It will just take perseverance and determination. I'll only regard it as a greater challenge."

"I know you will." Kendra smiled. "And that's what I told Maddie was needed. Someone who could meet the challenge. I've seen you conquer every one that came your way."

"Damn straight." She lifted her chin and turned toward Kendra. "And I'll conquer this one, too. But it will be my way, and you might end up owning this lion-dog yourself. So I'd better have your complete cooperation about finding him a good home." She put her cup down in the saucer. "Now, who takes Harley for the rest of the night? Do we flip on it?"

"It's almost five in the morning. I should go down to the FBI regional office first thing this morning."

"Don't quibble. My work is just as important to me." She frowned. "Though yours may be more urgent at this particular time. I might let you trade my keeping Harley during the day if you take him at night. I'll think about it. But that's not tonight. Do we flip for it?"

Kendra sighed. "We flip for it."

CHAPTER

4

Hell, Harley was barking again.

Kendra groaned and buried her head beneath her pillow to smother the hideous snarl.

"Get up." Olivia jerked the pillow from Kendra's head. "Jump in the shower while I make coffee." She turned and faced the barking dog. She pointed her finger sternly at him. "And you be quiet. You've caused me enough trouble this morning."

Harley broke off in mid-roar and sat down gazing expectantly at her.

"He's actually quiet." Kendra gazed at him, stunned. "Causing *you* trouble? He's been howling and barking off and on since I brought him up here from your condo."

"Serves you right," Olivia said as she left her

bedroom. "Did I mention that the super woke me up because he couldn't rouse you?" she called back over her shoulder. "He wasn't pleased with you, either. We've got to solve this problem. And a few others that I realized are on the agenda. Now get moving."

"I'm on my way." Kendra was staggering toward the bathroom. "I'll be right there. Ten minutes."

But it was twenty minutes before she could force herself to leave the warm flow of the shower after her sleepless night.

"Sorry. I decided to wash my hair," she said as she came into the kitchen. "And I had to make sure I didn't smell like a dog. I had to do a lot of petting and close contact to keep Harley quiet."

"And you still weren't very successful." Olivia put a plate with French toast and bacon in front of her. "Eat." She poured her a cup of coffee. Then she sat down opposite her with her own cup. She faced Harley, who was standing practically on her feet, and said sternly, "Sit. You've caused enough trouble."

He sat down and put his head on his paws.

"Any other orders?" Kendra murmured. "You appear to be the one in charge around here."

"Someone has to be." Olivia leaned back and cradled her coffee cup in her two hands. "One more order. I was so blown away when you told me about Elaine and then sprang Harley on me that I let you get away with avoiding my questions about Afghanistan. Now you're going to stop sidling away from the subject and talk to me." Her lips tightened. "And tell me if it had anything to do with Elaine's and Ronald Kim's murders."

"No!" Kendra said, shocked. She had never thought that Olivia would draw that conclusion. "Well, not really. Not the murders themselves. Just the opposite. I only became involved because Lynch wanted me out of Afghanistan. The bastard pulled strings with Griffin, and Metcalf came up with—" She drew a deep breath and said, "Okay, I can see how you might think that, but you don't have to worry about those scumbag contractors in Afghanistan having anything to do with Oceanside. What a nightmare it would be if I thought I'd brought that ugliness down on Elaine and Mr. Kim. I don't have any idea yet why they were killed, but I guarantee it had nothing to do with those sons of bitches who were trying to screw our soldiers over there. The timing of my arrival here was pure coincidence. One had nothing to do with the other."

"Then tell me," Olivia demanded. "Start at the beginning."

"Lynch," Kendra said bitterly. "Doesn't it always start with Adam Lynch?"

———◆———

"I can see why you were angry," Olivia said after Kendra had finished. "Lynch was totally outrageous and arrogant." She lifted her cup and took a sip of coffee. "You were perfectly right to be furious with him. I would have felt the same way."

"Yes, you would," Kendra said. "I knew you'd understand how I was feeling when I stood on that runway in Afghanistan."

"Of course," Olivia said solemnly. "I can definitely identify." Then she started to chuckle. "But it doesn't help me get the picture out of my head of you confronting that pompous general and ready to take on half our troops in Afghanistan to go after Lynch." She leaned back in her chair and started to laugh helplessly. "Lord, that's funny. I needed something to lift my spirits after the night we had, and you gave it to me. I can almost forgive you for bringing this lion-dog to torment me."

"I'm glad it amused you," Kendra said coolly. "Particularly since you said you would have felt the same way about Lynch."

"Oh, I would." Her face was still convulsed with laughter. "And I would have been deep in planning how to punish the son of a bitch for daring to interfere with my independence and lifestyle. But that doesn't mean I can't stand back and enjoy the show he put on when it doesn't concern me." She finally managed to stop laughing and shook her head.

"Come on, we both know you'll find a way to get your own back eventually. But you should have been more cautious when you were dealing with Lynch. You knew he was afraid for you. From the beginning he told you that he didn't want you to go there. He was probably only waiting for his chance."

"You mean 'excuse,'" Kendra said. "I didn't do anything wrong, dammit."

"He thought there was jeopardy. And we both know he's an expert. But that doesn't matter, he didn't want you to run the risk." Her smile faded. "And neither did I. You get into enough danger here without wandering into a war zone. I hated the idea that you were over there in Kabul. I worried about you every day."

"You didn't have to worry long," she said sourly. "It was only three weeks before Lynch arranged to get me kicked out. And the devious bastard had a complete plan in place to keep me here before I got off that C-130."

"Maybe he had the outline sketched in, but there was no way he'd know about Elaine and Ronald Kim. You can hardly blame him for that, Kendra."

"No." She shook her head. "Of course I don't. But I never know where I am with him. After we got to Kabul, I thought he might be willing to accept that I was there and could do my part to help Jessie and him capture that scum. He acted just like he always did when we were working a case together." That was what had hurt her most when she realized that he'd betrayed her. She had thought that he accepted her as part of the team. Yes, she had known he was afraid for her, but she was also afraid for him and Jessie. She hadn't tried to get them tossed out of the country, had she? By staying together, they could protect each other. And in the beginning, she thought she'd managed to persuade him to her way of thinking. Those first weeks he had been amusing, knowledgeable, listening to her and Jessie with equal attentiveness. Being Lynch at his most fascinating. It was painful to think it might have just been lies and manipulation to get his own way. "He didn't get uptight until that last night."

"You mean when he thought the Taliban might decide to pay you a visit? That would do it, considering how he feels about you. You're lucky his patience lasted for three weeks."

"Patience?" The word irritated her. "I was *contributing*. As for what he feels for me, it evidently doesn't include respect or understanding."

"I believe it's in the mix somewhere." Olivia shrugged. "But he's a complicated man and what he feels for you is complicated, too. If you didn't like complications, you wouldn't have stayed and worked with Lynch during these last years. You would have found someone like Metcalf. You're not simple, either. You probably put Lynch through hell every now and then."

"No more than he deserved. I generally treated him as a trusted partner and colleague." She ignored Olivia's gentle snort. "And he had no right to do that to me. I'm going to find a way to go back and finish the job."

"I'm sure you will," Olivia said quietly. "But not until you finish solving the job you're on now. I believe everything can wait until we get justice for Elaine and Ronald. As far as I'm concerned, that's the most important thing on the agenda." Her lips tightened. "And at the moment, I don't care how pissed off you are with Lynch. He's smart, he has contacts, and he's innovative as hell. If he were here, I'd have you go to him and ask him for his help."

"And I'd do it," Kendra said quietly. "I'm not about to put anything ahead of Elaine. I know my priorities." She threw her napkin on the table. "But Lynch isn't here and not likely to be. He said he was staying to wrap up the investigation in Kabul, though I wouldn't be surprised if that means he's going after those bastards by himself. But I am here and I'll do everything I have to." She pushed back her chair and stood. "Now I've got to get dressed and get out of here." She started for the door and looked back at Harley, still at Olivia's feet. "He looks very contented. He's been like that ever since you came this morning. Does that tell you anything?"

"It tells me that you're still ruthlessly trying to pawn him off on me."

"Maybe." She tilted her head, still gazing at him. "I think he's falling asleep. Neither of us got much last night."

"Well, he'll have to wake up. I have to go back to my condo and work." Olivia nudged him with her foot. "Come on, lion-dog. I have to get you some dog food and then I suppose I'll have to take you for a walk."

Harley instantly jumped to his feet and ran out of the kitchen in the direction of the front door.

"You speak, he obeys," Kendra said. "Dog food is beside the table in the foyer. I brought it from Maddie's along with a couple of Elaine's notebooks about Harley that she'd found with the dog kennel. Training manuals and personal history." She was heading for her bedroom. "*Please* be merciful and keep him awake as much as you can today..."

◆

Kendra leaned back in the triangular-backed chair at the FBI regional office's fifth-floor conference room. She'd just viewed Metcalf's PowerPoint presentation on the wall-mounted monitor at the room's far end, and as promised, it provided a concise overview of the case, the victims, and the crime scenes. She turned toward Metcalf, who was alone with her at the long conference table.

"Well done, Metcalf."

"Thanks."

"But the musical number was a little much, don't you think?"

"Very funny. You know, there is a guy here who's fond of lens flares. You're lucky I didn't do that to you."

"I guess I owe you one." She thought about what she'd just seen. She was glad she'd visited the crime scenes first, since it helped frame everything more correctly in her mind. She was still exhausted from the long plane flight and the restless night worrying about Harley, but seeing those corpses in the presentation had jolted her wide-awake. "Anything on that fence post yet?"

"They're working on it now. That is human blood at the bottom and the top, and it should be more than enough to extract DNA. So far, your theory of the victim using it as a weapon is holding up."

"Good. Now we just need to get a DNA match." She looked at the last PowerPoint slide, still displayed on the screen. It showed the Woodward Academy at night, much as she'd seen it the evening before. "I only wish we knew why Ronald Kim was spying on the access road."

"Me too. We've talked to some friends of his, and no one had any idea that anything unusual was going on in his life."

"Where did he live?"

"The Convoy District, in Kearny Mesa."

"Near the medical examiner's office?"

Metcalf nodded. "You could practically walk to his house from there. It's become a trendy neighborhood for the Asian community. Some good bars and restaurants have popped up there in the past couple of years."

"Mr. Kim never struck me as a trendy guy."

"He wasn't. After his wife died, he pretty much kept to himself. He ate most of his meals at a small diner connected to a Korean grocer. He was friendly with some of the other customers there, but that's about it."

A wave of sadness suddenly hit Kendra. In all the years she'd known Mr. Kim, she'd rarely given any thought to his life away from the school, to his hopes and dreams. As with anyone she met, she'd made observations about him. But overall, she'd always looked at him through the eyes of the little girl she'd been when they first met. Most of the time he'd treated her with an almost-old-world formality and called her Ms. Kendra. In return, he had always been Mr. Kim to her, even when she had grown older. His whole life seemed to be at the school, tending to the flowers and bushes. She remembered his voice, sometimes kind as when he'd put one of the blooming irises in her hand so that she could feel the textures, sometimes stern if she'd accidentally stomped on his precious white pampas grass. But wasn't that how most children viewed adults? A series of small impressions and memories mainly concerned with how their presence impacted their own lives? Still, memories of the velvet touch of flowers, fresh, fragrant scents, and a voice teaching her bad from good was surely a way most people would like to be remembered.

"Kendra?" Metcalf said gently.

She snapped out of it. "Yeah. Did Mr. Kim have a cell phone on him?"

"No. And we still haven't found it. He used an old Samsung flip phone, and it wasn't in his car or his home."

"Too bad. How about Elaine? Did she have a phone?"

"Yes. Also missing. It was an inexpensive Android phone. She used it for email but it wasn't connected to her Cloud account."

"Huh. So his wad of cash and her expensive watch were untouched, but both of their phones are missing."

Metcalf nodded. "That's about the shape of it."

"I'd like to see Elaine's house. Would that be possible?"

"Yes. It so happens we have a key. We got it from the school. She listed them as her emergency contact after her divorce."

"Good." She stood up. "I'd like to go now. *Right* now."

Metcalf smiled. "Of course you would."

———◆———

Less than half an hour later, Kendra and Metcalf pulled up to the modest one-story Mediterranean house in San Marcos, a community located in northern San Diego County.

"Nice place." Metcalf turned off the engine.

"A few of the teachers from Woodward live in this area. It's only a fifteen-minute drive from campus, and the housing is still somewhat affordable."

"Affordable? In Southern California, that's a relative term."

They climbed out of the car and walked toward the front door. Metcalf started to put the key into the lock, but Kendra stopped him, pressed her fingers against the door, and gave it a shove. It swung open.

"The door was ajar," Kendra said. "Is it possible one of your people forgot to lock up behind them?"

Metcalf pulled his automatic from his shoulder holster. "No. Our guys don't make that kind of mistake."

She went still. "Is that really necessary?"

"Probably not. But stay here while I clear the premises."

"Sure."

Metcalf stood ramrod-straight with his jaw clenched and eyes narrowed. He looked like a different person, she realized. Not the sweet, amiable Metcalf, but someone else entirely.

It was a good look for him.

He extended the gun and called out: "FBI! Anyone in the house, show yourself immediately."

He disappeared into the back rooms, repeating his message twice more before falling silent.

The silence continued for a moment longer.

And a moment after that.

She cocked her head. No trace of his footsteps or any motion at all.

"Metcalf?" she finally called out.

No response.

"Metcalf?"

She felt a tapping on her back. "Worried?"

She whirled around and instinctively cut loose with a kick and a pair of punches.

It was Metcalf, and he doubled over in pain. "Oww!"

Kendra grabbed his arm. "What in the hell are you doing?"

Metcalf straightened up and holstered his gun. "I wanted to make sure no one ducked out the back door after we got here. So I checked out the yard and came around." He gingerly touched his stomach. "I didn't expect *that*."

"Sorry, but you kind of had it coming. That was idiotic."

"I knew you'd say that." He nodded toward the open front door. "After you. The house is clear."

Kendra stepped inside. "No idea why the door was ajar?"

"No. Nothing looks disturbed or out of place. I wasn't part of the team that came here before, but I saw the photos."

"Yeah, I saw one of them in your PowerPoint. Evidence Response didn't remove anything?"

"An address book, a laptop, and a wireless telephone. They're back at the fourth-floor lab. We've already pulled some numbers from the phone's caller ID memory, and we should have IDs worked up for everyone on the list soon."

Kendra glanced around the kitchen and living room. She hated this part probably more than any other stage of a murder investigation. Even worse than seeing the corpse, she thought. This is who Elaine Wessler *was*. It's where she spent her last morning on Earth, never dreaming her life would soon come to a horrific end.

Kendra looked at the coffee cup and oatmeal-encrusted bowl in the sink, right where Elaine had probably left them before dashing off to work. On the kitchen counter, mementos of a life cut short. A Symphony by the Bay subscription package. An invitation to a baby shower. Reminder card for a hair appointment.

Kendra looked at a collage of framed photos in the short hallway that bridged the kitchen with the living room. Elaine appeared to come from a large family, kept a broad circle of friends throughout her life. She obviously loved to travel, mostly in western Europe.

Kendra moved into the neat living room, taking in the potted plants and stacks of gardening and pet care magazines.

Kendra shook her head. "Things hadn't been easy for Elaine since her divorce."

"What makes you say that?"

She gestured toward a bookshelf. "Lots of recent self-help books, all in the love and relationship category. Titles that suggest she was working through some serious self-doubt." She picked up one of the books and showed it to Metcalf.

He read the title aloud: "*Not My Fault: A Guide to Loss in Love.*" He winced. "Ouch."

"And right next to it is something called *Broken*

Hearts, Broken Dreams." She put the book back on the shelf and motioned toward the framed photos hanging in the hallway. "And it's obvious a few of those pictures have been replaced recently."

"Obvious how?"

"The wall is slightly sun-faded, but if you look carefully you can see fresh patches where larger-size photos once hung. I'd bet they were pictures that included her husband." She turned back into the room. "None of this is unusual for someone who had just faced the end of a long marriage, but she was obviously struggling with it."

"Anything else?

"She fostered at least four different types of dogs in the past six months."

"Dog hair on the couch?"

"Yes. Very good, Metcalf." She nodded. "And the same types of hairs are on that tracksuit jacket hanging near the front door. Harley is represented by those gold, straight, wiry hairs that have already found their way onto my living room sofa."

Metcalf nodded. "And the slacks and jacket I was wearing last night. They pierce the fabric. You pretty much have to pull them off one at a time."

"Something to look forward to. One more reason for Olivia to be unhappy with us."

"Unhappy with *you*," he corrected. "I was just an unwitting participant."

"You're not willing to take some of the heat?"

"Absolutely not."

"Coward."

"And Olivia knows better."

"You're right, not much I can do about it. That reminds me . . ." Kendra walked over to the coffee table, picked up the TV remote, and pressed the POWER button. After a moment, an episode of *House Hunters* appeared on the screen.

"Aha," Metcalf said. "So that's where Harley acquired his HGTV addiction."

"One mystery solved." Kendra turned off the TV and looked around the room again.

Come on, Elaine. Show me something, anything, that can help us . . .

Kendra fought another overwhelming wave of sadness.

Detach. Concentrate.

There had to be something here that would—

Wait.

It's not something that was here. It's something that *wasn't* here.

She turned toward Metcalf. "There were pictures and video of this room in your PowerPoint. Do you happen to have any of those with you?"

He pulled out his phone. "I was very proud of it. The entire presentation is right here."

"Of course it is."

"Unless you need it bigger, in which case I can get my iPad from the car."

"This will be fine. Can you pull up the shots of this house?"

Metcalf's fingers slid across the screen with a dexterity reserved for teenage texters and the most ardent *Angry Birds* competitors. Within seconds, his phone screen displayed an HD video of the room in which they were presently standing.

Kendra tapped it to freeze the image. "Look at this."

He studied the screen. "What am I looking for?"

"There are some things missing in here. When this video was shot, there was a camera on a hook at the side of the bookshelf. Now it's gone."

Metcalf looked from his phone, to the bookshelf, and back again. He walked over and looked at the floor.

"It's not anywhere," Kendra said. "I just checked. And it also looks like there was a hoodie on the coat-rack, which is also gone. And could you scan back to the kitchen?"

"Sure. Why?"

"There was a key hanging from the side of the refrigerator, held by flower magnets."

Metcalf glanced into the kitchen. "The magnets are there."

"The key isn't."

"Are you sure about this? I don't remember seeing—"

"Check the video."

Metcalf scanned back through the presentation until he finally saw the kitchen. "I'll be damned. There was a key there."

Kendra took another look around, making sure she hadn't missed anything. "Let me look at the rest of the place. Stay close with your phone in case I need to double-check something, okay?"

"You got it."

Kendra quickly scanned the rest of the rooms. There was a guest bedroom and bath that was decorated with an overabundance of paisley and lace, and another bedroom that had been repurposed as a project room with a low table and a taller artist's workbench.

"Interesting," Kendra said. She reached over and thumbed through a pile of decals, word balloons, and decorative borders. "She was a scrapbooker."

"Not uncommon these days," Metcalf said. "Both of my grandmothers had sewing rooms. Nowadays, it's all about scrapbooking."

"Fine. But where are the scrapbooks?" Kendra opened the closet, which was loaded top-to-bottom with more craft materials. "I haven't seen one in this entire house, though there are dozens of photo and border trims next to the paper cutter over there."

Metcalf nodded. "You're right."

Kendra pointed to a tall barren bookshelf in the corner of the room. "She kept them there. There's a fine layer of dust that begins about a foot up on the interior sides of each shelf." She picked up a blank scrapbook page and held it upright on one of the shelves. It matched up almost perfectly with the faint dust line. She turned back to Metcalf. "Someone took them."

"But why? What could they have been? Vacations? Seeing Eye dogs she helped train?"

"I don't know. It could be nothing more than someone wanting something to remember her by. Or it could be...something else."

"Well, somebody came in here after Evidence Response made their sweep. I'd like to know who it was."

"Same here."

Metcalf's phone vibrated in his pocket, accompanied by the five-note *Close Encounters of the Third Kind* motif.

Kendra smiled. "That's your new ringtone? Sorry I ever questioned your geek credentials. You can have your membership card back."

Metcalf fished the phone from his jacket inside breast pocket. "It means I got a text. Usually it's just a worthless—" He looked at the screen and froze.

"What is it?"

"We need to go. If we hurry, we can meet the data tracker team downtown." He started for the door.

"What in the hell is going on?"

He showed her the text. "Ronald Kim's phone popped up on the grid. Someone just turned it on."

CHAPTER
5

Kendra saw the three black FBI vans as they turned into the Embarcadero Marina Park North, adjacent to the San Diego Convention Center. The tech team was using it as their staging area, and they were clearly preparing to move out. Metcalf pulled to a stop next to the basketball courts, and they climbed out of the car.

They approached John Hyde, a tech specialist Kendra recognized from an earlier investigation. He was a slender man with gray slicked-back hair.

"What's the story?" Metcalf asked.

Hyde checked a scanner in his left hand. "The wireless providers were advised to notify us if either of your victims' phones came online, but you know how that is."

"Yeah, they might let us know a day later," Metcalf said sourly.

"Not this time. We heard from them within minutes. Ronald Kim's phone is pinging a tower downtown."

"Still?" Metcalf asked.

Hyde checked his scanner again. "Still active."

"Is it being used to make a call?" Kendra asked.

"Not as of a few minutes ago. But it's powered on. It's an older phone, which makes our job more difficult. If it was an Apple or Android phone, I'd already have an address. We're about to go out and do a manual sweep." Hyde motioned toward one of the vans. "If you want to come along, I've got room in my van."

Metcalf turned to Kendra. "Ever been on a Stingray sweep?"

"A *what?*"

He smiled, took her arm, and led her back through the open side door of the van. Inside, there were two other agents, a man and a woman, seated at a long bench seat that faced a wall of gear lining the left rear side. Both agents wore headphones. They nodded their greetings and turned back toward their instrument panels.

Metcalf pointed to a small silver box in the equipment rack. "Today, that's the only thing that matters. It's called a Stingray."

"I've been part of investigations that have used them, but I was always sequestered away in a command center."

"Oh, this is much more fun." He pulled down a bench seat that backed up against the front driver's and passenger seats. "Buckle up."

Hyde climbed in behind the wheel and started up the van. After another couple of minutes, they were on the road.

Metcalf pointed at the lines of people snaking around the convention center. There were thousands, many wearing elaborate costumes. "I should be there, you know," he said glumly.

Kendra gasped. "Comic-Con. I totally forgot. I usually don't go near the place around this time."

Metcalf unfastened the top two buttons of his shirt and pulled out a laminated convention badge attached to a lanyard. "I thought I might get a chance to take a whirl around the dealers' room today." He sighed. "Maybe tomorrow."

Kendra rolled her eyes. "And to think I questioned your geekiness in any way."

"You do that at your own peril. If you want any Hasbro exclusives or Funko figurines, I'm your man."

The female tech instantly turned around in her chair. "Funko? Actually, Metcalf, we'll speak."

"Sure thing." Metcalf turned back to Kendra. "See? I'm not the only one."

"Obviously."

Within minutes, they had traveled through the Gaslamp district and were in the heart of downtown.

Kendra leaned toward the Stingray box, where several indicator lights were flashing. "What's happening here?"

"It's sending out a signal that makes it appear to be a cell phone tower," Metcalf said. "Phones automatically connect to the strongest tower in the area, so hundreds of mobile phones are now connecting to this box as we drive along. But we're only interested in one, so the Stingray immediately cuts the others loose."

Kendra nodded. "So what happens when we find Ronald Kim's phone?"

At that moment, a red indicator light flashed.

"*That's* what happens," Metcalf said. "We lock on and don't let go. Now, as we move down these streets, our system is constantly measuring the strength of the phone signal. If it gets weaker, we know we're moving away. If it's getting stronger, we know we're getting closer."

Kendra nodded. "Kind of a digital version of 'hot and cold.'"

"You got it. We have two other vans doing the same thing. Whoever has that phone now, we'll find him."

With directions from the two techs, Hyde drove up and down the city streets until they finally turned down Fifth.

"This is it," the female tech shouted. "Probably less than two hundred yards."

Kendra's breath caught in her throat. "Metcalf... This is *my* street."

He looked out the front windshield. "I know. And two hundred yards would put us..."

"...right at my front door."

Metcalf leaned toward Hyde. "Take us to that white building on the right. Now!"

Hyde gunned the engine and raced toward Kendra's building. They skidded to a stop.

"This is it!" the female tech said tensely.

Kendra stared in bewilderment at her building's main entrance. What in the hell? She started to get out of the van.

"No," Metcalf said. "The killer could be in there waiting for you. We'll have half a dozen agents swarming that place in just a few minutes."

Hyde was already talking into his headset with the other mobile units, informing them of the location.

Kendra shook her head. "But why me?"

"It's no secret you joined the investigation," Metcalf said. "I'm sure everyone at the school knows it."

"My place is locked down," Kendra said. "No way anyone gets in there without me knowing about it. My phone would be shrieking right now."

"They could be in a hallway. Or the elevator. Or—"

Kendra's breath left her. "Olivia!"

She grabbed the door handle, but Metcalf blocked her. "Two minutes, Kendra. Agents are on their way."

Shit! Kendra looked up at the second-floor windows. Olivia was home. *Is it possible that—?*

Kendra pulled out her phone with shaking hands and voice-dialed Olivia's number.

She listened. Why in the hell was it taking so long to connect? Finally she heard the first ring. Then the second.

Come on, Olivia . . .

A third ring. A fourth.

Voicemail.

Shit!

She left a message. "Olivia, it's me. Don't let anyone in your place until I get there, you hear me? No one but me! I'll explain later."

Kendra cut the connection.

The other two vans rolled up behind theirs. "The teams are here," Metcalf said. "Wait in here, and we'll—"

"Like hell," Kendra said. She slid open the van

door and jumped out onto the sidewalk. "I'm going up to Olivia's. If your agents want to follow me, tell them to keep up."

"Kendra..."

But she had already thrown open the main door and was moving through the lobby.

Kendra bypassed the elevator and sprinted toward the stairwell. She looked behind her. Metcalf and two other agents were running behind her with guns drawn.

Please, please, please let Olivia be okay.

Kendra ran down the second-floor hallway to Olivia's condo. She pounded on the door. "Olivia, it's me! Open the door, please. Olivia!"

No answer.

"Olivia!"

The dead bolt was thrown and the door swung open.

It was Olivia. She appeared to be fine. Her phone was pressed against her ear.

She was frowning and mouthed the words *radio interview*.

Kendra smiled with relief. Just another workday for Olivia, promoting her website with a radio interviewer from Australia, England, Des Moines, or somewhere else on the planet.

"Sorry," Kendra whispered. "We're going to search your place."

Olivia wore a puzzled expression, but she waved them in and walked back toward her desk.

There was a time when Olivia would have been more surprised, Kendra thought.

Then all of a sudden Olivia whirled to face her, violently shaking her head. She pointed to her bedroom door and made a silent woofing motion with her pursed lips.

Harley! Kendra thought. She'd completely forgotten the dog was here. She held up her hand to tell the agents to freeze. Then she ran over to the bedroom and silently opened the door. Harley was on Olivia's bed watching the flickering screen of her TV, totally fascinated. *House Hunters*? Kendra wasn't about to determine that right now. She just wanted to get out of here before Harley saw her and his barking ruined Olivia's interview. She was in enough trouble with her friend as it was. She soundlessly closed the door, nodded, and motioned to Metcalf for the agents to continue their search.

It took only a couple of minutes to search the rest of the condo, and the agents were surprisingly respectful of Olivia's need for silence. "Clear," one of them finally whispered.

They filed out into the hallway and closed the door behind them.

"Your place," Metcalf said in a normal speaking

voice. "But you have to let us do our jobs. You stay out while we clear it."

"Fine."

They walked upstairs and Kendra gave Metcalf the keys. She waited in the hallway with one of the agents while they cleared the condo.

"See?" she said. "Told you no one could get into my place."

Metcalf's cell phone rang and he answered it. "Yeah? Okay. Okay. We'll be right down." He cut the connection.

"That was the sweeper team," he said as he headed for the stairwell. "They found Ronald Kim's phone."

"Where?"

Metcalf shook his head. "You're not gonna believe it."

———◆———

Two minutes later, they ran from the stairwell into the underground parking garage, where the sweep teams had already converged. Kendra shook her head at the surreal sight before her. No less than half a dozen investigators were clustered together, aiming their flashlights in front of them.

At her car!

"It's here," one of the techs shouted. "Right on the dash."

Kendra, Metcalf, and the other agents gathered around. As promised, an ancient, worn flip phone was open on her car dashboard, where no one could possibly miss it.

"The car was locked," Kendra said.

"Still is," one of the techs said, aiming his flashlight at the interior door handles. "And we've checked the doors and trunk. No obvious point of entry."

"Do you have the key on you?" Metcalf asked.

Kendra reached into the pocket of her slacks and pulled out the electronic key fob. She extended it to Metcalf, but before he could take it, she snapped her fist closed. "Wait."

He wrinkled his brow.

She leaned over the hood. "Everyone turn off your flashlights. Now!"

They powered off their flashlights.

Kendra looked through the windshield, holding up her hand to block the reflection from the garage's overhead lights. She squinted. There, on the floor in front of the driver's seat, she saw a faint green glow. "See that?"

Hyde was the first to see it. "Oh, shit."

Metcalf automatically backed away from the car.

"It's coming from underneath the seat," Hyde said. "It looks like it could be from an LED bulb."

Metcalf nodded. "Like a detonator's ready light?"

"Can't say for sure. I'm just glad you didn't unlock this car."

Metcalf stood straight and once again assumed the leadership role. "Okay, split up. No one goes near this car. I need a door-to-door on the entire building. We're evacuating and calling in the explosives unit. Move!"

"Right." Kendra turned and headed back into the building. "I'll get Olivia."

"Just get out of the building, Kendra," Metcalf called. "Our people will take care of that."

She didn't look back as she threw open the door and bolted into the lobby. She heard Metcalf mutter a curse as the door slammed closed behind her.

Tough luck, Metcalf.

Kendra bounded up the stairs and once again ran to Olivia's condo. She pounded on the door, and Olivia answered. This time she wasn't on the phone.

"Hi," Kendra said breathlessly. "Get Harley. We need to get out of the building."

"Whoa, whoa, whoa. You need to explain. First you bring half of the FBI San Diego field office here without a word of explanation..."

"You were on the phone. I didn't want to interrupt your interview." Kendra looked around. "Is his leash in here?"

"It's on my desk. What in the hell is going on?"

"We traced a murder victim's phone to this building. I was afraid the killer might have been coming after you."

"That obviously wasn't the case. Really, Kendra, it's not as if I'm constantly at risk." She added suspiciously, "Or was this just another ploy to prove how invaluable Harley might prove if I needed protection?"

"I wouldn't go to those lengths. We found the phone in my car. Along with what may be an explosive device."

"A *bomb*? In this building?"

"Don't know. We're evacuating just to be sure." Kendra turned to Harley, who had come out of Olivia's bedroom to see what the excitement was about. "Ready to go for a walk, boy?"

Harley yawned.

Kendra grabbed the leash from Olivia's desk and clipped it to Harley's collar.

Olivia ejected a USB drive from her computer. She turned back to Kendra and shook her head. "Never mind the bomb. If I were you, I'd be more worried about the condo association."

"Ah, you'll vouch for me."

Olivia's brows rose. "Again?"

They took the stairs down and crossed the street, where several of their neighbors had already begun to gather. From the snippets of conversations

Kendra overheard, they clearly hadn't been told why they'd been rushed from their homes.

An elderly neighbor, Irene Mero, who lived across the hall from Kendra, glared at her. She was protectively holding her white Persian cat as far away from Harley as she could manage. "This is because of you, isn't it?"

Kendra sighed. "Hi, Irene."

"It's always because of you. Care to tell me what's going on?"

"I'm really not at liberty to say."

"And I suppose you won't tell me if it's anything I should be concerned about?"

"They're just being cautious," Kendra said soothingly. "I'm sure we'll all be back in our condos very soon. This is all much ado about nothing."

Kendra heard a swell of excited chatter from residents on the sidewalk behind her. She turned. A large black truck had pulled in front of their building. Bold lettering on the side read FBI BOMB TECHNICIANS.

Kendra shook her head. "Subtle," she said under her breath. "Real subtle."

"Shit!" Irene grabbed her cat tighter and started pushing her way toward the nearest policeman. "Cautious!"

"What am I missing?" Olivia asked Kendra.

"Not much. Just the FBI doing what they do best. Scaring the hell out of people."

"That must be their truck I heard roll up in front of our building."

"Yep. And they don't mince words. 'Bomb Technicians' is in bold, scary lettering. I think the font is Helvetica 'You're All Gonna Die.'"

"Awesome." She suddenly flinched. "Ouch, I think Harley just stepped on my foot."

Kendra looked down at Harley, who was constantly maneuvering himself between Olivia and everyone who walked by on the crowded sidewalk. She smiled. "He's just doing his job, and doing it pretty darn well. He's protecting you."

"Is that what he's doing? I wish he could do it without stepping on my toes. I thought he was just agitated from all the activity."

"No, only when anyone comes near you. It's pretty crowded here and he probably couldn't avoid stepping on you. He's really bonded with you."

Olivia clicked her tongue. "He probably bonds with anyone who feeds him."

"I doubt that. I told you his history, he's very loving. He almost died of grief when he lost that little boy in the explosion. He hasn't bonded with anyone else since then, not even Elaine. He accepted her, but she wasn't his chosen person."

"Knock it off, Kendra," Olivia said, exasperated. "I get what you're doing here. How many times do I have to tell you that I don't need a guide dog?"

"Of course you don't *need* one," Kendra said quietly. "But maybe he needs you. He was selected and trained for only one thing. To serve and protect. Perhaps with you he's realizing instinctively it's time for him to reach out again and do what he does best. It just seems... right."

Olivia was silent. "Damn, you're good. Now I'm supposed to perform therapy on Harley? Not likely. You might be right, but it only means we'll have to find him someone else he'll accept to guide him through his therapy sessions." She held up her hand. "No more. You struck out again. Now talk about something else."

Kendra shrugged. "Okay, it just occurred to me that it could be a reason for Harley's occasional rather peculiar behavior."

"It's because *he's* peculiar," Olivia said flatly. "Now change the subject."

They stood on the sidewalk for another thirty minutes until Metcalf stepped outside with a bullhorn and made a brief announcement. "You may now return to your homes. Thank you for your cooperation. Have a good night."

"That's it?" Olivia asked.

Most of their neighbors waited a few minutes until they saw the bomb technician truck start up and roll away. Then they slowly crossed the street and moved back into the building.

Kendra patted Olivia's arm. "Go home. I'll give you an update when we're done, okay?"

Olivia smiled slyly. "Hey, need a bomb-sniffing dog?"

"Bye, Olivia."

Kendra entered her garage and ducked under the yellow crime scene tape stretched near her car. Metcalf and the other agents were still there, hunched over a small plastic container.

"No bomb?" Kendra called out.

"No." Metcalf turned to face her. "Not in your car, not anywhere around here. The bomb techs swept the whole place."

"Then what was it?"

Metcalf angled the container toward her. "Check it out."

Kendra looked down. It was a simple circuit board with a single green LED bulb mounted on its top surface.

Kendra shrugged. "It's not a bomb, but it's meant to look like one."

Metcalf turned to the techs. "Okay, let's bag it." He turned back to Kendra. "Sorry, but we're taking your car."

"What?"

"A tow truck is on the way."

"Aw, come on."

"Right now, your car is the best lead we have.

The only person likely to have Ron Kim's phone is his killer, and for some reason he broke into your car, placed it on your dashboard, and turned it on. He knew it would bring us here."

Kendra nodded. " . . . and probably knew what a stir his green light would cause."

"Someone's taunting you." Metcalf's lips were tight. "I hate to say it, but that could be why Woodward Academy was targeted. They knew it would bring you on the case."

"Maybe. We can't be sure."

"In any case, the killer was probably in your car today. I want our guys in the garage to examine and swab every centimeter."

Kendra bit her lip in frustration. The fact that Metcalf was right didn't make the news any easier to hear. She'd be without wheels for the next couple of days. Still, a small price to pay if it got them any closer to catching that monster. "Okay, but don't let them take the whole damn thing apart. I know how much your guys like to do that."

"I'll do my best," he said solemnly. "But whatever parts they have left over after reassembling your car, I'll make sure they box 'em up and give them to you."

"Thanks a lot, Metcalf."

After Kendra reached her condo she took a long, relaxing shower. She heard her phone ring but she didn't bother to answer it. *Let it ring.* It had been a rough day and she deserved a little pampering. It rang again after she'd finished and was blow-drying her hair. When she glanced at the caller ID, she wished she could ignore it entirely. But you didn't ignore Lynch; he only went around and came at you from another direction.

As he had on the way back here from Afghanistan on that C-130. She supposed she was lucky that she hadn't heard from him before this. *Get it over with.*

She pressed the ACCESS button. "Hello, Lynch. I can't talk to you now. I'm going to go down and have dinner with Olivia."

"An engagement of infinite importance. I won't keep you long," he said, amused. "I realize I'm not your favorite person these days. I only wanted to make certain you were settling in properly."

"As well as can be expected." She paused. "Don't you really mean that you wanted to know if I'd made any strides on getting my visa back?" Then she snapped her fingers. "Oh, that's right—you're much too influential with the Justice Department to worry about that. You believe I'm stuck wherever you want to put me."

"Not true," he said softly. "I know eventually you'll find a way to get what you want. I'm only hoping that I'll make enough progress here so that I'll be able to make it safer for you when you do."

She couldn't resist the temptation to ask, "And have you made progress?"

"A little. I don't want to move too fast and scare anyone off."

"Well, I'm sure that won't happen. You're very good at manipulating situations. Look how you finessed Griffin and his team to get what you wanted from me. You picked the perfect case to bring me running."

"I didn't pick it," Lynch said quietly. "It would never have been my choice. I just threw Griffin an offer and he went full steam ahead as he usually does. That's why I'm calling you. I phoned Griffin this morning and he told me about Woodward Academy. He said you knew the victims. I'm sorry, you've told me how much those teachers meant to you. This must be hurting you. If I'd known, I would have told Griffin to go anywhere but there."

"But you didn't know, you just knew you wanted your own way." She had to steady her voice. "And yes, it *is* hurting. I cared about them. They were part of who I am in ways you can't even imagine."

"You're wrong, I can imagine," he said roughly. "That's why I'm feeling so damn rotten. I can't help it. It bothers the hell out of me. I want to be there for you."

He meant it. There could be no mistake. In spite of the anger and indignation she had been feeling toward him, she knew that he would never do anything to hurt her. They had been close for too long; she had shared confidences and stories with him that she had never shared with anyone else. They had saved each other's lives, watched each other's backs, and lately she had even made the idiotic mistake of having sex with him. You couldn't go through all that with a man without knowing him. And she wouldn't pretend she didn't believe him because he'd been a complete asshole to her. "Okay, you know how I feel," she said curtly. "Two wonderful, caring people died for no good reason. None of it makes sense. But I've got to make sense of it or I won't be able to stand it."

"I know you won't." He paused. "Any clues?"

Blood on the fence posts. That bit of malicious mockery in her own car today. "Nothing definitive. Sorry to disappoint you. But you only threw me into this case yesterday. What can you expect?"

"You hesitated. Which means I might expect practically anything. And you know I didn't mean to throw you into a situation that might hurt you. You realize I'm apologizing."

"An apology from you is so rare that I'm having trouble recognizing it. I didn't get one when you got me kicked out of Kabul."

"And you won't get one. I did what I thought was best. This is different."

"You bet it is," she said wearily. "And I can only deal with one problem at a time. Getting back to Afghanistan will have to wait. I'll accept your apology for getting Griffin to drag me into this particular case because I would have become involved the minute I heard about the murders anyway. So forget about it, Lynch. This is my show now and I won't have your interference. Think positive. For once I'm doing exactly what you wanted me to do."

"No, you're not. But that might come with time and effort." He said softly, "Have a good dinner with Olivia. I'm glad she's with you. Let me know if you want to talk. I promise I'll accept any tongue-lashing, keep quiet, and not offer advice."

"Yeah, that's not going to happen."

"You can never tell." He chuckled, and she could almost see those brilliant blue eyes gleaming with mischief. "Try me."

He cut the connection.

And she felt suddenly alone without that vibrant, crackling presence reaching out to her. Very dangerous sign. It meant, though she found it hard to admit to herself, she might have become accustomed to the thought of Lynch's betrayal. Not that it mattered. The anger was still there, it just meant that she was remembering Lynch as a whole personality and in spite of herself she'd been touched that he'd called when he'd realized she might be in pain.

But that might not be a good thing.

I can't help it. It bothers me like hell.

And what bothered Lynch quite often ended up with interference and manipulation. All she needed was to have him looking over her shoulder and calling every night to check on her progress. Had she said anything that might have triggered his curiosity?

You hesitated.

It was what she hadn't said, she realized with exasperation. And it was only a matter of time before Lynch tapped one of his sources and heard about that bomb scare today. If he hadn't called Griffin this morning instead of later today, he might already have known about it.

Considering Lynch's contacts, she couldn't stop that from happening, but she could delay it.

She quickly punched in Griffin's home number.

"I just got home, Kendra," he said impatiently. "Couldn't it wait until tomorrow?"

"I have no idea, but I'm not taking any chances. I just had a call from Lynch, and I didn't want him phoning you and demanding a report. Since you seem to be in his pocket I figured you'd be the first one he'd call."

"I'm not in his pocket," Griffin said sourly. "We

just have a mutually profitable arrangement that benefits us both. Though the bastard was almost nasty about all my efforts to do that when he phoned this morning. What did he expect? I gave him what he wanted." He added, "And I gave you what you wanted, too."

"Yes, you're completely misunderstood. You acted just as we should have expected you to act considering that you have an FBI badge where your heart should be. And you did give me what I wanted, and I want you to continue." She added curtly, "But I want that report to be the last one you give Lynch about this case. And I want you to call Metcalf and tell him the same thing."

Silence. "That might be difficult."

"I don't give a damn. I don't know how you're going to do it, but if you ever want me to work another case for you, I won't have Lynch involved in this one." She continued, "I'm not going to make false threats about pulling out of the Woodward case. You'd know that would be bogus, but I keep my promises. I've just made you one. Believe it, Griffin."

"I believe it," he said slowly. "You're a valuable asset and I don't want to lose you. But Lynch can be—"

"Difficult," she repeated his word. "And profitable. Make your choice."

"I'm not Lynch's only source. It would only be a matter of time until he finds out what he wants to know."

"That could be the time I need to come to terms with what's happening without his interference. Stopping you would be the first line of defense."

"You speak as if he's your enemy. We both know that's not true, Kendra. Why not be reasonable and let me discuss—"

"Make your choice."

Silence. "I suppose I could avoid talking to him for a while. After all, I'm not at his beck and call."

"It only seems that way. Remember to call Metcalf. I'll be in touch tomorrow, Griffin." She cut the connection.

Done.

It wouldn't be a permanent fix, but it would have to do. It might keep Lynch from taking any action for a day or two and free her from his machinations.

Machinations was such a hard, soulless word, and it reminded her of what Griffin had said.

You speak as if he's your enemy.

He was not her enemy. He could never be her enemy. But sometimes it felt safer to treat him as if he was.

◆

KABUL, AFGHANISTAN

Voicemail.

It was the second time Lynch had called Griffin, and both times the calls had gone to voicemail.

Lynch leaned back in his office chair and stared at the green glow of the lampshade illuminating the papers on his desk. The voicemail could mean nothing, but Griffin usually picked up his calls right away.

He punched in Metcalf's number and waited.

Voicemail.

He shook his head and smiled slowly. Kendra had worked quickly to slam those particular doors in his face. But then she was always efficient, and she'd been very clear that she didn't want him to have anything to do with this case involving friends from her childhood. He'd actually considered waiting in the wings to see if there were problems.

Until he'd realized she was hiding something.

If Griffin had reassured him, he might still have stayed in the background. But Griffin had not reassured him and it was probably because Kendra had not wanted him to talk to Lynch.

Trouble?

Possibly. But even if it was only that Kendra wanted to avoid his interference because of her emotional attachment to these friends from her past, he had to be certain. Everyone needed privacy, but he couldn't let allowing Kendra her personal space to put her at risk.

So do what had to be done, but do it in the least aggressive way possible. He reached for his phone again.

On the other hand, the nuances of being aggressive could sometimes be many-faceted, intricately complicated . . . and ultimately satisfying.

He quickly dialed the number and listened to it ring.

CHAPTER

6

Damn traffic.

Kendra had woken up, showered, thrown on her clothes, and grabbed an Uber car to the Woodward Academy. She thought she'd be traveling against the flow of rush-hour traffic, but the I-5 freeway had a way of quashing any foolish notions of hope or optimism. Still, the ride did give her time to catch up on emails and rearrange her day's appointment schedule.

She needed to go back to Woodward and see the crime scenes in daylight, though she doubted she'd missed anything during her initial sweeps. And now maybe she could learn something from the other teachers and staff members.

Her phone vibrated in her hand. Probably a

callback from one of her music therapy clients. Hopefully they'd be willing to move their appointment to a time when—

DO I NEED TO COME BACK THERE?

It was a text message from Lynch.

She typed her response: ABSOLUTELY NOT. WHY? ASSISTANCE STILL NOT NEEDED. MUST GET OVER ONESELF.

He responded: YOU'VE SOMEHOW FROZEN ME OUT. UNEASY WHEN UPDATES DRY UP.

She typed back: TOLD YOU TO STAY OUT OF IT.

His response came quickly: USUAL SOURCES SURPRISINGLY UNRESPONSIVE.

She smiled and typed: SURPRISING TO GREAT AND SELF-SATISFIED ADAM LYNCH, PERHAPS.

HMM. PROBABLY DESERVED THAT.

PROBABLY?

OKAY, DEFINITELY. WHAT DID YOU DO?

ONLY WHAT THE PUPPETMASTER WOULD HAVE DONE.

ONCE AGAIN, NOT APPRECIATING USE OF VAGUELY INSULTING NICKNAME.

She laughed out loud in the back of the car. She responded: INSULTING PERHAPS, BUT NICKNAME ACCURACY NOT IN DISPUTE. WILL CONTINUE TO USE.

WONDERFUL. NOW HOW DID YOU ENFORCE BLACKOUT OF ALL TRUSTED SOURCES?

Kendra hesitated before revealing her strategy. She shrugged. Surely, he knew already. She typed: THREATENED TO WITHHOLD ONE THING OF VALUE TO THEM.

His response was immediate. She imagined his fingers flying across his phone's keyboard: OF COURSE. YOUR ASSISTANCE IN FUTURE INVESTIGATIONS.

BINGO.

EXACTLY WHAT I WOULD HAVE DONE. AFRAID YOU'VE BEEN COR-RUPTED BY MY BAD INFLUENCE.

NO WORRIES. BAD INFLUENCES PREDATED ADAM LYNCH BY MANY, MANY YEARS.

RELIEVED TO HEAR. MUST TELL ME ABOUT THEM SOMETIME. I ALWAYS LIKE TO HEAR ABOUT YOUR WILD DAYS. SO WHERE TO NOW? UNLESS BLACKOUT STILL IN EFFECT.

She thought for a moment. No harm in telling him. ON WAY TO ACADEMY.

WITH METCALF?

NOT TODAY. WILL ACCOMPLISH MORE ALONE.

WISH I WAS THERE WITH YOU.

She had a sudden wish he was, too. He was everything that was entertaining and amusing and always exactly on her wavelength. But there was no way she'd tell him that.

WHAT PART OF "ALONE" DO YOU NOT UNDERSTAND?

UNDERSTOOD PERFECTLY. JUST NOT CRAZY ABOUT CONCEPT.

I'LL BE FINE. NEARING SCHOOL NOW.

GOOD LUCK. LOOKING FORWARD TO HAVING BLACKOUT LIFTED.

She smiled and typed: NOT IN FORESEEABLE FUTURE.

HMM... PERHAPS IF I RAMP UP CHARM OFFENSIVE...

YIKES, WOEFULLY UNDERMANNED ON THAT FRONT. ALTERNATIVE STRATEGY RECOMMENDED.

She closed the conversation.

Typical Lynch. He knew she was still angry with him but thought he could make her forget with a little humor and his sheer force of will.

And for an instant he'd almost done it.

But you'll have to do a lot better than that, buddy.

She looked up at the academy's main house as her car rolled up the long driveway. The stone finish had recently been cleaned, and the shutters had been given a fresh coat of paint since her last daytime visit. She, like the other blind students who had attended Woodward, had no idea how stunning the campus was. It wasn't until Kendra had gained her sight that her mother had told her it gave her great sense of peace to drop her daughter off in such a beautiful place—though she regretted that Kendra could not see it. But there was more than visionary beauty here; there was also the wonderful scent of the flowers over which Ronald Kim had labored. There was the sound of the surf and the wind in the trees, and there was the friendship and challenges of teachers like Elaine.

The car stopped in front of the building, and Kendra climbed out and tipped the driver through the phone app. She looked around. She knew she should probably check in at the front office, but she wanted to take another look at the crime scenes without a school administrator hovering over her.

She started at the south lawn where Ronald Kim's body was found. Nothing she hadn't already seen the night before except for a few more shoe impressions on the outskirts of the scene. Probably from school employees venturing out to the spot to see where their colleague had spent his last moments on Earth. It was a common phenomenon at crime scenes, one that often led to flowers, cards, and other small mementos being left in tribute.

She looked over the short wall at the access road that for some reason had captured Ronald Kim's attention in the minutes before his death. Was he waiting for someone?

She walked back, making an ever-widening arc as she scanned the ground. Nothing of note.

She crossed the campus to the Slide, where the lowest railing post still had not been replaced since its uprooting two nights before. She sat on Big Rock, trying to imagine Elaine Wessler's battle to survive on this grassy slope. What in the hell had brought her out there in the middle of the night? Had she sat on this very rock, waiting to meet her killer?

Or had she been chased from the campus above?

What am I not seeing here, Elaine?

"Hello, Kendra."

Kendra whirled to see Allison Walker descending the steps behind her. "Dr. Walker…Allison. Hi. I wanted to get a better look."

"Seems to me you got a pretty good look the other night."

Kendra stood. "I was afraid I missed something."

"I don't think much gets past you," she said dryly. "It was true when you were a student here and it's even more true now."

"In any case, I haven't found anything else."

"Maybe you don't need to. Did they get DNA off that bloody post?"

"I haven't heard anything yet. I'll check in after I leave here."

"Good."

Kendra joined her on the steps. "The parking lot was full. I take it you still haven't canceled classes."

"No. Half the students still haven't come back, but the families of our resident students live hundreds and even thousands of miles from here. Twenty-six come from Europe, and eight are from Australia. It's difficult for them to just swing by and whisk their kids away, though I certainly don't blame the ones who did. We've increased security, which is how I knew you were out here. I'm afraid your Uber driver got a grilling before he was able to leave campus."

"Great." Kendra smiled. "There goes my customer rating."

"Desperate times. The sooner you can solve this, the better."

"No pressure or anything."

"There's plenty of pressure to go around, believe me. Maxine Rydell will be here later in the week."

"What?" Kendra's eyes widened as her head swiveled to look at her. "She's coming *here*?"

"For the first time in over five years."

Kendra let that sink in for a moment. Maxine Rydell was one of the world's wealthiest women, her fortune made by her great-grandfather's oil holdings in California's Central Valley. Her financial support was key to the Woodward Academy's continued operation and success.

"She lives in Switzerland, doesn't she?" Kendra said.

"She does. She rarely leaves Europe, though we talk on the phone almost every week. I guess this warranted a special trip on her private jet. She's disturbed by the events of the past few days. As we all are." She grimaced. "She says she wants to discuss the future of the academy."

"What does she mean by *that*?"

"Your guess is as good as mine."

That answer was too noncommittal. Kendra felt fear rush through her. "She's not withdrawing her support, is she? Has she said anything?"

Allison pulled her long sweater around her as the ocean breeze blew harder. "No, she's not said anything other than she's giving all solutions a good deal of thought." She smiled bitterly. "Does she think I'm not? But how can I fight against what happened here?" She straightened and lifted her chin. "Maybe it will be fine. We'll know soon enough. In the meantime, we'll navigate this crisis as best we can. Just as we have since Woodward Academy was founded." She turned to face Kendra. "Is there anything I can do to help you?"

"I'd like to see Elaine Wessler's office."

"It's on the second floor of the Brockmire Building. I'll call the custodian and send him over there. He'll unlock it for you."

"Thank you." Kendra thought for a moment. "You said Elaine had no special contact with Ronald Kim. Was she close to anyone here? Who knew her best?"

"I don't know if they were especially close, but Elaine did occasionally eat lunch with another teacher here. Layla Shaw."

Kendra frowned. "I don't know her."

"She's only been here for about five years. She's a PE instructor, very good with the students. If Elaine had a friend here, it was probably Layla."

"Can I talk to her?"

Allison checked her watch. "She has a class at the pool now. You can find her there."

"Good. Thank you."

Allison hesitated, then spoke in a guarded tone. "I have to warn you about something."

Kendra's brows rose. "That sounds ominous."

"It isn't, really. It's just...Layla Shaw is not your biggest fan."

Kendra looked at her in bewilderment. "I just told you, we've never met."

"I know. But everyone here knows you and your story. Our students have always been inspired by you."

"But not Layla Shaw."

She shrugged. "I shouldn't have said anything."

"The hell you shouldn't. Does she have some kind of problem with me?"

Allison motioned up the narrow stairway. "I should get back to my office. I have a few calls to make before my meeting."

"Come on. You're the one who brought it up."

"It's nothing you need to be concerned with. I'm sure she'll help you any way she can as far as Elaine is concerned." Allison turned and quickly made her way up the stairs. "Let me know if you need anything."

"Allison...?"

But she was gone.

What the hell...?

Kendra shook her head, trying to make sense of the bizarre end to her conversation with Allison.

She'd never known her to have much of a sense of humor, so she didn't think it was a joke.

Oh, well. There were more important things to worry about.

Kendra bounded up the stairs, strode across the east lawn, and took a shortcut down a grassy hillside to the athletic field and aquatic center. Twenty vision-impaired children were standing on the field wearing swimsuits.

Three instructors were also there wearing red swimsuits emblazoned with the Woodward Academy logo. One of the instructors, a tall, toned, thirtyish woman, was clearly in charge of the others.

Kendra approached her. "Layla Shaw?"

The woman turned toward her. "Yes."

"My name is Kendra Michaels. I'm here to—"

"I know who you are and why you're here," she snapped.

She wore a distinctly pinched, annoyed expression.

"I'd like to talk to you about Elaine Wessler," Kendra said warily.

"The police and FBI investigators have already interviewed all the teachers and staff. I don't think I can add anything."

"You might be surprised. Sometimes thoughts and memories just seem to come out of the blue."

"I'm very busy, Dr. Michaels. As you can see, I have a class here."

"I'll wait."

Layla rolled her eyes in exasperation and walked away.

Allison was right, Kendra thought. Definitely not a fan.

"It's a nice day," Layla said to one of the other instructors. "Let's open the shell."

One of the other women unlocked a gray box at the edge of the center's concrete periphery. She gripped a red lever and shouted to the students. "All clear."

The kids casually moved back until they reached a set of pebblestone pavers. They had this routine down.

The instructor pulled the lever and the ground vibrated from a hidden mechanism. The aquatic center's aluminum shell swung away, revealing a large rectangular-shaped swimming pool. The shell finally docked on a long rail. Layla blew her whistle and the students made their way into the pool.

The sport of the day was water polo.

Two teams each stood in chest-deep water on opposite sides, trying to score points against each other with an inflatable ball. The ball emitted a high-pitched pulse tone that enabled the sightless players to zero in on its location and send it toward their opponents. The teams were divided up along gender lines, and as far as Kendra could see, the girls were far better players.

After about twenty minutes, Layla walked the length of the pool toward Kendra. She was still wearing that annoyed expression, and Kendra was sure that she'd been hoping Kendra would give up and leave. "Okay, can we just get this over with?"

"Sure, when was the last time you saw Elaine?"

"Tuesday. She was killed that night."

"How was her mood?"

She shrugged. "Same as always. She was usually a happy person. She was talking about that guide dog she was fostering. I'm ashamed to say I kind of tuned her out. She always liked to tell stories about her dogs and I've never been much of an animal person." For an instant a flicker of regret touched her expression. "I had no idea it would be the last time I'd ever see her."

"Was there anyone new in her life? Or something she may have been doing that was different than usual?"

"Like what?" she snapped. Her moment of humanity was obviously over. "Nothing was ever different with Elaine. I can't believe she did anything that would make anyone want to kill her. For any reason."

"She was divorced. Were there bad feelings between her and her ex-husband?"

"Define *bad*. She was sad about that, but it doesn't

seem like there was any real anger or resentment.
They just grew apart. She took her maiden name
back after the divorce, but I think they still got
along. The academy holds a couple of weekend
retreats every year, and her husband would actually
feed and walk her dogs when she was away."

Kendra thought about this. "So he had a key to
her place?"

"I suppose," she said impatiently. "Is that why
the FBI brought you in, to make painfully obvious
deductions like that one?" The woman's tone was
practically sneering.

And Kendra had enough. She shook her head.
"No, they brought me in to do everything I could
to find out who killed two very good people. Now
what in the hell is your problem with me?"

"Are we finished here?"

She wasn't about to let her go. "No. What have I
ever done to you?"

Layla crossed her arms. "Nothing. Nothing at all."

"Then what's the problem here?"

Layla didn't answer, but she was looking back
toward her students still playing in the water.

"*What* is it?"

Layla finally turned back toward her. "You're a
hero to a lot of those kids, especially the girls.
Every time you come back and talk to their classes,
I hear about it."

"That's ridiculous. I don't sell myself as a hero."

"You don't have to. They're all online with their text-to-speech apps. They know your story and they know about your cases long before they meet you."

"That's hardly my fault, I never even give interviews. So what's the issue?"

Layla hesitated and then burst out, "Because of you, these kids are spending their lives dreaming of the day they can see. They think they're only a miracle operation away from becoming the next Kendra Michaels."

"Who's to say they won't be? The medical team that gave me my sight have done the same for hundreds of others."

"Hundreds? Out of how many tens of thousands of hopefuls?"

"I don't know the answer to that. But I do know the odds are getting better with each passing day."

"Come off it," Layla said. "You know the chance of any of these kids ever seeing is close to zero."

"Whatever the odds, there's always room for hope."

"They need to focus on being the best they can be with the hand they've been dealt. Not spending their days and nights dreaming of a life they'll never have."

She stared at her in disbelief. "I never stress anything else but learning and challenging themselves at every moment, every path, in their lives. Yet you still think I'm keeping these kids from being the best they can be?"

"I know you are, Dr. Michaels. I'm on the front lines here. I've seen thousands of blind children come through this school. I know what I'm talking about."

"You're *wrong*. The kids I've met, and I'd bet the kids in that pool, are amazing. You don't give them enough credit. They're strong and resilient and just plain wonderful. They know how to make the most of their lives and hold on to their dreams, whatever they might be." Her voice was suddenly passionate. "And I'll keep telling them to dream of miracles. Because somewhere out there in the world there's a med student who's having dreams of his own about how to make those miracles come true."

For an instant Layla looked taken aback. Then she said harshly, "Just what I'd expect of you. Keep thinking that. But just know I won't ever invite you to come speak to my students."

"Noted."

Layla turned and strode back toward her class. She blew her whistle and resumed her callouts.

Kendra took a deep breath and shook her head. Wow. Definitely a new one for her. Allison's opinion of Kendra's contributions had not been particularly encouraging, but she'd realized how deeply Kendra wanted to help. Layla's blunt rudeness had caught her off guard. Maybe she should have been more controlled and not responded that sharply to the blasted woman.

But perhaps Layla's arguments weren't entirely without merit. Could the woman have a point? Everyone had a right to their opinion.

No time for self-doubt. Not here, not now. She could tussle with it later.

Kendra turned and walked away from the pool.

But she found herself thinking about it anyway, because it kept gnawing at her all the way to Elaine Wessler's second-floor office in the Brockmire Building. Although it was one of the newer buildings on campus, it was made to appear quite old, with a classical design and dramatic columns lining the front side.

Kendra climbed the staircase and looked down the long hallway. Classrooms were on the right and teachers' offices lined the left. As promised, a custodian was working on the floor, adjusting a water fountain.

Kendra approached him, and even before she could get a word out, he spoke. "Yes, ma'am. Ms. Wessler's office is this way." He led her to a door halfway down the corridor. He pulled out a ring of keys, each of which was black and topped by a red rubber jacket.

"Do all the keys on campus look like that?" Kendra said.

The custodian showed her the ring. "Just faculty and staff offices. Classroom keys have red jackets, and plumbing, electricity, HVAC, and maintenance closets have black jackets."

"Interesting."

He unlocked Elaine Wessler's office and opened it. "Such a shame," he said under his breath.

"Did you know her?" Kendra asked.

"A little. I used to pet her dogs when she'd let me. Depending on where they were in their training, you know. She'd sometimes bring them with her to school. Nice lady."

"She was." Kendra glanced at the name tag stitched on the upper-left-hand side of his jumpsuit uniform. "Thank you, Gary. I won't be long."

He lingered for a moment as if expecting to enter the office with her. But she stood in the doorway and he took the hint. Gary walked back toward the water fountain, where his tools were neatly arranged on a towel on the floor.

Kendra stepped into the office, appealingly cluttered with framed photos, mostly of former students and fostered dogs. There were a pair of plaques on the wall—awards in a countywide debate competition. On the desk, a tin cup with a dozen pencils, each sharpened down to the exact same length. An empty place on the desk marked where Elaine's computer had been. The laptop was at the computer forensics lab at FBI headquarters, and Kendra knew the hard drive contents had already been copied. The techs were combing her emails for any signs of a threat.

There were no signs of a threat in her office. A Sonos music player, a filing cabinet, and a chair on each side of the desk, perfectly positioned for student–teacher conferences. The phone was angled awkwardly for any real use, but that could have been attributed to custodial staff cleanings or the FBI Evidence Response Team moving it as they examined the desk.

She tensed. A scraping sound in the hall behind her. Footsteps.

She spun around, leaned into the half-open door, and peered through the opening.

It was a little girl.

She appeared to be about twelve years old, blind, and the scraping sound was her white cane sweeping across the floor. She was holding flowers. She bent over to place the flowers in front of the door, but she suddenly froze.

She looked up. "Hello?"

"Hi," Kendra said.

"I didn't know anyone was here. I'm sorry." The girl quickly turned away.

"Wait." Kendra stepped into the hall. "Don't

go. Those flowers are beautiful. Are they for Ms. Wessler?"

The girl stopped. "Yes."

"They smell heavenly. I know she would have loved those."

She turned. "They're carnations. They were her favorite."

"Really? She told you that?"

"She didn't have to. I could always smell them from a vase on her desk in class."

Kendra smiled. "That's very sweet and you're smart to remember that. What's your name?"

"Ariel. Ariel Jones."

"I'm sorry about what happened to your teacher, Ariel. She was a nice lady."

Sadness fell over the girl's face. She had a dimpled chin, high cheekbones, and long blond hair, and her bright blue eyes were misting with tears. "She was the best. I miss her so much."

"I feel the same way, Ariel. I knew her from the time when I was a little girl."

"Really?"

"Yes. I was a student here until I was thirteen."

"Are you blind?"

"No, but I was then."

Ariel gasped. "Jeez. You're Kendra Michaels."

"I am."

"Whoa."

Kendra chuckled. "You make me feel like a rock star." Then Kendra remembered Layla's harsh words. "Unless being Kendra Michaels isn't such a good thing around here anymore."

Ariel smiled. "You *are* a rock star. And you're gonna find out who killed Ms. Wessler. And Mr. Kim."

"I'm trying."

"You *will.*"

Kendra looked around. "You shouldn't be in here alone. Shouldn't you be in class?"

"Recess." She beamed. "And I'm not alone. I'm with you."

"You should stay close to your classes and teachers, especially now. Or at least have a friend with you if decide to wander off."

"I don't have that many friends." She made a face. "I'm sort of a computer geek, and the other kids think it's kind of weird that I want to spend so much time working and trying to figure out stuff. But that's okay, sometimes being alone is kind of...comfortable. No one gets in your way if you're concentrating or just thinking. You know?"

"Yes, I do know. But I believe you could dig up a friend or two to hang out with if you tried during this situation. Right?"

She shrugged. "I guess so."

"Though I was told that a lot of the parents are keeping their kids home."

"They are. Most of the kids I know still haven't come back. But my mom and my brother live in Pennsylvania and it would cost too much for me to fly home. Besides, I'm not scared."

Kendra studied her. It wasn't just youthful bravado; Ariel *wasn't* scared. She spoke with defiance, standing her ground against the beast that might still be lurking nearby. But a little fear might be a good thing for her right now. "Well, *I'm* scared. You need to be careful. Do you understand?"

Ariel nodded. "I just wanted to put these flowers in front of Ms. Wessler's office. Because *she* was my friend. And I think flowers always made her happy. She didn't seem happy the last few times I was with her."

"What do you mean?"

"She wore glasses attached to a chain around her neck. There were beads or something on it. I could hear them when she moved."

Kendra remembered the crime scene photos of the glasses and broken chain near her corpse. She shook off the memory. "I don't remember Ms. Wessler wearing glasses when I was a student here."

"She put them on only when she was reading something to us. But in her last few classes, she was fidgeting with her glasses a lot more. I could hear the beads."

"Fidgeted...like she was nervous?"

"Exactly," Ariel said gravely.

"She didn't do that before?"

"Never. And she took a lot of deep breaths between sentences. And they were kind of jagged. She was upset or nervous about something."

Kendra nodded. She knew what the girl meant. She'd been able to pick up on such subtle cues since childhood, as could most blind children. If there was anyone to take seriously about this, it was Ariel and Elaine's other students.

"Did she say why anything could have been wrong?"

"No. I thought maybe something happened to her foster dog, but I don't think that was it."

"I don't think so, either." Kendra took one last look around the office. "Thanks for your help, Ariel. I think I'm done here."

"You're welcome. If I think of anything else you should know, I'll be sure to call the FBI."

Kendra could imagine Metcalf taking that call, and she didn't want to chance this child being hurt by a brush-off. She found Ariel's odd mixture of glowing fragility and toughness very appealing. "Suppose we keep it between ourselves?" She handed Ariel her card. "But you've already been very helpful and you mustn't feel bad if you can't remember anything else."

"I know that, but I have to be ready in case I do." She tucked the card in her jean pocket. "Now, where are we going?"

"*You* are going back to your class. I'm walking you back and making sure your teacher keeps a closer watch on her students."

"Are you gonna make a scene?"

"Would it embarrass you if I did?"

She thought about it. "Nope, not a bit. Go for it."

Kendra laughed. "You're a strange little girl, you know that?"

A luminous smile suddenly lit her face. "Oh, you have no idea."

———

Kendra delivered Ariel back to her class without making too much of a scene since the recess supervisor was already mortified that one of her charges had slipped away unnoticed. Kendra called Metcalf as she walked back to her car.

He was in the middle of a meeting, but he answered her call and continued the conversation in the hallway outside the conference room.

"You didn't have to leave your meeting on my account, Metcalf."

"Aah, it was getting dull anyway. What's up?"

"The missing key in Elaine Wessler's house...It was a spare key to her office at the academy."

"How did you find that out?"

She told him about the academy's colored-jacket system for their keys. "And since there was no sign of a forced entry at her house, I'd say that it and the other items were taken by someone with a key to her place. Like maybe her ex-husband."

"Her ex? We talked to him on the phone because he was in Tokyo on business. You have the interview notes in the case file. No bad blood there, and he had a great alibi since he was on the other side of the world." He paused. "How do you know he had a key to her place?"

"He still walked and fed her dogs when she was away."

"Nice."

"Maybe. But if he took those things from her house after Evidence Response did their sweep, I'd sure like to know why."

"Me too. I'll talk to him about it tomorrow morning."

"Why not now?"

"He just got in from Tokyo early this morning. He made an appointment to come in and talk to us to-morrow. Besides, I'm tied up here for the rest of the afternoon. But first thing tomorrow we can—"

"Is his address in the interview notes?"

"It should be." He paused. "You're not going to wait until tomorrow, are you?"

"Thanks, Metcalf. Gotta run."

"Come on, Kendra..."

"I'll let you know what I find out. I promise."

She cut the connection.

CHAPTER

7

It was almost sunset when Kendra's Uber car rolled up in front of the Bayside Lofts complex within sight of the Coronado Bridge. It was one of several warehouses south of downtown that had been converted to "artists' lofts," code for bare-bones living quarters hardly fit for human occupancy. They were situated along a stretch of shoreline where several marine maintenance and repair firms had once operated massive shipyards. Following a period of consolidation, several of the shipyards had been deserted; the loft conversions were the first step in what city fathers hoped would be a rejuvenation of the grimy, run-down area. For the moment, however, the complex's residents saw little of the WORK-LIVE-SHOP-PLAY promised by signs all around the two reconditioned factory buildings. The rest of the area still looked very much like the deserted shipyard it had been for years.

Kendra double-checked the address in her case file. This was where Elaine Wessler's ex-husband, Kit Randolph, lived. According to the interview notes, Randolph had seemed anxious to meet the authorities upon his return to the country. Maybe he had something to say.

Kendra entered the building lobby where the two elevator doors had well-worn developer signs reading ELEVATORS COMING SOON. Not *too* soon, she guessed.

Fine. She'd take the stairs. She climbed to the fourth floor and moved toward unit 416 where Kit Randolph lived. She pressed the doorbell button but heard no sound from inside the apartment.

She rapped on the door.

Still nothing.

She could have called first, but she usually got better results if she showed up unannounced.

Only, of course, if the interview subject was home.

She pulled out her phone and punched the number she had just seen on Randolph's interview report.

As she counted the rings, Three Dog Night's "Joy to the World" echoed from . . . *somewhere*. Kendra cocked her head. It could have been coming from the apartment. Could it be Kit Randolph's ringtone?

She cut the connection and punched his number once more.

Again, "Joy to the World."

But it wasn't coming from the apartment.

She spun around, trying to get a fix on the sound. From one of the other apartments? No. It almost sounded like it was coming from...

She looked at an open window at the end of the corridor. *There.*

She moved toward it, keeping the phone connection open. The song grew louder and more distinct. But four floors up?

She stood before the window for a moment, then stuck her head out.

No sign of Randolph. Just a fire escape and a depressingly ugly view of an abandoned shipyard.

But still that song was playing.

She looked down. It wasn't coming from there. That only left...

She craned her neck upward. It was coming from the building's rooftop. Was Randolph trying to hide from her or other unwanted contacts there?

The music stopped and she looked at the phone in her hand. Her call had gone to voicemail.

Kendra looked at the fire escape. It had been freshly painted, but that was probably only to hide multiple layers of rust. It was obviously seventy or eighty years old, but it should still support her weight.

Right?

She climbed out the open window and took a tentative step. The fire escape creaked and groaned, but it held. Kendra climbed a dozen short steps and hopped off onto the roof. It had been recently resurfaced and sealed. Curved metal vents jutted from the building in the shape of dozens of question marks. Fitting.

She glanced around. No sign of Randolph. She punched his number again.

"Joy to the World" blared. This time it was close. Almost on top of her.

It was coming from behind one of the large vents. She walked around one, then another. No dice.

Then she reached the third. This was it, she realized. The music was there.

She ducked around the other side, prepared to give chase if he bolted. She threw herself forward, and—

Shit!

It was a very bloody corpse!

She'd stumbled, almost falling on top of him.

The man was seated, leaning against the vent. His throat was cut from ear to ear and he was covered in blood. The wounds were fresh. His face was battered, his eyes swollen shut, but his features matched the picture on the interview sheet. Kit Randolph. She knelt beside him to make sure he was dead.

Dammit. No question.

"Joy to the World" was still playing over the awful sight, blasting from the phone in his breast pocket. She cut the connection and stared at him for a moment longer as the sun set behind her. Without the blaring song, it suddenly seemed very quiet, with only a gentle wind and sounds of the harbor in the background.

And the reverberation of footsteps coming toward her from behind.

Not good.

Move!

Kendra scrambled away, toward another one of the tall vents. She ducked behind it.

Had she been spotted?

No. She heard two pairs of footsteps, probably both men. And their pace hadn't quickened since she dove for cover.

She leaned low and peeked from behind the vent.

The men carried a large blue tarp as they walked toward Randolph's corpse.

Kendra strained to get a better look at them. It was impossible to see their faces in the shadows where she stood because of fast-encroaching darkness, so she focused on their builds, gait, hairstyles, and anything else she could gather. The taller man breathed through his front teeth, emitting a slight whistle. The shorter of the two men had long, dark sideburns, and his gait was lithe, graceful.

"I know I heard someone up here," the smaller man said, his speech clipped. British? "You heard it, too."

"Don't know what I heard." The second man with that whistle had a Southern accent, probably Tennessee Valley. "We just need to get the hell out of here."

"Wait. Be quiet."

Both men went still.

Kendra quickly ducked behind the vent.

Mustn't move.

Mustn't breathe.

The smaller man finally spoke. "Let me check something. His phone kept going off."

Kendra heard the rustling of fabric and the crumpling plastic tarp as she imagined him kneeling over their fresh kill.

After a long moment, he finally spoke. "Kendra Michaels!"

She jerked and felt an icy chill. But he was only reading the caller ID screen on the dead man's phone.

"She called over and over again, Kendra Michaels. Three times in four minutes." He called out, "Is that you we heard up here, Kendra?"

She held her breath.

"I think it was!" His voice dropped to a menacing purr. "And you're still here."

She cocked her head. Footsteps.

They were on the move. The men had separated, searching the rooftop for her. It was only a matter of time before they—

RING-RING-RING-RING-RING!

Her phone, still in her hand, blasted the ringtone. The call had come from the dead man's phone.

The man with the sideburns had redialed her. They now knew exactly where she was.

"Over there!" he yelled.

She got one clear, brief glance at the faces of both men as they ran toward her.

Shit!

She tossed her phone, leaped to her feet, and bolted across the rooftop. They were already close and gaining on her.

She only remembered seeing one rooftop exit into the building, and it was behind her.

Keep running.

Keep pushing.

Keep thinking.

Another fire escape! Just ahead!

The footsteps pounded louder.

Shit.

The edge of the fire escape loomed only yards away.

But she couldn't see what was beyond the edge. She didn't know if there were actually steps, or if she'd be jumping into nothingness.

No time to stop. No thinking it through.

Just take the shot.

She leaped over the edge and landed hard on the metal stairs of the fire escape four feet down.

BAM!

Damn, that hurt.

She rolled over and flew down the stairs of the fire escape, searching frantically for an entry point into the building.

She passed window after window blocked by a rigid metal mesh, until she finally stepped down...into nothingness. The dilapidated fire escape simply ended...and left her dangling four stories above the concrete below!

She frantically gripped the handrail, trying to regain her footing.

BAM! BAM!

The men jumped onto the fire escape above her. They'd be on her in seconds.

Down, there was only pavement. To her right, the impenetrable windows. To the left...

She took a deep breath. To her left, there was another building. Another abandoned factory, another fire escape, and dozens of accessible windows.

At least seven feet away. Could she make it?

The men's footsteps clanged on the metal fire escape above her.

She *had* to make it. But she needed a running start.

She followed the fire escape around the front corner of the building. There she had an eight-foot straightaway to build up some speed before going airborne.

She turned to face the other building. That seven-foot abyss looked even farther from here. This was insane.

But it was more insane to stay here and risk getting her throat cut like Randolph.

She crouched in a sprinter's position and got ready. She raised her chin.

Raised her chin? As if that would keep her from splatting on the sidewalk below?

The men were getting closer.

She couldn't wait any longer. She just had to *do* it. Time to fly.

Kendra ran with all the speed she could muster, then launched herself from the very edge of the fire escape with all her force and strength. *Dear God, let it be enough.*

For a few seconds she felt as if she were lost in a bizarre dream.

Wind slapping against her cheeks.

Her pursuers yelling curses behind her.

The odor of decades-old shipyard oil catching in her throat.

SMASH. She hit the neighboring catwalk, rolled, and shattered the factory window with her right shoulder. She rolled back, trying to avoid the glass guillotines slicing downward.

SMASH-SMASH-SMASH-SMASH! She buried her head in her hands, feeling the glass spray pierce any exposed skin.

She looked at the backs of her hands. Cuts on both the backs and the palms. Blood.

But she was *alive*.

She hurtled through the open window and found herself on an interior catwalk. It looked like an old machine shop, with a massive main floor where ship engines were once built or repaired.

That smell...machine oil vapors. Dizzying, overpowering.

Ignore it. Fight through, find a way out...

She stumbled down the catwalk, weaving through a maze of old machine parts.

SMASH!

She turned back. At least one of the men had followed her crazy building-to-building leap. He stood silhouetted against the factory windows. He appeared to be the taller one.

Guess it was too much to hope for him to have been decapitated by falling glass, she thought regretfully.

He staggered through the same opening she'd entered, looking one way, then another.

She crouched low and moved behind a machine panel. She grabbed a steel pipe.

The man was now walking toward her, shaking the catwalk with what sounded like a limp.

THUMP-thump. THUMP-thump. THUMP-thump.

He stopped.

She peeked around the panel. He was obviously injured. She could *use* that.

Which leg was he favoring?

THUMP-thump. THUMP-thump.

The injury was to his right leg. It was bleeding.

He had stopped again and he was looking down.

He was tracking her, she realized. Using the bloody trail from her cut hands.

She reached down and slowly, quietly, raised the metal pipe. It was heavy.

Good.

THUMP-thump. THUMP-thump.

Gotta make this count.

She jumped to her feet and swung the pipe at the

man's good knee. He howled in pain, but before he could recover, she swung at his already-bleeding right leg.

He went down in a torrent of curse words.

She *ran*.

Her eyes were now adjusted to the darkness, but it still took a moment to see the stairs that led to the complex's main floor. She jumped over a small sign and half ran, half slid down the stairs.

Light from the streetlights outside filtered through the floor-to-ceiling painted-over windows at the factory's main entrance. She could do this, even if she had to break some more glass to do it.

She stopped halfway down.

Oh, shit.

The other man was down there waiting for her. He stood at the bottom of the stairs.

Behind her, the still-howling, still-cursing man had pulled himself to his feet.

She was boxed in.

She sized up her opponents. She'd take her chances with the downstairs guy first. The man behind her was still nursing his wounds, so he might not be such a—

CRASH!

A Toyota SUV burst through the front of the factory, shattering at least a dozen windows.

Kendra froze, stunned. What in the holy hell?

The man at the bottom of the stairs was clearly as surprised as she was. He spun around.

They stared at the still-running SUV. Its headlights blazed in the dark factory.

The man on the floor shielded his eyes from the glare with his forearm. He stepped toward the vehicle.

"Hello?" he shouted.

No answer.

The man above yelled down at him. "Who is it?"

"Hell if I know."

"What do you mean?"

The man on the floor was standing next to the driver's side door peering inside. "No one is in there."

"What?"

"The car's empty."

"Bullshit."

"Get your ass down here."

In the darkness behind her, Kendra heard what sounded like a choking sound, then a man's scream. She turned just in time to see her pursuer on the catwalk hurtle over the railing and fall to the factory floor.

And a familiar lithe form appeared at the top of the stairs.

Jessie Mercado was in the building.

Kendra stared at her in disbelief. "Jessie?"

Jessie ran down the stairs to meet her. "Get in my SUV as soon as you can," she whispered.

Kendra was still incredulous. "What in the hell?"

She shrugged. "You're welcome."

Then she was gone, melding with the darkness as she slid under the railing and moved hand-over-hand on the metal stairs' underside.

The man on the floor was still dazedly trying to get a fix on what had happened. Then a window-pane shattered behind him. Then another. Then another.

The large wall of painted-over windows was getting smaller by the second.

The effect was that of sniper fire, but Kendra knew it was likely from Jessie's odd stock-in-trade: ball bearings from her jacket pockets hurled at maximum force.

The man ducked for cover.

Kendra's cue. She ran for the SUV's passenger door and slipped inside.

She looked around. What now?

Stupid question. With Jessie, the show was probably just beginning. She glanced out the window.

Kendra gasped. The man was no longer cowering on the factory floor. She spun around. Where in the hell was he?"

For that matter, where was Jessie?

WHAM! WHAM!

Kendra jumped and turned around. The man who'd been on the floor was swinging an old fire extinguisher against the car window, trying to get to her.

Kendra threw herself into the SUV's backseat, where Jessie kept her private-eye tools of the trade. Binoculars, listening devices, camcorder... Where was a good stun gun when you needed it?

Amazingly, the man still wasn't making much headway against the glass of the window. Kendra squinted into the shadowy darkness behind him as she glimpsed something... Was that—?

FWAPP! Jessie snapped her leather jacket over the man's head, pulling the ends of the collar over his throat like a garrote.

He struggled, but each of his movements was met with a knee to his kidneys. Jessie finished by repeatedly slamming his head against her SUV roof.

She pulled the jacket from his head, revealing that the man was now unconscious with a bruised and bloodied face. His nose and right cheekbone appeared to be broken. He fell to the floor in a heap.

Jessie ran around to the driver's side, climbed in, and put the SUV into gear. She backed up, spun the car around, stomping on the accelerator as she headed south on Harbor Drive.

She checked the rearview mirror. "I don't think we're being followed."

Kendra looked at her dazedly. "What are you doing here?"

Jessie smiled. "Saving your sorry ass."

"No, I mean—"

"I know what you mean." She shrugged. "I just got into town a little while ago. I dropped in at FBI headquarters because I thought you might be there and Metcalf told me that you were headed here to talk to the victim's ex-husband. I thought I'd join you."

"Just like that."

"Yeah. But then I saw you running across a rooftop with those two thugs after you. I thought you could use a little help."

"A little help..." Her heart was still beating so hard it was painful. "Did you kill that man?"

"Nah. He won't be posing for class pictures anytime soon, but he'll live."

"What about the man you threw off the catwalk?"

"Oh, him. No guarantees there. Would you like to tell me what happened?"

Kendra picked up Jessie's phone from the console and started dialing. "I need to call Metcalf. I think those were the men who just killed Kit Randolph. I found his body and I have to get someone out here to arrest them." She rubbed her aching temple. "And I should meet Griffin and Metcalf here at the crime scene. We should go back and make certain the evidence isn't—"

"Hold it." Jessie took the phone away from her. "We're not going back and letting you hold that corpse's hand until your FBI buddies get here. I'm taking you home." She spoke into the phone as Metcalf picked up. "Jessie. I'll let Kendra talk to you in a minute when she's thinking straight. Randolph has been murdered and she ran into the assholes who might have done it. They might still be on the premises, so you and Griffin get out here and take care of the situation. She's not in great shape. I'm taking her home and getting her patched up, providing I don't decide to go to the ER if the bleeding is too bad. Just tell her she's barred from the crime scene and you'll give her a report later." She handed the phone back to Kendra. "Now you can talk to him. Give him all the information you think he needs. By that time I should have gotten you back to your condo. But try not to get blood all over my phone."

The advice came too late, Kendra realized. She'd forgotten her cut and bleeding hands. "You made it sound as if I was really hurt. I'm fine. Just a few cuts." She spoke into the phone. "Jessie was just being difficult, Metcalf. But you should really come quick and I'll try to be there when you—"

"We're on our way. And you do exactly what Jessie says." He paused. "How bad is it?"

"I told you, she's just being difficult." However,

she could tell from Jessie's expression that she fully intended to continue being difficult. "But perhaps I'd better fill you in on what happened tonight. You'd better record it while it's fresh because I'm a little blurry. It was pretty bizarre. And I don't exactly know what happened to those men who were chasing me..."

———◆———

KENDRA'S CONDO

"Get into the shower and clean yourself up so that I can see what I'm working with," Jessie said brusquely as she led Kendra into the living room and slammed the front door. "But be careful of the hands and lower body. You were limping a little when you were going from the car to the garage elevator."

"Because I'm sore." She headed for the bathroom. "I'm not like you. I'm not accustomed to jumping off fire escapes. It's not in my job description."

"Keep it like that," Jessie said dryly. "Or get a hell of a lot more training. You almost got yourself killed."

"It's not as if I had a choice. I did okay." She looked back over her shoulder. "I'll be right out. Metcalf and Griffin should have reached that crime scene by now. Call Metcalf and get a report while I'm in the shower."

Jessie nodded. "But I won't be in a hurry. You might take a little longer than you think." She made a shooing motion. "If you need me, give a shout."

"I won't. I'm fine."

"Until the adrenaline runs out." Jessie grinned. "I'll make coffee. The caffeine will work as a substitute."

Difficult, Kendra thought again as she carefully removed her clothes and got in the shower. Jessie was treating her like a child who needed a bodyguard. Well, maybe she had needed Jessie in that moment before she'd exploded into the factory. She was certainly grateful, but it was time for Jessie to back off and treat her with—

Shit!

Pain.

She fell back against the shower wall as the warm water hit her hands.

It took her a moment to get her breath before she held up her hands to look at them. Several cuts had lacerated both hands on the backs and the palms. The blood was running down her hands to her wrists, washed off by the water from the shower. The cuts didn't look too deep, and she couldn't see any glass shards. She was probably going to be fine, as she'd told Jessie.

But she'd have to go very slowly during this shower if she didn't want to experience that agonizing pain again. She reached out and tentatively picked up the washcloth, then looked warily at the soap.

It was going to sting like hell.

Yes, definitely go very, very slowly . . .

———◆———

"Go sit down over there at the dining table," Jessie said when Kendra came back into the living room. "I need to watch you walk and then bandage those hands." She was digging into her backpack and brought out a first-aid kit. "I gather from the length of time you were in that shower that I'm not going to have any trouble convincing you to let me do it."

"No, that would be stupid. You told me once you were trained as an army medic. You know what you're doing. But I don't think there's any glass in the cuts, they're just painful." She moved slowly across the room toward the table. "And the only reason I was limping is that my hip and buttocks hit that fire escape so hard. I have mega-bruises, but I'll be fine tomorrow. The warm shower helped with that problem." She sat down and looked up at Jessie. "Did you call Metcalf?"

Jessie nodded as she laid out the bandages and

ointment on the table. "You gave me plenty of time. It seems that the perpetrators were gone from the factory by the time they got there."

"Shit! I should never have left the scene."

"Yes, you should." Jessie was examining her left hand. "You weren't in great shape. Besides, we couldn't be sure that they were the only ones in that building."

"I didn't see anyone else."

"You mean when you were sliding down the fire escape? I wouldn't bet on your focus at the time. And I was a little busy, too. Anyway, they recovered the husband's body and searched his apartment. They found all the items that had been taken from Elaine's house except the camera. Maybe that was stolen." She was examining Kendra's other hand. "But between us we might have managed to spill enough of their blood to get a DNA profile to send to CODIS. That might help, and, if it doesn't, you did get a good look at those two goons who are the prime suspects. You'd remember them."

"It would be hard to forget them. I probably should go down to the FBI office and look at mug shots and have one of their artists draw—"

"Tomorrow," Jessie said firmly as she started to clean and bandage her right hand. "I'll take a few notes now and call Metcalf back if you come up with anything important. Did you get a good look?"

Kendra nodded. "I saw both of them. I can help the sketch artist generate a fairly accurate drawing."

"Good."

"Though I got a better look at the guy you tossed off the catwalk. I was able to pull a few things about him but I don't know how much help it will be."

"What do you mean?" She put salve on the first cut.

Kendra winced as pain stabbed through her hand.

"You okay?"

"Yeah, it just hurts like hell."

"It'll pass. Get your mind off it. You were about to tell me some things about that asshole."

Kendra closed her eyes.

Detach. Concentrate.

"He drives a BMW Series 7."

"You saw it?"

"No, not at all," she said impatiently. "And he has what looks like day-old stubble. But it's not natural. He uses a Conair swivel-head stubble trimmer."

"There are a lot of stubble trimmers out there. Trust me, most of the actors in Hollywood use them."

"I know, but this guy uses the Conair. And he's been in a high-end hair salon in the last week. If it was this area, it was probably Renata or Suriya."

"Good." Jessie started working on the cuts on

Kendra's left hand. If she was curious about how Kendra had arrived at her conclusions, she hid it well. "What else?"

"He's left-handed. He probably spent some time in Europe recently, including the U.K. I'd say he was there last summer. And he usually alternates between two different styles of sunglasses: Wayfarer and round rimless. Though he wasn't wearing either today." Kendra thought for a moment. "That's all I got. See? Not much help."

Jessie had finished applying the salve and was scribbling on a scratch pad she'd picked up from Kendra's kitchen counter. "I wouldn't say that. There are things here they can follow up on."

She made a face. "Maybe. I might have to take your word on it. I'm not thinking too clearly."

"Not maybe, definitely. But they'll want to know how certain you are and how you picked up on this stuff. Let's start with the car."

"A BMW Series 7."

"But you said you didn't see it."

"I didn't."

"And I assume he wasn't showing off pictures of it as he attacked you?"

"No, but I saw a distinctive bulge in those tight jeans of his."

Jessie grimaced. "This is starting to get ugly."

"His key fob. It's an elongated six-sided fob, very

distinctive. Like no other fob I've seen. It goes to a BMW Series 7."

"Got it." She jotted down the info. "And the Conair trimmer?"

"His beard is too even to be natural. Hair grows at different rates on various parts of the face, but it's the same short length for guys who use a trimmer. And that particular model is the only popular trimmer with a swivel head that helps keep it uniform. Otherwise, the chin hair would tend to be a shade shorter than the neck skin immediately below."

"What a tragedy. And I'm guessing his hairstyle is leading you to the salons?"

"Yes, he's wearing what's called a messy quiff. It's a European style you can't get at a Supercuts. If he got it here in town, those two salons are a good place to start."

Jessie consulted her notes. "And he's left-handed because..."

"...because that's what he used to pick up something off the factory floor to try to beat my brains out."

"Of course." Jessie nodded. "That would do it. How do you know he's been to the U.K.?"

"Two things. First, he was wearing a Boden Alderley overshirt. Boden is an English company, even though they do sell clothing in the U.S. I get their catalogues. But far more of their product is sold there. And he was wearing a pair of Adidas sneakers. They were a pair of commemorative shoes with the Union Jack plastered over them. I think they may have been tied to the World Cup, which means they were sold all over England last summer."

"And the sunglasses?"

"Tan lines on his face. I'm pretty sure about the Wayfarers, but even more positive about the wireless round lenses. He wears both fairly often."

Jessie finished her note taking and placed the scratch pad on the table. "Very good. Metcalf should get something from that. I'm not sure about the sunglasses, but there was all that about the car, and the fact that he might be a Brit could be—"

"Whoa," Kendra said. "I never said there was a possibility he was a Brit. No way." She rubbed her temple. "Though I can see how you might have thought that. I forgot about the speech patterns. I told you I wasn't thinking straight. He was almost surely a U.S. citizen who grew up in the South, probably the Tennessee Valley. It was the other guy on the roof who had the British accent. If I had to guess, I'd say there's reason to think our Southern gentleman might have possibly even been recruited in the U.K. last summer. Metcalf will have to check on it."

"And I'm sure he'll jump on addressing all your notes first thing in the morning."

Kendra grimaced. "For whatever they're worth."

Jessie smiled and said softly, "Yeah, for whatever they're worth." She reached into the first aid kit and picked up a roll of gauze. "But right now I think you need to forget about it and try to relax. Metcalf said to tell you to just rest and he'll have everything ready for you when you show up in the morning. He was worried about you."

"You probably intimidated him. You shouldn't have done it." She looked at her inquiringly. "Those cuts are no big deal, right?"

Jessie nodded. "Painful but superficial. No stitches. I'd judge it won't even scar. And I don't see any sign of glass. Of course, we could take you in for X-rays and be—"

"No, I probably washed any glass out in that damn shower. If anything shows up later, I'll go in and let them take a look at it. Just put on a temporary bandage." She waved her hand impatiently. "You know what to do. I trust you."

"Do you?" Jessie murmured as she bent over Kendra's hand and started to wrap it with the gauze. After a few moments, she added, "Then why did I see a hint of wariness when you came out of that bathroom? I should have known when you had time to think that it would all come together.

When did gratitude fly away and suspicion knock on that shower door?"

"About halfway through the shower," she said coolly. "I was having to concentrate on thinking about other things to forget about the pain." She paused. "And gratitude didn't fly away. I'm still grateful, but I might be a little pissed off, too. I have a few questions to ask."

"I figured that would be a possibility." She was quickly bandaging the other hand. "Though I think you've got most of it figured out. Go ahead."

"Why did you come back from Kabul so quickly? And why did you go directly to the FBI office after you arrived here from Afghanistan instead of going to the condo? I'm sure you started asking them questions in your own inimitable super-sleuth way. They both know we're friends and that you worked with me and Lynch, which would give you access to see them." Her lips tightened. "Tell me. Did they fill you in on the entire case?"

She chuckled. "Be for real. They'd never tell me anything if it meant pissing off Lynch or you. I'm very low on the totem pole when it comes to Metcalf or Griffin. No, they just politely told me I should go to your condo and talk to you. But Metcalf likes me and did mention you might be a little late since you were going to interview Kit Randolph at his apartment."

"How nice for you."

"And for you," Jessie added quietly. "But yes, I'm glad that I decided to go hunting for you instead of waiting for you at the condo. I don't have so many really good friends that I can afford to lose one." She shrugged as she got to her feet and got them both a cup of coffee. She set Kendra's cup down on the table beside her and then wandered over to the couch with her own. "Even if you're royally pissed off at me at the moment. Okay, have at me and we'll get this over."

"What are you doing here?" Kendra asked bluntly. "Lynch sent you, didn't he?"

"Of course he did. You closed down on him. He was going to send me back home anyway in another week or two. But you made him edgy and he gave me a call."

"And he told you to butt into my business?"

"He knows better than that. He left it up to me. He just said that he thought I might want to make sure everything was all right with you. He would have done it himself, but he's involved with a few things that are a little...touchy."

"Touchy?" Kendra stiffened. "What's that supposed to mean?"

"What I said. Something about the Taliban. You know Lynch doesn't talk if a situation is ongoing and tight."

Shit! *Taliban*.

"And that didn't send off alarm bells?" Kendra asked. "You should have asked him what was going on."

"Like he asked you if there was a problem with you?" Jessie shook her head. "You can be damn touchy yourself. And you were almost accusing me of acting as Lynch's spy. I don't deserve that, Kendra." She suddenly chuckled. "If I'm going to spy, it's always going to be on my own behalf."

"And you do it so brilliantly." Kendra smiled sheepishly. "I didn't really believe you'd do that to me. I guess I'm a bit on the defensive. But we both know how manipulative Lynch can be." Her smile faded. "And how damn nosy. He can't expect to get me thrown off the job in Afghanistan one day and then try to control what I do with my life and career stateside the next. He can just stay out of it."

"He'll find that hard to do." Jessie paused. "Particularly when he hears about that bomb scare in your car. Now, that might arouse his curiosity even if he doesn't find out about it tonight."

"It wasn't a bomb, the most it could have been was a threat." She frowned. "And how did you know about it if Griffin or Metcalf didn't tell you anything?"

"I took my time getting up to see them after I arrived at the FBI regional office." She stretched her booted legs out before her, crossing them at the ankle. In her black leather garb and that gleaming dark pixie-cut hair, she was lithe and gracefully strong, and yet also appeared oddly exotic as she lifted her cup to her lips. "I stopped and chatted up a few agents I knew in other departments. That bomb scare created quite a stir even if it was a dud."

"And there was no reason for them not to talk to you. The case wasn't confidential," Kendra said wryly. "And you knew Lynch always went through Griffin and Metcalf for his information and didn't bother with the lower rungs at the FBI."

"He probably would have started plumbing those sources if I hadn't been available. Lynch is nothing if not determined." Jessie finished her coffee and set the cup on the coffee table. "But I was available and he decided to send me. That way either he'd get the information he wanted or he'd have someone he trusted on hand to look out for you." She shrugged. "Though I didn't think I'd have to make that decision quite so soon. I had no idea you'd be stumbling over bodies and dodging over rooftops."

"What can I say? I always like to make an impact." Her eyes were narrowed on Jessie's face. "And why were you 'available'? Why come now when you could have stayed another few weeks? I know how much you wanted to nail those Brock Limited contractors to the wall. It was almost an obsession with you."

She nodded. "They hurt a lot of my army buddies when I served in Afghanistan, and I want to see that they don't have a chance to hurt anyone else." Her lips tightened. "But Lynch is right, this isn't the time. Things have altered just in the past few days. Every information source is drying up and with the Taliban forging a partnership with Brock, it's getting too dangerous to tap any new ones. It's time to step back and wait until Lynch sees an opening. I'll get my chance." She met Kendra's eyes. "We'll both get our chance. We just have to be patient."

"That's hard for me," Kendra said. "I don't want to wait."

"I know." She smiled. "Lynch always said you were on fire to take down Brock from the moment you arrived in Kabul."

Kendra said grimly, "Well, he's doused that fire fairly thoroughly for the time being."

Jessie shook her head. "Just put it on simmer. I know you too well to believe anything else. Now, what are we going to do about Oceanside?"

"I know what *I* intend to do. I don't know what you're going to do." Kendra tilted her head. "Are you going to call Lynch?"

"Hell, no. That was a last-case option if the situation was going down the tubes. I think Lynch and I both knew it wasn't in the cards. I've decided to go with Option B."

"Specify the details of Option B."

"I stick around and make certain no real bombs show up to take you out and that you don't decide to have another marathon jaunt skipping from building to building. You don't really have the experience to handle that type of ninja hijinks." She thought about it. "Though you did do pretty damn good for an amateur. Maybe after a few months of working out in that training camp where I went to train for the *American Ninja* competition." Then she shook her head. "Nope, you'd never leave those autistic kids you're working with again so soon." She grinned. "And if I get bored, I can always help you solve this case you're working on. I'm obviously eminently qualified. How's that for Option B?"

"Fine." She added quietly, "But there is an Option C, you know. You can forget about me and go back to your own profession...for which you're, indeed, eminently qualified."

"Nah, there never was an Option C." Her smile deepened and illuminated her face. "Not since Lynch told me about the scumbags who killed your friends. So you're stuck with me." She got to her feet. "And now I'm going to go down and see if Olivia can put up with me for a few days."

"Olivia?" She frowned. "Why? You can stay here."

She shook her head. "I'd be tempted to hover and you'd hate it. Besides, I'll probably be seeing you all the time on this case. You know Olivia and I are best buds. We don't get a chance to hang together, and this will give us an opportunity to catch up." She headed for the door. "See you in the morning."

"Well, just tell her I'm tired. Otherwise she'll be up here checking me out. You know Olivia." Then as Jessie reached the door she said sharply, "Wait. It will probably be before that." She'd just remembered Harley. "I'll have to go down and pick up the dog from her."

Jessie's brows rose. "Dog? She's got a dog?"

"Not if she has her way. She has certain issues with Harley. Come to think of it, so might you. It's probably just as well I take care of him at night."

Jessie shook her head. "After the night you've had, you need your rest. I'll tell her I'll take care of this Harley dog."

"I . . . don't really think that would be a good idea."

"Sure it would. I like dogs and they like me. I once had a stray beagle follow me to the finish line on a marathon race in Patagonia." She made a face. "Very inconvenient. He lost me the race— I had to keep slowing down for him because I was afraid he'd die from exhaustion. Do you know how short a beagle's legs are? But what could I do? He wouldn't stop. He obviously had a mission. And when we *finally* dragged our butts over the finish line and the media got hold of the story, he had people standing in line to adopt him. Hell, I wondered afterward if maybe *that* was his mission. Anyway, Harley and I will work out just fine." She glanced over her shoulder with a mischievous grin. "After all, how on Earth could I ever resist a dog named for a motorcycle?"

CHAPTER

8

C ome on. We're getting on the road," Jessie said curtly when Kendra opened the door the next morning. "*Now.*"

"What's the hurry?" Kendra grabbed her handbag before she ran after Jessie toward the elevator. "I was just coming down to Olivia's to get you. You know she usually likes to make breakfast when she has guests."

"I'm not a guest. I'm a victim." She punched the button. "And I refuse to look at that smug, malicious expression on her face even for breakfast. We'll go to Starbucks."

Kendra's gaze was raking her face. "Circles under the eyes. Tiredness . . . Harley?" She couldn't keep her lips from twitching. "I take it he didn't love you enough to follow you across the finish line? Don't feel bad, maybe that only works for beagles."

"Shut up. You're as bad as Olivia. I could tell she wasn't pleased when I told her I was going to take care of Harley for you, but she didn't say anything. And the dog was fine with me while Olivia and I were sitting around talking before we went to bed. I liked him. He liked me. It was when she handed me Harley's leash and sent him into the guest room with me that it all went to hell." She shuddered "I've never heard a sound like that outside of a torture victim in Afghanistan, and he kept it up all night. When I knocked on Olivia's door for help, she only smiled and said that I had to accept the consequences if I interfered with her arrangements with you about Harley. And then she wished me a good night and shut the door."

Kendra was laughing helplessly. "Lord, she's tough. Harley must not have wanted to leave Olivia. I told you that she has issues with him. She set up firm rules and made me promise to share custody, but I didn't realize she'd get that upset about you interfering. That's all she said?"

Jessie nodded glumly. "And I wish you'd stop laughing."

"I'm sorry. It's just that I would have thought she'd have a little mercy on you and tell you the one thing that would have saved you."

"And what is that?"

Kendra punched the button for the garage. "That HGTV has twenty-four-hour programming."

———◆———

Kendra was holding on to her patience by a thread. She was sitting in the FBI regional office's fifth-floor conference room and relating the evening's events to Metcalf, Griffin, and a pair of SDPD homicide detectives she'd never met before. The cops needed to be brought up to speed on the Woodward Academy investigation, which was a source of annoyance for all involved. Apparently there was some dispute on control and jurisdiction over the murder and attack the previous evening. Kendra made it a point never to get involved in petty squabbles, which arose in a surprising number of her investigations. But this time it was getting in her way.

After the cops and Griffin left, Metcalf brought her a cup of coffee and sat down next to her. "I'm sorry, Kendra. I feel awful."

She wrinkled her brow. "Why?"

"I knew you were going there. I shouldn't have let you go alone."

"The choice wasn't yours, Metcalf. You told me to wait until today."

"But I knew you wouldn't do that." He shook his head. "When I think what could have happened..."

"It didn't."

He was looking down at her bandaged hands. "It did. And it easily could have been worse if Jessie hadn't been there for you. I would never have forgiven myself."

He was actually upset. Kendra put her hand on his arm. "Don't beat yourself up. I know you're always there when I need you."

He nodded. "And I always will be. You're... very special to me, Kendra."

Kendra looked away. It was the closest he'd ever come to expressing the feelings she suspected he had for her. Damn. She patted his arm, leaned back, and tried to speak casually. "Yeah, we make a good team."

His face flushed. Obviously not the response he'd hoped for. He immediately awkwardly tried to change the subject. "Uh, we need to have you sit down with our sketch artist. He'll be in after nine tomorrow, so if we can have you come back?"

The last thing she wanted was to have this stretch out any longer than necessary. "I'd rather see if I can get together with Bill Dillingham and have him make the sketches."

"Bill Dillingham?" he repeated in surprise. "Is he even still alive?"

"Of course he is." Kendra made a face. "At least, I think he is."

"He's what, a hundred years old?"

"Don't be ageist. I think he's only eighty-seven or eighty-eight."

"Only? Maybe you'd just better come to the office tomorrow and—"

"No. Age doesn't matter. If Bill will do it for me, he's the one I want. He's still the best. One way or another, I'll make sure you get the sketches tomorrow, okay?" Kendra stood. "Well, I guess I'll hit it. Can I get a ride home?"

"Sure. I'll take you myself."

"I hate to ask it. This is very annoying. Can't you do something about them returning my car? If you're so sorry, then get me my car back by the end of the day."

"I'll do everything I can. Kendra..." Metcalf paused for a long moment.

Too long.

Don't let him say anything, she prayed. She hated the thought of embarrassing him or making their professional relationship awkward. She smiled politely but very impersonally. "Yes, Metcalf?"

He finally shook his head. "Nothing. I'll get my keys."

———◆———

Kendra received a phone message late in the afternoon that her car had been delivered to the parking garage.

Yes.

But that was the only thing that was moving with any degree of speed. It took Kendra several hours and half a dozen phone calls before she finally tracked down Bill Dillingham. She'd feared the worst when she discovered his house had been sold and no new address appeared on any of the online databases, but an old coworker at the San Diego PD finally pointed her toward a senior living community in Rancho Santa Fe, about a thirty-minute drive north of the city. By that time it was early evening and Kendra reluctantly decided to wait until the next day to visit him.

"Maybe you should have called first," Jessie said as they exited the freeway after ten the next morning. "Even if Bill Dillingham is able, he might not be willing. Maybe the guy just wants to stay retired. Didn't you tell me he wasn't in the best of health the last time you saw him?"

"Yeah, it was sad. But he was weak in body, not of mind. He was very, very sharp. And if I had called him, he might have said no."

"He could still. Even if he's alert and has all his wits about him."

"Work is always good for a person, and someone

as talented as Bill would have trouble giving it up. I'm willing to take that chance. And we can always go back and use the FBI's sketch artist if we have to."

"True." Jessie frowned. "I used to visit relatives who lived in retirement homes. I always thought those places were depressing."

"I hope this one isn't." Kendra turned onto El Camino Real Drive, which would take them to the facility. "If that's the case, maybe we can stay a little longer and try to make today a little less depressing for Bill. After all he's done for me, it's the least we can do."

———◆———

Fifteen minutes later, Kendra and Jessie stood slack-jawed in front of a massive, beautiful fountain that fronted acres of well-manicured grounds. In the distance, a spirited golf match was under way. A group of elderly women power-walked by them, wearing earphones and fluorescent workout clothes. On another field, a man flew a drone helicopter with his two grandchildren.

"Wow." Jessie gave a low whistle. "Not what I was expecting."

"Yeah, me neither. The people at the front desk said Bill isn't in his room."

"Do they have any idea where he is?"

"He double-booked himself for two activities on the grounds this morning. He's either at tai chi or curling."

"They have a curling court here?"

Kendra showed Jessie the printed yellow map the receptionist had given her. "Yep. She said she'd page him."

"Kendra!"

They turned to see Bill Dillingham walking toward them. He looked nothing like he had the last time Kendra saw him; he was now tan and fit, and his eyes' former twinkle had been restored. His hair was neatly coiffed, and he sported a jaunty mustache. He wore white slacks and a bright red shirt.

"Bill?" Kendra hugged him. "You look fantastic."

"I feel fantastic. Good to see you, my dear."

Kendra stepped back, still amazed at the smiling, healthy-looking man in front of her. She motioned toward Jessie. "Bill, this is Jessie Mercado. She's a good friend and an amazing P.I. She's helping me on a case."

"Delighted." His gaze was raking Jessie's face. "She has an interesting aura. Bold, yet complicated. I'd like to paint her." Bill took Jessie's hand and kissed it. "And if that's sexual harassment, I'm afraid you'll just have to take me to court."

Jessie smiled. "Pleased to meet you, Bill."

Kendra once again took in the beautiful surroundings. "This place is incredible. I want to move in here myself. Today. Right now."

"You're too young. I'm afraid you'll have to wait a few decades. But it sure is a nice place to wake up to every morning."

"Nice? That's an understatement." Kendra lowered her voice. "It must cost a fortune to live here."

He shrugged. "I came into some family money and I've always been a good saver. I realized that being by myself was detrimental to my health and I needed interaction. So I decided to stop being careful and start spending that money. I figure if I can't be good to myself now, when can I?"

Kendra nodded and laughed. It felt good to see Bill so vigorous and happy. "Absolutely."

"And around the same time I moved up here, I got new doctors. They changed my medications and it's made all the difference in the world. I feel like myself again. I've taken up cycling. I ride over three miles a day. And there's always something to do around here. There are shuttles every day to the beach whenever we want a change of scenery."

"Wow." She added with genuine sincerity, "I'm so happy for you, Bill."

He studied her expression. "Yes, you are. But something tells me you're here to intrude on that happiness."

"I'm afraid so." She raised her bandaged hands. "I had a run-in with two creeps the other night. They killed a man. I'd like to catch them."

Bill grabbed her wrists and held up her hands. "What did they do to you?"

"Nothing broken. Just cut. It would have been much worse if Jessie hadn't come along."

Bill nodded approvingly at Jessie. "I told you she had an aura."

"I want to give the FBI sketches of the guys," Kendra said. "And there's nobody better than you."

"I agree with you. Hardly a week goes by that I don't get a call from somebody wanting me to make a sketch. I'm officially retired, Kendra. You may find this hard to believe, but I don't even keep a pad anymore."

Jessie thrust a large sketch pad toward him. "Will this work?"

Bill laughed. "Pencils?"

Jessie reached into her jacket and produced a fistful of pencils. "We wanted you to have a choice."

"You get extra points for being prepared." Bill sighed and motioned toward an outdoor table near the fountain. "We can set up here. Did you get a good look at the guys?"

"Good enough."

They sat around one of the round tables, and Bill flipped open the pad. "This won't take long. You're always so clear and specific about everything you see, Kendra."

"It's because I couldn't see the first twenty years of my life. Now that I can, I want to soak in every detail."

"So I gathered. I always thought you should be able to just draw these yourself."

"No way. I'm the worst artist you've ever seen. Blind kids don't grow up drawing like other kids do. No crayons, no coloring books. My artwork hardly rises above the level of stick figure."

"Well, I guess that's what I'm here for." Bill selected a pencil and put the rest down on the table. "Let's start with the shape. Was it a long face, round face, or somewhere in between?"

———◆———

It took Bill less than forty-five minutes to generate sketches of both men with enough character and detail to rival a good photograph. As always, he was able to tease the tiniest details from her memory and perfectly reproduce them onto the sketch pad pages, as if a laser printer had been hardwired to her brain.

Kendra held up the sketches side by side. One of the faces was heavier, with thick lips and bushy eyebrows that she recognized as the man who'd jumped after her into the factory. The other was sleek, with a thin nose, high cheekbones, and wide-set eyes. Both of them appeared to be somewhere in their thirties or forties. "These are good. Too good. Just seeing these faces again makes me a little sick."

"Good. It means I did my job." Bill stood. "Now, if you ladies will excuse me, I have a conversational French class to get to."

"French?"

"*Oui.* A group of us are going to Paris next spring." He tipped an imaginary hat toward Kendra and Jessie. "Good luck. And be careful."

Bill turned and walked away with a decided bounce in his gait.

"Hard to believe that's the same guy you were just talking about," Jessie said.

"Tell me about it. That's how I want to be in my retirement years."

"Ah, you'll never retire, Kendra. You'll still be walking into crime scenes and dazzling police detectives well into your nineties."

"Don't say that. I don't want to dazzle anyone. And I can't imagine being able to stand those kinds of depressing scenarios for that long a time. That's definitely not where I want to be." Kendra laid the sketches on the tabletop and used her phone's camera and scanner app to make two PDF files. She sent both to Metcalf. "These sketches are good enough that the FBI might be able to use their facial recognition systems to see if either of these matches anyone in their database."

Jessie clicked her tongue. "That's a real long shot."

"It may be the only one we have." Kendra took one last look around and suddenly frowned. "I wish every retirement facility was like this one. There should be better care for all our seniors. Life should be lived to the fullest like Bill is doing."

"I'm with you. But not everyone is lucky enough to come into a little extra money," Jessie said gently. "I know you're all set to mount your soapbox and see what you can do about correcting a massive problem, but put it on hold for the time being. Just enjoy it for Bill until we get this case solved."

Kendra nodded. She was right, of course. "I know. Think about the good and not the problems until you can solve them." She smiled. "Then we'd better go soon before I try to become a permanent resident here. I could get used to this."

◆

Bill had been so quick that when Kendra got back to the condo, she still had time for a leisurely shower before she went down to Olivia's for dinner. The shower took almost forty-five minutes, and then she spent another forty minutes washing and blow-drying her hair. It shouldn't have taken her that long, but she found herself lingering because it was blissfully peaceful compared with what she usually had to endure in the morning when Harley was impatient to get down to Olivia.

But she'd rather face Harley than keep Olivia waiting after she'd taken the trouble to make dinner. She could be far more intimidating. Kendra quickly slipped on her robe and then headed for her bedroom to dress.

"It took you long enough. Though I admit I've been enjoying the scent of that lemon shower gel. It seems as if it's been a long time since I've been able to smell it."

Lynch!

She froze, her gaze flying to the half-open door leading to the living room. The door she knew she'd closed when she'd gone into the bathroom. She strode quickly to the door and threw it wide.

Lynch was sitting on the couch drinking a beer. He was dressed in what looked like army gear. A khaki shirt open to reveal his white T-shirt. Khaki jeans and desert boots that were rough and stained. "Hello, Kendra." His smile deepened, and immediately that military look took on charisma. "You're looking well. I do approve of that tousled look."

She instinctively reached up to touch her mussed hair. "I was drying it." But she could tell by that mischievous movie-star grin that he knew that. He'd probably been sitting here listening to the dryer and drinking his beer while she was naked and thought she was alone. The picture it brought to mind was...intimate. It automatically put her at a disadvantage. Which, of course, was exactly what he'd intended. "What the hell are you doing here? How did you get in?"

"Why, I used my key. I knew you wouldn't like it since you only gave it to me because there was a serial killer after you at the time and it was the practical thing to do. Actually, I was thinking about going over the rooftop of the condo next door and then coming in that way. But I was tired. It was a very long flight and I didn't sleep because I was working the entire trip." He smiled. "So I was pleasantly surprised you hadn't changed the locks."

"I didn't think I'd have to," she said bluntly. "Not if you knew I didn't want you to use that key. Which I most certainly did not. Now, what are you doing here?"

"Having a beer." He got to his feet and moved over to the bar. "And starting on number two. I'll get you a glass of wine. You wouldn't want me to drink alone." He poured her a glass of Merlot and brought it to her. He took a long sniff as he handed it to her. "You smell even better close up." He wrinkled his nose. "I'm sorry I can't say the same. I went straight from Tangi Valley to the jet, and then I came straight here when I landed." He looked down at her terry robe. "Your belt's coming untied. I probably startled you when you came out of the bathroom." He reached down and slowly tightened it. "Pity. I hate to let an opportunity like that pass. But in your present mood you'd probably blame me if it came open. Right?"

"It would be your fault," she said coolly, trying to ignore the warmth of his fingers through the material. "As you said, you startled me and you shouldn't have been here. You weren't invited, Lynch." She gazed impatiently at her wine and then put the glass on the occasional table next to her. "And I don't give a damn if you drink alone. I just want to know why you're here. Just tell me and then get out."

"Rude. Very rude." He strolled back to the couch and sat down. "I was hoping to have the time to let you get over the fact that I'm not exactly your favorite person these days."

She made a crude sound.

He chuckled. "Exactly. It wasn't going to happen." His smile faded. "Particularly since no one appeared inclined to let me know about bomb threats and you dodging murderers and flying through glass windows. It made me realize that I couldn't afford to wait until hell froze over or you forgot about being pissed off at me. I figured my chances might be the same for either one."

"You had that right." She went still. "How did you know I had a few…problems? I know it wasn't Jessie."

"No, she was completely silent where you were concerned. Which was suspicious in itself. I thought I was going to have to dig deeper, but it turned out not to be necessary." He took a sip of his beer. "As a matter of fact, you helped me along with it yourself."

"I did not," she said flatly.

"Not intentionally. Heaven forbid." His lips twisted. "But you did it just the same. I had no idea you had so much influence on Metcalf, but it seems he was worried about you after that last incident. He contacted me and told me that it might not be a completely bad idea if I came back on the scene since I'd pitched you into this case."

"He didn't!" She couldn't believe it. "Metcalf is a professional. He wouldn't do that, particularly against Griffin's orders."

"What can I say? I've always told you he has a crush on you. He was very surly about it, but he obviously wanted you to have all the help you could get. Even if it came from me. As you said, he's a professional and he knew he had to be on the job and wouldn't be able to devote the same attention I would." He tilted his head. "I actually respect him for it. I'm sure he would rather have been the hero than the whistle-blower. It wasn't easy for him to do it."

"I don't give a damn. He shouldn't have done it. I don't need your help," she said through set teeth. "It's humiliating that you'd think I'd take it."

"You may not need it. But I need to give it," he said quietly. "Metcalf was right, I was the one who pitched you into this, and now I have to be there with you until we find who killed your friends. You know what a good team we are, Kendra. I'll be there beside you, working just as hard as you. Give me a chance to help find the bastard who did this." He added coaxingly, "Don't throw me into outer darkness until later. Let me do this one case with you."

"Don't you understand? I don't want you to—" She stopped and tried to smother her anger and indignation. He meant what he said. They had been together long enough for her to know the difference between sincerity and manipulation in Lynch. He might be superbly talented at the skill that had given him the nickname he hated, but he'd always been careful not to use manipulation on Kendra. Until that time he'd had her jerked out of Kabul and then tried to run her life, she thought bitterly. That was why it had hurt so badly and made her feel betrayed. "And I'm supposed to believe we can still work together? Every time I look at you, I remember what you did to me. If you had a problem, you should have talked to me, not sicced that pompous general on me."

"I actually felt very sorry for General Kotcheff. Though I'm still determined to find out about those bright red shorts." He grinned. "But I decided I couldn't afford to wait." He put his beer down on the coffee table and the next moment he was standing in front of her, gazing directly into his eyes. He said softly, "And you know we can still work together. You're the smartest woman I've ever known and you're not going to let the fact that you think I acted like an asshole interfere with what you consider important. I'm good and you know it. For God's sake, *use* me."

He was too close and she didn't feel at all smart at the moment. Heat. That smoky male scent mixed with the spice of his aftershave. Her breasts were growing taut, her body readying as it always did when he was near. She wanted to take a step back, but that would be too revealing. Lynch had always been able to read her. She took a moment to steady her voice. "You mean like all those multinational business conglomerates and heads of state? Should I be flattered?"

"Yes, because I'd never give them the service I'd give to you." He repeated, "Use me."

He's smart, he has contacts, and he's innovative as hell. If he were here, I'd have you go ask him for help, Olivia had said that first day.

And Kendra had known then that she was absolutely right.

And now Lynch was here and offering his help. What the hell could she do? She had no right to consider how difficult his presence might make it for her on a personal basis. Not if it meant she was ignoring an asset that might help bring Elaine's murderer to justice.

She looked away from him. "It's not going to be easy for me."

"Yes, it will. I'll make it easy."

She took that step back. "My rules, Lynch. All the way."

"Of course, that goes without saying. Unless I feel I can contribute something."

"All the way."

He inclined his head. "Whatever you think best. Would you like to fill me in on what's been going on? Metcalf was very sketchy, and you and Jessie probably didn't confide everything to him anyway."

"No, we didn't. It's a good thing, since he evidently can't keep his mouth shut."

"Ouch. Poor guy. He thought he was doing the right thing for you."

She shot him a razor glance. "As you did?"

"No comment. Do you want to fill me in or not?"

"Not right now. Tomorrow will be soon enough. I'm supposed to go down to Olivia's for dinner." She added hesitatingly, "I suppose you could join us. You did know Jessie is staying with Olivia?"

He shook his head. "You've had enough of me for the time being. I'd really prefer to take a shower up here while you're having dinner and then you come back and we talk." He raised a brow. "But that's not going to happen, is it?"

The last thing she wanted was to imagine Lynch naked and in her shower all during dinner. Though she was tempted to see his reaction when she brought Harley up for the night. She repeated, "Tomorrow morning will be soon enough. Go home, Lynch."

"Fine. I should really go check over the security measures there anyway. It's been a while since I've had the time to do it. I only want to do one more thing and I'll let you banish me." He took both her hands and looked down at the cuts. "Nasty. But they appear to be healing. You're still keeping them bandaged?"

"Of course, when I'm not in the shower." She tried to pull her hands away but he held them firmly. "They're doing fine. After tomorrow I won't have to bandage them at all. I'll rewrap them before I go down to Olivia's."

"Would you like me to do it? I'm something of an expert these days."

She knew that was true because she had seen the bullet and knife scars on his body. "No, thank you." She had no desire to have Lynch touching her for that length of time. She was having enough trouble with just the small intimacy of his hands holding her own for these few minutes. She tried again to pull them away but he was still examining them. He traced a jagged cut on her palm with his forefinger. "I can see why Metcalf was so upset." His lips tightened. "I'm a little pissed off myself." He released her hands and turned away. "We might have to do something about it." He headed for the door. "What time tomorrow?"

"Eight." And his mention of security measures at his home had reminded her of something else. "But can I even count on you to be here? Jessie said that you were temporarily shutting down the investigation into Brock Limited but that you were still involved yourself with the Taliban. You told me yourself you were at Tangi Valley, which is notorious Taliban country, just yesterday. Yet here you are today knocking on my door as if nothing had happened."

"I didn't knock, I used the key," he reminded her as he grinned at her over his shoulder. "And, yes, the Brock investigation is definitely on hold for the foreseeable future. There are CIA complications that have to be dealt with first. But it's just a postponement, Kendra. We'll get them, I promise." He paused. "And you'll have me on your doorstep as long as you want me. I belong to you until you're ready to toss me away. That's why I had to go to Tangi Valley yesterday—to clear the decks."

"That's bullshit. You don't belong to anyone," she said. It was scaring the hell out of her to realize he'd made that trip into Taliban country and probably would never tell her why. She had to admit it was almost a relief to know that he was here and she'd know what was happening to him. "But at least I can count on you being around for a while and not flying off somewhere again." She turned to go back into her bedroom. "I'll see you tomorrow, Lynch."

"Yes, you will. Say hello to Olivia and Jessie for me."

He was gone.

She stopped and took a deep breath as the door closed behind him. It was foolish to let him shake her like this. Hold on to the anger and the disappointment that was rapidly slipping away. At the end of that conversation she had only been aware of the fact that she had never had a greater friend and partner nor a more exciting lover. The rest had seemed unimportant and of course it was not. There was dignity and self-worth and not ever being taken for granted.

And dammit, there was Lynch not letting her be with him in that valley when he'd risked his life with those Taliban.

———

Kendra's phone rang at seven forty-five the next morning.

"Come down to the parking garage," Lynch said when she picked up his call. "The parking attendant is giving me a hard time about my car and I need you to smooth him down."

"Since when do you ever need help smoothing anyone down?" Kendra asked incredulously. "You wrote the book on diplomacy."

"Don't argue. The guy is nuts about Lamborghinis. He says the guest space is too close to the exit and he wants you to move your Toyota so that there won't be danger of anyone hitting my loaner and damaging it."

"What? And what about my humble Toyota? I just got it back from the FBI shop."

"It will be quicker if you just come down and ask him that. You're the condo owner."

He was right, Kendra thought crossly. But it was an irritation she didn't need this morning when she was nervous about working with Lynch anyway. "I'll be right down." She caught sight of Harley sitting by the front door with his leash in his mouth. "Right after I get rid of him."

"Him?" Lynch repeated.

She didn't answer and quickly hung up the phone. "Come on, Harley." She quickly leashed him and opened the front door. "I'm not about to leave you to start howling. I'll drop you off with Olivia." She ran down the stairs, pushed Harley in the door at Olivia's condo, and took the elevator to the parking garage. All this trouble and she hadn't even seen Lynch yet this morning. Why would a car be so blasted disruptive?

Then the elevator doors opened and she saw the Lamborghini Aventador.

Sleek red brilliance that almost lit up the entire garage. The lines were magnificently crafted and totally stunning. She could feel her jaw go slack at the sheer breathtaking beauty of the car.

"There you are." Lynch pulled her out of the elevator and led her over to a uniformed attendant. "I've told Herb here that I won't hold him responsible if the Lamborghini gets a scratch or two but he still wants permission to move it to your spot when we take the Toyota out. He appears to be a bit nervous."

"A scratch would be sacrilege," Herb murmured,

his hand reverently caressing the hood. "I've never seen a car like this."

"Neither have I," Kendra said. "I thought that Ferrari you had before was dazzling, but this is spectacular. Is this going to be the next Lynch incarnation?"

"I haven't decided. I just picked it up as a loaner after I left you last night. Do you like it?"

"I might, if it came with sunshades."

"It's fantastic," Herb protested.

Lynch was gazing at it critically. "It might be a little too attention getting. But he's right, the lines are splendid."

"I can see you're beginning to fall in love," Kendra said. "And why should it matter if it attracts attention? The Ferrari that went to car heaven was every man's dream car."

"Maybe I don't want to appear not to be in mourning," Lynch said with a sigh. "Out of respect, I'll take my time about replacing her." He added, "And the Lamborghini did get a little bit too much scrutiny this morning. That may not be a good thing considering that we're on the job and have no idea where we're going. That's why I thought I'd leave it here and let you drive the Toyota."

"I'll take good care of it," Herb said eagerly. "Is it okay if I move it to your spot, Dr. Michaels?"

"By all means, we wouldn't want to blind someone coming down that ramp." She gave him her
car keys. "Just park my Toyota on the street and
position Lynch's car wherever you want. I have to
go see my friend Olivia. I should be down in ten
minutes."

"I'll take care of it." His hand was still caressing
the Lamborghini. "I'll keep an eye on it all day,
Mr. Lynch."

"I'd appreciate that," Lynch smiled. "Thank you,
Herb."

"My pleasure..."

"And it will be," Kendra said as she got on the elevator. "He's so besotted I doubt if he'll do anything
but gaze at the damn thing all day."

"You never did appreciate the wonders of fine
mechanical workmanship." He punched the button.
"Who is *him*?"

"What?"

"When you were on the phone, you said you had
to get rid of him. Who is *him*?"

She blinked. She'd never thought he'd make that
assumption. What the hell, why not go with it?
She shrugged. "I guess I should have told you
this before, but I have a roommate now. A male
roommate."

"Really? You've only been back for a few days."

"I work fast."

"Obviously." He studied her expression. "You're trying to make me jealous, aren't you?"

"That would be childish and I pride myself on being an adult. He absolutely adores me. When I'm away, he spends the entire day just rolling around on the floor and moaning."

"Aw, that's nice. You've finally given Metcalf a chance?"

"Stop it. It's not Metcalf."

"That crazy guy at the end of your street who bums for change while singing bad show tunes?"

"No. My roommate's actually very sweet. He likes to lick my face and neck."

Lynch leaned in close. "Well, that has potential for being erotic. If that's what you're into, you should have told me before we—"

"And his breath smells like sour liver."

"Are you sure we aren't talking about Metcalf?"

"Ugly. Do you want to meet him?"

"Of course. Why wouldn't I want to meet this moaning, face-licking, halitosis-ridden rival for your affections?"

"He's with Olivia at the moment."

Lynch nodded approvingly. "He gets around. I'm starting to like him."

She was suddenly tired of playing this game. She gave a half shrug. "I'm not sure if he'll like you. At least not at first."

Lynch dismissively waved his hand. "Come on, everyone likes me."

"You're right, they do." She added coolly, "Until they get to know you."

"Even after they get to know me. Admit it."

She met his eyes. "All that means is you're really good at fooling people."

"No, it means you may need to realign your perception of me."

"Hardly. No one really knows you, but I thought I knew you better than most, Lynch."

"You did, Kendra," he said quietly. "You do."

"Until you suddenly turned around and I found I didn't know you at all."

"You don't believe that or you wouldn't have let me back in the door today. No one knows everything about a person, because everything around us keeps changing. Then we have to decide if we want to change, too, or accept that we can't go down that path." He smiled faintly. "You've been growing and changing ever since the day I met you, and I've welcomed every single one."

"Well, I didn't welcome that change you pulled on me in Afghanistan."

"I had a reason, but we'll both have to decide if it will prove to be a good one in the long run. I'll definitely have to think about that."

"Don't think anything. If Adam Lynch suddenly

engages in any meaningful self-reflection, the Earth may spin off its axis."

His lips quirked. "I wouldn't want to be responsible for that."

"Of course not." The elevator slid open at Olivia's floor and they started to walk down the hall toward her condo. "Fortunately, I have the perfect thing to take your mind off it."

An unearthly half moan, half roar echoed toward them from the direction of Olivia's door.

Lynch froze. "What was that?"

Kendra rapped on Olivia's door. "New roommate."

Olivia unlocked the door and opened it. "Finally. Our friend didn't like that you tossed him in with so little ceremony." She cocked her head. "Hello, Lynch. Welcome home."

Kendra knew she'd most likely identified him by his Ambre Topkapi aftershave.

"Hi, Olivia. Good to see you."

At that moment, Harley muscled Olivia out of the way and hurled himself at Kendra. He raised himself on his hind legs, slapped two large paws on her shoulders, and licked her face and neck.

"You weren't joking," Lynch said. "Sour liver."

Kendra raised her head to avoid the large tongue lapping at her nose. "Olivia thinks his breath smells more like rancid poultry. But I told her that was unkind."

Olivia nodded. "We're going to take care of it. I'm exploring the possibility of healthy dog mints."

Kendra sputtered as Harley's tongue caught her lips. "By all means."

Lynch mouthed three rapid clicking sounds and made a quick lowering motion with the flat of his right hand.

Harley immediately pushed back from Kendra and sat on the floor.

Kendra stared at Lynch in surprise.

He made the clicking sounds again, extended three fingers, and lowered them.

No response.

He clicked again and made a downward sweeping motion with the same hand.

Harley immediately dropped to the floor with his head propped on his front two paws.

Kendra looked between Harley and Lynch. "How in the hell did you do that?"

"Your roommate and I came to an understanding."

"Huh... Lynch, meet Harley."

"Nice name."

"Jessie liked it, too. She said that when he barks, he sometimes sounds like her motorcycle revving up. But you didn't answer my question." She turned to Olivia. "He used some kind of hand signals to get him to obey. How did you do that, Lynch?"

Lynch knelt and stroked the back of Harley's

neck. "I spent some time in Syria last year, and I had a friend there who went everywhere with an exceptionally well-trained bomb-sniffing German shepherd. He often found himself in situations where it was inconvenient, maybe even dangerous, to use verbal commands. So he used hand signals. I decided to give it a shot."

Kendra shook her head. "I wasn't aware there was an international sign language for dogs."

"There isn't." Lynch stood. "Though there are some standard signs that are used frequently by trainers. But often owners develop their own signals, and they can be very diverse. That's why I just had to try a couple before I found one that worked for 'lie down.' But most dogs like discipline and structure. That's why he responded so well to it."

Kendra looked at Harley. He certainly seemed happier and more relaxed than she'd ever seen him.

"I need you to teach me those hand signals," Olivia said. "If I had known that's all we needed to do, these last couple of days would have been much more bearable."

Kendra bit her lip. "Strange."

"What do you mean?" Lynch said.

"This dog was living with one of the victims in the murder case. Elaine Wessler. She fostered a lot of guide-dogs-in-training over the years, but I've never known her to train them to respond to hand signals."

"Do you think he picked it up from somewhere else?" Lynch said. "A previous owner?"

"Maybe. All I heard about was a little boy who owned him before he was killed. I don't know anyone else."

Lynch clicked his tongue and tried a few hand motions until he found one that elicited a response from Harley. The dog jumped to his feet and wagged his tail. He looked very happy.

"I guess that's 'at ease,'" Kendra said.

"Looks like it." Lynch patted Harley's head. "We should spend some time and see what he's capable of. The signals he knows may give us a clue about where he was trained before your victim took him in."

Kendra turned to Olivia. "He's all yours. We've got to get going to the FBI office. I just wanted to introduce him to Lynch." She suddenly realized someone was missing. "Where's Jessie?"

"She took off early this morning to L.A. to retrieve her motorcycle. You know she can't live without it for more than a couple of days." But her mind was still on Lynch and Harley and she said, "When you come back tonight, I want Lynch to teach me those signals the minute he walks in the door."

"You got it."

Lynch clicked his tongue and patted his thigh.

Harley bounded over to him, tail wagging and tongue practically flopping out of his mouth.

Kendra shook her head. Dammit. Everyone *did* like Lynch.

Even that crazy dog.

———◆———

Kendra's phone rang as they were walking toward her Toyota, parked at the curb. She picked up the call.

"Kendra, it's Griffin. I have Metcalf here on speaker."

Kendra hit a button on her phone screen. "Fine. I'm on speaker, too. Lynch is here with me. It's a party."

"I don't think you'll feel like celebrating," Metcalf said.

"Okay, so it's not *that* kind of party. What's up?"

"We got a CODIS hit on some blood left behind by one of the thugs who killed Kit Randolph," Griffin said.

"And almost killed you," Metcalf added.

Kendra glanced hopefully at Lynch. "You've got an ID on him?"

"Yes," Griffin said over the shuffling of papers. "His name is Justin Hayes. He served a six-year prison stint a while back for assault. He was acquitted on another case and was suspected of a hit against a witness in a civil trial, but the DA couldn't make their case."

"Charming guy," Kendra said. "Your basic thug for hire, I assume."

"Yep. And his face matches one of the sketches you gave us. This is definitely the perpetrator."

"Good," Lynch said. "Do we know where to find him?"

"That's the tricky part," Metcalf said. "It's rather awkward. You see . . . Justin Hayes has been dead for three years."

CHAPTER

9

Kendra and Lynch followed Metcalf quickly through the maze of hallways at FBI regional headquarters. "We've been pulling together everything we can about Hayes. Stuff is still printing out as we speak."

"Printing out? You mean we're not getting one of your famous PowerPoint presentations?"

"Sorry to disappoint you, but there isn't time. We're gathering the info in Griffin's office. That's where we're headed now."

"I looked up a photo of him online on the way here," Kendra said. "It's definitely the man I saw the other night. I have to say, he was pretty spry for a dead man."

Metcalf gave her an amused glance. "I guess you

just have a way of bringing that side out in people, Kendra."

They rounded a corner and entered Griffin's glass-walled office, where two other agents and an assistant sorted through stacks of paper still warm from the printer. Griffin was seated at his desk finishing up a phone call. After a moment, he slammed down the handset. He picked up a grainy printout and showed it to Kendra. It looked like a driver's license photo. "So this is the guy?"

"Yep." Kendra nodded. "That's the one Jessie tossed off the catwalk."

Griffin dropped the printout. "I figured. That's where we picked up the blood sample."

"So his name is Justin Hayes," Lynch said. "Why do people think he's dead?"

Griffin picked up another piece of paper and tossed it to Lynch. "Maybe this death certificate had something to do with it."

Lynch and Kendra looked at the certificate.

"Malta?" Kendra said.

"Yes. Boating accident." Griffin rummaged around his desktop until he found another photo printout, this one of a small sailboat. "Pleasure craft versus cargo ship." He picked up another photo printout of the sailboat's wrecked hull washed up on the coast.

"Let me guess," Lynch said. "No body ever found."

"No. But a pair of eyewitnesses saw it happen and

swore they saw him impaled with a piece of his mast and go down spurting blood from his mouth."

"Kind of a gruesome detail," Kendra said.

Lynch nodded. "Specific and memorable. Perfect for getting a rubber stamp at a coroner's inquest."

"Which is exactly what happened even without a body," Griffin said.

Lynch studied the wreckage photo. "Do we have names and addresses for the witnesses?"

"We're still working that up."

"What about known associates?"

"He was very much a freelancer. At the time of his so-called death, he was under investigation for some dirty tricks on behalf of the Cardinelli crime family."

"Cardinelli . . ." Lynch repeated thoughtfully.

Griffin looked at him. "Did you ever have any contact with them?"

"Not directly. But there's some overlap between them and the MacDougal syndicate." Lynch turned to Kendra. "In my FBI days, I spent a year undercover with the MacDougals."

"I heard about that," Kendra said. "It was one of the first things I ever heard about your work. You were still with the FBI then. Everyone says you pretty much brought down that organization single-handedly."

Lynch shrugged. "Aw, shucks. I don't want to brag."

Griffin made a sour face. "The dozens of men and women who worked on that case for over four years might not want you to brag, either. Even if there's an element of truth to it."

"The point I'm trying to make is that I met people who did work for both organizations," Lynch said.

Kendra held up another photo from Griffin's desk. "People like Justin Hayes?"

"No, I've never heard of him before tonight. But his elaborate faked death has a familiar ring to it. There aren't many people around who could orchestrate something as elaborate as that. Offhand, I can only think of one."

"Rick Zales?" Griffin said.

"Bingo."

"Who's that?" Kendra said.

"Rick Zales pulled similar stunts for the Mac-Dougal organization while I was undercover there," Lynch said. "But he also worked for the Cardinellis at the time of Hayes's so-called death. This stunt reeks of him."

"I agree," Griffin said.

"Then we need to talk to him," Kendra said.

Griffin shook his head. "That won't be easy. Zales testified against the Cardinellis in several of the trials. He refused witness protection because he didn't trust us to keep him safe. I wouldn't even know where to look for the guy."

"I would," Lynch said. "Mexico."

After waiting a moment for him to elaborate, Metcalf said dryly, "Any particular part of Mexico? It's kind of a big place."

"Playa Ensenada, last I heard. He was running a hole-in-the-wall cantina that caters to locals, mostly. I know the woman who helped broker the sale."

Griffin picked up his phone. "I'll reach out to the Mexican authorities."

"Don't," Lynch said. "They might tip him off and then he'll be in the wind. You'll never find him."

"We can't cross the border without contacting local law enforcement."

"You can't," Lynch said. "But Kendra and I can. We'll find Rick Zales and talk to him."

"I can't permit you to do that."

"It's not your decision," Kendra said. "As private citizens, we can travel when and where we want. Unless you're prepared to put a freeze on our passports."

Griffin looked between the two of them. "Shit. I don't want to know about this, okay?"

Lynch nodded. "Unless we find Zales and get some information we can use. Then I assume you'll be most anxious to know about it."

"That's a safe assumption, Lynch. But for now, get the hell out of here before you say something else that can get me in trouble."

Even with a stop by Kendra's condo to pick up her passport, Lynch and Kendra made it past the Mexican border in less than an hour.

As they sped down the 10 Highway, Kendra looked out at the Pacific Ocean. It was a clear day, and the water was sparkling.

"It'll only be another forty-five minutes or so," Lynch said. "It's only a short hop to Ensenada and El Hobo Muerto Cantina."

Kendra slowly turned to look at him. "That can't be the name of the place."

"Sure it is."

"Seriously, El Hobo Muerto? The Dead Hobo?"

"Yes. They serve strong drinks in tall glasses."

"What kind of clientele would spend an evening out at a place with that name?"

"You're about to find out. Don't be such a snob. From what I understand, they do a very good business there."

"Trust me, in my wild days after I got my sight, I hung out in lots of scary places. I'm not above any of them."

"You'll have to take me to some of them someday." He gave her a sly glance. "Maybe the bartenders will give me some embarrassing Kendra Michaels stories."

"I don't embarrass easily. But I'm sure you'd be very amused."

"No doubt."

Kendra smiled, imagining Adam Lynch in some of those dive bars where she'd spent her early twenties. But the more she thought about it, the more she realized he'd probably find a way to fit in. He always did, wherever he found himself. She turned back toward him. "How well do you know this Rick Zales?"

"Not very. During the year I spent undercover, I saw him maybe a dozen times. I actually helped him dismantle a small airplane one night. The boss had seized it from a competitor and wanted to send a message. So Zales and I took it apart, ran it through a compactor, and delivered it to the rival's front yard."

Kendra was almost afraid to ask. "With the pilot still inside?"

"No. Though that was discussed. Zales stole the plane from its hangar. Resourceful guy."

"Sounds like it. Are you sure he's gone straight?"

"Hard to say. People in that world have a hard time leaving it, even though Zales has a strong incentive to lie low. He testified against half a dozen men who would now very much like to kill him. Even this hole-in-the-wall bar in Mexico is probably too high-profile for his own good."

"Once we find him, I hope he's in a talkative mood."

"He will be. I've found that I'm pretty good at putting people in that mood."

She studied him warily. "That sounds ominous."

"It doesn't have to be. Depends on how cooperative Zales will be for us."

"No matter how painful it becomes for him?"

"Just the fine art of persuasion. It's an art that can take many forms. If one doesn't work, you just move on to the next."

"Did you employ this art during your FBI days?"

"There were times when it became necessary, particularly when I was undercover. But let's just say that my palette was much more...limited."

"What about your employers now?"

"It's an advantage of being freelance. My employers are much more results-driven. They're not overly concerned with how I get the information I do."

"My guess is that they'd rather not know," she said soberly.

"I'd guess the same thing." He added cheerfully, "But why dwell on the negative? Maybe the three of us will have an easy, productive conversation over some ice-cold Coronas at El Hobo Muerto Cantina."

They arrived at Zales's bar less than an hour later, which was located, oddly, in the middle of a residential neighborhood. It was a brick building painted in bright red and yellow hues, with a neon sign depicting a classic hobo figure with a stick and kerchief over his shoulder. The eyes were closed, suggesting that the hobo was indeed dead.

"Unbelievable," Kendra said.

"You'll never forget it, will you?"

"Never."

"Then Zales is a marketing genius. A tasteless son of a bitch, but a genius."

"If you say so."

They parked on the street and walked through a gravel parking lot that looked as if it had once been two house lots. Lynch stopped and pointed to a Tesla Model X parked near the back door. "That's his, or at least I think it is. It's registered to the business."

"Nice car. Did you think of getting one of those instead of that Lamborghini you're driving?"

"I briefly considered it." Lynch pulled out his phone and spent a few seconds typing something into his screen.

"What are you doing?"

"Just checking something. Let's go inside." He put away his phone and led her around front, where half a dozen outdoor tables were occupied with patrons watching a soccer game projected on a large white tarp. They walked inside, where the same game was playing on a pair of wall-mounted televisions. The place was packed, with the customers gathered around a long bar that looked to Kendra almost like a deli counter. Then it dawned on her: The place had once been a diner, only slightly modified for its current use as a dive bar.

A short, curly-haired man in his fifties greeted Kendra. "*Hola, bella dama!*" Then he saw Lynch. "Oh, shit."

Lynch clasped his shoulder. "What kind of greeting is that, Zales?"

"Vincent," he whispered. "My name is Vincent Seles now. You're gonna ruin everything."

Lynch smiled. "I wouldn't do that to you. Not after all we've been through together."

"You almost got me killed."

"I persuaded you to do your civic duty."

"You didn't give me a choice."

"Sure I did. Testify or go to jail." Lynch looked around. "You've done well for yourself. Much better than jail."

Zales nervously glanced around the bar. "What do you want?"

"I want to talk about Justin Hayes."

"Never heard of the guy."

"Come on."

"Sorry. Name doesn't ring a bell."

"Don't lie to me. Part of your agreement with the U.S. Justice Department is that you would divulge all illegal activities. If you left even one out, that could mean years in jail for you. I'm not trying to jam you up. I just need some information."

"I'm *not* going back."

"You don't need to. Just tell me what you know about Justin Hayes and what you did for him. Then I'll leave you alone."

"Ohhh . . . *Justin* Hayes. It's all coming back to me."

"I thought that it might."

Zales pointed to the doors behind the bar. "I need to go to the kitchen for a second. But I'll tell you what you need to know, okay? That's all you need? Nothing else, no hidden strings?"

"No hidden strings. You'll never see me again for the rest of your life."

Zales gave him a sour look. "That's what you said after I testified at my last mob trial."

"Circumstances change, my friend. By the way, this is my friend Kendra."

Zales gave her a nod much less enthusiastic than the greeting he'd given her earlier. "Charmed. I'll be right back."

He circled around the bar and disappeared through the swinging doors to the back.

Kendra turned toward Lynch. "I'm surprised you're letting him out of your sight."

"Why, don't you trust him?"

"Hell, no."

"Good instinct. Neither do I."

"Then why are we sitting here?

Lynch chuckled. He pulled out his phone, tapped the screen, and looked up. "Let's go talk to him." He stood and strolled out of the bar.

Kendra jumped to her feet and ran after him. She followed him around the bar and back to the gravel lot where they'd been only minutes before.

Lynch gestured toward Zales's Tesla. "Oh, look," he said, in mock surprise.

Zales was in the driver's seat, frantically pounding on the window.

Lynch leaned against the car and crossed his arms. "Why, Zales. Oh, sorry, I mean *Vincent*. Or can I call you Vince?"

"You son of a bitch!" Zales yelled from inside the vehicle. He slapped the window again. "What did you do to my car?"

"I took control." Lynch held up his phone. "A custom app I had a friend make for me. Like it?"

Zales frantically tried the door handle again. "I can't get out of here!"

"You're fine where you are."

"I can't freakin' breathe!"

Lynch tapped the phone again, and the driver's side window cracked open. "How's that?"

"You bastard." Zales jammed his foot on the brake and repeatedly punched the start button. Nothing.

"Bastard?" Lynch laughed and jerked his thumb toward Kendra. "She's called me that once or twice. That's why I prefer to think of it as a term of endearment."

"It isn't, trust me," Kendra said reassuringly. "I feel your pain, Vince."

"Nice vehicle you have here." Lynch turned to admire its sleek lines. "The trouble with upscale cars these days is that they're really computers on wheels. Are you enjoying the Wi-Fi and Bluetooth upgrades? Because that's what's letting me into your car's operating system without even touching it."

"You've made your point. Let me out."

"Not yet. Listen, the same thing happened to me recently. It was no fun. I lost a Ferrari I loved very much. Just heartbreaking."

"It's true," Kendra said. "We almost died, but of course that didn't matter to him nearly as much as the loss of that car."

"I don't give a shit." Zales was trying to loosen his collar. "I'm kind of claustrophobic. I'd appreciate it if I can continue this conversation outside."

Lynch shook his head. "I remembered that phobia from the old days. But I'm afraid you've already violated our trust. You're right where you need to be."

"Okay. Fine. What do you need to know?"

"You staged a rather spectacular phony death for Justin Hayes a few years ago. Off the Maltese coast. He was a killer and all-around thug for the Cardinelli crime family."

"Who told you I did that?"

"I have sources. I found you, didn't I?"

"Okay. Ancient history. I may have helped him start a new life, so what of it?"

"I need to find him."

"Now? You know guys in that line of work . . . He may not even be alive."

"He is," Kendra said. "He tried to kill me a few nights ago."

"Damn. Sorry about that."

"Touching," Lynch said. "So tell me, do you think he's still working for the Cardinellis?"

"No way. They were kind of pissed at him. They thought he'd gotten sloppy. They wanted me to stage his death so the authorities would stop looking for him. They were afraid that if he got pinched, he might somehow lead the FBI back to them."

"Lucky man," Lynch said. "That wasn't like the Cardinellis to go to such extremes, especially when their own hides were on the line. Normally in circumstances like that they'd just snuff him out."

"That's what I thought. And that's not a service I provide. But he'd done good work for them and I guess that was part of their severance to him."

"A mob benefits package. I like it. So where did he go?"

"How the hell should I know? It's not like I was married to the guy."

"No, you just staged his death. Tell me, how did you rig the mast through his chest?"

"There was no broken mast in his chest. We piloted the boat into a cargo ship and paid a couple of college-kid tourists to act as witnesses and tell the story to the cops and coroner. I basically paid for their spring break."

"And you have no clue who Hayes may have gone to work for later?"

"None. Can I get out of here now?"

"I don't think you're being entirely forthcoming with me." Lynch tapped his phone, and the car's engine roared to life.

Zales's eyes widened. He grabbed the shifter, but the car wouldn't engage. "What are you doing?"

"My Tesla-driving friends just *love* showing off how their car automatically pulls out of their garage and rolls down their driveway without them being in it." Lynch swiped his finger across the phone screen, and the car suddenly went into reverse. It slowly backed out of the parking space.

"Lynch...!"

"And I have to admit, it's a pretty neat trick. But do you want to see a neater one?"

Zales beat on the window with his fists. "Come on, Lynch. It's not funny."

"A neater trick is if I waited for a truck to roll down the street, and I suddenly backed you out into its path. It wouldn't even have time to stop."

"What more do you want from me?" Sweat was beading his forehead. "I told you everything I know!"

"I don't believe you." Lynch slid his finger back, and the car lurched out of the parking lot.

Zales looked around frantically. "Shit!"

"Lynch," Kendra whispered. "What are you doing?"

"Watch." He and Kendra walked closer to the car, which was now slowly backing down the street. He called out to Zales, "There's a railroad track down here, isn't there?"

"Please, man!"

"And if you'd stop whining long enough to listen, I think I heard the sound of a train horn in the distance. It's almost like it was meant to be, isn't it?"

Zales stopped to listen. Sure enough, a train horn blasted and a locomotive engine rumbled closer.

A moment later, the white crossing gates dropped across the road. Zales looked back at Lynch with panic in his eyes.

"Stop it!"

Lynch quickly walked alongside the driver's side window with his phone extended in front of him. "I'm sure I can put you over the tracks before the train gets there. And your car will snap those crossing gates like twigs, don't you think?"

"Oh, God! No!"

"Give me something. Where can I find this guy? Who may he be working for?"

"The Cardinellis paid me for that job. They'd kill me if they knew I ratted the guy out."

"Everyone already wants to kill you." Lynch pushed the control button, and the car rolled faster toward the train tracks.

"No! Stop!"

"Give me something, Zales."

"Padres! Padres!"

"You're calling for your dad?"

"No! He was working for the Padres baseball team!"

Lynch slowed the car. "Doing what?"

"Security. He was like a bodyguard. I saw him about a year ago. He was bragging about it. He said he was working for a company that was doing security for them on their away games."

"What company?"

"I don't know! Stop it! Please!"

The train's roar was getting louder. The car rolled closer toward the thin gates.

"Is that all?"

"Yes! Please! Believe me! That's all I got!"

Lynch tapped his screen and the car stopped. "See, Zales? Was that so hard?"

Zales lunged out as the doors unlocked and rolled away from the car. The train roared past only seconds later.

Lynch pocketed his phone. "Have a good day." He took Kendra's elbow and led her toward the Toyota. "You should really take better care of your vehicles, Zales. You almost damaged a fine piece of machinery."

Zales was still swearing helplessly as he watched Lynch and Kendra drive away.

"That was . . . interesting," Kendra said when she could get her breath. "What if Zales hadn't had anything to tell you?"

He shrugged. "I had to go the limit. I knew I had at least another thirty seconds before I could be sure that he didn't know anything else."

"Oh, thirty seconds. That's different." She moistened her lips. "I was afraid it was really close."

"Only if the Tesla hadn't performed as well as I thought it would." There was a sudden twinkle in his eyes. "But as I told Zales, it is a fine piece of machinery."

"Bastard."

"You can't convince me that there's not a hidden term of endearment buried in that word somewhere. Particularly when I've just performed every bit as well as that Tesla. Don't I deserve it?"

"You'd deserve it more if you'd given me warning ahead of time." She added grudgingly, "But that would probably be too much to expect considering who you are. And you did get us the information we needed. Where do we go from here? What do you know about the Padres?"

"That I lost quite a bit of money on them last year. I'm hoping for better things this season." He held up his hand as she opened her lips. "And as far as I know, the franchise would have no reason to hire a thug of Hayes's caliber in a security capacity. But there are always possibilities to explore. I think we should go to Petco Park and talk to the Padres security department about why they'd do that."

"I only hope none of their executives drive a Tesla," Kendra said. "At least the interview should be comparatively tame in comparison." She looked at her watch. "It's only the middle of the afternoon. We should be able to get across the border and to the stadium before five or six. That should be—" She stopped. "Shit!"

"What?"

"I can't go with you. You'll have to go by your-self. Olivia's had Harley all day and she'll be upset if I don't take him over on schedule."

"Can't you call for an emergency dispensation?"

"I could, if I could prove it to her. But she wouldn't consider an interview with a bunch of sports executives as any kind of emergency. And you have no idea how tough she could be if she thought I was avoiding my obligation. Ask Jessie."

"I will." He smiled. "I definitely want to hear that tale. I suppose I can do without your company, but it does leave me wondering who's in charge of whom where Harley is concerned."

"Don't go there. We're trying to work it out." She changed the subject. "I suppose you want me to take you to my place to pick up your Lamborghini before you go to the stadium?"

"By all means. I'm already suffering withdrawal symptoms from riding around in this Toyota. Maybe I was wrong about needing a less showy vehicle."

"Color me surprised," she said dryly. "But Herb will be devastated that you're taking it away from his loving care. You'll call me about what you found out later tonight?"

"I'll report in person."

She looked away from him. "That won't be necessary."

"I always believe the personal touch is best. Besides, I promised to go over hand signals with Harley. Olivia seemed excited about it."

Yes, she had, Kendra thought resignedly. It seemed she was going to get the personal touch whether she wanted it or not...

———◆———

"Where's Lynch?" Olivia asked the minute Kendra entered her condo. "I told you I need him to—"

"I know what you told me," Kendra interrupted as she knelt to pet Harley. "But he wasn't finished for the day. He said he'd come by later to work with him."

"And me," Olivia added. "Hand signals are important and might keep Harley's barking to a minimum. I've noticed lately that he seems to get upset whenever anyone flinches away from him. He doesn't understand it." She was frowning. "We have to do everything we can for him."

"And we are," Kendra said. "Lynch promised he'd drop by. He keeps his promises."

"I know he does." Olivia went to the desk and signed out of her computer. "How did it go today? Did you find out anything?"

"Well, I found how close you can get to extermination in a Tesla," she said dryly. "And no, it wasn't me. It was Lynch's way of interrogating one of the bad guys from his shady past. I'll tell you all about it over dinner."

"I can hardly wait." She went toward the kitchen. "Lynch stories are always entertaining. I told you his contacts would be—"

"Excuse me." Kendra was getting an email and she glanced at the signature in case it was Lynch. It was not Lynch. *Praxidike.* "What the hell?"

Olivia stopped. "What's wrong?"

"It's an email on my business account and it's weird. It's signed Praxidike and it's only two lines." She read it to her.

"It's important you meet me at the grove near where Mr. Kim was killed this evening at 6 PM. Please do not notify either the FBI or any school officials of this email. Sincerely, Praxidike."

"Very weird," Olivia said. "What the hell?"

"I believe that's what I said," Kendra glanced at her watch. "And he didn't give me much time to make up my mind what I was going to do about it. It's ten after five right now."

"You're not thinking about going?" Olivia asked. "May I remind you that you came close to getting yourself killed a few days ago? Now you're supposed to go along with this message that says you're not to tell anyone who might possibly protect you what you're going to do? Not smart, Kendra."

"But it's the *school*, Olivia. That meeting place he

chose is out in the open. It will still be daylight at six and no one will be hovering, ready to pounce. This sounds more like someone who wants to give information and is afraid to do it. Look, he even said please."

"So he's a polite murderer."

"No, I mean it's just not something anyone with bad intentions would naturally say." She was nibbling at her lower lip. "I think I'd regret it if I didn't go."

"Then call Lynch."

"He's busy. Besides, he can be . . . intimidating. He might scare Praxidike away." She made a face as she repeated the name. "Whatever that means. No, it's better if I go alone." She went to Olivia's desk and pressed the combo to release the lock on her security drawer. "But if it makes you feel better, I'll borrow your gun and take it with me. That's what I was planning anyway. I just don't want to have to run upstairs and get mine." She tucked the Smith in her handbag. "Now I'm great. No problem with going alone."

"Absolutely not," Olivia said flatly. "If you're going to do this then I'll have to go with you. Let's get on the road."

"No." Kendra shook her head. "This isn't your job. I'll be fine without you—"

"Be quiet, Kendra. I know every inch of the grounds of that school just as well as you do. Don't argue. I haven't been able to help since Elaine and Mr. Kim were killed. If you think there's some reason you might be able to find out something from this bizarre message, then we have to go for it." She smiled over her shoulder. "Besides, you need me to protect you."

"Protect me?"

"No school officials. No FBI. But he didn't say anything about me." Olivia clipped the leash to Harley's collar. "Or my friend here who we know can be very protective when the occasion calls for it." She led him toward the door. "Providing no one knows what a complete softie he is."

CHAPTER
10

S ee? I told you that there would be no threat,"
Kendra said to Olivia as they rounded the corner that led down to the gate. "No scumbags
waiting in the shadows to take me down. Feel that
sun on your face? No shadows. And you can even
hear the choir practicing over at the chapel."

"I definitely heard them," Olivia said dryly. "It
made me nervous that Harley might decide to join
in and start caterwauling. And then all hell would
break loose and whoever is down there waiting for
you would take off in fear for his life."

"It's something to think about," Kendra said. "But
he usually sticks close to you, and he's seemed
content enough, even familiar, with the grounds
ever since we got out of the car. I think Elaine

must have taken him for walks here on the campus when she brought him to work with her." She had another thought. "I wonder if she introduced him to Mr. Kim? It would have been natural for him to have run into—" She stopped as they came over the hill and she was suddenly staring down at the grove. "I don't see anyone." She felt a rush of disappointment. "Maybe our Praxidike got nervous and decided to stand me up. How rude of him. I was hoping that—" Then she saw a man getting to his feet from a kneeling position near the hydrangea bushes. He was wearing jeans and a blue work shirt and had glossy dark hair that shone in the sunlight. "I spoke too soon, Olivia. There's a man working down there in the bushes, I think he was digging. He's got a spade in his hand and looks like a gardener." She was starting down the hill. "Stay here. We don't want to scare him off. I'll call you if I need you and you can loose our fierce Harley to go on the attack."

"I don't like this, Kendra."

"It's why we're here. He looks harmless. Just listen and be my trusty backup. Okay?" She didn't wait for a response but took off at a trot. Better to get this over quickly before Olivia got anxious and decided to come to her rescue. As she drew closer to the man, her confidence grew. Well, not really a man; he looked like a college kid and had the same golden skin and slightly almond-shaped eyes as Mr. Kim.

"Hello," she said. "I'm Kendra Michaels. You wanted to speak to me?"

He jumped and whirled to face her. "What?"

If he was a college kid, he was a very nervous one. "Don't be afraid. You're doing the right thing. If you have information, you should tell us about it."

"Information?" His gaze was raking her face. "You're not one of the blind students, are you? You can see me."

"I can see you. You must know that if you contacted me. I told you, I'm Kendra Michaels."

"I didn't contact you." He appeared sincerely bewildered. "But I know who you are. My grandfather used to tell us about you. You're the one who works with the FBI."

"Yes." Now she was the one who was confused. "Your grandfather?"

"I'm John Kim." He wiped his hand on his jeans so he could shake her hand. "My grandfather is...was Ronald Kim. I took a break from my classes at UCSD to help out at the school until they could get someone qualified to replace him." He cleared his throat. "Not that anyone could. But I knew he wouldn't want his gardens here to suffer while they tried. He loved every plant, every blade of grass."

"I realize that," Kendra said gently. "I'm sure he'd appreciate what you're doing. We'll all miss him." She paused. "And you didn't send me an email asking me to meet you here at six?"

He shook his head. "No, the only reason I didn't leave earlier was that I needed to trim the hydrangeas." His gaze went to the yellow barrier tapes several yards away. "And I kept putting it off because it was...here...too close to where he died. It hurt too much." He added, "But they say the police are done now and won't be back. Maybe it will be better now." He started to turn away. "It was nice to meet you, Dr. Michaels." Then he turned back. "You really shouldn't have come here alone. Please don't do it again. Like I told you, my grandfather always talked about you and the other kids. He wouldn't want anything to happen to you."

She was touched. "Thank you, John." She gestured to Olivia and Harley a short distance away. "I'm not alone. And I'm so sorry for your loss."

He lifted his hand and headed for the gate.

She watched him leave. Mr. Kim had been such a part of her youth and who she had been during her growing years, and yet she couldn't remember him ever speaking of his family. When he was here with them, it was as if he were one of the strong, beautiful plants that he nurtured so carefully, giving everything, taking nothing.

"He's nice, isn't he?" Ariel Jones came out of the shrubbery behind her. She had her white cane and was carrying a bouquet of the same white hydrangeas that John Kim had been trimming. "His name's John and he's Mr. Kim's grandson. He gave me these flowers when I was up here before. He said that he was trimming them anyway and I might as well enjoy them."

"He's very nice," Kendra agreed. She fixed the girl with a stern glance. "But you shouldn't be out here without someone with you. I thought we addressed the buddy system the last time we talked."

She nodded. "But you didn't use it. I heard John tell you that you shouldn't be alone here. Does that mean I shouldn't have told you to come?"

"What?" Kendra frowned. "First, I have a friend and a dog up on the hill. I'm not alone. And does that question mean what I think it means? You're the one who sent me that email message? Was it some kind of joke?"

"No, I wouldn't do that. If I did, you wouldn't pay any attention when I did need you. It would be like that boy-and-the-wolf story. I just wasn't sure what I should do so I wouldn't get in trouble."

"You made it sound very dramatic. No FBI? Really, Ariel."

"Well, I think the FBI puts hackers in jail. And maybe I should have told you about Ms. Wessler."

She stiffened. "More than you already told me?"

"Not about the hacking. I told you I was nervous."

Kendra tried to stifle her impatience. "Okay. Tell me about the hacking and everything else. Who hacked whom?"

"I did. I get bored sometimes and I'm really good at hacking. You find out so many things that are more interesting than all the things they let kids know. It doesn't seem fair. Well, I was sitting in Ms. Wessler's class and I'd finished my work and I was trying to find something to do."

"And you found it," Kendra said grimly.

"Ms. Wessler had one of those old-style flip-top phones, and she had to use the hard buttons with that beep I could hear when she logged into the faculty bulletin board. I memorized it and later, I used it to log in and use my text-to-speech app to read all kinds of interesting discussions between the faculty members."

"*Private* discussions," Kendra said pointedly.

"Yes, but I'm telling you about it now, aren't I? Anyway, I could also read private messages between Ms. Wessler and other faculty members, including unsent drafts. It was kind of exciting." She hesitated. "But then I sort of got carried away and I listened and managed to pick up Ms. Wessler's email password. That way I could hack into her email account."

"Ariel!"

"I know I shouldn't have done it. It was an experiment. I was only going to do it for a little while. But then stuff started to happen and I didn't know what to do."

"What 'stuff'?"

"Ms. Wessler emailed Mr. Kim about something strange she'd thought she'd seen while she was up on the cliff path the night before. She said it looked like people moving back and forth on the north shore. But the beach is private and she thought she must have been mistaken. It was dark, and it had only been for a minute, but she was still uneasy so she asked him to check it out if he got the chance. She said she knew he sometimes worked late in the gardens to avoid the heat of the day and hoped it wouldn't be an inconvenience for him." She frowned. "That was really interesting. And I was waiting for him to answer her back, but if he did, it wasn't by email." She swallowed. "And then two days later I heard that he'd been killed and it scared me real bad. I didn't know what to do. It scared Ms. Wessler, too. She emailed her ex-husband right away even though he was in Tokyo and told him that she was feeling guilty, that she should never have asked Mr. Kim to do something she could have done herself. She asked if there was any way he could come home and meet with her so that they could talk it all out before she went to the police. She said the day before Mr. Kim was killed, she thought she saw movement down on the shore again and she'd tried to take pictures. And the day that Mr. Kim was murdered she was sure she and her dog had been followed. That's when her husband told her not to wait until he could fly home to be with her, but to take the pictures right to the police." Ariel whispered, "But she didn't do it. I think she really liked her husband and wanted to see him. She must have felt kind of alone. I waited and kept checking all night to see if she emailed the police or maybe Dr. Walker. But she didn't do it." She moistened her lips. "And then the next day she was dead, too."

Kendra stared at her, stunned. It was a secondhand experience of horror, but that didn't mitigate the terror and confusion this little girl must have felt. "I'm sorry, Ariel."

"Was it my fault? Could I have done something to stop it?"

"It wasn't your fault. You're a child and it was the responsibility of the adults you were monitoring to take care of their own situation." She reached out and grasped her arms. "You mustn't think that you could have changed anything just because of those emails. Do you hear?"

"I hear." She was frowning. "I just thought that

because I'm smarter than most people, I should have been able to stop it from happening."

"Well, there is that." Kendra found herself smiling in spite of the gravity of the situation. "But even Einstein might have had trouble balancing guilt and responsibility. I know you feel terrible about Mr. Kim and Ms. Wessler, but they wouldn't blame you. They loved children and understood them."

"You're *sure* it's not my fault?"

"I'm very sure."

Ariel gave a deep sigh. "Whew. When those terrible things happened to both of them, I wondered if maybe I should have let someone know about it. Even if I got into trouble for hacking."

"I'm not saying that the hacking wasn't wrong. It certainly was wrong and you should have gotten in trouble for doing it. I'm only saying that it wasn't your responsibility to run the lives of the people you chose to hack. That would have been an even greater intrusion."

"But if I hadn't been hacking, I wouldn't have had anything to tell you and that would have been bad, too." She gazed at her hopefully. "And everything is important in a murder case, isn't it? So didn't that kind of make up for it?"

Kendra couldn't argue with that logic even if Ariel had twisted it to suit herself. "Maybe. As long as you don't do it again. It's true the FBI should know everything you've told me about Ms. Wessler and Mr. Kim. I want you to give me copies of those emails." She tilted her head. "Now, is there anything else you haven't told me?"

She shook her head. "I don't think so." She thought about it. "Except I don't know if I shouldn't feel guilty just because I'm a kid. If I'm smart enough to hack emails, shouldn't I be smart enough to know what to do with them?"

Kendra was silent. "You'll have to decide that for yourself. I've given you my opinion. Anything else?"

She shook her head. "But I'll let you know if I think of something."

"Please do." She took her hand. "Now I'm taking you back to the residence hall and dropping you off." She was leading her up the hill toward Olivia. "And you're going to remember the buddy system from now on. Right?"

She nodded. "But a buddy would have gotten in my way today." She stopped abruptly. "What's that sound?"

Oh, Lord, Harley was *barking*.

"That's our dog, Harley. Don't pay any attention to him. He won't hurt you. He just sounds odd."

But Harley had broken free of Olivia's leash and was tearing toward Ariel, and the barking was fiercer than Kendra had ever heard it. He was acting as if he was going to tear her apart. Kendra instinctively stepped in front of the child to protect her.

But Harley streaked past Ariel and Kendra and tore through the brush, howling and growling. Was he trying to attack John Kim? She ran through the brush after Harley, but she could see that Kim's grandson was no longer in sight.

And neither was Harley. He'd gone under the yellow barrier tapes and was in the crime scene area where Kim had been killed. He was tearing around the brush, sniffing and growling, pawing and digging at the ground.

"Harley, stop it!"

Harley was paying no attention to her. He was whimpering, sniffing, and growling, running excitedly from place to place.

"Harley!" Olivia called. "Come!" She'd made her way down the rest of the way to stand beside Ariel. "Now!"

Harley halted, freezing. Then he was darting out under the yellow tape straight to Olivia. But he didn't stop; instead he ran circles around Olivia and Ariel, still barking and growling.

Kendra caught up with him and grabbed for his leash. "Tell him to stop, Olivia. He's going crazy and he's not paying any attention to me. I think he's trying to protect you and Ariel."

"Stop!" Olivia yelled. "Idiot dog. Everything's fine."

Harley stopped. He was still panting, but he was leaning against Olivia's knee and that weird aggressiveness was gone.

"Or is it?" Olivia turned to Kendra. "Harley doesn't act like that. What happened?"

"He ran into Kim's crime scene area and was sniffing and digging and I couldn't get him to quit. Then he ran back toward you and Ariel." She gazed at Ariel. "I'm sorry if he frightened you. He's really a very gentle dog. He'd never hurt you."

"Of course he wouldn't." She reached out for the dog, ignoring the horrendous sounds he was making, and began to stroke him. "Anyone can tell that. I've read about police dogs like him. He was just looking for clues to help the FBI find the people who did those bad things to Mr. Kim. I think he must be very clever to make those horrible sounds so the bad guys would be afraid of him."

"I'm glad you think so." She looked at Olivia and shrugged in bewilderment at Ariel's total acceptance of both the situation and Harley's hideous caterwauling, which usually frightened everyone. "And this is my friend Olivia Moore, Ariel. I told you about Ariel, Olivia. It seems she was the one who sent me the message. I'll tell you all about it later. Right now we're going to take Ariel back to the residence."

"Olivia Moore?" Ariel froze, transfixed. "You're

the one who created *Outasite*. I go there all the time. You're *awesome*."

"Thank you. It's nice to be appreciated." Olivia smiled. "Particularly since you seem to be such a fan of my friend Kendra, who has a much more glamorous image."

"I didn't even know you were friends. How cool is that?" Ariel's cheeks were flushed with excitement. "Appreciated? I was standing in line to attend your Advanced Computer Savvy lecture last year. I had to get special permission because I was a little young for it. I learned so much. Are you going to give another one this year?"

"I'm sure I will. It's just not set up yet."

"Then could I help you do it? I still have lots of questions I need answered."

It was obvious Kendra had been forgotten, and she just stepped back and enjoyed the adulation Olivia was receiving.

"You could always email me." Olivia was smiling at Ariel with amusement. "You're clearly very good at that. I'll give you my email address."

"Would you? That would be great. I'll try not to bother you too much." She suddenly thrust the bouquet of flowers she was still carrying at Olivia. "You should take this bouquet. It will be like someone in the audience giving flowers to a great artist."

Kendra could see Olivia was touched, and her friend didn't make the mistake of refusing the offering. "That's kind of you." She lifted the hydrangeas and breathed in the fragrance. "It's a lovely gesture and it makes me feel very special."

"You *are* special." She turned toward Kendra as if suddenly remembering she was there. "You're both special and it's wonderful that you're friends." She went still, and then she was suddenly beaming. "I bet you email back and forth all the time."

Oh, shit.

"No!" Kendra said sharply. "We live in the same building. We hardly ever email. We just run back and forth when we have something to say."

"Really?" Ariel said, disappointed. "But I'd think it would be more convenient to—"

"Wrong." Olivia stepped in, as she sensed there was more to Kendra's answer than appeared on the surface. "Sometimes it's good to forget about technology and just reach out and touch." She glanced at Kendra. "You're right, we should get Ariel back to her residence hall so that you can fill me in on what's been going on." She turned back to where Ariel was petting Harley. "But not until we get Harley to be a little quieter before he disturbs the entire campus. He likes her entirely too much." She put her hand on his muzzle and said firmly, "Hush, Harley. No more."

He gave a low growl and then was silent. But he

ambled contentedly beside Ariel until they got to the residence hall. Ariel gave him a pat and then turned to Kendra. "You'll tell everyone I helped and the FBI won't arrest me for the hacking?"

"I believe they'll let you be on probation," Kendra said solemnly. "As long as we see you're on good behavior."

"I thought so. Thanks."

"You're welcome." She had another thought. "Providing that you tell me why you called yourself Praxidike in that email."

"Oh, I ran across that name in Greek mythology. Praxidike was the spirit of Justice." She frowned. "Though maybe I shouldn't have called myself that when I always thought the name should belong to you, Kendra."

Olivia choked.

"You will *not* mention that to Lynch, Olivia," Kendra murmured between set teeth.

Olivia was trying to smother a smile. "We'll see..."

"It seemed perfect for you." Ariel grinned. "But I couldn't resist using it for our first big case together. And maybe I'll deserve it myself someday." She gave Harley one final pat. "Goodbye, Harley. He's really a great dog, isn't he, Kendra?"

"You wouldn't want to adopt him, would you?" Olivia asked. "You're really getting along well with him."

Ariel laughed. "Don't be silly, Olivia. Anyone can tell that he's *your* dog."

She turned and ran into the residence.

"I thought she was a very bright little kid until she said that," Olivia said. "Did you bribe her?"

Kendra held up her hands. "Innocent." She turned and started back toward her car. "But she was bright enough to understand nobody should be afraid of Harley but the bad guys. Maybe all her other instincts are equally good. A police dog he's definitely not. But from what Ariel just told me, it could be that we were right about Harley being more familiar with the campus than we thought. Maybe today he was recognizing the scent of the murderer who killed Mr. Kim."

Olivia was remembering something else. "Hacking? You were afraid she might hack our emails to each other?"

"I thought it might be a possibility that I wanted to discourage."

Olivia smiled slowly. "It would be interesting to see if she could do it. I'd like to see how much technical skill she acquired and could apply from my lecture last year."

"I'm not sure that I want to know. Now stop trying to gauge if she has the ability to be a future Olivia Moore and I'll tell you what else I found out while I was grilling our hacker. Then we really have to call Metcalf and Griffin and let them know the same information, and tell them about Harley's sudden transformation into Ariel's idea of a police dog."

———◆———

Lynch didn't arrive at Kendra's condo until almost nine, and it was clear he was not in a good mood.

He used his key to open the door and then slammed it behind him. "Don't say it. I don't want to hear it." He bent down and did a series of hand signals to Harley that instantly quieted him. Then he went over to the bar and poured himself a whiskey. "The only thing I want to hear is why you didn't tell me when you went out to Oceanside today."

She instinctively braced herself. "It wasn't necessary. I could handle it. You'd already left to go to the stadium and you might have found out something important. Did you?"

"Later. Why didn't you call me and give me the choice? And what happened to that Harley emergency block?"

"Olivia was there when I got the message. She realized that this was something unexpected and unavoidable and there wasn't much time." She repeated, "And I knew I could handle it. The meeting was at the school in broad daylight for goodness' sake. I thought I'd tell you how it went when you showed up tonight." She frowned. "How did you find out about it anyway?"

"Metcalf. You called and told Griffin and him what you'd learned about Mr. Kim and Elaine from Ariel Jones." He took a swallow of his whiskey. "You casually mentioned that I was following up on another lead and he called me an hour ago to see what luck I'd had with the Padres. He was a bit surprised that I didn't know about Oceanside."

Metcalf again, she thought impatiently. He hadn't seemed in the least curious or critical when she'd given them the report, but that call to Lynch was a little too coincidental. "I told you, I was planning on telling you tonight. It's not as if I was keeping something from you." She was sounding defensive. It was beginning to piss her off. "And you have no right to charge in here treating me like this. I was following up on a lead and there was no reason for me to run to you when I could do it myself. As I said, the meeting was to take place at the grounds of the school, and I could have called out if there had been a problem. I'd taken Olivia's gun so I was armed. In addition, Olivia came with me and brought Harley for additional protection."

"One question. Did Olivia tell you to call me?"

"She suggested it. I told her I could handle it myself. The message sounded tentative, not threatening."

Her hands clenched. "And I did handle it. It turned out to be even less dangerous than I expected. A college kid trying to honor his grandfather and a little blind girl who had stumbled on something she didn't know what to do with. I went to the meeting, I got the information, and no one was hurt. It was the right thing to do."

"Like it was the right thing to do for you to go back to the poppy field that night in Afghanistan?" he asked coldly.

"Yes. Don't go there, Lynch."

"Okay, I won't." He finished his whiskey and set the glass on the bar. He came toward her, his words coming like bullets. "Because only the potential for risk was the same because you were so damn reckless. Shall we go down the list? You received the email very close to the time you had to meet. No time to make advance preparations, encouraging you to act on impulse. You felt safe because the meeting was to be at your old school? Didn't you realize that was the most logical location for an attack to take place? Particularly for a professional with experience. I'd choose somewhere the target has been before and preferably has pleasant memories of, which would banish any sense of threat. A college-kid persona appearing would be perfect to lull her into thinking that everything is rainbows in Oz. The gun? You wouldn't pull it unless you suspected something, and I would have had time to take it away from you and drag you into the bushes before you could get it out. You're not unfamiliar with weapons these days but there's no way you're near to being an expert. Your backup? A blind woman who might be very sharp but has obvious drawbacks and a dog who I doubt would ever make a K-9 team."

"Are you finished?" She glared at him. "Because your tearing my reasoning to shreds doesn't alter the fact that my judgment was right and I got what I needed. If you'd shown up, Ariel probably wouldn't have trusted me and run away. She's not some mob hoodlum you can slap around or threaten with a damn runaway locomotive."

"It wasn't a runaway and it was the Tesla that I used—" He stopped and drew a deep breath. "We're going to disagree on this no matter what I say, but I had to get it out because I don't want it to happen again. Yes, nothing happened this time, but you can see it had the potential. Admit it?"

"But judgment and instinct can be *everything*," she said fiercely. "And I'm not going to think that I have to believe bad of people in every situation. Why do you think I refuse so many cases and just teach my music classes? I couldn't live that way."

"I know you couldn't," he said softly. He reached out and touched her cheek with his index finger.

"And it scares me to death you might make a wrong call someday. So why not admit that it could have gone south today?"

That touch was incredibly gentle, and his expression held the same depth of feeling. No one could doubt his sincerity. Her anger abruptly vanished as she gazed at him. She said jerkily, "I admit you could be correct if everything on the planet had gone wrong with the situation. I'm surprised you didn't bring up the possibility of little Ariel jumping out of the bushes with an AK-47 and blasting me."

He suddenly smiled. "No, that would have been a little too much even for me. But from what Metcalf told me, I'd say that she might have to be watched closely for the next few years to see where that curiosity will take her."

Kendra nodded ruefully. "It will only be dangerous if she gets bored again." She added, "But you did go overboard. There was no reason why you should have been that upset."

"There was every reason. Because it showed just how tentative you are about working with me. We had a fairly successful day in Mexico, and I thought you were coming around to accepting me as a partner again. But the minute you got a chance to jettison me and go off on your own again, you took it." He met her eyes. "You knew I'd come back if you called me. You knew I'd *want* to come back. But you fed yourself all that bullshit so that you'd have an excuse not to let me be there for you."

"It wasn't bullshit."

"Close enough. Be honest, Kendra. We've always been honest with each other."

"I would have called you if I'd thought there was a reason to do it." But she wouldn't lie to him when she'd just realized that she might have been lying to herself. "I might have been reluctant to have you around twenty-four seven. You can be ... overpowering."

"You can handle me."

"I know I can," she said quickly. "I just don't like to go to the trouble."

"And it will only be until we find those butchers of your friends. Then I'll let you go your own way again ... maybe. But I can't worry about you doing this kind of nonsense just to avoid me. You can be as trusting of the human race as you want to be as long as you let me be there to strike a balance. So will you promise me that you'll give me the chance to protect you even if it's only from Ariel Jones with her machine gun?"

"AK-47."

"Whatever." He smiled. "It's important to me. Will you do it?"

She couldn't look away from him. He was using

every bit of that charisma that was his stock-in-trade. And what did it matter? Lynch very seldom asked anything from her. It was no defeat because it was her conferring the favor. "I suppose it doesn't make any difference. I promise I won't avoid you unless you become completely obnoxious."

He chuckled. "I'll attempt to make sure you won't find me too disgusting to bear. I guarantee I'll make every effort."

He was doing that right now, and she had to do something to break free. She took a step back and said, "But you have to admit I found out valuable information from Ariel. A connection in the deaths of Elaine and Mr. Kim, the presence of strangers down on the shore, Elaine being stalked..." She frowned. "But Metcalf said that they'd searched the entire campus area including the shore after Mr. Kim's death and they hadn't seen any sign of any trespassers. No footprints, nothing. He said he'd go back and look again."

"I'm sure he will. And yes, Ariel's information was valuable. I never said it wasn't."

"No, because you were so busy yelling at me that you didn't concern yourself with the important things. You still haven't told me what you found out from the Padres. Did you get anywhere with them?"

"Yes and no. They're still not doing anything to

shore up their rather disappointing infield, if you're interested."

"Not in the slightest."

"Then you must want to know if Justin Hayes really did do any work for them. And the answer to that is that I still don't know. The bodyguards who were employed by the Padres for their away games last season are no longer with them."

Kendra's brows rose. "Trouble?"

"No one wanted to talk about it at first, but I finally got a secretary to give me a little information."

"Of course you did."

"It turned out that those bodyguards were selling access to the players to autograph dealers, tipping them off to their schedules, their comings and goings. It was a lucrative sideline for them, but of course it compromised the players' security. So the entire bodyguard detail was fired."

Kendra thought for a moment. "Kind of scuzzy, but nothing to suggest any of them could be a murderer."

"If Hayes is low on money, he could just be an opportunist who would do anything for the right price. I flashed his photo around but no one in the office recognized him. Not that they necessarily would, since the security team only worked while the Padres traveled to away games. The team's in St. Louis now but they'll be coming back into town tonight. I thought it would be a good idea to show up at practice tomorrow at Petco stadium and flash the photo to the players and road manager. We can see if they recognize Hayes and can give us the name he's using now."

"What about the name of the security company itself?"

"Johnson Security. It was a small firm and it disbanded right after the firings. They didn't have much future after that. The Padres were anxious not to have any adverse publicity, which is why we hadn't heard anything about it. I tried to reach them by phone but it was disconnected. We'll have to follow up on it tomorrow."

"You have a busy day planned for us tomorrow."

"Unless you have something more productive to do, like helping Mr. Kim's grandson in the garden or teaching Ariel better ways to hack. I know your friend Sam Zackoff, that hacker genius with Homeland Security, might be able to show her a few tricks."

"Not funny," Kendra said. "Sam might turn her into a superstar if he had her for a few months. She needs no encouragement." She looked down at Harley, whose head was now resting on her foot. "But talking about skills, it reminds me that you have a job to do yourself." She headed for the front door. "We have to go down to Olivia's condo. We can't disappoint her. Grab Harley's leash. You have a few lessons to give to both of us."

———◆———

PETCO PARK
NEXT DAY

"It looks a little like a ghost town," Kendra said as she and Lynch climbed the ramp from the attached parking deck and followed the signs that would take them to the field. With the shuttered food vendors and cavernous, empty corridors, the stadium looked almost nothing like the bustling place it was at game time.

"How long's it been since you've been here?" Lynch asked.

"A few months."

"You're a baseball fan?"

"Well, I was here for a concert. I saw the Eagles play here. Good show."

"I'm sure."

"Nothing against baseball, but I've always thought it more fun to play than watch."

"You play baseball?"

"Beep ball, actually. I was pretty good."

Lynch looked at her as if he hadn't heard correctly. "Beep ball? Come on. You made that up."

"You never heard of beep ball? It's a big deal. There are leagues all over the world. When I was twelve, I was on the Woodward Academy team that played in the Beep Ball World Series in South Korea."

"Okay, let me see if I have this right. It's like baseball, but the ball beeps so you know where it is?"

"Well, it isn't exactly like baseball. In beep ball, teams pitch to their own batters. And the pitcher isn't blind. There are six outfielders who get help finding the ball from sighted spotters. A lot of work goes into establishing a rhythm and shorthand with your spotters. The ball, of course, never stops beeping, which also helps you zero in on it. But you don't round the bases like in regular baseball. When you get a hit, one of the bases beeps in its own distinctive tone. You run toward that one and if you make it before one of the outfielders picks up the ball, then your team scores a run."

Lynch nodded with approval. "Cool."

"It's been around since the 'seventies. It's a lot of fun. I watch the championship games on ESPN sometimes."

"Next time invite me over. We'll make popcorn and I'll watch with you."

She was gazing speculatively at him as they continued to walk. What would it be like to hang out with Lynch in ordinary circumstances, away from the murder cases and life-or-death stakes that so frequently brought them together? Would they find themselves as drawn to each other in the course of a mundane, everyday life? Watching a ball game or a Netflix movie in front of her TV on a Saturday night?

It was difficult to imagine. But at this point in her life, it was difficult to imagine that with anyone. She might shy away from the ugliness that was an integral part of dealing with the cases the FBI brought to her, but she wasn't certain if she could exist without the accompanying rush and sense of living on the edge.

Maybe she needed these cases more than she cared to admit, even to herself.

That was a depressing thought, and she dismissed it. Of course she could live without her FBI work. It was only a question of making the adjustment and a different mind-set. Which would probably not happen as long as she was around Lynch.

They walked through the empty club level until they found the field access ramp. A few yards later, they were on the grass field, gazing up at the empty stadium surrounding them.

"Kind of takes your breath away," Lynch said.

Kendra heard the cracking of the bat even before she saw the two lines of players waiting their turn. The team was in the middle of batting practice drills in front of half a dozen people whom Kendra assumed to be journalists. A small camera crew was near the dugout interviewing the team's star player, whom Kendra recognized only from his television deodorant commercials.

"Can I help you?"

Kendra and Lynch turned to see a stocky man with a distinctly annoyed expression. He'd probably dealt with one too many gate-crashing fans, Kendra thought.

Lynch flashed his ID. "We're assisting the FBI in a murder investigation and we believe someone here can help us identify a suspect. I'm Adam Lynch, this is Kendra Michaels."

If Lynch thought this would soften the guy's attitude, he was wrong. If anything, the man looked even more pissed. "I'm Joe Beacham, bullpen coach. And we're trying to get ready for a game."

"Understood," Kendra said. "We'll try not to take too much of your time." She pulled the Justin Hayes photo printout from her jacket. "Do you recognize him?"

The coach hardly glanced at it. "No. Are we done?"

"Look again," Lynch said crisply; it was more an order than a request. "You go on the road with this team, don't you?"

The coach nodded.

"Then you should recognize this man. Look at him."

The coach took a few seconds to study the photo. "Okay. Maybe he looks familiar."

"That's progress," Kendra said. "But we'll need to run this by each and every one of your players until we get an ID. I'd recommend we start with your smartest and most observant guy or else it's going to be a long morning."

The coach whistled and crooked his finger at one of the players waiting for his turn at bat. "Ganz, get over here!"

"Oliver Ganz," Lynch whispered to Kendra. "Damn good catcher."

Ganz ran over and looked at Lynch and Kendra with a slight bit of wary trepidation, obviously wondering if he might be in trouble.

"Don't worry," the coach said. "This isn't about one of your road groupies. They just got a picture they're flashing around to see if any of us recognize the guy. You were celebrating a little less than the other guys here last night, so I thought I'd let you take a look first. Capiche?"

Ganz smiled. He was a handsome man, part Latino but with striking blue eyes. Kendra imagined he had quite a few road groupies trailing after him. "Sure, no prob. But you're wrong about the celebrating, boss. I just did it in a different way."

Kendra showed him the photo, and his face immediately lit up in recognition. "That's Davey!"

"Davey," Kendra repeated. "And you know him from where?"

"He was one of our road bodyguards last season."

The coach cursed. "He's right. That's why he looked so familiar to me."

Ganz shrugged. "I always liked those guys, especially Davey."

The coach rolled his eyes. "That's because he helped smuggle groupies into your hotel room without the press finding out about it."

"You knew about that?"

"Everyone knew about it, Ganz. And your low-life buddy probably sold tickets."

The smile faded from Ganz's face. "Yeah, I heard about the crap he and the other guys pulled. Is that what this is about? Is he in trouble because of that?"

"What's his last name?" Lynch asked.

Ganz thought for a moment. "Lambert. David Lambert."

"Would you happen to know where he lived?"

"Afraid not. But I got the feeling he was new in town."

"What makes you say that?" Kendra said.

"He didn't know much about San Diego or the team. I thought he might have moved here just to get the job. But he didn't talk all that much about himself. And once he and the other guys were fired, we never saw them again."

Kendra pulled out a copy of the sketch that Bill Dillingham had made of the other man she'd seen. "Recognize this man?"

Ganz took the paper from her and studied it. "I don't think so."

"Are you sure?" Lynch asked.

Ganz angled the drawing so that the coach could also see it. The coach shook his head no. "Positive. He definitely wasn't one of the other bodyguards, if that's what you're getting at."

Kendra took back the drawing. "Is there anything else you can remember about David Lambert? Anything that might help us find him?"

"Well . . . I know he worked out near here. Within walking distance."

"At a gym?"

"Yeah. I remember him bitching about not being able to use the team gym here at the stadium. But it's players only, so he had to join a club. It was somewhere nearby, though."

Kendra nodded. "You've been very helpful. Thank you."

Ganz winked at her. "Sure thing, doll." He ran back to join his teammates.

She turned toward Lynch. "Did he just call me 'doll'?"

"Indeed he did."

"Just checking."

They thanked the coach for his time and walked back through the empty concourse toward Lynch's car.

"That was productive," Lynch said. He tapped out a message on his phone as they walked. "I'm texting Metcalf and Griffin, giving them the David Lambert aka. Depending how far he went in setting up his new identity, there may even be a driver's license with an address. But these days, law-enforcement facial recognition software makes it a dangerous prospect to pose for any kind of official government ID photo, even under an assumed name."

"Wouldn't he have needed a license or passport to fly with the team?"

"They usually fly charter so there's no airport security screening to worry about. But even on flights where it's an issue, a good fake will get you past any TSA agent."

"That's kind of scary." She frowned. "But we aren't going to sit around waiting for the FBI to get back to us, are we?"

"Of course not. That's never been my speed. Reason number four hundred seventy-two why I couldn't continue to work as an employee there." He tilted his head and smiled. "But I didn't want to be pushy so I thought I'd let you take the lead. However, I'm definitely open to suggestions. What did you have in mind?"

Kendra pulled out her own phone and launched the Google Maps app. "I'll pull up all the fitness clubs in a three-mile radius. We'll pound some pavement, visit them all, flash some pictures, and see if they have a member on their rolls by the name of David Lambert."

He snapped his fingers. "I like it. Very mid-twentieth-century gumshoe."

"As much as we can be, I guess," she said dryly as she turned and headed for the exit. "Considering that we're both holding network-connected super-computers in our hands."

CHAPTER
11

Kendra's search turned up six fitness clubs and a boxing gym, and they set out on foot to visit them all. They didn't get a hit on the first club, and the second told them to come back with a warrant. The third club, a shabby little facility on Seventh Street, finally gave them some promising news.

The attractive, red-haired woman at the front desk typed the name on her keyboard and got an immediate hit. "David Keith Lambert. It says here he joined in May of last year."

Kendra showed her the photo. "Great. Would you know if he looked like this?"

The receptionist smiled. "Like this?" She swiveled her desktop monitor around to let them see.

Kendra froze. It was him.

For some reason, this was even more of a punch to the gut than when Griffin and Metcalf had shown her his old driver's license photo. This was the man who had come very close to killing her. If luck and Jessie hadn't gone her way, she would be dead, and he would have been able to go about his life with little or no threat of reprisal. But that was no reason for her to be this shaken, she told herself. Maybe it was because she could see that this picture was taken right where she was standing right now.

In a place where he could appear at any moment.

Maybe he was even here now.

Detach. Concentrate.

Kendra leaned closer to the photo. "His hair's a little longer now, but that's definitely him." She smiled. "Wow. Check out his T-shirt."

Lynch squinted at it. "Does that say what I think it does?"

"Absolutely."

The red shirt was adorned with a colorful logo for THE PUB—ISLAND OF MALTA.

"Malta," Lynch said. "The site of his supposed death. Either he's not very bright or he likes living on the edge." He looked at the last check-in date. "He was here four days ago, right?"

The woman swiveled the screen back around and

looked at the member record. "Yes. Before that, he was here almost every weeknight."

Lynch patted Kendra's arm. "I don't blame him. After you and Jessie worked him over, it appears he hasn't been in the mood for lifting weights."

"Did he give a home address?" Kendra asked.

The receptionist glanced around. "I'll probably need a manager's permission for that."

"Come now," Lynch said. "If you really need manager approval for this sort of thing, you shouldn't have given us the information you already have." He leaned close to her and whispered, "I'd hate to see you get in trouble."

She half smiled. "And I'd hate to feel blackmailed by you."

"Blackmailed?" He glanced at her name tag. "Such an ugly word, Lara."

"Isn't it?"

"And not at all fitting this situation."

"Okay. Extortion?"

"Even uglier," he said softly. "And still not true."

"You threatened to get me in trouble with my boss."

"Not at all. I felt it was my duty to warn you. A lovely woman always arouses protectiveness in me. I was only reminding you of the precarious position in which you'd placed yourself."

"By helping you."

"For which we are *very* grateful."

"Funny way of showing it." The young woman flipped back her long hair.

Kendra resisted the temptation to roll her eyes. The receptionist was clearly enjoying Lynch's flirtatious banter. Why not? It was a game in which Lynch had expert credentials. Did she know she was being played?

Probably. But she didn't seem to mind.

The Lynch Effect at work.

"I'd appreciate it if you could help us just a little bit more," Lynch said.

"By further compromising a member's private information?"

Lynch leaned closer. "Would it help soothe your guilt to know he's a very, very bad man?"

"Parking tickets?"

"Worse."

"Bank robbery?"

"Definitely worse. Your manager doesn't want this kind of member. You'll be saving him from himself."

"You'd be surprised. As long as the dues are paid..."

"Trust me."

"Well..." The receptionist punched a letter on her keyboard and once again swiveled the screen around to him.

It was a member information page, with name, address, phone number, and even personal fitness goals. Kendra raised her phone and snapped a photo of the screen.

"Happy now?" the receptionist whispered to Lynch with a smile.

"Extremely," Lynch replied. "Thank you." He gave her his card. "If he happens to come in while you're working, do you think you could make a discreet call?"

She put the card on the desk in front of her. "I'm very discreet."

"Very good. Thank you, Lara."

Kendra and Lynch walked out the front doors and didn't speak until they were on the Seventh Street sidewalk.

"Wow." Kendra smiled. "I think you enjoyed that a little too much."

"Enjoyed what?"

"You know what. That intense flirting was getting so hot, I felt like fanning myself. And she *really* enjoyed it."

"Nonsense. She probably gets hit on ten times a day."

"But usually not by Adam Lynch. She's going to call you, all right. I'd be surprised if she even waits until we get back to the car."

"I think you overestimate my—" Lynch's phone

vibrated in his pocket. He looked at the screen. "Oh."

"What?"

"A text from Lara, the receptionist. She says she enjoyed meeting us both."

"Really?" Kendra said skeptically.

"Not really. Just me."

Kendra laughed. "Exactly what I thought. Well, she'll definitely be looking for him now."

"If Hayes gave them a real address, we may not need her. It's on Twenty-Sixth Street?"

Kendra raised her phone and looked at the information page she'd captured. "Yes. Looks like it's near Broadway. Golden Hill."

"Good. Let's go."

"Wait. We need to loop Griffin and Metcalf in, you know."

"Must we?"

"Yes."

He sighed. "Oh, all right. We can call them on the way there. But after what that asshole did to you, I was really looking forward to a little one-on-one time with him before I had to turn him over."

—◆—

Fifteen minutes later, Kendra stood in a smoothie store near the intersection of 26th and Broadway, staring at a three-story apartment building where, by all indications, a killer lived.

Lynch hunched over the intercom pad at the building's front doorway and then turned and ran across the street. The next moment he was entering the store to join her.

"Well?" she asked.

"There's a D. Lambert on the building directory in apartment three twenty-nine, just as his gym membership shows us. He's obviously secure in this new identity of his." Lynch glanced around the store and then down the street. "I thought the FBI would be here by now."

Kendra raised her phone. "I just got a text from Metcalf. They're four minutes out."

"What's their play?"

"We're meeting them around the corner, in the parking lot of a strip mall. A tactical team is on the way."

"We don't even know if he's home." Lynch shook his head. "I'm not entirely comfortable with this. Sometimes a direct, smaller-scale approach is best."

"You just want to bypass Metcalf and do your own thing. Take it up with the FBI. Ready?"

"Sure."

Kendra and Lynch walked quickly to the next block, where they turned and immediately saw a sad mini-mall that was mostly vacant. The only busy tenants seemed to be a nail salon and a karate studio. Within two minutes, three unmarked vans and a pair of cars squealed into the lot.

Metcalf climbed out of one of the cars and nodded toward Lynch. "Griffin's already taking bets on whether you would really wait for us before storming into the place yourself."

Kendra nodded. "It almost happened. How did you bet, Metcalf?"

"I didn't. I know better than to wager my hard-earned government salary on anything as unpredictable as the two of you."

"Smart man," Lynch said. He surveyed the two vans, which featured large magnetic signs for a local cable TV company. "Are these surveillance-equipped?"

"Yes. And there's another one already in front of the building. A couple of our guys dressed as exterminators are covering the exits."

"Good. How about exterior windows?" Kendra said.

"We're on it. The county sent us scans of the building plans on our way over, and we know exactly which windows are his. Top floor, fourth window from the left. The shades are closed right now."

"And your guys have the perp's photo?" Kendra said.

"Plus the sketch you provided of the other guy," Metcalf said. "If either of them is in there, he's not getting out."

Kendra nodded. As usual, Metcalf seemed to have all the bases covered. But she could tell Lynch was still uneasy, and it was making *her* uneasy.

Metcalf tapped his almost-invisible earpiece, which Kendra knew was hooked up to his cell phone via a Bluetooth connection. He cocked his head, then made a hand signal to the driver of one of the vans in the parking lot. The vehicle sped away.

He returned his focus to Kendra and Lynch. "That team will be covering the garage and rear entrance. We'll head out two minutes later, park on the street, then go in through the front door."

"Got a key?" Lynch said. "Surely you're not hoping for him to buzz you in."

"No key, but we have permission from the building owner to jimmy the front-door lock."

"Good," Lynch said. "Who's handling the door?"

"Special Agent Roberts."

"He's good, but I'm faster," Lynch said. He reached into his jacket's inside breast pocket and produced a thin wallet of lockpicks. "I'll take care of the door."

"Roberts has already started prepping." Metcalf pointed to a man inside the van's open side door whose name tag read SPECIAL AGENT DON ROBERTS.

"That may be so, but I'll do it much faster," Lynch said impatiently. "Ask Roberts, he'll tell you."

Roberts, who had obviously heard the exchange, looked at them and shrugged.

"Whatever," Metcalf said. "I don't have to ask him. I've seen your work. Okay, you're on the door." He turned toward Kendra. "You take the front passenger seat. If we bring him out, I need you to make an immediate positive ID."

"It will be more immediate if I'm inside with your team."

"That's not going to happen."

She made a face. "I thought I'd try."

"Forget it." Metcalf raised his index finger and made a twirling motion to his team. "We roll in sixty seconds. Be ready!"

———◆———

"This is Charlie, your trainer from the gym, Mr. Lambert. You said there would be fifty bucks in it for me if I kept an eye out for anyone asking about you. Does that still go?"

Hayes's grip tightened on the phone. "Hell, yes. Someone was there?"

"This morning. A man and a woman. Lara at the front desk was getting real chummy with them."

"Did she give them any information?"

"She spun the computer around so they could read it. I think they left happy. When do I get my money?"

Hayes cut the connection.

Shit! Shit! Shit!

He could feel his heart beating hard as the panic jolted through him.

This morning?

And he didn't have to guess who the woman was. It had to be that bitch, Kendra Michaels.

How much time did he have? He ran over to the window and looked down at the street.

Only to see Kendra Michaels getting into the front seat of that black van parked in front of his apartment building.

That was his answer about how much time he had. None.

He ran out of his apartment, down the inner staircase exit, and then followed the emergency plan he'd put in place when he'd first moved into this apartment. He'd learned a long time ago when he was working for the Cardinelli crime family to always have a convenient escape route and never leave a car where anyone expected it to be. He'd rigged too many car bombs himself to take that chance. And this situation with those damn FBI agents might be just as explosive.

His Audi was parked on the curb just ahead.

As he dove into the driver's seat and slammed the door, he could hear other car doors slamming at the front of the apartment building. Those FBI assholes must be starting their assault.

Damn, that had been close.

Justin Hayes stomped on the accelerator as he looked behind him to see if he was being followed. Not yet. But it could happen any minute. One of those people in front of his apartment building had been Kendra Michaels, and she had been bad news from the minute they had run across her after the Randolph killing. There was no way she should have been able to track him to his apartment. For all he knew, she might have put a GPS tracker on his car before the FBI team entered the building.

Maybe not. It didn't appear as if they'd found this car, and there was still no obvious pursuit. But that didn't mean he was off the hook. This job should have been so easy and it was turning into pure shit! What was he supposed to do now?

Dietrich.

Hayes shouldn't have to go through this alone. Dietrich thought he was so smart, let him get him out of this mess. He hesitated for an instant. Dietrich had told him no contact for the next couple of weeks, and he wasn't a man Hayes ever wanted to go up against. Not that he was afraid of the bastard. Well, maybe a little nervous around him. There were things he'd heard about Dietrich that sent a chill through him. Screw it. He needed *help*. He punched in Dietrich's number on his phone.

Dietrich answered in two rings. "You weren't supposed to phone me. It had better be an emergency, Hayes."

"Do you call being on the run from the FBI an emergency?" he asked sarcastically. "Kendra Michaels and some other Federal dudes showed up at my place. I just got out of my apartment to my car by the skin of my teeth. They're probably going through all my stuff right now."

Silence. "What stuff? You didn't leave anything that might be awkward for me, did you?"

"Am I stupid? I know what that would mean. You've made it clear enough to me. They won't find anything that would lead anyone to you. But now it's your turn to help me. I did everything you told me to do and they still found me."

"That's because you probably left a trail that a blind person could follow," Dietrich said harshly. "Well, Michaels isn't blind any longer. Whatever possessed you to go after her through that glass window? You'd have still been in that factory if I hadn't yanked you out before the police got there. Mistake after mistake. And now you're wanting me to save you again?"

"Hell, yes. Why not? You're the one who told me

we had to go after Randolph because we couldn't be sure he hadn't already met with Wessler. Now things are all going to hell. You said we'd be partners. But I'm the one who's getting the shaft. *Do something.*" Another silence from Dietrich, and for a moment Hayes felt a chill again. Had he gone too far?

Then Dietrich said, "You might be right. Okay, let's look at the situation. You must have tipped your hand again and done something to put you on the run. Michaels and the FBI aren't going to stop looking for you now. That means we have to find a hideout for you where you'll be safe until the heat dies down."

"All I need is money to get me out of town."

"You already took half the money for the job. You have to finish it before you get any more. No, that's not the solution." He paused. "I know a safe house where I can send you for the next few weeks until we can regroup and finish what they paid us for. Then we'll come out of this with a gigantic bankroll and can hit the trail. But you can't be driving around in your own car, they'll track you in a heartbeat. Where are you now?"

"Fifth and Main."

"Pull over to the curb and I'll be there to pick you up in ten minutes and take you to the safe house. You should be okay there." He added caustically,

"Providing I can trust you to not blow your cover like you did this time."

"I didn't do anything wrong," Hayes said defensively. "I only did what had to be done. It was that Kendra Michaels witch. She's pure bad luck. I knew it from the minute I saw her flying off that damn fire escape into the factory window. She's not going to ever give up on us."

"Really? That's a bad attitude, Hayes," Dietrich said silkily. "You should have known and accepted that she might cause us problems. If you'd done the research I did, you'd realize that the minute Oceanside became involved there was a chance she might be, too. Now you have to look on the bright side: She wants you so badly, she might get reckless and make mistakes. That's always a way to turn bad luck into good." He added softly, "Then you just have to make the preparations to remove her altogether."

◆

"Shit!" Metcalf's voice crackled over the earpiece Kendra had been given. "We're inside his place, but the subject is gone. I repeat, the subject is not in the apartment. Keep watch on all building exits. We have reason to believe he was just here. All stations, report in."

Kendra listened as the stationed agents reported in, one by one, from each building exit.

No sign of their man.

Kendra shook her head. Lynch's unease had definitely been justified.

After another few minutes of back-and-forth chatter on the radio, Metcalf's defeated voice finally came over. "All stations, keep an eye on the building next door. To the west. We have indications that our subject jumped from a stairwell landing to a window next door. There are two torn screens. We may have lost him."

After another few minutes, Metcalf's voice came back on the frequency. He didn't sound happy. "The apartment is clear. Roberts, bring Dr. Michaels up, please."

Special Agent Roberts, whom Lynch had booted from the lockpicking detail, slid open the van's side door. "You heard him." His voice sounded as disgusted and surly as Metcalf's. "It sounds as if Hayes slipped away from us, Dr. Michaels."

"Well, at least you didn't miss anything by being stuck down here with me," she said ruefully as she jumped out of the van. "I'm feeling pretty flat, too."

"I didn't mean to be rude," he said quickly. "I respect you, very much, I just wanted to—"

"I know." She stopped him mid-sentence. "You

just wanted to be where the action was. Me too." She smiled. "So let's go see if there's anything we can do to salvage this botched operation, Special Agent Roberts."

"Right." He smiled back at her. "But please don't mention to Metcalf that the word 'botched' was used."

———◆———

Kendra stepped into the one-bedroom apartment, which was swarming with FBI Evidence Response personnel. A photographer covered every inch of the place while techs lifted fingerprints and swabbed for DNA trace evidence from a telephone handset, doorknobs, windows, and the refrigerator handle.

Lynch and Metcalf stood in the small dining room area, populated only by a four-seat dinette set and a low-hanging light fixture. The rest of the apartment was just as sparse, with a single sofa and coffee table situated opposite a fifty-five-inch flatscreen television on a black lacquer stand.

She extended her hands to Metcalf and wiggled her fingers.

He tossed her a pair of evidence gloves. "I could give you a box of these things. You can keep 'em in the trunk of your car, like the rest of us do."

"It's not gonna happen." Kendra snapped on the

gloves. "You know it, I know it, and most of the people in this room know it. I need to cling to my delusion that these violent and depressing murder cases are part of my past and someday I won't need those gloves."

"That is a delusion," Lynch said. "You know you'd miss the bloody corpses, the psychopathic killers, and Metcalf's goofy grin."

"Goofy?" Metcalf said. "I thought it was more suave and devil-may-care."

Lynch shrugged. "Whatever gets you through the day."

"Not goofy," Kendra said. "That's not kind. Infectious."

"Like Ebola?" Lynch said.

"Absolutely not." Kendra glanced around the room. "I thought you guys were going to hang back until Justin Hayes came back home."

"That was the plan," Metcalf said. He looked seriously bummed. "A neighbor in the laundry room saw him go in here just a couple of minutes ago, but when we burst in, he was nowhere to be found. We thought he might be hiding in one of the other apartments, but then one of the agents discovered the torn screens in a third-floor stairwell and in a corresponding window in the building next door."

"So you think he got away through that building?" Kendra said.

"Most likely." He was frowning with disgust. "I thought we had him, dammit. We have agents swarming all over the street, but if he slipped out of that building before we knew what had happened, he could be anywhere in the city by now. He probably had his vehicle parked on the street."

Lynch gave Kendra an I-told-you-so look. She was impressed with his restraint in not calling Metcalf out for the botched operation. She figured it was probably because Lynch, like most law-enforcement agents, knew firsthand how painful it was to suffer a bungle like this one.

Kendra took a quick spin around the apartment, paying special attention to the stove, microwave, and a half-eaten bowl of soup on the coffee table.

She finally turned to face Lynch and Metcalf. "He was just here. Or at least someone was."

"How do you figure that?" Lynch said.

"That bowl of ramen noodle soup is still warm. The whole apartment smells like it, meaning he cooked it in the microwave with the flavor packet already in the water."

"Even I picked up on that," Metcalf said. "Hot and Spicy Chicken flavor. I wouldn't have made it through my college years without it."

"He's had a guest here. There's Coke and Diet Coke in the fridge. People generally don't drink both."

Kendra strode toward the small countertop in the opening between the kitchen and living room. She started to look quickly through a stack of mail. "Has anyone found anything we can use yet?"

"No pay stubs or anything indicating where he might have been earning a living for the past six months." Lynch held up a key ring. "But we did find a spare car key. An Audi."

Metcalf nodded. "Which jibes with his auto registration. He owns a silver Audi TT RS. It isn't in the unit's parking space. We have a BOLO out for the car everywhere in the city."

"Good."

Metcalf nodded at the stack of mail. "Are you finding anything there?"

"Afraid not. Grocery store circulars, Shoppers Value envelopes of coupons, mostly." Kendra moved into the kitchen, where she started looking through the drawers. A corkscrew and two stained bottle stoppers in the top drawer showed a preference for red wine. A few tools rattled in the second drawer. Kendra reached for a pair of needle-nose pliers, gripping the steel tip with her gloved hands. She moved it close to her eyes and inspected it.

"I know that look," Lynch said. "What are you seeing?"

"These pliers have an unusual grip pattern. The FBI probably has techs who can identify it instantly, but I'd guess it was made by a foreign manufacturer."

"So Hayes likes to use foreign tools," Metcalf said.

Kendra nodded. "That he used to make a phony bomb."

Metcalf went still. He stared at her for a moment. "You think he used those pliers to—"

"I'm almost sure of it. I've seen this grip pattern only one other place and it was on a green wire on that fake bomb we found in my car."

"I was going to ask if you're sure but I guess I know you better than that."

"Don't take my word for it. Is the case file still up to date on your iPad? Look at the high-res photos of that device."

"My iPad's in the van downstairs."

"Okay, then *do* take my word for it. This unusual pair of pliers—or a pair exactly like them—was used to make that fake bomb."

By this time, two techs had come over to look at the pliers she was holding.

Metcalf turned to them. "Bag it. We'll check any imperfections against the impressions in that wire she's talking about. We may be able to get an exact match."

Kendra surrendered the pliers to one of the techs, who placed it into a clear plastic evidence bag.

"Good work," Metcalf said to her. "Anything else catch your eye?"

Kendra stepped into the living room. She took a closer look at the coffee table, which was topped by magazines that included *Guns and Ammo*, *Tactical Weapons*, *American Handgunner*, and *Soldier of Fortune*.

"Nice that he supports printed media, but it's kind of a scary collection to a gentle soul like me," Lynch said.

"What do you expect from a guy like this?" Kendra asked. "*Good Housekeeping*?"

"Good point."

Kendra noticed a thin sliver of white protruding from behind the cover of one of the magazines. She picked it up and slid out a glossy photo.

She froze in shock. "What the hell?"

"What is it?" Lynch crossed to where she stood. "Find something?"

"I'll say I did." She thrust the photo at him. "Something completely unexpected. And I don't know what on Earth it means or why Hayes should have it. It's Harley."

"What!"

"My response exactly."

The dog was leashed and walking through a wooded area, accompanied by a woman who could only be seen from the waist down. A large red *X* was scrawled across Harley, drawn with such force that the photo was torn in places.

Lynch nodded. "It certainly looks like him."

"It *is* him," Kendra said. "No doubt. You can tell by the coloring on his ears and paws."

Metcalf glanced at the photo. "I'd know that furry face anywhere. It's definitely Harley."

"And that may have been Elaine Wessler walking him," Kendra said. "We can ask her coworkers to see if anyone recognizes the shoes and maybe even her slacks."

Lynch squinted at the photo. "This looks like it was taken with a zoom lens. And if this was Elaine Wessler, it means someone was stalking her before she was killed. It was no random act of violence."

"Elaine told her ex-husband that she and her dog had been followed. That's how this looks to me." Kendra frowned. "And I'm disturbed by this jagged red X practically carved over Harley. What in the hell is that supposed to mean?"

"It looks...violent." Metcalf was gazing down at the photo. "Almost...an attack. I don't like this. Harley wasn't all that fond of me, but I liked the mutt."

"He liked you. He likes everybody. He just didn't like that you were keeping him from Olivia." Kendra turned over the photo. A phone number was inscribed on the back, written in the same red ink.

(619) 555-8422

Kendra pulled out her phone and tapped in the number.

"You're not calling it, are you?" Lynch said.

"No. Google search." She looked at the results page. "Nothing."

Metcalf took the photo from her. "Don't worry. The FBI's databases are far better than Google's. Awesome. We'll find out who has this number."

"Thanks." Kendra started tapping another number in her phone. "But I just had another thought."

"Now what?" Lynch asked.

"I'm calling Olivia. She has Harley with her and she needs to know about this." The phone was starting to ring. "And we might not have to wait to check with the FBI's 'awesome' capabilities if Olivia has been her usual numbingly efficient self."

CHAPTER
12

"A photo of Harley?" Olivia repeated. "That doesn't make sense. Why would Hayes have a photo of Harley? I can't see an asshole like him as a dog lover."

"Neither can I," Kendra said. "And that photo is hardly affectionate. There's a big cross slashed across Harley's face in red pencil that looks like it was done in anger. And on the back of the photo is that phone number I gave you scrawled in the same heavy red pencil. That number isn't Elaine's. Will you check the documents Elaine got on Harley from the vet when she agreed to foster him and see if the number is on any of them? You did transfer them to your Tactile text-to-Braille converter?"

"Of course I did," Olivia said curtly. She went to her desk, took out the folder, and began to verify the numbers. She didn't find anything until she reached the fourth page in the packet. "It's the phone number for Ace Dog Training Farm. Brian Miller, president." Her fingers flew over the script. "This Brian Miller evidently trained Harley for the first eighteen months of his life before he turned him over to the service dog organization. It's curious that your scumbag would want to talk to him. And it's also curious that he'd actually print out this photo as if it had some importance. Not Elaine, just the dog." She added thoughtfully, "Though I remember that when we were out there at Oceanside the other day, we both thought it was possible that Elaine had taken Harley for walks on the grounds when she brought him with her to the school. And Ariel said Elaine was frightened because she thought she and her dog had been followed."

"We need to talk to this trainer and see if he knows anything. Lynch and I have to go back to FBI headquarters this afternoon to go over the forensic evidence we found here in the apartment, but we'll try to get to him tomorrow."

"Don't bother," Olivia said. "I'll take care of it." She was putting Harley's documents back in the folder. "Go do your FBI stuff. But I don't care for the idea of Hayes doing ugly things to that photo of Harley. Anyone who defaces a picture might do equal harm to the animal itself. Particularly someone as violent as Hayes. I won't tolerate even the thought of cruelty to any animal. I'm in charge of Harley and I'll get to the bottom of this right away."

"Okay." Kendra was thinking, trying to find a solution. "Maybe Lynch and I can split up and I'll come back to your condo and pick you up and we'll—"

"Don't be ridiculous. I don't need you. Jessie called me after you left this morning; she should be back from L.A. within the next half hour or so. If I can get her off that motorcycle, I'll use the extra keys you gave me to your Toyota and have her drive me and Harley to see this trainer. She's a P.I. and shouldn't have trouble getting him to answer questions."

"Neither would you. But you could send her on her own."

"Harley's in my charge," she repeated firmly. "My responsibility. We made an agreement, Kendra. I'd accept you if you could do it, but no one else. Jessie is only a guest star in this miniseries."

Kendra chuckled. "You must remember to tell her that. Jessie isn't accustomed to taking a backseat for anyone."

"Oh, I will. Now I have to go put Harley's leash on him. Goodbye, Kendra." She hung up the phone, turned to Harley, and gave the hand signal for him to kneel. "It seems you might have been fooling around in bad company lately," she murmured as she leashed him. "You'll have to be careful about that. Remember, not everyone knows what a pushover you are..."

———◆———

"Guest star in a miniseries?" Jessie repeated as she glanced at Olivia while she made the turn into Ace Dog Training Farms. "I've been thinking about that. Couldn't you have at least given me full costar status? It's not as if Harley and I haven't gotten along very well after that first night. And that was partly your lack of communication."

"Granted." Olivia smiled. "But I was enjoying it far too much to be kind to you. And you might not have been demoted to guest star if you hadn't decided to run off to L.A. and leave Kendra in the lurch."

"Come on," Jessie said quietly. "We both knew when Lynch appeared on the scene that I wasn't going to be needed. I'm very good at what I do, but they're a matched set. When they're together, they don't need anyone else. Kendra might have difficulty admitting that to herself, but that's her problem. There's no way I'd get between the two of them." She shrugged. "So I went back to L.A. to take care of my own business and kept my phone handy in case of an emergency. I didn't get a call, so I assume she didn't jump off any fire escapes while I was gone?"

"No. Lynch didn't like a couple of moves she made, but nothing happened. She said he was just overprotective and told him to back off."

"It was like that in Afghanistan, too. I always found the dynamic interesting but explosive. So I'll let him take the heat and just be on hand to help out when needed." She glanced at Harley in the backseat, who was lifting his head to enjoy the wind blowing in the open windows. His big ears were lifting like small balloons, and there was an ecstatic look on his face. "In the meantime, maybe I'll help you train Harley. Though you're doing great. Those hand signals are magic. Where did you learn them?"

"Lynch."

"See? What did I tell you?"

"You didn't have to tell me anything. I'm just saying that it's all hands on deck from now on. You want to stay in the shadows? Fine. I know what a powerhouse Lynch can be, but I'm not willing to let him take over," Olivia said. "I'll take whatever he has to give to Kendra and me, but two of my friends died and I have to be there to make sure the people who did it are punished."

"And I'll be there to do that, too," Jessie said quietly. "Because both you and Kendra are *my* friends and your fight is my fight. Why else am I here, Olivia?" She drew up before the wire dog pens adjoining the neat brick residence. "And there's a nice gray-haired man in that dog pen who seems to have a few friends of his own. Those German shepherd pups are all over him." She opened the car door and called, "Mr. Miller? Jessie Mercado. I phoned you before we left the condo and you said you'd be glad to speak to us."

"Because you said you had one of my favorite students." He'd left the pen and was walking toward the car. He was smiling when he saw Harley suddenly straighten as he caught sight of him. "How are you doing, Harley," he said gently. "Good to see you, boy."

Harley went wild. He barked, he howled. He jumped out the open back window and loped toward the man.

"No, Harley," Jessie said. "You'll knock him down."

"Harley!" Olivia jumped out of the car and headed in the direction where the barking was a cacophony of sound. "You can't do—"

"Down," Miller said quietly. "*Now*, Harley."

Harley instantly lay down, but his tail was a riot of wild wagging. And the barking was still horrendous.

Olivia's hand made the signal for silence with authority in every motion.

Harley fell silent except for an eager whimpering.

"You're very good," Miller said to Olivia as he knelt down and stroked the dog. "Miss...?"

"Olivia Moore." She knelt beside the man and the dog. "And he'll be much better once we get a chance to train him a little more. He's only been learning hand signals for a couple of days. He's gone through a lot, and I'm afraid that he's a bit confused and wild right now."

"I'm just glad to see that he's still alive," Miller said. "I was afraid he wouldn't make it when I visited him with his vet, Dr. Napier, after his former owner died. Napier thought Harley might have some kind of response to me and asked me to come by and see him." He grimaced. "It didn't work. I wasn't the boy, Terry, so he just went deeper into depression." Then he smiled as he changed the subject. "And a couple of days to teach him hand signals—that is very good, Ms. Moore. I was starting to teach them to him myself just before I turned him over to the service dog people. I usually don't release a dog until he's thoroughly trained, but Terry Calder's parents were pressuring the guide dog organization for a dog and Harley was special. I told them I'd come back and teach him on my own time whenever they called me."

"That was kind of you," Olivia said. "I'm sure they appreciated it. Why did you think Harley was so special?"

"He was the ideal companion dog. He and the boy were perfect together. Anyone could see it. Sometimes it happens like that. He's always been something of a wild child but not when he was with Terry. He was everything he should be." He was gently stroking Harley's throat. "Since he was so intelligent, I thought he'd make an exceptional K-9 candidate. I even started teaching him the skills. He had a great nose and was an amazing tracker. But he was a complete failure at tactical, he wouldn't attack on command. He was very protective, but he'd attack only if he thought I was about to be hurt. Not exactly what the police want to intimidate the bad guys." He lifted the dog's chin and looked down into his eyes and said softly, "But the perfect amount of protectiveness for a dog who only wants to love and care for a person in need. So I had to change gears and start training him as a service dog. He was terrific at that." He glanced at Jessie. "But you said you wanted to ask me a few questions, Ms. Mercado? I'm sure that it wasn't all about Harley's failure as a K-9. You appear to be doing very well with him in his present role."

"We've been having a few problems." She grinned. "And, who knows, it might have something to do with what you've told us. We'll have to see. But we really want to know if you've ever seen this man before?" She handed him her phone with the photo of Hayes pulled up. "Has he ever been here? Do you recognize him?"

Miller shook his head. "Never saw him before."

"Second question. Have you had anyone call you recently and ask you questions about Harley?"

"Only the tech from Dr. Napier's office last week. I thought he must have been the one who referred you to me."

Jessie shook her head. "No, we haven't contacted the vet yet. What day was it?"

"Thursday."

"And what was the tech's name?"

Miller's forehead wrinkled in a frown. "Benton, I think. Paul Benton. I wasn't paying much attention. He interrupted one of my advanced training sessions. I would have put him off if I hadn't wanted to see if Harley here had made it. I hadn't heard anything from Dr. Napier since the day I visited his office."

"Benton," Jessie repeated. "You said he interrupted you? Was he rude? What kind of questions did he ask?"

"No, pleasant enough...kind of...smooth. But he was just firing questions at me one after the other. He said that they needed to update Harley's past history because of his recent operation and traumatic illness." He added, "And he was very interested about his K-9 training and tracking experience. That was why I mentioned that to you right off the bat."

"Was he?" Jessie asked thoughtfully. "Anything else? Any specific questions about the training?"

"No, he just wanted to question Harley's proficiency in both areas. Then he let me get back to my training class." He tilted his head. "I hope I didn't do anything wrong? It's not as if this information was top secret or anything." He chuckled. "As I said, Harley is hardly qualified in that direction."

"No, you didn't do anything wrong. It's only that the person who called you might not have been who he told you he was and the FBI would want to know why." Jessie gave him her card. "If you can think of anything else that was unusual about him or if he calls you again, I'd appreciate if you'd let me or Dr. Kendra Michaels know right away."

"FBI?" Miller's lips were quirking as he looked down at Harley. "Talk about a leopard changing his spots! Was I wrong about you, boy?"

"No, you weren't," Olivia said. "You were absolutely right and you did exactly what you should have done. You gave that boy and Harley the love they both needed before it was taken from them. As you said, they were perfect together." She got to her feet. "This FBI thing is nothing you should worry about." She held out her hand to him. "But we thank you for taking the time to talk to us. It's clear that what you're doing is important to a good many people."

He took her hand and shook it. "And thank you for bringing my friend Harley to see me. It's good to know he got lucky a second time after the loss of the boy. If you want any help training this dog of yours, come back and I'll be glad to fit him into my schedule."

She stiffened. "He's not my—"

"I'm sure she will," Jessie interrupted as she pushed Olivia toward the car. "But you can see she's doing a pretty good job herself. Goodbye, Mr. Miller."

He waved his hand and started back toward the pen with the German shepherds.

"I told you he was a very nice man, and he obviously cares about his dogs," Jessie said as Olivia snapped her fingers to bring Harley running, and then got into the passenger seat. "And I didn't see any reason to disappoint him when he obviously wanted his story for Harley to have a happy ending."

"I'm not arguing. It's not that important. You might be right." She fastened her seat belt. "I'm just getting extremely irritated with people making that mistake."

"Would it be dangerous to suggest that you might be the one making the mistake?"

"Definitely," she said coldly.

"Then I won't do it," Jessie said. "Instead, while we're on the road, I'll ask you to call Harley's vet and ask if he has a tech named Benton who made a call to Miller on Thursday of last week."

Olivia nodded. "It was too coincidental. It sounded phony. And if the tech doesn't exist?"

"Then we call Kendra and tell her what we've learned and ask her to have the FBI put a trace on all incoming calls on Miller's phone that day to get a phone number." She added, "And an address if we get lucky."

"We might already have an address. Don't you think that call probably came from Hayes?"

"Maybe. But there's someone else out there and if I were Kendra, I wouldn't forget about mystery man number two. Whom I so efficiently took down in that factory . . ."

———◆———

Kendra and Lynch followed Metcalf and two of the FBI vans back to the regional office in a veritable caravan. They'd been on the I-8 freeway only a few minutes before Lynch pulled ahead and left the others in his dust.

"This Lamborghini could be a keeper," Lynch murmured. "As unfaithful as it makes me feel, I'm not missing the Ferrari nearly so much anymore."

"Nice car," Kendra said absently.

"You're thinking about Harley."

"Of course I am."

"If someone meant to do him harm, they could have targeted him with a high-powered rifle as easily as they did with that camera zoom lens."

"The same could also be said for Elaine Wessler, and we know what happened to her." Kendra leaned back against the headrest. "It's sickening to think of her being stalked for days by a man who would eventually kill her. And Mr. Kim... two days and he was a dead man."

"He had to have found out something he wasn't meant to know. This doesn't impress me as anything else."

"Possibly." She shivered. "But I've had several cases where murder victims were tailed before their deaths. Prep work for a certain type of cold, methodical killer who likes to get a handle on time schedules and personal habits as they plan their kill. Not only do they consider it efficient, but it gives them a sense of power." She cursed under her breath. "We should've had this guy. Now both those men are still out there, planning who knows what."

"We'll find them," Lynch said quietly. "Metcalf will start searching for that tech who called the trainer as soon as he gets back to the office. It almost certainly had to be either Hayes or his partner. I'm hoping it will be the partner so that we can open a new lead. And we just missed Hayes because of this snafu. But he's clearly not overly bright. Forensics might even turn up something from that search of his apartment."

There was such certainty in his voice that she felt better even though the response was totally irrational.

Her phone rang. She fished it out of her pocket and looked at the caller ID screen. Metcalf. She answered and put him on speaker. "Please tell me one of your guys picked up Hayes hiding in a trash dumpster down the street."

"Next best thing. We got his car. SDPD just found it parked a few miles from his apartment."

"Where?"

"Grant Hill. On Twenty-Eighth, near L. We're on our way now."

Lynch was already exiting the freeway.

"Good," she told Metcalf. "We'll see you there."

"Maybe a little brighter than I thought," Lynch said. "At least he knew it was smarter to ditch the car."

———◆———

Kendra and Lynch parked in front of a Twenty-Eighth Street liquor store and walked the half block to the spot where Metcalf and several of his crime scene techs were already standing. A San Diego PD cruiser was on the street with flashers on, forcing passing cars to go around.

As they came closer, Kendra could see that it was indeed the silver Audi TT RS Metcalf had described earlier.

Kendra placed her hand on the car hood. "Still warm. But not *that* warm. Car's been here maybe half an hour."

Metcalf nodded. "Soon after we raided his place. It looks more and more like he just managed to get away from us by the skin of his teeth."

Lynch peered into the passenger side window. "Have you gotten inside yet?"

"Our warrant covers his apartment and car. We have a guy on the way who can get us inside. He's a wizard at this stuff. Even you couldn't get us inside as fast as he can. Just wait and you'll see that—"

CLICK-CLICK-CLICK-CLICK.

All four doors unlocked. Lynch pulled the passenger side handle and opened the door. "You were saying?"

"Holy shit," Metcalf said. "How in the hell did you do that?"

Lynch raised his phone, which had a black fob attached to its underside. "A custom software app coupled with an outboard RF transmitter."

"You should see what he can do with a Tesla," Kendra murmured.

Metcalf still looked stunned. "I'm not sure I want to know. Plausible deniability and all that."

"Smart man," Lynch said. "Keep that attitude and you'll have a long and successful career in the Bureau."

"I think that was a dig." Metcalf turned to Kendra. "Was that a dig?"

Kendra nodded. "That was a dig."

Lynch leaned into the car. "Looks like finger-prints on this wheel, the touch screen, and maybe the glove compartment."

Metcalf motioned to the Evidence Response techs. "You've given us what we needed. Now please get out of there and let my guys get their samples." He added with pointed formality, "And thank you for your cooperation."

Lynch lifted his hands and backed out of the car. "Anytime."

As the techs went to work lifting prints and swabbing for DNA, Kendra walked around the car. "That was a bit chilly," she told Lynch as he followed her. "But you couldn't expect him to let you take over. You have a tendency to be a trifle flamboyant. It's probably difficult for Metcalf to maintain a businesslike persona with his fellow agents when you're strutting around pulling tricks out of your hat."

"I don't strut. That would be ridiculous." He thought about it. "Though I'm guilty of pulling an occasional stunningly clever trick to dazzle the mind. But that's only because I'm a gadget freak and so is every agent on Metcalf's team. And I backed off when Metcalf got his feathers ruffled, didn't I? I realize I can be a hard act to follow."

She made a rude sound.

"I take it that you're trying to burst my bubble so I'll change the subject." He tilted his head, watching her examine the car. "Anything?"

She pointed to the left-rear quarter panel. "Traces of mud just above the tires, but the color and consistency aren't unlike what you'd find almost anywhere in Southern California. Not much help there."

"Too bad."

She looked through the side windows. "The driver's seat is adjusted all the way back and the steering wheel is angled upward, indicating a tall man, well over six feet. That's in line with Hayes's height. The passenger seat probably sat someone a few inches shorter."

"Like the man who was with Hayes when you saw him? You described him as being shorter."

"Yes." She looked at the driver's side door. "A few light scratches here. They're fairly high up, just under the door handle. Most likely it was dinged by another vehicle parked right next to it. Always the same vehicle, since each scratch hits at exactly the same height. A tall vehicle, maybe a jeep or SUV. We should check his parking space at the apartment complex and see who he might have been meeting."

"The FBI team may already have photos of that. I'll ask."

Kendra suddenly leaned over and studied the side-view mirror. "Tell Metcalf that Hayes is wearing black tennis shoes, jeans, a gray hoodie, and aviator sunglasses."

Lynch looked at her curiously. "You mean, when you saw him the other night?"

"No." She snapped, "Right *now*."

Lynch stared at her. "The car is telling you that?"

She nodded. "Stop asking questions. Please go tell Metcalf, dammit."

"Not before you tell me how in the hell—?"

"I'm looking at him in this side mirror, that's how." Her voice was shaking. "He's watching us from behind that food truck half a block back. He just walked up and stopped short when he saw us. I don't want to tip our hand. Tell Metcalf to have his guys take positions."

Lynch casually nodded. "Got it." He started strolling in Metcalf's direction.

Kendra circled around the front of the car, trying not to reveal that she had Hayes in her sights. The temptation was almost overpowering to glance in his direction. Why the hell was he taking this risk? Why didn't he run? Maybe Lynch was right about him not being very smart. Or maybe there was something in this car that he didn't want to be found. Either way, all she cared about was keeping him here until they could get their hands on him. This could be the man who had stalked and killed Elaine. How many times had he followed her, watched her, and planned how he was going to do it? And she had never known, never realized, someone was there, ready to take her life.

You son of a bitch, I see you.

Lynch had reached Metcalf and spoke quietly. Metcalf played it perfectly, registering no surprise at the news.

But a nearby ERT tech wasn't so smooth. He turned to steal a glance back toward the food truck.

Shit!

Hayes caught it. He bolted away, running toward a row of storefronts behind him.

Lynch was off in a shot, pounding the pavement before anyone else realized what was happening.

Instinctively, Kendra ran after him. Metcalf shouted into his radio, barking commands to the other agents and police officers on-site. Within seconds, the block had erupted in a chaotic scene with agents scrambling toward the storefronts, shouting as the police cruiser's siren blared.

Kendra rounded the corner. Nothing.

Where in the hell had Lynch gone? And Hayes?

One of the storefronts had a glass door with open shades. The pull cords swung back and forth.

There!

Kendra bolted through the door and found herself in a Thai restaurant. A table had been knocked over, and two spilled water pitchers rocked on the carpeted floor. The staff and customers were obviously disturbed by some commotion.

Kendra charged through the dining room and pushed through a red curtain. She ran through the kitchen.

Pots and pans rolled across the floor, which was cluttered with broken bowls and soup.

A helpful but obviously confused cook pointed toward the back door.

Kendra nodded and ran outside to the alley. Still no sign of Lynch or Hayes.

She stopped to listen.

Pounding footsteps. But from where?

And was it from Lynch and Hayes or the half dozen FBI agents and cops now swarming the area?

BAM!

A trash can tipped over. Somewhere...

She turned. It came from the left. She ran down the alleyway following the sounds of plastic bottles hitting the pavement. It was most likely a recycling container, she realized.

She stopped.

The green plastic container was between two buildings, knocked on its side.

She ran toward it, slowing as she moved down the narrow opening between buildings. Only then did she wonder what in the hell she would do if she found Hayes. She had no gun, no weapon of any kind. What would happen if—?

A strong pair of hands covered her mouth and yanked her to the ground.

She tried to scream, but the sound was muffled by the palm pressed over her lips. She was about to bite down when she became aware of a familiar scent.

"Quiet," Lynch whispered into her ear. "He's near."

She relaxed as he pulled his hand from her mouth and then drew a shaky breath. "Risky," she whispered back. "Your bitten-off fingers almost ended up on the ground."

"Worth the risk." His eyes darted down the narrow

opening between buildings. "I think he's down there somewhere." Lynch picked up the handgun he'd obviously put down to grab her and drew her behind the nearest dumpster. They crouched there, their gaze narrowed on the opening.

More police sirens wailed in the distance.

Lynch nodded to a pile of shipping cartons. "He could be there. Or maybe in one of the other dumpsters."

Kendra shook her head. "All those dumpsters have locks."

"Good point." Lynch picked up a crate lid and hurled it toward the stack of cartons. They tumbled to the ground, scattering across the narrow walkway between buildings.

No shots.

No wild scramble to escape notice.

Lynch peered at the scattered boxes. "No Hayes."

They got to their feet and slowly, carefully made their way down the walkway.

Suddenly Kendra stopped and cocked her head. "Do you hear that?"

"The sirens?"

"No. Listen." She listened again herself. "Water. Drizzling, running water. Just ahead."

"Oh, I hear it," Lynch said. He took two steps forward and kicked aside the largest carton on the pavement in front of them. "It's damn familiar."

There, under where the cartons had been, was an open manhole. The iron cover was askew, moved just to the right.

Lynch cursed and began lowering himself into the manhole. He said to Kendra, "Call Metcalf. Tell him that Hayes is in the sewer system. He's going to have to pop up somewhere."

"But we don't know where and we have a chance to get him while he'd still down there." She moved toward the manhole. "I'm going with you."

"The hell you are."

"Shut up, Lynch. Don't be sexist." Kendra's fingers flew across her phone's keyboard. "I just told Metcalf where we're going. These sewer lines are monitored, aren't they?"

"Some, not all. We can't count on that." Lynch disappeared into the sewer.

Kendra was two seconds behind. She climbed down the iron rungs, which were slimy and cool to the touch. A moment later the awful smell overcame her.

She fought an immediate gag reflex. She'd seen sewer workers wearing goggles and filter masks, and now she knew why. Her nose burned and eyes watered. She had a taste in her mouth that matched the awful stench.

"You okay?" Lynch called up to her.

"No, but I'll live."

"Just a warning. When you step off the rungs, you'll be ankle-deep in sludge."

"Great. This keeps getting better."

Lynch helped her make her final step onto the sewer floor. Her feet landed with a sickening *squish*. She took one step, then another, each time pulling suction on the foul-smelling ooze.

"Which way?" Lynch asked.

"Listen."

Kendra turned her head until she heard the faint sound of footsteps in the sludge.

Lynch heard it, too. It was coming from the east. In the distance, they saw the faint glow of a cell phone.

"He's using GPS to map his position," Lynch whispered.

"I recognize the sound of that limp," Kendra said. "I think I helped give him that."

"Well done."

They navigated the dark sewer, working their way through each length. The odors changed every few feet, depending on the character of the streets above. Sometimes sickly sweet, sometimes sour, all of it almost unbearable.

The phone light ahead abruptly extinguished itself.

The footsteps stopped.

"He knows we're on his tail," Kendra said.

BLAM!

A gunshot rang out. A bullet ricocheted in the sewer's darkness.

Kendra dove for the wall and her shoulder slammed against it.

Pain. Stabbing, excruciating pain.

BLAM! Another gunshot. This time the ricocheting bullet seemed to hit closer to Lynch.

"Hug the outer wall," Lynch whispered. "Put away your phone."

"Not a problem. It's already in the bottom of that muck." She paused to listen. "He's on the move again."

"Then let's go get him."

They quickened their pace as they reached somewhat firmer ground. The muck gave way to a thinner covering that was slicker, but at least they could move faster.

A metallic scraping sound echoed in the sewer.

They froze. The scraping sound continued, and a shaft of light suddenly appeared ahead.

Kendra turned to Lynch. "He's going back up to the street."

They ran toward the light, but before they could reach it, another metallic sound filled her ears.

It was dark once more.

"He's gone," Kendra said. "And he put the cover back."

Lynch pulled out his phone and dropped a pin in

their GPS location. "I'll send the map to Metcalf, but it'll take them a few minutes to get here."

Kendra ran for the iron rungs that would take them back up to the street. "He could be gone by then. We almost lost him before. We can't wait."

"Agreed. Let me take the lead."

She scowled impatiently. "Because you're a man?"

He pulled out his Beretta semiautomatic. "Would I dare say that? Because I have a gun. And because I'm incredibly well trained for situations like this. Can you say the same?"

"No, you're right. After you."

Lynch swiftly climbed the rungs, managing to maintain a grip on his gun as he worked his way up to the street. He pushed up on the manhole cover and slid it off to one side. He popped his head up and looked in every direction.

"See him?" Kendra said from below him.

Lynch climbed up to the street. "Afraid not."

Kendra gripped the rungs and pulled herself up. Her fingers throbbed in pain, and only then did she realize that one of the cuts on her left hand had reopened. A little blood was soaking through the bandage.

It was probably nothing. Work through the pain. She could take care of the wound later.

She scrambled the rest of the way up the rungs and joined Lynch on the street above. They were on Nineteenth Street in front of a row of empty storefronts.

"Shit," Lynch said. "We lost him."

Kendra stiffened in panic. Then she smiled. "No way. He was trudging through the same muck we were. Look at the sidewalk." She pointed to a set of footprints leading down the street. "Though I guess he could have erected a big neon sign reading, 'Killer this way.'"

"Too subtle."

Then they set off down the street at a run, following the trail of green-brown ooze for a block and a half to Pacific Arms, a dilapidated six-story downtown hotel that had been partially converted to low-cost government-assisted housing. A muddy pair of sneakers sat outside the front door.

"Considerate," Lynch said. "And maybe not as subtle as I thought."

Kendra threw open the door, and they ran through the musty lobby. Lynch grabbed her arm and pointed to the elevator, which had an old-style analog indicator above the door.

The elevator was on the third floor.

"Stairs," Lynch said.

They ran into the stairwell, which smelled even mustier than the lobby. They flew up the stairs to the third floor, where the stairwell opened at the end of a long carpeted hallway. The walls were a dark burgundy color, topped by a gold crown molding that was chipped and peeling.

"Okay," Lynch whispered. "He could be in any one of these rooms. We'll hold down the fort until Metcalf gets here. I'll text him now."

It seemed like a good idea until she had another thought. "What if Hayes goes out a fire escape? He's shown himself to be very comfortable doing that."

"Then what do you propose?"

"I'll just tell you which room he's in." She started down the hallway.

"How?"

Her head moved from right to left and back as she progressed down the long hallway. "Keep your distance. Give me ten feet or so."

He held his gun in front of him. "I don't like this."

"Just be ready. I don't want him to get away."

She pressed on quietly down the hallway, continuing her sweep. She stopped at the halfway point.

No. False alarm.

She resumed her journey until she finally found herself at the second-to-last door to the right. She turned back to Lynch and pointed at the door.

Are you sure? he mouthed.

Positive, she mouthed back.

He looked confused, but he motioned for her to step back. He silently tried the doorknob. Locked.

He put his hand out and mouthed, *Stay here.*

He counted down with his fingers.

Three . . .

Two . . .

One!

Lynch kicked in the door and body-rolled into the room before the doorframe's splinters had even hit the floor.

No sound from the interior of the room.

Kendra instinctively moved toward the broken door. "Lynch!"

Lynch muttered a curse. "Stay where you are, dammit."

She froze as she heard doors opening and closing then the sound of window blinds.

Lynch cursed again before calling out. "Kendra . . . All clear."

She ran into the room. No Hayes. "He got away? How could he have possibly—"

She stopped in her tracks, shocked.

Holy shit.

Because Hayes *was* there.

He was dead.

Hayes was on the floor of the room, glazed eyes open, with a gunshot wound that pierced his fore-head and blew apart the back of his skull.

He was still shoeless with his pant cuffs drenched from sewer sludge.

"What in the hell?" Kendra said, dazed.

"Good question. He fought awful hard to get to a place where he'd just get his head blown off." Lynch motioned toward the window. "And you were right to be afraid of the fire escape. Looks like that's how his killer got away." Lynch holstered his gun. "By the way, how did you know Hayes was in here?"

She moistened her lips. "It was the only room on the floor that smelled like a sewer. Of course, you and I smell the same way so it wasn't easy. That's why I asked you to back off."

He made a face. "Should have figured out that one myself."

Kendra was still staring dazedly at Hayes's corpse, where blood was spreading slowly onto the carpeted floor. "Shit. All of this was for nothing. We *needed* him."

"That's probably why he died." Lynch pulled out his phone. "I'll call Metcalf. At least his Evidence Response Team is nearby. Maybe we can get some answers."

CHAPTER

13

An hour later, most of the floor had been cordoned off as a crime scene and FBI Evidence Response had already dusted and swabbed the room. The medical examiner had also done his preliminary work and was tapping notes into a tablet computer while waiting for the go-ahead to cart away Hayes's still-warm corpse.

Metcalf turned away from talking to the M.E. to join Kendra and Lynch at the door. The stare he gave Lynch was distinctly cool. "Promise me you didn't shoot this guy."

Lynch literally laughed in his face. "Are you serious? You think that I—?"

"I'm not thinking anything," Metcalf interrupted. "I asked a question. I know how I'd feel if I came face-to-face with any dirtbag who'd hurt Kendra."

"Then you know I'd get far more pleasure making the rest of his life a living hell," Lynch said softly. "You're being very simplistic, Metcalf."

Kendra stepped forward. "I was there, remember?" she said impatiently. "For goodness' sake, Lynch didn't shoot him. And we're trying to crack this case, not get revenge for anything that happened to me. That's over and done with. Lynch is a professional, and he wouldn't let personal feelings get in the way of finding out what happened at Oceanside. And unless your team found something we can use, his death is a big setback for us."

"Well, I might let my feelings get in the way a little bit," Lynch said. "But not to the extent of an execution-style bullet to the brain."

"I know." Metcalf scowled. "I guess I'm sorry. But I had to ask. It's my job."

"And you enjoyed it since it was aimed at me. Now that I've been hopefully eliminated as a suspect, did your team find anything?" Lynch asked.

Metcalf glanced back into the room. "It doesn't look good. The entire place had been wiped down. Except for yours, there isn't a single fingerprint to be found anywhere. Not on any of the doorknobs, not on the faucet, toilet handle, phone... The place is clean."

"There wasn't time to do it after he was shot," Kendra said. "We weren't more than a couple of minutes behind him. His death had to have been planned before he even walked in there." She stared into the room for a moment.

"What's the story with this room?" Lynch asked. "Did Hayes book it under his alias?"

"No," Metcalf said. "We talked to the receptionist and the management company. It was leased for six months by a New York firm. The rent is paid monthly by a mailed money order. The account name is ABCD."

"What? You're joking. That's the guest's name?" Kendra said.

"Yep. Probably phony, of course. Since most of the other guests probably pay cash and register under the name John Smith, I guess they really didn't care. We're already trying to track it down."

"How long has this room been booked?"

"They received the booking three months ago. No arrangements for maid service, no employee access of any kind. The dead bolt is a different brand from every other lock on the floor. It looks like it was installed by the renter."

Kendra nodded slowly. "What the hell did Hayes have going on here?"

"I have no idea." Metcalf raised his iPad. "But it might not be Hayes at all. I have something to show you. It came in right after I got here."

"Tell me it's something good."

"Depends on how good your sketch artist is."

"Bill Dillingham? He's the best."

"Then we have a chance of identifying the other man who came after you at the factory. It took longer than I would have liked, but I got a hit of about fourteen possible matches with photographs in the FBI database. I'd like you to take a look and see if you recognize any of these guys."

"Right now?"

"Unless you're too upset? We can wait."

She glanced at the door of the room where Hayes had been killed. "No, we can't. He might have killed Hayes to keep us from knowing who he was. Every minute we wait makes it a win for him."

"Okay." Metcalf displayed his iPad screen to her. "Swipe right to look through the pictures. Kind of like looking for a Tinder date, but far sicker."

She tried to smile. "You would know, Metcalf. Let's see what you have here." She swiped her finger across his iPad screen, displaying a succession of men who looked remarkably like the man Jessie pulverized against the car the other night. But it wasn't until Kendra reached the end of the photo lineup that she finally saw *his* face.

She inhaled sharply. "That's him."

"Positive?"

"Yes. His eyes, the thin nose, the set of his jaw . . . No doubt."

As chilled as Kendra had been to see the sketch when Bill had first produced it, seeing the photo only made her angry. Angry for what he'd done to Elaine Wessler's husband, angry for what he'd tried to do to her. She couldn't wait to bring this son of a bitch down. She looked up at Metcalf. "Who is he?"

He turned the iPad around and double-tapped the photo. "His name is Lance Dietrich. He entered our system four years ago as a suspect in an espionage case."

"A suspect?" Lynch said. "No conviction?"

"Not in this case. But Kendra just identified the guy. We haven't had a chance to investigate him in-depth. I'll turn everyone loose to dig deeper once I'm back at the office. I'm ready to leave now." He glanced at Kendra. "I believe you know that I'll do everything that can be done. I won't stop until I—"

But Kendra was no longer listening to him.

She stepped closer to Hayes's corpse and looked down at him.

Execution-style.

The words echoed in Kendra's mind.

Cold. Efficient. Brutal.

Kendra shuddered as she remembered her first sight of Hayes when she'd come into the room. Death was always a shock even if it happened to a criminal like Hayes, but knowing the icy callousness of the man who had killed him was overpowering. "Lance Dietrich," Kendra repeated. She was trying to connect Hayes's death with the man she'd seen so briefly on that rooftop. "And you think this Dietrich killed Hayes?"

"It's a possibility," Metcalf said. "If they were partners, maybe Dietrich thought we were getting a little too close to Hayes and was afraid he might talk." He paused. "It was odd you just happened to catch sight of Hayes and he led you right here, where he took the bullet himself. Almost as if he was trying to get you to follow him. As I said, we'll know more once I get back to headquarters and start doing an in-depth search on Dietrich. We should know all the basics about him and any known associates within an hour or two, and then we'll go from there. I should be able to call and give you an initial report tomorrow."

"Tomorrow?" Suddenly the anger and frustration that had been brewing within her erupted. "No, I want to go back to the office with you. I want to know the minute you know."

Metcalf frowned. "You're not being reasonable. It's much better that you go home and take a shower and rest. Let us call you when we have a complete—"

"I'm going with you," she said fiercely. "I don't feel like being reasonable. We almost *had* Hayes. We were so close. Dietrich had to be one of the sons of bitches who killed Elaine and Mr. Kim, and now he thinks he can clean up his mess by putting a bullet in Hayes's head? Screw him!"

Metcalf took a step toward her. "I know you're disappointed, but that doesn't—"

"Drop it," Lynch said quietly. "You're going to lose this one, Metcalf. It's been a rough day for her. Give her what she wants in the most convenient way possible for you." He reached in his pocket, pulled out his car keys, and handed them to him. "We'll meet you back at the regional office. Have someone drive my Lamborghini back to the parking lot. I'll take one of your vans parked at the curb that you can fumigate later." He took Kendra's elbow. "Let's go. Battle's won. Metcalf was only trying to be considerate." He smiled. "Or maybe the aromatic fumes we're emitting are going to his head. But arrangements can be made to take care of that. What about it, Metcalf?"

"I still think I'm right." Metcalf forced a smile. "But whatever you say, Kendra. And I agree you do *desperately* need a shower. Take her to the forensics department on the second floor where there are shower stalls, Lynch. I'll call ahead and have them dig up some clothes for both of you."

"With 'FBI' blazoned prominently on the back?" Lynch asked. "See? One way or the other, they're going to recruit you, Kendra."

She ignored him. "I'm just grateful that you're being cooperative, Metcalf," she said. "This is important to me. Maybe I was a little curt."

He smiled. "No problem. Like Lynch said, you've had a rough day." He turned away to talk to another agent.

"You actually apologized," Lynch murmured as he led Kendra from the hotel out to the street. "Incredible. You were throwing so many sparks around that I didn't believe it possible. I was just hoping to yank you out before you hurt poor Metcalf's feelings."

"Yeah, that was going to happen. When I calmed down, I realized that it wasn't Metcalf's fault I was so upset. And you certainly didn't have to step in and make explanations for me. That pissed me off more than Metcalf's stubbornness. I could have handled him."

"Right. But I did manage to get Metcalf to offer you a shower and clean clothes. Doesn't that earn me forgiveness?"

"It might." She thought about it. "Yes, I'd forgive the devil himself if he offered me a shower right now. It's going to feel absolutely fantastic." She headed for the van parked at the curb. "But he'd have to get me in that shower really, really fast."

FORENSICS FACILITY

FBI REGIONAL OFFICE

But the shower didn't feel as fantastic as Kendra thought it would. That fall against the wall of the sewer had really done a number on her, she realized. The muscles of her back and shoulders were becoming more sore by the minute, and the sprays pounding against them were like little needles. She thoroughly washed her body and hair and then got out of the stall as quickly as possible.

Pain.

She had to balance against the vanity for a moment to catch her breath before she was able to dry off...very carefully. She glanced at the cut on her left hand. It had stopped bleeding under the water of the shower and would probably be fine. She took a bit of paper towel and put it on the cut in case it started bleeding again.

It took her ten minutes to put on the black shirt, slacks, and shoes Metcalf had supplied her. Another five minutes to brush her damp hair back from her face. But then it was necessary to spend another few minutes to stand there and recover once again. She grimaced as she glanced in the mirror. She looked like a drowned rat, but at least she was clean.

She took a deep breath and squared her shoulders. Bad move. She flinched with pain and had to take another minute. Then she crossed to the door and opened it.

Lynch was standing there. He was dressed in a black FBI sweatshirt and pants and looked disgustingly good in them.

"Okay?" His gaze was searching her face. "It took you a long time."

"Of course I'm okay. I told you I was looking forward to that shower."

"Well, it gave Metcalf enough time to have one of his guys retrieve your phone from that muck." He handed her the phone. "And properly sterilize it. Don't worry, it's as clean as you are now." His eyes were glinting mischievously. "Though I knew that wouldn't be good enough for you. I can see you cringing. So I told them to arrange to get you a new one, enter all your info, and have it here in a couple of hours." He added solemnly, "But you can use this one until then, if you like."

"I'll borrow yours instead."

"I thought that would be your decision." He handed her his phone. "Enjoy. Though some of my calls tend to be a bit unusual."

"I can imagine. Metcalf should never have made that poor agent go after my phone." She shuddered. "They should give him a medal for wallowing in that muck." She moved past him to the elevator. "Is Metcalf back here yet?"

"Yes, and he hopped right on the Dietrich file." He punched the button. "It's not going to take long to get the initial info if he keeps on at this pace. I think I'll give him a little nudge now and then to remind him that you're here and waiting..."

But when the elevator doors opened Kendra realized that would be redundant. The entire office was crackling with the whir of machines, special agents on their phones, and Metcalf in the center of it all. She even saw Griffin out of his office and talking to him. "Leave him alone. I don't think he needs nudging. Griffin appears to be doing a good enough job." She sat down in a chair at a desk near the elevator. "First, I'll take a minute to call Olivia and let her and Jessie know everything that happened today. After that you can have your phone back until I need it again. Then, when Metcalf gets time to take a breath, I'll ask him if I can help."

"I doubt if you'll get a yes. You don't know the protocol and you don't have the contacts." He was moving across the room toward Metcalf. "But he'll probably enjoy giving me orders since I have both. Stay here and I'll let you know..."

But Kendra was delegated to just sitting there waiting for another three hours before Metcalf and Lynch started across the office toward her.

She straightened in her chair. "Dietrich?"

"There's still information streaming in but here's

what we know so far," Metcalf said as he waved a handful of printouts in his hand. "The most interesting thing is that he's not in the U.S. at all. At least not according to the State Department travel and immigration databases."

"Where's he supposed to be?" Kendra said.

"London. Supposedly born and raised in Elsworth, near Cambridge, but his current address is London and there's no record of him leaving the EU in the last six months at least."

"He *was* here," Kendra insisted. "I didn't make a mistake. That was his photo."

"I believe you," Metcalf said. "His partner was supposed to have been dead for years, remember? These guys are fairly proficient at gaming the system."

"What's his background?" Lynch asked.

"Cambridge-educated with a degree in finance. He got in on a rugby scholarship. He was good. He was also a star kickboxer. He placed second in the European championships."

"Impressive," Kendra said. "And even more impressive that Jessie was able to mop the floor with him."

"What about since college?" Lynch asked.

"Equally impressive. He worked for one of the top brokerages in London."

"He was a finance whiz?" Kendra frowned. "That

doesn't make sense. How did he get from there to chasing me across a shipyard rooftop?"

"Well, there was that industrial espionage arrest four years ago. He was suspected of being a corporate spy, stealing technology secrets from a defense contractor. The charges were dropped before the case went to trial. The company evidently didn't want to press it." He shrugged. "It could be that they weren't entirely on the up-and-up and didn't want to stir the waters."

"What's he been doing since?" Kendra asked.

"Nothing," Metcalf said. "At least as far as we can tell. No company would hire him after his arrest. He hasn't drawn a paycheck since then."

"In four years?" Lynch asked.

"At least officially. We're having our friends at the British NCA follow up for us. We do know he's visited Paris several times during that period. Lynch called a few of his buddies with the Paris office of the CIA and got them to go through some of their records. He had contacts with several known smugglers and drug dealers on those visits. But it appears he was very smart and no one could pin anything on him."

"Any history of violence there?" Kendra asked.

"Again, no proof. But the word is that he's a bit wacko and likes to take chances. He was known to have a bad temper, and people had a habit of disappearing when he was displeased with them. One of those drug dealers was later found dead on the banks of the Seine. And there was a pilot for Air France who was killed on a layover in Lisbon after he'd agreed to meet with Dietrich about smuggling artifacts out of Cairo." He paused. "Both of them had bullets in their heads."

"It seems he likes the idea of executing his partners," Kendra said dryly. "Anything else?"

"As I said, there will be more streaming in all the time," Metcalf said. "The CIA promised Lynch they would keep on digging. But we've found out that Dietrich is clever, has contacts, and won't be easy to catch. No matter what he does, he researches the job thoroughly before he dives in." He paused. "Also, he likes to keep his own hands clean and he's willing to kill to do it."

"And that he has a background of smuggling and drugs," Kendra said. "Could the Oceanside deaths have anything to do with either?"

"I don't see how, but we'll take another look."

"Please." She moistened her lips. "Though I'm just guessing and throwing out possibilities. He's an ugly customer. Much worse than Hayes. Very cold. Who knows how many other people Dietrich eliminated when they got in his way? But all that horror still doesn't tell us why he'd kill Elaine or Mr. Kim. They didn't have anything to do with smuggling or drugs. And he might be a murderer, but he's evidently not some psycho serial killer."

"We can't be sure of that. He might be many things. That report Lynch got from the CIA showed definite psychotic tendencies," Metcalf said. "That's why we have to go even deeper. But is this enough to persuade you to go home and let us keep on digging?"

She nodded. "It's not enough. It will never be enough, but it's something I can work with. I know him better now. He's not a complete stranger." She got to her feet. "Thanks for letting me hang out here until you finished." She made a face. "Even if I was totally useless."

"It was kind of nice looking over and seeing you in that FBI shirt." Metcalf grinned. "I know Griffin liked the idea."

"Then it's definitely time I went home." She headed for the elevator. "Are you ready to give me a lift, Lynch?"

"Just waiting for you to say your goodbyes like a good chauffeur." He followed her into the elevator.

"Thanks, Lynch," Metcalf called after them. "I hate to admit it, but those calls you made to Paris speeded up the search enormously. The CIA is never fond of sharing with us."

"Only here to serve, Metcalf," Lynch said as the elevator doors closed. He added to Kendra, "I'm going to owe Gabe Laurent with Paris CIA big time. No choice. I needed to tap that information to get you out of here sooner, and Laurent was the only one who could give it to me." He frowned. "Though I have a hunch he wasn't telling me everything about Dietrich." Then he shrugged dismissively. "How are you doing?"

"Fine. Why shouldn't I be? All I did was sit around and wait."

"That's right. What was I thinking? And you can do the very same thing while I drive you home..."

———

Forty minutes later Lynch pulled into her condo garage and parked the Lamborghini. She was vaguely aware he'd been unusually silent all the way from the FBI office, but she was too tired to care.

"Thanks, Lynch." She got out of the car. "Now I've got to call Olivia and tell her that I'm on my way up to her condo to pick up Harley." She moved quickly toward the garage elevator. "I'll see you tomorrow."

"Yes, you will." Lynch got out of his car and strolled after her to the elevator. "But you can't get rid of me just yet. I have a few duties to take care of that require my attention." He took out his phone and punched in the number. "Olivia? Kendra is on her way up to assume Harley duty but she's exhausted, bruised, and trying to hide the fact that one of the cuts on her left hand is bleeding again. Do you really want her taking care of a fine canine like Harley? I have to warn you it would be a disservice to him." He put the phone on speaker and handed it to Kendra. "Over to you."

"Olivia, he's just being—"

"Don't be stupid, Kendra," Olivia said curtly. "Of course you don't have to take care of Harley. Can't you see everything is changing? The minute you told me about Hayes being shot, my first thought was that things were beginning to shift out of our control. We've got to get it back. That means Harley is my responsibility from now until we find the person who put a bullet in Hayes...and probably Elaine. The dog's probably safer with me anyway. You just concentrate on doing what you need to do. Lynch, I assume you're listening to this? You wouldn't want to miss knowing that you got your own way even if it's your fault that Kendra is in such bad shape. You should have taken better care of her."

"I'm well aware of that, Olivia. She's just difficult to—"

"No excuses. Just take care of her now and make sure she doesn't get an infection." She cut the connection.

Lynch flinched. "Sometimes getting my way with Olivia can be very confusing. I'm never sure whether I won or lost."

"Well, thanks to you, I'm sure I lost," Kendra said through set teeth. "She didn't even let me get in a word edgewise. And you had no business telling her all that bullshit. I made a deal with her, I keep my promises, and I'm just fine."

Lynch pressed the button for her condo. "Did I lie to her? Are you exhausted, bruised, and bloody?"

"I'm fine," she repeated.

He looked at her.

"You exaggerated," she said, in exasperation. "If it were you, you wouldn't have even noticed a cut or a bruise. You would have laughed about it."

"But it's not me." He nudged her out of the elevator and toward the front door of her condo. "And I'm not laughing. For some reason I never find it amusing when I see you hurt and bleed-ing. I'm working on it, but I'm not there yet. It seems to be happening entirely too often lately." He unlocked her door. "I don't even like to hear about it, which is why I got a bit upset when Metcalf told me about you swinging through the glass window at that factory. Or when you showed me that bullet wound in your arm that night in Afghanistan."

"I don't want to talk about that night." She

went past him into the condo and turned on the overhead lights. "It only makes me angry."

"I know. But we may have to talk about it anyway." He smiled. "Not right now, though. I've made you angry enough just delving into current events. You're right, I shouldn't have indulged myself by saving you from Harley just because I didn't want to think of him keeping you awake." He chuckled. "Maybe I was afraid I'd be forced to offer to take care of him myself."

"It would have served you right." She grimaced. "But you would have probably spent the night teaching him some more miraculous tricks that would make Olivia forgive you anything."

He shrugged. "I might be out of tricks."

"You're never out of tricks." She reached up and wearily rubbed her temple. "Go home, Lynch. You've saved me from Harley and all I want to do now is get to bed."

"I can't do that. I'm under strict orders. You heard Olivia, I have to take care of you." He held up his hand as she opened her lips. "Don't stress it. I promise I'm not going to make anything difficult for you. Consider this a time-out. I'm just going to take a look at your hand and rebandage it. It's all part of the service."

"What service?"

"When you agreed to let me come back to

work on this case, I told you I'd watch your back."
He added lightly, "You can see how patching up
wounds is essential to doing that. Now go sit down
at the dining room table while I get the first-aid kit
out of the bathroom vanity. It's still there?"

"Yes." She stood watching as he went into the
bathroom. Of course he knew where she kept the
first-aid kit. She'd known him a long time, in so many
ways, and binding each other's wounds had been a
part of it. But so was trusting each other's promises,
and he'd given her one not to cause her any stress
tonight. Right now that was far more important.

She went to the chair at the table and dropped
down on it. She winced as the back of the chair
pressed the bruise on her spine.

"Here we go." Lynch set a bowl of water and
the first-aid kit down on the table beside her.
"Shouldn't take any time at all." He sat down in the
chair next to her. "Okay?"

"Sure. Just get it done."

"As soon as I take this bit of paper towel off your
palm and make sure the wound is clean. Paper towel?"
He shook his head. "What were you thinking?"

"That I'd take care of it when I got home," she
said defensively. "It was barely bleeding."

"And you had too many other things to worry
about at the time. Like Dietrich, and how banged
up you were in other places." He carefully removed

the towel that was sticking to the cut. "Not too bad. You broke the scab but you probably didn't bleed much. Why didn't you get Metcalf to fix it at the FBI office? He would have been delighted."

"It wouldn't have been professional. Everyone was too busy. Besides, I didn't need anyone to bandage it. I'm not helpless and I'm tired of being treated as if I am. First Jessie and now you? I told you that it only bled a little." She looked him in the eye. "I can do it myself. It's not as if I wouldn't have done that anyway if you hadn't caused such a fuss."

"I realize that you don't need me," he said soothingly. "Just lean back and let me feel important for the next few moments and then it will be over." He was carefully cleaning the wound and then adding salve and a new bandage. "There." He got to his feet, went to the bar, and poured them both glasses of wine. "All better." He handed a glass to her. "Now drink it down and maybe it will help you sleep. You're moving very stiffly and I'd suggest that you take another hot shower instead, but I don't know how steady you are right now." He grinned. "And I don't think you'd let me take one with you to make sure you don't fall."

"You've got that right," she said dryly. "And I didn't think I was moving all that stiffly. No one else noticed it."

"No one else has my eagle eyes." He lifted his glass

in a half toast. "Or my total dedication to watching your back." He set his glass down on the table and got to his feet. "Which led me to seeing that you need a little more service than I originally intended. Bend your neck and look down at the table."

She instinctively tensed. "Why?"

"Because Olivia wouldn't be pleased with me. I didn't do a good job. You could hardly turn your neck when you took that glass from me. Do what I tell you."

She slowly bent her neck. Then he was behind her, his thumbs on her nape, massaging. The first few minutes were painful and then it became... magical. All of the stiffness disappeared and she felt as if she were melting. "You're very... good at this."

"Yes, I am. I learned the technique from a madam in a house in Beijing that specialized in 'special' services. Madam Nadia spent two years studying it with a tribe in Mongolia, but I persuaded her to give me some pointers in the three months I was hiding out there." His fingers were kneading, twisting. "Give me another few minutes and you'll be okay."

Okay? She felt as if every muscle in her upper body was warm... flowing. Even the beat of her pulse seemed to be slowing. Her eyes were closing...

Then his fingers were gone. "The wine should do the rest. I'd much rather keep my hands on you, but I made you that damn promise."

She took a deep breath and then forced her lids to open. "I definitely don't need this wine to soothe me." She took a sip anyway. "I was almost hypnotized. But I feel much better. Thank you."

"You're welcome." He tilted his head. "Now I wonder if I've gotten you in a relaxed enough mood to return the favor." When he saw her tense, he chuckled. "Don't stiffen like that. If you're not careful, you'll ruin my therapy. I just want you to satisfy my curiosity." His voice lowered dramatically. "The general's infamous bright red underwear."

"Oh, for goodness' sake, don't you ever give up?" She sighed. "That was easy. There was a single red thread caught in the general's zipper. I hate to think where else it might have come from, but red underwear was the likeliest candidate. So I went for it."

"You certainly did." He grinned. "Do I dare ask about all the other personal information you hurled at him?"

"No, you said favor. Singular. Tit for tat. You'll have to earn anything else. Besides, you were only intrigued by the underwear." She smiled as she slowly rotated her neck and felt no pain. "Though I believe I got the best of the deal. I really am grateful, Lynch."

"My pleasure." He grimaced. "Sort of." He sat

down again and studied her. He added softly, "At least this moment is a pleasure. Your cheeks are flushed and you're glowing. You look like you do after we've had sex." He held up his hand. "I know, wrong thing to say. It just came out. I can see you're already drawing away from me. I won't follow up on it. I don't want you jumping up and running out of here." He took a sip of his wine. "Which you probably would have done already if you weren't so mellow at the moment. But it's difficult not to comment on how much I love sex with you when I think about it a hell of a lot of the time. So I thought I'd get it out and then go back to being my discreet, stoic self again."

"I'm not that mellow anymore, and I've never seen you stoic," she said unevenly. "But regardless, I think this sudden burst of frankness from you is going to be a deal breaker. I've told you what we had was a mistake. I could be a friend, I want you for a partner, but there's no way I want an emotional relationship that could tear me apart. I can't handle it."

"Sure you can." He bent forward and brushed his lips against her temple. "You can handle anything and anyone."

"Then I don't want to handle it. Not with you." Her grasp tightened on the stem of her glass as her eyes blazed up at him. "Anyone would be crazy to let herself become involved with a man who might disappear any minute if he gets a call from some government to help bring down a dictator or negotiate the rescue of hostages from a Somali pirate who's already said he's going to kill them anyway." She leaned closer to him and spat her words like bullets. "You've built a gorgeous house that's like an armed camp because of all the people who want to kill you. I've seen the scars on your body from the hit men who have tried." She punched her forefinger at his chest. "I'd never ask you to change the insanity you call a life. That's your choice. But I'm not like all those other women who think it's exciting to watch you skate on thin ice so they can applaud you when it doesn't break. Someday it will break, and I don't want to be there to see it."

"Are you finished?" he asked quietly.

She swallowed. "Yes, I think you should leave now."

"I don't." He smiled. "Because that rant almost ruined the effect of the massage I performed on you. Now I'll have to go to step two. And it's not as if I didn't realize the problem you have with me." He added softly, "But it doesn't make any difference, because it can't. It's too late. Half measures suck and neither of us will be able to stand it for long. It's going to happen. We can't stop it. But I'll try not to push it." He got to his feet. "Now let me put you to bed and then get out of here. Do you want to finish your wine?"

"No." She put her glass on the table. "And I have no intention of letting you put me to bed. You haven't been listening to me. I'm serious about this, Lynch."

"I know you are." He pulled her out of her chair and lifted her in his arms. "And I respect what you're saying, but there's no way you're going to throw me out when we're getting closer to this Dietrich." He was carrying her toward the bedroom. "So I still have time to make you forget I blew it for a little while and get back in your good graces."

"Let me down. This is like some scene from a cheesy soap opera. You're being ridiculous."

"I'm never second-rate. But if I'd made you walk, you'd be tottering and that would offend your dignity. Your back is hurting and it will have stiffened up again after you sat that long. As soon as I get you to bed, I'll take a look and see if it's only a bruise or if it needs an adjustment."

"Courtesy of your Beijing madam? I don't need an adjustment."

"We'll see. Only she wasn't really a madam, that was a cover. She was a Russian agent who'd been sent to infiltrate the brothel to gain information from a North Korean colonel about their nuclear program. It was supposed to be a joint international operation with me doing the leg-work at the silos to confirm her information." He sat Kendra down on the bed and was unfastening her shirt. "Needless to say, Nadia got what she wanted from him. As you can see, she was very talented." He stripped off her shirt and carefully rolled her over on her stomach. He took off her bra and turned on the bedside light. He gave a low whistle. "Nasty bruise. That must have been where you hit the wall."

"I told you it was just a bruise."

He was gently probing. "Yes, you did. And everyone knows you're usually right. Let's just be sure..."

She screamed as an agonizingly sharp pain shot through her. When she could get her breath, she said, "Sorry, I wasn't expecting that. Is something broken?"

"No." He was still probing, "You knocked your vertebrae out of alignment and pinched a nerve. I could take you to the ER or I could fix it myself. Which do you prefer?"

"You. The last thing I want is to be dragged to the hospital tonight. And I've begun to trust Madam Nadia."

"So did I." His fingers were moving lower on her back. "Until she tried to kill me."

"What?"

"It got complicated." He continued to gently probe as he said, "It seemed she didn't understand the concept of *joint mission*. She decided that in order for her mission to succeed, she had to kill me to show her colonel how devoted she was to him. I had to stop her. Pity. I'd learned a lot from her." He'd found what he was looking for. "There it is . . . This is going to hurt like hell. Ready?"

"No." Her hands clenched the pillow. "Do it anyway."

"I think you should reconsider the—" He made the adjustment with lightning speed in mid-sentence.

This time she managed to bite her lower lip to smother the scream. "Is it done? It still hurts."

"It's done. And I've seen worse. Though it will hurt for a couple of days. But I'll get you an ice pack for tonight, and it will feel better by tomorrow morning. Then I'll give you some of the medication Nadia used as a substitute for narcotics, and you'll be able to work if you don't ram yourself into any more walls." He got up from the bed. "I'll be right back. Stay where you are."

"With pain so bad I can hardly move? Was that a joke?"

"Yes, see, you're already better if you can recognize it." He disappeared and was back in five minutes with an ice pack and a thermal ice bucket filled with ice. "No heat. It's an ice regimen. I'll let Olivia know I was even a greater disappointment than she imagined so that she can get you some help." He deftly stripped off the rest of her clothes. "You'll be able to change the ice in the ice pack during the night yourself, but be careful about moving too quickly." He paused. "Or I could stay around and do it for you. I should really check on you occasionally to make sure I haven't done any damage."

"I'll be fine. I'm not afraid of any damage you could do me." Not any physical damage. "You've been very efficient. I'll be all right in no time."

"I'll make sure you are. I can't disappoint Olivia. Now I'll go get your phone and put it beside you on the bed." He was heading out of the room. "If you need me, just call." Then he was back and placing the phone beside her pillow. "Do you want the lamp on or off?"

"Off. Just leave the light on in the living room and the door cracked on your way out." She turned her face away and said haltingly, "I think I owe you again. I'll tell you all those things you wanted to know about the general now if you like."

"Tit for tat?" He turned off the lamp. "I think we'll skip all that tonight. Maybe later." Then he sat there for a moment in the dimness before he reached over to slowly stroke her shoulders and back. Not with any hint of sexuality, but with perhaps the most exquisite gentleness she'd ever known. "Call me," he repeated. His index finger was touching the top of her spine and running slowly down her back to her buttocks. "I have your back. This way, every way." He pressed his lips to the very center of the hollow of her back. "But I prefer it *not* be this way."

He placed a towel on her back and positioned the ice pack where his lips had been, then covered her with a light blanket.

"Good night, Kendra. Try your best to sleep well." He was already at the door. He was looking back at her and she suddenly felt very naked and vulnerable and yet totally... protected. "Tomorrow..."

He was gone.

Heat.

Ice.

Emotional chaos.

Pain.

Lynch.

She buried her face in her pillow.

There was no way she was going to sleep well tonight.

CHAPTER
14

Jessie showed up at Kendra's door at eight the next morning. She knocked and then called to Kendra as she unlocked the door and let herself in. "Hi, Olivia gave me her key with orders to get you up and dressed and down to her place for breakfast in an hour." She poked her head in the bedroom and grinned. "Which may be a major task to look at you. Should I go back down and get Harley to help?"

"Don't you dare." Kendra carefully sat up and swung her feet to the floor. "Fond as I am of the big lug, I've no desire to deal with him before I get dressed."

"I doubt if Olivia would let me bring him anyway. She doesn't want to let him out of her sight since you told her about what Hayes did to that photo of him. So I think I'm on my own." She found Kendra's robe and put it on her. "You're moving very slow. How do you feel?"

"Just the way I look." She thought about it. "But better than last night. Lynch said I would, but for most of the night I was doubting him. It took me a long time to get to sleep. But you're right, I'm moving too slow. If you'll help me shower and dress, I'll be ready to go by Olivia's deadline."

"That sounds like a plan." She helped Kendra to her feet. "Because Lynch called me right after he phoned Olivia and filled me in on Dietrich. He told me he wanted me to cruise over to that hotel where you found Hayes's corpse and ask a few thousand questions of anyone I ran across. I'll have to leave right after I turn you over to Lynch." She was guiding her gently toward the bathroom. "He sounds like a son of a bitch but very interesting. I had no trouble putting him down at that factory, so he must have lost some of the skills he had at Cambridge. It's intriguing that he's fascinated by guns now. They aren't nearly as satisfying. Maybe he got lazy."

"Or maybe his true nature came out and there wasn't anything sportsmanlike about him," Kendra said bluntly. "He's just another murderer."

"No, I believe he might be much more." Jessie

turned on the shower and tested the water. "At any rate, I can't wait to renew my acquaintance with him."

Kendra and Jessie arrived at Olivia's condo ten minutes earlier than Olivia's schedule for Jessie had demanded, and it was Lynch who opened the door. His gaze raked Kendra's face; he nodded approvingly. "A few dark circles and your color isn't the greatest, but not bad on the whole. How do you feel?"

"Like I'm tired of answering that question." Kendra came into the condo and carefully knelt to pet Harley. "There's something vaguely humiliating about being taken down by a sewer system anyway. It's even worse being treated as if I'd gone through a major catastrophe. I'm fine."

"My apologies," Lynch said solemnly. "I can see you're at least well enough to be bad-tempered. May I remind you that there were bullets involved in your attack by the killer sewer system, so it's not quite as humiliating as you're making out?" He handed a hypodermic case to Jessie. "She shouldn't have a narcotic, but this medication should help her get through the day, Jessie. I was going to give it to her, but I believe I'll yield that duty to you. A shot in the butt certainly won't make her any more pleased with me. I'll go help Olivia make coffee."

"I don't need you," Olivia said as she came out of the kitchen. "Did Lynch take good care of you, Kendra?"

"Not bad." She looked up from stroking Harley and met Lynch's eyes. All the colors and shadings of last night's events were suddenly flowing back to her. "No, he took great care of me," she said quietly. "I couldn't have asked anything more."

"Amazing," Olivia said. "Then I guess I'll give him breakfast."

"I'm humbly grateful," Lynch said.

"You should be." Kendra looked quickly away from him and down at Harley. "Olivia, Harley didn't bark once when I came in just now."

"Of course he didn't. He knew there was something wrong with you," Olivia said. "He realizes that his bark is disturbing, but it's what dogs do. It's natural. But his trainer said he was a born service dog. He senses everything. He wants to give everything. So he's giving you his silence. And you'll find when you sit down at the breakfast table, he'll sit beside you and not with me as he usually does."

"That's kind of wonderful," Kendra said softly.

"You bet it is," Olivia said fiercely. "And yet slimeballs like Hayes and Dietrich targeted him? *Why?*"

"We don't know yet. We assume Hayes took the photo but we're not sure about that, either. Metcalf will check it for fingerprints." She started to get up and found Lynch beside her, helping her to her feet. "Thank you. It was easier going down than getting up."

"It happens that way sometimes." He gave her a little push toward Jessie. "Your shot. Either go in the bathroom or bare your butt here." He turned away and headed toward the kitchen table. "While I keep Olivia entertained by telling her how all the forensics experts were holding their noses to keep from breathing our stink at the crime scene yesterday."

———◆———

"You're very quiet." Lynch glanced at Kendra as soon as he got on the highway. "Don't tell me that shot didn't work. I'm an expert at pain management in all forms."

"You've had enough practice," Kendra said dryly. "All I have to do is look at all your scars to see your credentials. No, that extremely illegal shot worked fine. Only enough ache to remind me to be careful."

"Then why are you so quiet?"

She ignored the question. "Was it illegal? You didn't answer. You said it wasn't a narcotic."

"It wasn't precisely illegal. It's an experimental medication from China that Beijing is trying to keep a lid on until they can situate themselves to gain dominance in the world market. No more adverse effects than a few Tylenol. They're going to make a bundle. But it depends on the country you're in at the time, or the organization you're working for when you dispense it." He smiled. "But it's safe, and I've used it many times before. You know I wouldn't put you at risk."

"Never mind. I needed a clear head and a mobile body and it's entirely my responsibility anyway." She paused. "What I told Olivia was true, you know. You were very kind to me last night." She added lightly, "So it's only fair I do payback. After all, I made you a promise. I know you don't really care about all that General Kotcheff business, but it's something I can do now. So you'll just have to put up with it while I rattle it off and get it over with. Serves you right for using it as a bargaining chip. Ready?"

"I'm always ready for you, Kendra," he said quietly.

"I'll go right down the line," she said brusquely. "How did I know the general was spending time out of uniform at Kolula Pushta Road? Answer, he has fresh calluses on the lower knuckles of his thumb and the middle two fingers of his right hand. Bowler's calluses. There's no bowling alley on the base, but there is one on Kolula Pushta Road.

You and I passed it a few times while we were there. I was curious and read that it was the only one in the entire country. And I could see from his tan lines that he often wears a shirt other than his military uniform. I doubt he wears it on base, so it wasn't a stretch to figure he wears it on his in-town bowling jaunts."

"Very good. What about the fact that he had a boat on Lake Huron?"

"I'm getting to it. He has fishing lures hanging from the rearview mirror on his jeep. Very elaborate, very well made. I assume he made them himself. In any case, it shows an interest in fishing. He wears a diver's watch and on his right wrist he has another tan line. It's for the flexible wrist bracelet that most divers use to hold a key to their boats so that someone can't come along and easily take it. I can recognize a Detroit accent from a mile away, and Lake Huron offers the best fishing and diving in the area. It's not the only one, but it's the biggest and the best lake for that. The bracelet tan line was very fresh so I knew he must have been back there recently. He wears a wedding ring so it was likely that he'd been there with his family." She took a breath and then realized she had forgotten something. "By the way, I could pick up a faint Alabama twang in his speech, so that's how I knew he probably spent his younger years there."

"No, we shouldn't forget that twang I never even noticed," he said solemnly. "Are we finished?"

"Almost. The diabetes. He has tiny red spots on his retina. It could indicate diabetic retinopathy. I was angry with him, but I still thought he should know about it."

"By all means." He shook his head. "And you followed that act of concern and thoughtfulness by blowing his mind when you threw the bright red underwear at him."

"Well, I never said I was perfect. Can we forget about all this now?"

"No, I never forget anything about who you are, Kendra." He paused. "Particularly when you try to distract me by dazzling all those deductions in front of me."

She stiffened. "You said you wanted to know."

"Yes, it amuses me. But not if it means you avoid telling me what I want to know. Why were you so quiet?"

"Never satisfied."

"Not true. On many levels."

She was silent and then burst out, "Jessie." She moistened her lips. "You sent Jessie to dig deep and find everything she could about Dietrich. I wish you would have talked to me first."

"You disapprove?" he asked. "What's the problem? I thought it was going to be an all-out effort to nail Dietrich. Metcalf is going at it full force and we both know what an excellent investigator Jessie is when she gets the bit in her teeth. She'll be a major asset."

"I know she will. And she's definitely got the bit in her teeth. She's curious about Dietrich and she'll go the extra step to get him." She paused. "I'm just afraid she'll go too far. Investigating him is one thing. What if she finds him and goes after him?"

"She's a professional, Kendra. She wouldn't do anything to scare him off."

"I know that." She was silent again and then said haltingly, "I don't want her to run the risk, dammit. She's my *friend*. I've already lost too much to that son of a bitch. I don't want to go into some room and see her lying there with a bullet in her brain."

Lynch was silent. "I'm not going to tell you it couldn't happen. You wouldn't believe me. I'm just saying that considering how sharp she is, the chances are minimal. Do you want me to call her and try to get her to stop?"

"It's too late. I should have sent her away when she showed up at that factory. Just as I should have sent you away. I was just so angry and upset about Elaine and Mr. Kim that I reached out and grabbed any help I could find. It didn't matter that this was my fight and I might get you killed."

"It mattered," Lynch said. "You're not thinking straight. We know who you are. We had to twist your arm to get you to let us help you. And I'm the one who got you sent here to Griffin and involved in your own personal nightmare. So quit blaming yourself and blame me. It will be much more fun for you."

"No, it won't." She drew a shaky breath. "And I'm thinking straight, I'm just being emotional. I have a right now and then. It's probably your fault for giving me that shot."

"Absolutely. I deliberately spiked it."

"And I just want to say one more thing. In the end, I have to be the one who goes after Dietrich. I can't have you or Jessie pushing me aside like you did when we were in that sewer. I don't care how much more experience you have than I do."

"We'll talk about it," Lynch said warily.

"No, we won't." She added, "Though you did have another argument that I'll agree is a winner. I brought my gun with me today and I won't be leaving it behind until I get Dietrich."

"Great. Then you can protect me. I always appreciate a woman who—"

His phone rang, and Metcalf's name flashed on the dashboard monitor. Lynch punched a button on his steering column that would answer the call on speaker. "What's up, Metcalf?"

"Is Kendra with you?" Metcalf's voice came through the car stereo system.

"I'm here," Kendra said. "We're heading to the FBI building right now. We'll see you there in fifteen."

"No, you won't. I'm not there."

"Where are you?"

"Back on the campus of Woodward Academy. Listen ... You should get down here as soon as you can."

Kendra didn't like the way that sounded. "Why?"

"There's been another murder here on the grounds."

God, no.

She almost didn't want to ask. "Who ... Who was it?"

She could hear voices in the background before Metcalf finally replied, "We just got here ourselves. We don't have an ID yet. Just get yourself to the campus."

———◆———

Less than half an hour later, Kendra and Lynch were walking across the Woodward Academy campus, just a few hundred yards from where Elaine Wessler's body had been found. The uniformed police officers staffing the gate had directed them to the campus's west side, where a long and winding path led down to the access road that fed into the Pacific Coast Highway.

Kendra steeled herself for the sight that awaited her on the other side of the hill ahead. Woodward had always been a source of comfort, of support to her, but that had all changed in the past few horrible days. Could it ever go back to the way it was?

Lynch squeezed her arm. He knew how this was affecting her. He always knew.

She nodded. "I'm okay." She swallowed. "Not really. This is scaring me. Another death. Allison must be barely holding on right now. All this scandal and horror... And I don't understand it. Why would anyone want to kill someone here at Oceanside? It's a place that only wants to heal kids."

"Who knows? And this is a beautiful spot," Lynch said, gazing at the dramatic beauty of the Pacific glittering in the distance.

"Yes, it's called Lookout Point." She tried to regain her composure. "Kind of a funny name for a school with so many visually impaired kids. I think it was called that long before the academy was here."

As they climbed the gentle slope, the crime scene came into view, a little bit more with each step.

The yellow tape. The FBI investigators in their suits and polyester-blend blazers. A pair of uniformed officers, doing little but keeping onlookers away.

And finally, the corpse.

Kendra's eyes narrowed on it as they ducked under the tape.

It was a man, probably Latino, in his early forties. He was lying on the path faceup, his head cradled in a puddle of blood.

No one she recognized. She felt immediate guilt for the wave of relief that brought her.

Metcalf, who was kneeling next to the body, stood and turned toward Kendra and Lynch as they approached. "Campus security found him at about six thirty A.M. One shot to the head, execution-style."

"Like our friend Hayes," Lynch said.

"Exactly like that. We found a shell casing that looks like a match. It's a .44."

Kendra studied him for a moment longer. She could see that his hands were stained with fingerprint ink. "You took prints to ID him?"

"Yes," Metcalf said. "He had no wallet, no identification on him."

"Get a match?" Lynch asked.

"Yes." Metcalf lowered his voice as he stepped away from the other investigators. "His name is Victor Cardona. Unlike the first two victims, he has no connection with this place as far as we can tell. He's a known drug trafficker."

"A very successful one," Kendra said. "At least

judging from his choice in clothing. Armani shirt, tailored pants, Gucci loafers. And that Yurman bracelet doesn't exactly come cheap."

"Which is unusual in itself," Metcalf said. "Since he must have arrived here in the speedboat we found pulled up a little way down the shore. You'd think he would have been dressed more casually."

"Do we have a time of death?" Lynch asked.

"The M.E. puts it between two and four A.M., based on body temp."

Kendra nodded. "And I take it no one saw or heard anything?"

"We've just started a canvass of the resident students and staff, but no one reported anything. We're trying to talk to everyone while they're still here."

"Here? What do you mean?" Kendra asked.

"The administrator just told me that they may close the academy down until this case gets wrapped up. They're still weighing their options, but no one's especially anxious to keep a couple hundred special-needs kids around when murder victims are dropping all around them. I'm surprised they've kept this place open as long as they have."

Kendra nodded. "This is probably going to be the last straw. Allison told me that she was having problems." And of course, until they knew they could keep the kids and faculty safe, evacuating the campus was the only reasonable thing to do. "She's going to have to concentrate on getting her students to return when it's safe."

"Dietrich is also involved in the narcotics trade," Lynch said. "Is Cardona a known associate of his?"

"Not as far as our records show, but details are sketchy." Metcalf pulled out his phone and zoomed in on a document he'd already opened. "Victor Chase Cardona worked for the Gonzales cartel in Mexico. We believe he facilitated the transport of hundreds of tons of heroin across the border. Mostly in Hidalgo, Texas, but lately there'd been indications that he moved his operation west, moving product through Southern California."

She shook her head in disbelief. "Through this school?"

"I don't know." Metcalf turned and looked out at the ocean. "We did find a kilo of heroin under the seat of that motorboat. I've been thinking... What if the merchandise was being transported up by boat? This might be the last spot you could land before you hit the waters off Camp Pendleton. The marines keep a tight net over there. But here..." He shrugged. "Just a theory."

"A theory without any actual proof," Kendra said.

Metcalf gestured toward the corpse. "Unless you count the dead guy over there."

Kendra walked back over to Cardona's body. His

face had a bright, uneven tan. His left loafer was almost entirely off, revealing a sunburnt foot and ankle with no tan line. She could imagine he'd spent a lot of time on a boat.

She knelt beside him, brushing aside a pair of pesky flies buzzing around the corpse.

Come on, Cardona. Give me more.

A hairline that was too symmetrical, plus some tiny healed scars that indicated at least one hair replacement procedure. Possibly to alter his appearance, but most likely just for vanity's sake.

Nicely manicured fingernails, expensive haircut, and eyebrows that appeared unnaturally sculpted. Which all confirmed her impression that he was a looks-obsessed man of means, but little else. Except...

Kendra took a closer look at the Gucci loafers. Something coated the soles of both shoes. "Glove."

Metcalf handed her an evidence glove and she slid it on. She pressed her fingers against the soles. Tacky.

"What is it?" Lynch asked.

"Looks like some kind of oil."

"Motor oil?"

"Not the kind you put in a car. This is stickier." She glanced around. "It's fresh. I don't know where he would have picked it up. Maybe the motorboat?"

"We'll have it analyzed," Metcalf said. "Anything else?"

She stood up and pulled off the glove. "Nothing of any use. Thanks, Metcalf."

She turned and walked away.

"Where are you going?" Lynch asked.

"I'm not sure. I'll be around." She gazed up at the administration building. "Maybe talk to some of the staff. They must be so upset and afraid. And they might know something about this."

Lynch stopped. "Then I think my time will be better spent elsewhere rather than trailing after you."

"What does that mean?"

"Just because the FBI database doesn't show a relationship between that dead guy and Dietrich doesn't mean there wasn't one. I'm going to tap some of my other sources and see what I can find out. Will you be okay here?"

"Of course. It's probably better if I talk to the staff alone anyway." She glanced around at the familiar gardens, the buildings where she'd spent so many years. "You know ... If they close this place down, I'm afraid they'll never reopen. It would be a shame. No, it would be a tragedy."

"We won't let that happen."

"This is one time I wish I had your confidence, Lynch."

"Usually you'd call it arrogance," he said ruefully.

"I'll take whatever I can get right now."

He squeezed her arm. "I'll let you know what I find out, okay?"

"Yes. Thanks, Lynch."

He was still hesitating. "I can wait for you. I don't like the idea of leaving you here alone."

"Alone?" She looked at him in bewilderment. "It's broad daylight. Metcalf hasn't even left the crime scene yet. This area is crawling with the forensic response crew and FBI agents. I'm quite sure there's not going to be any of Cardona's pals still hanging around. I'm perfectly safe. Go away, Lynch."

"And you're packing a heater," Lynch growled in a guttural gangster snarl. "How could I forget about that?" He turned away. "Give me a call if you find out anything. I'll see you later at your condo." He headed toward his car.

Kendra immediately started up the hill toward the main facility. But when she reached the driveway, she paused before entering the glass doors of the administration building. Allison would be frantically busy dealing with police and parents, and she wasn't the one Kendra wanted to speak to anyway. She turned left and entered the dormitory area.

A few minutes later, she was knocking on the door of Maddie Turman, the dorm supervisor. It took a few minutes before the woman opened it.

She was pale but controlled and stood to one side to permit Kendra to enter. "I was wondering if you'd show up," she said unsteadily. "We've got to stop meeting this way. It's like a story by Edgar Allan Poe. I couldn't believe it when I found out about that murdered man they found this morning. This shouldn't have happened here. When will it stop?"

"I wish I could tell you," Kendra said gently. "That was my first thought, too. I know it's terribly upsetting to both the staff and the students."

"We may not have any students left after today," Maddie said. "Once the police release the premises, the parents are going to swoop down and whisk their kids to safety. Allison has been going crazy between fending off those parents and trying to make explanations to Maxine Rydell. She says we'll probably have to close down for a while." Her lips tightened. "And all we ever wanted to do was to keep them safe and give them a chance for a better life."

"And you did it. You're still doing it. This madness will pass and everything will be normal again."

"Maybe," Maddie said doubtfully. "But everything's crazy now. One of the security guards heard a rumor that the victim was some big drug dealer. Is that true?"

"It might be, but you shouldn't discuss it."

"Do you think I don't know that? All we need is to have the parents think we're allowing drugs into the school. Mr. Kim's and Elaine's deaths were bad enough, but this would be a horror."

"And we don't know anything definite about the circumstances yet. It could be a lie. We're going to investigate and try to clear up everything."

"Then do it soon," Maddie said. "The place where that drug dealer was discovered isn't five minutes' walk from here. The kids and their parents aren't the only ones who are afraid." She shivered as she crossed her arms over her chest. "I was wondering what would have happened if I'd gone for a walk last night? Would there have been someone out there watching me? Would I have ended up lying dead on that slope instead of that cocaine dealer?" She shook her head. "I never thought I was a coward before all this began happening."

"You're not a coward. You're just being smart and cautious. That's exactly what you should be until we catch this killer." She paused. "And that's why I'm here. You were very helpful to me when I came to see you before. But I might need more help if you can give it to me. We've found a possible connection between Elaine's dog, Harley, and what was going on here. You seem to have been more familiar with Elaine's schedule with her dog than anyone else. But you didn't mention whether she took Harley on walks when she brought him to Oceanside with her."

"Of course she did," Maddie said. "That dog was full of energy, and it was the only way she could keep him under control. Not at first, but once he began to heal and behave more normally, she started to take him for a long walk every evening before she went home."

"Here at Oceanside?"

"Yes, she only had a small yard at home and Harley needed to stretch his legs." She frowned. "Why are you asking?"

"Everything about what Elaine did in those last days is important, and if she took Harley with her, that's also important." She added, "Do you know where Elaine usually walked Harley?"

She thought for a moment. "Elaine always liked to take him along the cliff path. The students weren't permitted up there, and she didn't have to worry about Harley barking and scaring them."

"That makes sense. Anywhere else?"

"Not that I remember. Do you need to know anything else?"

Kendra shook her head. "You've been great. If I think of anything else, I'll call you." She turned toward the door. "I'll see you soon, Maddie. Take care of yourself."

"I intend to do that," Maddie said grimly. "But it

would help if you can persuade the FBI to get on the ball and offer a little protection, too. As I said, I'm a coward these days."

"They're trying their best. So am I, Maddie." Kendra lifted her hand in farewell as she left the room. She stopped as soon as she got outside and drew a deep breath. It had been no more depressing than she'd expected, but she hadn't anticipated the fear that she'd felt in Maddie. This latest killing had almost paralyzed the woman and probably the entire campus. The deaths were mounting and they were feeling helpless to stop it.

And Kendra was feeling a bit helpless herself. But she wasn't, she told herself. There was work to be done and she had to do it. She had gotten the information she needed from Maddie, and now she needed to follow up on it.

She turned and gazed toward the cliff path where Elaine had walked Harley. If that photo of Harley had been taken here at Oceanside, it had probably been done on that rocky cliff path that overlooked the sea.

And what had Elaine seen that had gotten her killed because she'd walked her dog on that cliff path? The only thing to do was to go up and walk that path and try to see what Elaine had seen.

She started across the campus toward the tree-lined path that bordered the trail. It took her another ten minutes before she made it through the stand of trees and reached the path. She stood looking out at the sea. No wonder Elaine had chosen to come here. Not only for privacy but also for this wonderful view. There was a stone wall that looked weathered and ancient following the line of the cliff and acting as a barrier against the steep slope. Not much of a barrier, she thought. It was only four feet or so high and sloped even lower in some places. Elaine would have definitely had to keep Harley on a leash. She took a step closer, her fingers touching the warm stone of the wall as she lifted her head to listen to the sound of the sea.

She suddenly stiffened. Because she was hearing more than the sea. She was hearing the dull roar of some kind of vehicle. She took another step closer to the edge of the cliff and looked down.

She inhaled sharply as she realized that from here she could also see the slope where Cardona's body had been found. The yellow barrier tape was still in place, but the forensics trucks and FBI vans were gone from the area now. And the engine sound she had just heard was the departure of the coroner's wagon with Cardona's corpse driving away from the property toward Highway 5.

Hideous death and magnificent beauty, side by side.

Totally unexpected. And what else was she going to find here?

She moved slowly around the curve of the path.

Surprise. Surprise. There was also a view of the shore that led up to the rocky flatlands. Not from the upper path, but only when she went around the lower bend of the trail. So this was where Elaine would have been able to see those shadowy figures she'd emailed Mr. Kim about, leading to his death. Who had been down there? Dietrich? Hayes? Cardona? Elaine had not even been sure that she'd actually seen someone, but the possibility had been enough to make her lose her life.

And what had happened here that made Hayes or Dietrich want to kill Harley? Had Elaine taken the dog down to the shore and run into Dietrich?

Or had there been something else on this cliff path that made them come after her?

Guesswork. Yet every possibility was in play now. She'd have to leave and try to put everything together later. She'd go back to her condo and talk to Lynch and perhaps they'd—

A rustling sound in the trees ahead of her.

She stopped short on the path, her gaze swiftly searching the brush and branches of the trees. No reason to be startled. Birds, small animals—it could be anything. That rustle could have even been the sea.

It was not the sea.

She knew that sound so well from her years of living here.

The wind?

Same answer: She knew every nuance of that sound.

Is someone out there watching me?

Maddie's words came back to her. A chill was running through Kendra as she gazed at the shadowy bands of trees on either side of the path ahead of her.

Imagination?

Concentrate.

Listen.

Don't close your eyes.

Too dangerous.

Keep looking at those trees.

Another rustle . . .

Define it. Take it apart.

Movement. Deliberate movement, not a small animal, larger, and surreptitious . . .

A stalking animal.

And she could be the prey.

She'd told Lynch that no one would be waiting to pounce on her when Cardona had only just been murdered. It would take a tremendous amount of arrogance and ego to run the risk of another death so close to Cardona's. Particularly with police and

FBI still milling around on the premises. But Dietrich *was* arrogant, and he had killed Hayes only feet from where she and Lynch had been standing. What if he'd decided that she was a threat and needed to be stopped? This deserted stretch of ground above the sea would be very convenient...

Someone out there is watching me.

Another rustle.

Okay. That was it. Assume she was right and it was Dietrich. Get the *hell* out of here.

That rustle had come from the far left of the path. She turned and ran to the right, off the path and into the trees bordering the trail leading to the campus. She darted in and out of the brush and trees so that he would lose track and not be able to get a bead on her; and to show him she wouldn't be an easy target. Her hand closed on the gun in her pocket and she drew it out in full view at her side.

A few more yards and she'd be away from this leafy dimness surrounding her.

The rustle was louder, breaking twigs and brush.

No longer watching.

Hunting.

Then she was out of the trees!

The next moment she was on the campus trail and hurrying down away from the cliff. Her heart was pounding as she looked back over her shoulder.

It hadn't been her imagination, she thought fiercely. She *knew* it. She could still feel it. Dietrich had been there, mocking, making her feel her own weakness and his power.

Would he have killed her if she hadn't realized he was there and started to run and evade him? The gun in her hand might have also given him reason to hesitate if his goal was a silent kill.

Stop questioning yourself and do something. He might still be back there in the trees. She took out her phone and called Metcalf. "I'm still at Oceanside, Metcalf," she said breathlessly. "Could you send security or a few of your people back here to search the area? I thought I saw someone on the cliff path..."

—————◆—————

Michaels might still be within range, Dietrich thought as he leveled down the barrel of his .44. She was moving fast, but she was on the phone now and distracted. That might give him the few seconds he'd need to take her out.

And he desperately wanted to kill the bitch. The white-hot anger was coursing through him. At first, he had only meant to follow her, find out how close she was getting, but that had changed when he'd realized she was on the cliff path where he'd stalked Elaine Wessler. So what if he knew he shouldn't take her down this soon after Cardona's death? He was an expert and could make it work. The desire to do it was like a fever inside him. He hadn't expected her to connect the dots this fast, but that didn't mean he couldn't take advantage when he found her this vulnerable. One quick, silent, accurate shot, and then drop her into the sea.

But that weird talent she possessed had screwed him up and now she was probably calling her FBI buddies.

He lowered his gun. She was no longer in range and he'd better get the hell out of here. He whirled and turned back into the trees, cursing beneath his breath. She probably thought she had beaten him— and nobody ever beat him. He was smarter than all of them, and particularly Kendra Michaels, who was so smug and satisfied with herself.

Enjoy it, bitch.

You won't get away from me again.

CHAPTER

15

KENDRA'S CONDO

A nd why didn't you call me, instead of Metcalf?" Lynch asked politely. "Isn't that what
partners commonly do? Or am I mistaken?"

He was clearly pissed off, and Kendra was too tired
to argue with him. "You were busy. I didn't want to
bother you. I wasn't sure that Dietrich was in those
trees. I had no proof. It seemed better to use the
FBI to investigate rather than bother you."

"You might not have had proof but you had a
damn good idea that he was there or you wouldn't
have called Metcalf. Isn't that right?" He leaned
back against the bar and took a drink of his whiskey
as he gazed at her across the room. "And Metcalf
thought the same thing once he examined the
footprints he found up there. Just how close was he
to you before you realized he was there?"

"Too close," she said curtly. "What do you want me to say? Everything I said to you before you left the school was true. This shouldn't have happened. Dietrich would have to be crazy to still be hanging around Oceanside after he killed Cardona. It doesn't make sense that he would have stayed around with the FBI on the property. It's even crazier that he would have actually gone after me when he thought he had the chance."

"But I told you that according to the CIA, Dietrich is a little wacko. He likes to take chances; the sensation of skimming close to the edge gives him a rush." He added grimly, "And this time he chose you to provide him with his buzz. Was Metcalf sure about the footprints?"

"He's double-checking. But the initial info is that the shoes of the man on that cliff path were made in Portugal. Didn't you say Lisbon was where Dietrich killed that pilot?"

He thought about it, then nodded. "You were probably right that it was Dietrich up there stalking you."

"Of course it was," she said impatiently. "Why else would I have called Metcalf if I didn't believe it was Dietrich? I didn't only hear him, I could *feel* him there, Lynch." She added, "And I did what I thought was best. Now will you please stop interrogating me. You haven't done anything else since you walked in that door fifteen minutes ago. I'm sick of it."

"I can see that." His gaze was narrowed on her face, and he turned to the bar and poured a glass of wine. "You're also very tired. Metcalf told me you spent another two hours trekking around that path after he brought his team to investigate." He crossed the room and handed her the glass. "How does your back feel?"

"Okay." She shrugged. "A little sore. I did a little running through those trees before I reached the campus trail."

"Running? You didn't mention that."

"I didn't think of it." She took a sip of wine. "It wasn't important."

"It was important." His lips tightened. "I don't like the picture it brings to mind of you darting through the trees like a frightened deer with that bastard after you."

"Then don't think about it. Think about how we're going to catch him." She looked him in the eye. "Because I didn't like the idea of running away from that son of a bitch, either. It made me feel helpless. I can imagine how Elaine must have felt with him after her."

"But Elaine Wessler wasn't killed on that cliff path."

"No, she wasn't. Why not? Was it because she

always took Harley with her when she walked that path? The trainer told Olivia that the bogus call he took from the vet tech was an inquiry about Harley's K-9 abilities. Were they thinking about the possibility of killing the dog to discourage Elaine from taking him up there? What if Elaine ran into Dietrich and Hayes on that path and Harley was aggressive?"

"All possible," Lynch said. "But then you have to ask yourself why they even chose to be strolling up there at the same time as Elaine Wessler. Did they realize she had seen them? Or had they just seen her and were taking preventive measures?"

She wearily shook her head. "I don't know. And surely Elaine would have reported trespassers if she'd actually run across them on the path. All the teachers are super careful of the students. That's why Elaine asked Mr. Kim to check out a possible intrusion on the private beach." She shook her head. "But Metcalf said after the murders that there was no sign of a disturbance down there, no footprints, nothing. Whatever they were doing, they cleaned it up as if it had never happened."

"Oh, you mean like Hayes's room at that hotel?" Lynch asked sardonically.

"Perhaps." She shook her head. "What else did you find out from the CIA about Cardona?"

"What we suspected. Cardona was an international

player who dealt principally with the cartels in Mexico, but a few years ago he and Dietrich had a profitable arrangement smuggling drugs out of North Africa to Rome."

"Drugs," Kendra said slowly.

"It seems to be the tie that binds Cardona and Dietrich together," Lynch said. "Though Dietrich prefers to operate out of Europe and Russia. He even recently bought a home north of Moscow. But maybe Cardona made him an offer he couldn't refuse. San Diego is right across the border from Mexico where Cardona did most of his business. They could have had a joint deal with one of the major cartels and then had a falling-out."

"Here on our doorstep at Oceanside?" She felt sick at the idea. "I can't believe it."

"Believe it," he said quietly. "Cardona is a big player. What would be a safer place for them to hide a multimillion-dollar stash of drugs than a wonderful, humanitarian school for special kids? No one would suspect it."

"Because the idea is hideous." But it was possible and she had to accept it. "And you think Mr. Kim and Elaine might have stumbled across them and were killed because of it?"

"I'm not that far along yet," Lynch said. "I don't know what to think. I'm just saying that it could be one explanation." He grimaced. "But Laurent isn't telling me everything about Dietrich. I told you before he's being very cagey. I have an idea Dietrich is on some kind of watch list or Laurent wouldn't have had the information about him so readily available."

"Can't you find out?"

"It's not that easy. I'll go back to Laurent if I can't do it any other way. But we might know more later after I hear from Metcalf."

"Metcalf?" She straightened upright on the couch. "Why are you expecting to hear from him?"

"After he told me about your get-together with Dietrich on the cliff, I asked him to go back there with a more specific search in mind. Such as places where a cache of drugs or cash could be hidden up on that cliff. Previously, he'd only been searching for Dietrich himself or proof that he was even up there. But now we have a drug connection between Dietrich and Cardona." He made a face. "He wasn't pleased at the prospect of going back. He'd just gotten home and was nursing a cold beer. But he said he'd do it. He didn't even ask if he could wait until morning. He came right here, which is when I knew he was really upset about you."

"And started yelling at me," she said. "He was right to not want to go. What do you think he'll be able to find blundering around in the dark?"

"I didn't yell. I merely expressed my displeasure.

And he might find Dietrich up there trying to re-move something valuable or incriminating after all the agents have left. Or he might find nothing at all, but then we'd know to look somewhere else."

She frowned. "Metcalf was sure Dietrich wasn't up there any longer. But if you think there's a chance of finding something, we should go back there, too."

"No, you've had enough for today. Did you eat dinner?"

"I wasn't hungry. Olivia made me a sandwich."

"Good." He took her glass from her and put it on the coffee table. "Then lie back down on the couch and try to take a nap. I know you won't go to bed until you hear from Metcalf, but it won't hurt you to rest." He was scooting her to a more comfortable position and putting one of the couch pillows beneath her head. "I'd massage your back but you'd probably object. I can tell you're edgy and brimming with independence at the moment."

He was wrong. She did feel driven, but she was also uncertain and disappointed and didn't want to be alone right now. "I wouldn't object." She rolled over on her stomach. "That would be stupid. The sooner I get over this pinched nerve, the better. Since she tried to kill you, Madam Nadia was obviously a terrible person, but she taught you well and I might as well reap the benefits."

"Always practical." He chuckled. "That's a phi-losophy I can understand." He fell to his knees on the floor beside her. He pushed up her shirt and unfastened her bra. "Close your eyes and relax your muscles. It's only a little different from the neck massage. It will hurt a little at the beginning but then it will all come together."

She flinched. "Ouch." Then she did as he'd told her and relaxed her muscles.

His fingers were rubbing, smoothing, deep cir-cular movements that were like nothing she'd ever felt before.

She was light-headed.

As if she were being whirled down and around...

Every muscle relaxed.

After a while, he fastened her bra and pulled down her shirt. "Okay?" he whispered. "Relaxed? No more aches?"

"If I was any more relaxed, I'd be unconscious." Her voice sounded slurred, even to herself. "But I have to stay awake until I talk to Metcalf when he finishes at the cliff..."

"I thought that would be the next objection." He brought her phone to her and set it on the coffee table beside her. "Metcalf will call me first and then I'll call you." He turned off the overhead lights. "I promise I'll keep ringing until you answer."

"You're leaving?"

"I think it's best. I can take only so much of Madam Nadia's hands-on therapy when it's you who's the subject. You've been very trusting today and I don't want to blow it."

"You wouldn't. You compartmentalize beautifully." She yawned. "I've always thought that about you."

"Have you?" He bent down and kissed her forehead before he asked softly, "And how do you think I do walking on hot coals?"

"What?"

He laughed. "Never mind. Just a thought." He headed toward the front door. "I'll call you as soon as I hear from Metcalf."

The next moment the door was closing behind him.

She lay there in the darkness, thinking. She hadn't meant to be a tease, but she probably has been. She had just been tired and upset, and she was accustomed to Lynch's iron control and the way he brushed off everything but what he wished to accept. She had needed not only that magic touch but the comfort of having him here, and she had taken it. That didn't excuse her, and she should be more careful. She couldn't tell Lynch one thing and then ask for another. It wasn't fair.

Stop thinking about it. There were a lot of unfair things in this world. It wasn't fair for good people to have to die. It wasn't fair that there were killers like Dietrich. All she could do was try to be as good and honest as she could be.

And watch out for moments of weakness like the one that had occurred tonight...

———◆———

Her phone was ringing...

Kendra could see the light blinking on the phone on the coffee table.

Lynch, she thought drowsily as she reached out for it. Lynch had promised to call her after Metcalf—"

"What did he say, Lynch?" she asked as she pressed the ACCESS button. "Did he tell—"

"Hello, Dr. Michaels. Or may I call you Kendra? I feel so close to you that I believe a certain intimacy is called for in our relationship."

She inhaled sharply. Not Lynch. She knew that voice even though she had only heard it one time, on the roof of the shipyard building. "Dietrich," she whispered.

"You see, you feel the intimacy, too, if you recognize my voice so easily. But you don't sound pleased that I'm calling you. I thought you looked so eager when you were running through those trees today." He added mockingly, "Oh, that's right, you were running *away* from me, weren't you? And it wasn't eagerness, it was terror. What would your friends at the FBI have thought if they'd seen you? You have such a fine reputation and it would have been ruined."

"They would have thought I was smart." Her hand was shaking as she pressed the RECORD button. "Because I was avoiding an ambush. You did have a gun pointed at me, didn't you?"

"Only toward the end. Though I had every intention of shooting you once I saw you heading for the cliff path. It would have been a shame to lose the opportunity."

"Why? Do you regard me as that much of a threat?"

"More of a nuisance than a threat. I never expected you to be this annoying when I started out. You were going to be just a minor challenge, the icing on the cake. I should have known you'd be tougher than that. You've been getting in my way and it's time I put an end to it."

"With a bullet in my brain as you did with Hayes and Cardona? Isn't that the way you usually handle nuisances?"

"Why not? Everyone needs a signature, and mine is so dramatic and unique. And neither Hayes nor Cardona expected it. They'd served their initial purposes very well, Hayes by obediently following my orders and Cardona with his contacts south of the border. But it was time for them to serve one last purpose for me. That was to remove the threat that they might be too talkative. Actually, you should be glad that my method of removal is usually very quick." He paused. "Your friend Ronald Kim didn't suffer long at all. Not at the end. Elaine Wessler was different. She decided she had to be brave and surprised me and I had to use the knife. Before the end she was shaking and crying and begging me not to do it."

"Shut up!"

"Does it bother you? Good. Then I'll tell you how she got down on her knees and pleaded with me. The slut said she'd do anything I wanted her to do if I just wouldn't kill her."

He was trying to hurt her, frighten her, she realized. And he was succeeding. But why was he doing it? There had to be a reason. "I don't believe any of this. Why did you call me? Were you angry because I got away from you today?"

"You didn't get away from me," he said quickly. "I don't make mistakes like that. I'm an expert. Everyone knows when I take on a job, I get it done. I could have killed you anytime I wanted if I hadn't wanted to toy with you later. I let you go on purpose."

He was lying, Kendra thought. The phrasing, the sudden harshness, the arrogance, were sure signs.

"We both know that's not true. You were clumsy and I picked up on it and I got away from you. Why don't you admit it?"

"Because it's not true, bitch," he said harshly. "I just called to tell you that your time's run out and you should get ready to die. Keep looking over your shoulder because I'm going to be there. I decided that you're not worth me wasting my time making you cringe and cry like Elaine Wessler. I'll just blow your head off."

He cut the connection.

Kendra's hand was shaking as she punched in Lynch's number.

"I haven't heard from Metcalf yet, Kendra," Lynch said when he picked up. "I promised you I'd call when I did. The good thing is that he must be doing a really thorough job of searching that area if he—"

"I want you to come back here," she said unevenly. "Right now. Will you do that?"

Silence. "What's wrong?"

"Dietrich called me."

"I'll be there in twenty minutes."

He arrived in seventeen minutes and she'd had time to make coffee and pull herself together before he walked in the door.

She pointed to her phone on the coffee table. "I didn't record the first part of the call, I was too shocked. But I got the rest." She was pouring coffee into two cups. "Listen to it. It's self-explanatory. Mostly intimidation and threats. I evidently pushed a button when I hurt his pride as an expert killing machine."

He was already listening to the call and Kendra tried to block out the sound of Dietrich's words and the viciousness of his tone. Once was more than enough. Every word, every inference, was engraved on her mind.

Lynch turned off the recording and walked toward her across the room. "Nasty," he said quietly. "Are you all right?"

"No. But I will be when we put that asshole away." She sat down at the table and picked up her coffee cup. "I was stunned that he called me, because I couldn't understand why. But then I realized he was furious and only wanted to hurt me. He has such a tremendous ego, he couldn't accept that I'd managed to escape him. He was angry that he wasn't able to kill me so he thought he'd strike at me in a different way. He kept talking about Elaine and what he'd done to her..."

"I caught that," Lynch said. He sat down opposite her. "And the fact that you were also taunting him."

"I couldn't let him think that he could hurt me." She lifted her cup to her lips. "And I thought if I kept him talking I might find out something I could use later."

"And did you?"

"I don't know. Maybe. I'll have to sort it all out." She frowned. "But I did find out that he knew a lot about Elaine and how I felt about her. He knew talking about her like that would hurt me. How did he know that?"

"I told you that Dietrich carefully researched all of his jobs. He was meticulous about every single aspect. Maybe when he realized she might be a problem, he began researching Elaine and found out she was your teacher."

"Maybe." She thought of something else. "You said Laurent with the CIA told you how clever Dietrich is and so careful that no one could pin anything on him. But this phone call wasn't clever. He wasn't watching what he said or considering he might be recorded. Several things he said could have incriminated him. He didn't *care*, Lynch."

"I noticed that," Lynch said. "Which means he felt protected because he has a safety net. Or that he wanted you to believe he was stupid enough to be vulnerable if you chose to lose your temper and go after him. He was clearly attempting to frighten or anger you enough to go that route." He took a swallow of his coffee. "Or both. Anyway he's bold as hell and not afraid. You agree?"

"How could I help but agree? He targeted me." She looked down into her coffee. "I *hated* it. There were moments when he was talking to me that I actually felt helpless. I'm not going to let him make me feel like that again." Her eyes lifted to meet his own and she said fiercely, "And I don't want to hear you tell me how you'll take care of me and everything will be all right. That would make me feel even more useless."

"I wouldn't dare." A faint smile indented his lips. "That would bring mega-destruction on my own head. I was only going to offer my services to locate the bastard so that you could perform whatever torture or dismemberment you deem necessary. Will you accept that?"

She couldn't help but smile. "I might."

"Then we'd better get started trying to find him. Not that we weren't before. But I'm definitely feeling an added sense of urgency after the bastard had the balls to actually call you." He reached in his pocket and pulled out his phone. "And I'm not waiting any longer for Metcalf's call. He's way overdue."

She tensed. "You think something happened to him?"

"Not with an entire forensics crew up there with him on that cliff. And Dietrich was too busy harassing you tonight to bother about a humble FBI agent." He was punching in the number. "I'm just curious and I'm looking for somewhere to start."

Metcalf's tone was sour when he picked up the call.

"Don't bother me, Lynch. I'm filthy, tired, and very bad-tempered. I won't put up with your crap."

"I'm not giving you any. Kendra is just a bit depressed and would like to know if there's any progress?"

"No. Yes. Maybe. I thought it was going to be a complete bust at first and I was planning your immediate demise. But then the high-beam lights picked up a mark on the northern slope down by the shore."

"A 'mark'?"

"That's as close as I can come to describing it. It looks like a large, heavy object was dragged on the slope down by the shore. We haven't been able to determine whether it was up or down or even the exact shape. I sent a photographer to climb the thirty feet down there but he came up with zilch."

"Large, heavy object," Kendra repeated thoughtfully. "A safe . . . ?"

"No way I can tell. I'll let you know if I do. But don't get your hopes up." He paused. "Depressed? Hey, we're doing all we can. I'm even going to bring dogs up here tomorrow to see if they can find any drug stash."

"Lynch exaggerates. Since I'm not dragging a safe up a cliff in the middle of the night, I guess I'm not doing too bad."

"And I might not be, either. Just tell Lynch after

I get that photographer back on firm ground I'm going home to bed and he's not to call me." He hung up.

"You heard him," Kendra said to Lynch. "Let the man go home to sleep."

"I didn't even mention Dietrich's call," he said virtuously. "I'll leave a message on his voicemail to-morrow." He shrugged. "But why should he sleep when I don't think you will. I can see the wheels turning in your head."

"That doesn't mean it'll do any good," she said in frustration. "There are too many things that have to be put together and we don't know enough. For instance, he said Hayes and Cardona had served their purpose for him and were still doing it. What was that supposed to mean? All I can do is go over what we do know."

"But that doesn't mean the wheels will stop," he said as he got to his feet. "So I'll leave you to it and go about my business."

"What business?"

"Locating Dietrich so that you can suitably punish him and keep me from doing it. That appears to be the name of the game. Metcalf is covering the cliff, so I thought I'd go talk to Jessie and see what she's dug up at the hotel."

"She's probably tucked in bed in Olivia's condo downstairs at this time of night."

He shook his head. "She's a night person and so are most of her contacts and clients. I'll bet she's still on the job." He headed toward the door. "So I'll wander down to that hotel with coffee and doughnuts in hand and we'll see if I'm right."

"Lynch." She'd just had a sudden thought.

He glanced over his shoulder.

"While you're plying her with doughnuts, ask her if she found out how long Dietrich has been hanging out in that hotel. It might be important."

"Because?"

"It would be a secure place for him to stay while he was 'researching' whatever he was up to at Woodward Academy. He was familiar enough with the grounds to find a way to follow me up to the cliff path without me knowing it." She was working her way through the thought process. "Though there are a few ways he could have done that. I came over the campus route, but I think the cliff path can also be reached from the chapel garden and the south gates. If he'd been here for a substantial length of time, that might mean he had time to learn everything about the place and the people who inhabited it. It would have been easy for him to stage the killing of Cardona and get away. He even felt comfortable staying on the property when any other killer would have run." She added, "Providing he had a reason to stay that was still there and couldn't be easily removed..."

"Go on." Lynch was smiling. "I'm enjoying this."

"I'm not," she said soberly. "Because if he was that confident, then he must have cause. And we need to know what he knows to keep him from doing any more harm. There are still teachers and students at the school, and if he can move that freely, then they aren't safe." Her lips twisted bitterly. "Elaine and Mr. Kim weren't." She got to her feet and went to get her computer from the sideboard. "So ask that question first, Lynch. I have to know if I'm right." She sat back down and flipped open the lid of the computer. "And in the meantime, I'll get to work, too."

"Doing what?"

"I've always thought I knew everything there was to know about Woodward Academy. But I didn't know any of the details about the cliff path because it was considered too dangerous for the students to go up there. That means there might be other things about the school that Dietrich knows but I don't. There are several classroom outbuildings, and the chapel, and the greenhouse Mr. Kim used in the winter. Probably a few others that were built after I left. Dietrich probably knows all about all of them in detail." She pulled up the page on Woodward Academy. "I'll find out everything I can on the computer and then when the school opens, I'll go to the library and ask Allison to get me more details." She made a shooing motion with her hand. "Go. Talk to Jessie."

"Yes, ma'am." His lips were quirking as he opened the door. "And it will be the very first question . . ."

———————◆———————

Lynch called Kendra thirty minutes later. "I'm still in my car, but I phoned Jessie to get your answer. You see how obedient I'm being? Jessie found out quite a bit about him. She thinks that he's the one who rented the room where Hayes was killed as well as another room for himself in another wing. But no one has seen him since he blew Hayes away, and Jessie thinks the chances are that he's done with the Pacific Arms. She'll keep checking, but she's looking for other leads."

"You still haven't told me how long Dietrich has been here."

"I was getting to it. From what she can gather, Jessie thinks at least eight weeks." He paused. "And that means a man as sharp and accustomed to research as Dietrich would have had time to practically memorize the entire property."

Kendra muttered a curse. "And that's probably what he did. Which means I'll be on my way to see Allison first thing this morning."

"Not finding anything on the computer?"

"Not much. I'm going to go to another site after this and keep trying. But the library at the school will have much more, and I vaguely remember seeing some reference books on the shelves in Allison's office."

"Then we'll go to the school." He added emphatically, "You notice I used the plural. After your lecture on Dietrich's knowledge of the place, I'm not about to let you go up there alone. I'll be unobtrusive, but I'll be there, Kendra."

"I'm not arguing. I've been thinking about the school—it can be like a rabbit warren. It might be comforting to have someone handy to negotiate all the twists and turns with me."

"Haven't you heard I'm famous for my ability with twists and turns? I'll pick you up in the morning and tell you if I find out anything else from Jessie. Try to at least get a nap tonight."

She ruefully shook her head as he hung up.

She'd had her nap for the night before Dietrich's call. There wasn't any way she could relax enough again after he'd tossed abuse and threats at her. Admit it, there had also been an element of fear. She'd felt as if everything was escalating at top speed and she couldn't stop it.

But all that negative bullshit had also brought a positive result. It had made her think and move and start to put facts together, and that was always a good thing.

She just had to keep on doing it.

She changed to a San Diego historical website and typed: *Building and construction of Woodward Academy.*

———◆———

10:15 A.M.
WOODWARD ACADEMY
OFFICE RECEPTION AREA

"I'm in a hurry, Kendra," Allison said impatiently. "I don't have time for this. I shouldn't even be here talking to you. I not only have to greet and apologize to every parent picking up their child, I have to beg them to return when we can assure them it's safe."

"I won't keep you long. I know it's inconvenient now that you're temporarily closing the school." She met her eyes across the desk. "But I'm glad you're doing it. Get everyone out of here as fast as you can. Then you go, too." She smiled with an effort. "I know you're like the captain staying with a sinking ship until the last minute. But don't let it be the very last minute, and make sure you have someone with you until you drive out the gates.

This man is dangerous, he's unpredictable, and he knows this academy very well."

"You mean it." Allison's impatience vanished as she stared at Kendra. "Actually, I'm sure every captain prefers to get off his ship in a timely manner, and I will, too. But I appreciate your concern. Now what can I do to get you out of here quickly?"

"Information," Kendra said. "I've been told Dietrich probably knows every detail of the academy school and grounds, and there's a possibility that he might choose to return here. I need to make sure I'm as familiar with it as he is. I'm going to the library after I leave you to go through all the books on the history and renovations of the school. But I thought I remembered you have books and pamphlets here in your office that the library might not have."

She nodded slowly. "I have a few books that I've owned since I first came here to teach." She frowned. "You're setting yourself a huge task. This mansion and property were originally donated by a parent who had a special child and the funds to renovate it. The plans have changed and altered several times over the decades. It's been a work in progress for the last seventy years."

"A wonderful work in progress," Kendra said. "And it makes me angry as hell that a man like Dietrich ever set foot on it."

"Me too." Allison got to her feet and strode over to her bookcase, selected four books, and crossed back to Kendra. "So let's kick the son of a bitch off our property." She handed her the books and turned back to the reception area. "Now get out of here and let me get back to work."

"Right." Kendra grinned and swiftly scooted out the door to the hall where Lynch was waiting. "Got them." She gestured to the books. "But she made me feel like a kid again bothering the teacher."

"What about me? I'm the kid you sent out in the hall for bad behavior. Why were those books important?"

"I ran across a few esoteric facts and quotes from them while I was on the computer. I called the county library this morning to ask to borrow the books and I found out that two of the ones I'd seen in Allison's office couldn't be found. The librarian put me on wait list for the books, but then I remembered these copies in Allison's library."

"Lucky break."

"We deserve a little luck. Everything about this is a long shot. Do you know what kind of odds those kids have to overcome every day?" She looked out the window at the long line of cars driven by the parents waiting to pick up their children. "And what happened here made every one of those kids' lives even harder. So don't tell me about long shots.

We'll just check it out and then go on if it doesn't get us to Dietrich."

"Just a comment, Kendra," he said quietly. "What do you want me to do?"

She grimaced. "Tell me to shut up. I'm a little overemotional right now after seeing all those children being yanked out of school. I know how I would have felt if I'd had to leave here when I was a kid. This place helped open up the entire world for me." She'd reached the library and turned to face him. "But what I don't want you to do is hover over me while I'm trying to find out how and why Dietrich is still here when he should be running like hell."

"We talked about this."

"No, you talked about it and I agreed. But I was very vulnerable at the time. I'm better now. Look, there's security all around this place, and they'll be here until all the teachers and children have left the property. You're not going to be able to help me go through those references in the library. There are only a few that aren't in Braille. You'd be of much more use to Metcalf and Griffin checking out the grounds. Metcalf said he was going to bring tracker dogs out here later today to see what they can find. You're very good with dogs."

"I'm better at getting rid of vermin."

"Yes, you are. But go do it somewhere else. I

promise I won't leave this library until you get back." She opened the door to the library. "And I have my gun even though I'm not about to pull it out with all these kids around."

He hesitated. "I'll have Metcalf assign an agent outside in the driveway."

"What a good optic when Allison is trying to play down the thought of any present threat here." She waved her hand. "Go ahead. Do it. We'll take care of optics later."

She watched him walk down the hall before she went into the library and closed the door. It was empty as he'd thought it would be. School had been declared officially canceled this morning at nine, and there wouldn't be any children permitted in the library or other outbuildings until classes resumed. She put her handbag and Allison's books down on a table before going over to the shelves and starting to look for the reference books she needed. There was an entire row of books concerning the purchase and renovations to the school and grounds of Woodward Academy over the years. More than seventy years, Allison had said. A huge task, indeed...

Stop standing here being overwhelmed, she told herself impatiently.

Get to work.

CHAPTER

16

An uproar!

Kendra lifted her gaze in alarm from the book she was reading.

Then she drew a deep breath and relaxed.

It was a familiar uproar.

The library door opened and Harley burst through it and tore across the room toward her, dragging his leash behind him. He was howling and growling and looking very happy to see her.

"Shh." She started stroking him as she gazed beyond him to where Olivia was standing in the doorway. "What are you doing here?"

"At the moment, trying to get Harley away from those kids in the driveway before he makes Allison's job harder." Olivia came toward her. "They didn't understand as Ariel did that all he wanted to do was love them, but then Ariel is fairly unique."

"What else are you doing here?" Kendra asked. "When I called you this morning, I told you they were closing down the school."

"You also told me that scum might still be here causing trouble, and you and Lynch were going to try to find him. By the way, I heard the FBI team and the tracking dogs up on the cliff when my Lyft dropped us off. It nearly drove Harley crazy. He wanted to run up there to play with them. His trainer was right, he doesn't grasp the hunt-and-attack concept." She reached out for one of the Braille books on the table in front of Kendra and sniffed. "This one smells very old." Her fingers traced the copyright date. "Only twenty-two years. Was it of value to you?"

"No." She paused. "Olivia?"

"I'm here to help you," she said simply. "I've let you push me into the background and been very frustrated. Handicap isn't just a word, it's a reality, and I had to accept it. But I can use that handicap to help you go through this mountain of books. I'm smart enough that you'll trust me to catch anything in them that might help us get Dietrich. It will cut your time in half, maybe more." She smiled. "Because I might even be a little smarter than you. Ask Ariel."

"I don't have to ask her. But I don't want you here, Olivia."

"Tough. You sound like Lynch. And it annoys me as much as it would you." She went around the table and settled in a chair. "Now, what you're looking for is a hiding place for drugs or similar valuables on the property? And you also want to know how Dietrich is playing Houdini and managing to move around the school without anyone noticing him? Also anomalies and things that seem odd or out of place."

"Piece of cake?"

"No, but not impossible, if we work hard enough. Suppose you feed me those books to read in the order you believe to be most promising."

Kendra sighed and pushed a book toward her. There would obviously be no budging her. "Well, at least you brought Harley to protect you."

"No, I brought him because this is where he should be right now. I would have preferred not to bring him. I'd like to keep on protecting him." She opened the book. "But someone wanted to hurt him, too, and he lost Elaine just as we did. If we have a chance of catching the man who did it, he should have a part of it." She added, "And I believe that you think we're getting very close."

"I could be wrong. There's nothing solid."

"Of course you could. But we'll think positive, won't we?" She frowned and closed her book. "But speaking of Harley, I'd better take him for his walk before I get settled in. Do you want to come with us?"

"No," Kendra said as she went back to her book. "But be sure to have the FBI agent out front go with you. I took a peek earlier and it's that Special Agent Roberts I met at Hayes's apartment. You won't find him a bother."

"Sure, I don't mind. It's always amusing to notice those big, tough guys' reaction to Harley. First, they're all mushy and then they want to go climb the nearest tree." She was leashing Harley as she spoke. "I particularly liked Metcalf's..."

"You definitely have a sadistic streak." Kendra heard Olivia laugh before she looked back down at the text of the book she'd been reading when Harley and Olivia had burst into the room. She didn't like the idea of either one of them being back here when everyone else was being shunted away to safety, but it was hard not to feel the warmth and comfort Olivia always brought with her. Just looking up and seeing her working at the library table reminded Kendra of the hours they'd spent here as children. Only then it had been a world of darkness for both of them. But there had also been music and whispers and talking about the magic of the books they had just been reading...

11:10 P.M.

Kendra carefully closed the library door behind her and moved silently down the hall toward the office reception area. All she needed was to have Harley hear her leaving and start barking.

But Lynch was there at the door, pulling her into the office area and then out into the driveway. "You called, I came. Silent as the proverbial mouse." He smiled down at her. "But I admit it was amusing to see you creeping down that hall like a teenager on her first date."

"Well, I would have been much more careful if you'd been that first date. Mom was very selective, and she would have considered you in the bad-boy category." She breathed in the cool night air and added, "But thanks for taking the trouble to be quiet. Olivia's sleeping on the couch and Harley's curled up at her feet. I didn't want to wake either one of them."

"Believe me, I didn't either. I spent entirely too many hours on that cliff path today with Metcalf's guys and four dogs. I was ready to come down when you called."

"They're still up there?" Kendra lifted her gaze to the lights still burning in the trees bordering the cliff path. "I didn't expect Metcalf to be that long."

"Neither did I. But he doesn't want to disappoint

you, so he's making sure that he's done everything possible."

"And did you find anything?"

Lynch shook his head. "Zilch. Nothing at all suspicious." He tilted his head. "You?"

"Not really. Olivia and I have gone over at least half those reference books and we haven't found anything that would connect Dietrich to Oceanside or any reason why he staked out the property." She rubbed her temple. "Though I've gotten terribly bored reading about the history of the Woodward family and their great generosity in giving the property to the foundation. All the society reporters of the era worshipped at their feet. I was getting discouraged and hoping you were having better luck."

"Sorry." His gaze was searching her expression. "I wish I could have given you what you wanted."

"You can't give me what's not there." She tried to smile. "And maybe I just wanted to get some air and see a fresh face. Even Olivia was getting discouraged, and she curled up on the couch and nodded off."

"Oh, I've got a very fresh face." He reached out his hand and touched her cheek. "But what we might need is fresh information. Maybe it's time I took my turn at doing a little research myself instead of trailing after Metcalf and all his grim, determined followers."

"What? I assume we're not talking about anything

as boring as what Olivia and I have been going through?"

"Not my cup of tea. I think I'll go after Laurent again and then get in touch with my less-than-legal contacts in Sonora, Mexico, and see what I can find out about Cardona's deal with Dietrich. That might lead somewhere."

She grinned. "Definitely somewhere more interesting than the high-society write-up of the last cotillion ball the Woodwards threw before they turned the property over to the charity foundation."

"Ouch. No wonder you were getting frustrated. I'll see if I can go a bit deeper and find something to keep you awake."

Her smile suddenly faded. "I didn't mean to saddle you with this. You seemed reluctant to go back to question Laurent before. I just wanted to see you and vent, I guess. I'm ready to go back and tackle the other half of those reference books now."

"You didn't saddle me with anything. You just saved me from putting up with Metcalf." He smiled. "And I'd much rather rescue you from boredom. I regard that as an essential duty connected to being your partner."

"But you're not rescuing me, I'll still go back and go through those books."

"I know, rescuing you does have its difficulties. But you'll at least know that I'm here for you." He gave the tip of her nose a quick kiss and turned away. "So go rescue yourself by finding another couch in that library to catch a few hours' sleep. I'll get to work right away and try to have something to show for it in the morning if I can."

She watched him stride away. Then she turned and walked back into the office.

But you'll at least know that I'm here for you.

And she did know that. He'd always been there. It was probably why she'd called him tonight when she'd been so frustrated and depressed. She hadn't wanted him to rescue her, she'd just wanted to be with him and share.

And instead he'd started to plot and plan to change what had upset her and craft it into what he wanted it to be. Typical Lynch. She could understand him going after Laurent. But that reference to his less-than-legal contacts in Sonora had disturbed her.

What the hell did he think he was going to find out in Sonora?

———◆———

SONORA, MEXICO
NEXT DAY

Raul Delgado!
Tonight?

Lynch was cursing beneath his breath as he slammed out of the cantina and strode across the street to his rental car. No wonder Laurent had been playing cat and mouse and dangling just enough bait to keep Lynch interested. Delgado was a prize Laurent wouldn't easily give up, and the bastard was balancing some very dangerous elements to keep under control.

As soon as he got in the car, he punched in Laurent's number.

Laurent answered him immediately. "Hello, Lynch. What are you doing in Mexico?"

"I believe you know or your contact down here wouldn't have let you know I might call you. Tell me about Raul Delgado."

"An interesting man."

"Don't bullshit me. I want answers."

"Answers can be expensive. I realize you can be a valuable resource, but you also have to cooperate. I want the credit for this. The FBI could get in my way."

"I'm not the FBI. You work that out between you. I only want to know about Dietrich and I want to know now."

"Because of your friend Kendra Michaels? I sympathize but I really can't let her interfere. We're too close to the objective. She'll have to accept the risk."

"No, she won't. Because you're going to tell me everything so that I can keep that risk away from her." He lowered his voice to silky softness. "You don't want me for an enemy, Laurent."

Silence. Then Laurent said, "No, I don't believe I do. So I'll be agreeable and deal. But I'll get what I want and a little on the side. I don't care about Dietrich."

"I do. So we'll start with him as far as answers are concerned." He paused. "Is it tonight or was that bullshit?"

"No bullshit. But we're not really sure. All we know is that it's going to go down soon. It could be tonight or tomorrow or the next day, but it will be very soon. Pedro gave you the worst-case scenario, because he's afraid of you. You would have known Pedro was lying, he's very transparent." He added wryly, "But if it does turn out to be the worst-case scenario, you'd better ask your questions quickly, hadn't you?"

———◆———

WOODWARD ACADEMY
6:40 P.M.

The first thing Kendra noticed was that Lynch was not driving his Lamborghini when he came up the driveway but a modest dark Volvo covered in dust.

"You're late, you said you'd let me know this morning," she said as she walked toward him. "Or maybe you said you'd try, but I was still worried."

"And impatient," he said. "Does that library have a refrigerator? I need a bottle of water. I feel as if I've been swallowing dust all the way from Sonora."

"Sonora?" She led him inside and gave him a bottle of water from Allison's compact office fridge. "I thought you were only going to call your contacts. Why did you go down there?"

"Dietrich would call it in-depth research." He drank half the water in three swallows. "I spent half the night on the phone with contacts in Mexico and trying to get in touch with Laurent. He was noticeably unavailable, so I decided to stir the pot a bit. I can always find out more in person."

"I imagine you can."

"Anyway I drifted around Sonora and asked questions and tried to get a grasp on what was happening with the cartels and what and how they were moving their products." He dropped down in an office chair and stretched his legs out before him. "Everyone was very guarded. And there were CIA operators that I recognized wherever I went. It wasn't hard to realize that something very hot was brewing down there. So I went to Pedro Amadez, a source that I knew I could 'persuade,' and squeezed very hard about what that might be."

"And you found?"

"Raul Delgado."

"What?"

"You know the name?"

"Of course I do. Who doesn't? Drug kingpin who controls half the drugs leaving Mexico and Central America."

"And a good portion of Colombia and Venezuela. He's a mega-billionaire and so powerful that he has more clout than the governments who are paying him just to stay in office." He paused. "But he's also had a target painted on his back for the last five years. There's a ten-million-dollar bounty on his head placed there by the U.S. and Mexican governments, his brother was blown up in his home last year, his wife was shot six months ago. No one knows how many attempts have been made on Delgado himself by the cartels."

"Am I supposed to be surprised? I've seen photos of his victims hanging by the neck off bridges."

"But evidently Delgado has a highly developed instinct for self-preservation. He's feeling cornered and doesn't know who to trust among his Latin brothers. He decided a change was needed so that he could regain control."

"What are you saying?"

"That Delgado wants to go to a place he'd feel safer and has made arrangements. Very careful and expensive arrangements. In a place not even in the same hemisphere."

"Where?"

"Do you remember that we heard Dietrich had purchased a new home outside Moscow?"

Her eyes widened. "Dietrich is in this? Why?"

"Because when I went back and grilled Laurent again, he told me one other job at which Dietrich was known to be very good. Extraction. He's spent time and effort on moving any number of unhappy people like Delgado and his followers to safe environments where they could prosper once again. He probably chose Moscow because there was no extradition and Delgado's money would make him a king in its mafia underworld."

"And that's why Dietrich is here? He's trying to move Delgado from Mexico to Russia? Why not just hop a plane?"

"Because Delgado is reputed to be paranoid and doesn't trust anyone but a so-called expert like Dietrich. Though I'm sure Dietrich has been told he'll be sliced into little pieces by Delgado's men if anything about his plan doesn't come off as it should. According to my source, Pedro, the word is Delgado has been moving from place to place around Mexico for the last few weeks. He's either very nervous or he's been waiting for word from Dietrich that everything is ready for him."

"Here?" She was frowning. "Why on Earth would Dietrich choose this place in an exit strategy?"

He shrugged. "I have no idea if it's here. My first thought was that Oceanside is directly on the ocean. And this place is now conveniently deserted. There are three entrances to enable someone to get on the property plus all the trees and flowering bushes to hide them once they pass the gates. If Dietrich found a safe way to get Delgado this far, then it would be easy to slip down to the coast to be picked up by a ship."

"And Dietrich would probably arrange to make very sure that the captain could get close enough to the shore," she said slowly. "Elaine's email to Mr. Kim mentioned someone or something down at the shore that she felt uneasy about. Could it have been a meeting between the captain of a ship and Dietrich?" She shook her head in frustration. "Guesswork. We don't know anything."

"Except that whatever is going to happen will happen very soon."

"Laurent didn't know when?"

He shook his head. "Or where. He said Dietrich was a wild card and just when you thought you knew how a deal was going to go down, he went the other way. No one can say that anything Dietrich's done here at the property has been an outstanding success. It should have discouraged him from using these grounds for his purpose. Those three deaths alone must have drawn attention. And Laurent said one of his agents saw Dietrich across the border near a private airport at Juarez last night." His lips twisted. "That's probably why Delgado is willing to pay Dietrich so much for his extraction. Unpredictability can be expensive."

Kendra went to the window and gazed up at the cliff path. "He was trying to fool me?"

"What do you think?"

"I think he wanted to kill me," she said. "And I don't think that he's going to go to Juarez. He may be unpredictable but I'm beginning to know him."

"Then we'll have to keep an eye out for the bastard, won't we?" He grinned. "I made Laurent promise to call me if and when he gets definite word of what Dietrich is up to. Not that he'll let me know much ahead of time. He wants Delgado in his sights before he gives me Dietrich. So can I talk you into going home?"

She shook her head. "No way. I'm going to go back to the library and thumb through those damn books again and try to figure out what Dietrich is going to do next." She added ruefully, "If I can get Harley to leave me alone. He doesn't obey me nearly as well as he does Olivia."

"Olivia isn't here?"

She shook her head. "I made her go home.

Though it was a tough fight and she even took some of the books back to her condo to keep working. But she insisted on leaving Harley here to protect me."

"Who else is here to protect you? Metcalf?"

"No, when the last students left the school, they closed down the crime scene and left a skeleton crew. Metcalf said Griffin was nagging him to go back to the office and fill out reports anyway. There are a couple agents at all the entrances, and Metcalf insisted on leaving Special Agent Roberts out front."

"Kind of him."

She smiled slightly. "He was afraid you were being irresponsible and leaving me here alone. He told me to call him if you didn't show."

"You told him how worried you were about that?"

"I just sighed and looked fragile."

"You don't do that very well." But he was frowning. "I think I'll go check the guards at the entrances and make sure they're set up and on the alert. They might think because the rest of the crew pulled out that they can let down their guard. Call me if you need me."

"Don't worry. Agent Roberts took very good care of us while you were gone." She headed for the library and closed the door behind her. She looked down at Harley, who had his head on his paws and was staring up at her inquiringly. "Please be good," she murmured. "Everything is going crazy and I have to figure out how to stop it."

———◆———

Harley was amazingly good for the next few hours, but it didn't help Kendra come up with anything fresh or new in that pile of books. She was beginning to believe that Lynch could be right to think Dietrich might have become discouraged about using this place to launch Delgado into his new existence. It was certainly practical that he would—

Her phone rang. Lynch.

She picked up. "I haven't found anything yet that—"

"I just got a call from Laurent. His agent at Juarez thinks that Delgado is in a hangar at the south end of the airport where a Gulfstream was taxied earlier today. There's all kind of muscle surrounding the place and Rico Lopez, who's Delgado's number one, was spotted going into the hangar with a briefcase an hour ago."

Yes!

Her hand tightened on the phone. "What about Dietrich?"

"Not there now. But that same agent caught a glimpse of him a few hours ago."

"Then he's probably not far away from Delgado. We should get on the road right away."

"Good thought. Forget it. We can't go near that hangar. As soon as Laurent verifies that Delgado is there, a combined task force of the CIA and the Mexican government is going to launch an attack and take him down. Laurent won't let us near there until Delgado is in custody. He promised he'd let me know the minute that happens."

"I don't want to wait. What if Dietrich gets away?"

"Then I'll inflict great bodily harm on Laurent. At any rate, if we cause a fuss at that hangar, Dietrich will know and slip away. We don't want that to happen."

No, they didn't, she thought, disappointed. "Do you trust Laurent?"

"If he gives me his word. He did promise me Dietrich. Otherwise it's marginal."

"Then we'll wait. But I'll *hate* it."

"I know you will. I'll let you know as soon as we can move. Just go back to those reference books and try to get your mind off what's happening in Juarez."

"Fat chance."

She cut the connection.

It was absolutely ridiculous having to sit here when she and Lynch could be on their way to Juarez. Besides being a waste of time staring at those boring books when she wouldn't find anything anyway.

But she would go crazy if she didn't have something to do until Lynch called her.

She grudgingly sat down at the table and shook her head as she stared balefully down at the pile of books. She felt as if she had the damn things memorized. Particularly all that family history and society stuff she'd been forced to glance through. It was probably a waste of time to scan it again when Dietrich would have had no reason to want to know anything that had happened here seventy years ago . . .

Her business email pinged and she glanced down at it impatiently. Just a notice informing her that her request was unavailable. She was about to ignore it when she caught the name of the sender. San Diego County Library.

She opened the email and scanned it. It was a polite regret that the two books she'd requested were unavailable. Unfortunately, since the books had been present during inventory two months ago and had not been lent out, it had to be assumed that they would be permanently unavailable.

In other words, stolen.

The library would have been one of the first places Dietrich would have gone to research. If those books had been stolen, he was the most likely candidate.

What had he found in them that made them

valuable enough to steal? She couldn't remember anything of substance in those lightweight history books. But perhaps Kendra hadn't been giving them her full attention because she'd assumed that Dietrich wouldn't.

But what if she'd been wrong?

Why all that research, Dietrich?

So close your eyes.

Concentrate.

Assume nothing.

Was there a reason why Dietrich would have wanted them?

Remember that text . . .

A few minutes later she gasped! Her eyes flew open and she scrambled to find the books on the pile on the table.

One of them was there. But not the right one, she realized impatiently. It must have been one of the books that Olivia had taken home with her.

She punched in her number and Olivia answered in two rings. "I knew you couldn't do without me. Do you want me to come back?"

"No, I want you to read me what's in that book you took home that was about the gift of the property by the Woodwards. I think I remember it all but I have to check. It was written by some society reporter, Helena Sanders, and it read more like a family tell-all than a historical document."

"Wait a minute." Olivia was gone from the phone. "I have it here." Kendra could imagine her fingers racing through the text. "I see what you mean. But the reporter is very gushy and verbose. I'll try to cut it down for you. The deed..." Silence as she read it. "It was very generous and pretty cut-and-dried. No stipulations except for a clause that refused permission for any renovations or outbuildings to be built on a small specified area of the property. Over later years there were several requests to overturn that clause but it was never permitted."

"Any explanations?"

"Not really. Some people including this reporter thought it might be because any building might interfere with the view of the sea." She paused. "But she mentions there were dozens of other gorgeous views on the property and there weren't any clauses forbidding building near them. Regardless, the Woodward family was adamant about it. Or rather, Noreen Woodward, the matriarch of the family, was adamant. Several years later, her son James filed a request to permit the deed to be altered if the custodians of the school gave the family a fat fee."

"Charming. Yes, that's what jumped out at me. Trouble in paradise."

"It didn't last long. Mama squashed James's request flat and he was immediately sent off to England.

She must have really been pissed off because she also disinherited him."

"Over that clause," Kendra murmured. "It must have been important to her..."

"Or her son might have been a total jerk she'd been putting up with for far too long anyway."

"Also possible. I've got to hang up, Olivia. I need to do some more research here. I think I remember another gossip book here written by Helena Sanders. I'll call you back if I need you."

"Just use me and toss me away."

"Sorry, I think we just got very, very lucky."

"Is Lynch there now?"

"Yes, he just got in and he's being Lynch down with the guards at the gates."

"And you're excited and in a hurry and I'm keeping you. I want to *be* there, dammit." Then she said quickly, "Forget it, call me when you can. But you'd better take care of my dog."

"I will. And he'll take care of me."

"Of course he will. He has more sense than you. Bye."

She cut the connection.

And Kendra went back to the shelves and rifled quickly through the books to find what else the very gossipy Helena Sanders had to reveal about the Woodwards.

CHAPTER
17

Kendra spent over an hour going through the books and photographs, but as fascinating as they were, there seemed to be little of relevance to her case. There were many photos of a young James Woodward who spearheaded the construction of the original buildings. Several photos showed him looking at blueprints with a bald, heavyset man with a mustache. The architect, perhaps?

One photo identified him as Alonzo Cortez. Kendra Googled his name and was surprised to see his face on an entire row of photos on the search results page.

There was actually a Wikipedia entry for him and she quickly read it. At the end there were more vintage photos. One of them made her gasp.

"Holy shit," she said aloud.

She sat there staring down at the book in front of her, breathing hard, her cheeks flushed with excitement. It had to be the answer. Why hadn't she seen it before? Suddenly a lot of things were making sense. Right down to the sticky oil on the bottom of Cardona's shoes, she realized.

She picked up the phone. Her hand was shaking as she dialed Lynch. "I've got it," she said the instant he picked up the call. "I was stupid. It was right there before me."

"What was there before you?" he asked. "Juarez? Talk to me."

"I'm trying to talk to you. No, not Juarez. You wanted me to forget about Juarez until you called me and maybe it was a good idea. I'm talking about what was in the deed to the property the Wood-wards turned over to the foundation to create the school. Not much, just a clause that said a certain area in the property couldn't be renovated or used by anyone. But it triggered my curiosity."

"And you decided to pull that trigger."

"I couldn't help it. Particularly since it started a family feud between the matriarch of the family and her son, James, that was so intense he was disinherited." She paused. "And sent him not only out of San Diego, but out of the country to England. Olivia and I agreed he had to have been a very bad boy to receive that degree of punishment, so I decided to check."

"And you found?"

"I had to access a hell of a lot of computer and library records to get his history, but I found out the most from a gossip writer, Helena Sanders."

"Not exactly a reputable source?"

"Be quiet. It made sense to me. James was pretty much the scum of the Earth from the moment he was born. He was spoiled rotten because his sister was born blind and his mother tried to give him everything he wanted to make up for the time she had to spend with her. He flunked out of several universities, became an alcoholic by age twenty, and was also addicted to gambling. Gambling takes money and what he couldn't steal from his family coffers, he earned running drugs across the border."

"Ahh, the plot thickens."

"But then he appeared to suddenly have a lot of money, a very steady income." She drew a deep breath and went for it. "So I was wondering if he'd started to transfer those drugs in another way."

"Well, their estate was right on the water."

"That's what I thought, but that stretch of coastline has always been heavily patrolled. I think he found a better way. When these original buildings were being constructed, he worked with a man named Alonzo Cortez. He had an unusual specialty. Tunnels."

He gave a low whistle. "Tunnels? As in all the way from Mexico?"

"We're not all that far as the crow flies."

"Or the gopher digs."

"Yes, smuggling tunnels have been built from as early as 1912, and though they didn't become really sophisticated until later in the century, they were always in high demand. Drug tunnels stretching even eighty or ninety miles weren't uncommon. A tunnel on this property would be less than half that." She paused. "And Alonzo Cortez was the expert who built them. The Woodward family was ultra-respectable and wealthy, and it would be a perfect cover...if James could get the big drug cartels to pay him for use of his tunnel."

"Indeed, they would," Lynch said thoughtfully.

"And it all could be true, because Mama Wood-ward abruptly decided to move the family from the property to another residence and build a special-needs school with the stipulation written into the deed." She was speaking quickly, trying to convince him. "As for the tunnel, who knows? She might have had it sealed up or maybe had a stick of dynamite thrown into it so that no one could ever use it for that purpose again. Because she seems to have been very smart and probably thought that as long as it existed, James would find a way to get what he wanted."

"And she finally sent him to England so that he could no longer stain the family honor?"

"Don't make fun. It could be true. It makes a good story."

"I'm not making fun of you. I'm impressed. I'm just trying to develop the story a little further." He paused. "And Dietrich was from Elsworth, U.K., a short distance from Cambridge. He could have been a relative of James or some other member of the Woodward family. Or maybe someone who just heard the story in the local pub? If James was an alcoholic, he might have done a lot of bragging. Whatever. It might have intrigued Dietrich enough that he considered coming down here to see if there still was a tunnel and what his options were. To use it to transport drugs . . . or to extract Delgado, which would earn him a hell of a lot more money."

"Delgado," Kendra said definitely. "And Dietrich did his research and found the tunnel, but when he decided that he wanted to cut Cardona out of the deal, everything started to go wrong. There was no way he wanted to kill him on the property. I'm betting he had no choice. Maybe Cardona found out what he was doing and showed up here and confronted him. Or maybe they were partners and he got greedy. Dietrich killed him and then had to make it look like a drug deal gone bad. All he could do was hope we believed that Mr. Kim's and Elaine's deaths may have happened because they'd stumbled on cartel business."

He was silent. "You're sounding very certain, Kendra."

"I am certain. He *found* the tunnel." She couldn't keep the excitement out of her voice. "Because I found it, too. Cortez hid the entrances to all his tunnels, but he always carved a symbol on a tree or wall nearby. I saw a picture of one of his tunnel entrances in Texas. A nearby tree had a very familiar carving. It was a four-leaf clover."

"So?"

"There's one just like it carved on Big Rock here on campus. I've felt it there since I was a little girl. When I found out what it was, I thought someone must have carved it there because they were wishing us good luck." She jumped to her feet. "The tunnel is *there* somewhere, Lynch. I know it. Well, I almost know it. Even if it had been dynamited or walled over, he could have drilled through and opened it up by himself. But it would have taken time, and he couldn't work in daylight." She was heading for the door. "But we'll know for sure after we go up there and take a look. I'm on my way. I'll meet you at Lookout Point. We can go on to Big Rock together."

"No. Stay where you are, Kendra. I can be back at the library in fifteen minutes."

"It will be quicker if I meet you. I don't want to wait. Because I think this may change everything, Lynch. I'll take Harley and Agent Roberts and you'll probably be at Lookout Point before I am." She disconnected and grabbed the leash. She ran for the door. "Harley, come!"

Harley barked ecstatically as he jumped up, followed her, and then streaked past her as he ran out into the driveway.

Agent Roberts backed away warily as he caught sight of Kendra and then watched Harley leaping toward him, then galloping off across the campus. "Is there a problem, Dr. Michaels?"

So much for leashing Harley, she thought ruefully. He had caught the excitement that was zinging through her and thought it was playtime. Well, maybe it was. She might know very soon. "No, there may be a solution, Roberts. I need to check something. Come with me!" She turned and ran toward the cliff.

———◆———

Agent Roberts aimed his flashlight into the brush. "We're going in *there*?"

Kendra stepped ahead of him on the almost-imperceptible pathway. "It's easier than it looks. I could do it blindfolded. Literally."

She high-stepped over a large clump of brush. "Be careful, that's actually a rock."

"You *do* know your way around here."

"Just like almost every other kid who's ever gone to this school. Duck!"

Roberts lowered his head just in time to avoid a low-hanging branch. "Thanks."

"That's a little lower than it used to be. This way." She led Roberts and Harley to the left as the path started a slow incline. Harley bounded ahead a few yards but always kept a watchful eye back to make sure Kendra was still within sight.

Roberts shone the flashlight around to get his bearings. "Are you sure this is the right way?"

"Positive. It's the fastest way to Lookout Point where I'm supposed to meet Lynch. And the safest, believe it or not."

"I'll take your word for it."

"We should be at Lookout Point in about ten minutes. And it won't be—"

Harley had stopped.

Something was wrong.

Kendra stopped short. "Harley?"

The dog sniffed the air and looked around in every direction. His ears folded back and his tail lowered.

"What is it?" Roberts asked.

Kendra knelt beside Harley. "What's wrong? What's bothering you, boy?"

Harley let out a low growl. He was tearing around in a circle, excited, growling, sniffing.

Kendra lifted her head, listening, every sense alert. *What the hell are you picking up, Harley . . . ?*

Then the dog sprinted into the brush, well off their path.

"Harley!"

Harley was gone.

Roberts aimed his flashlight into the dense foliage where the dog had disappeared. "Should we go after him?"

"We'd never catch him." She cocked her head, still hearing the crackling sounds of Harley moving through the dense brush. "But remember this spot. We'll come back with Lynch and the others if Harley doesn't show up."

"Are you sure?"

She wasn't sure of anything right now. She wanted to be out there with Harley, tracking down whatever had bothered him.

Focus. Stay on target.

"Yes. Let's stick to the plan."

She turned back toward the main path and pushed on. It had become more overgrown than she remembered. Did the current generation of students even use it anymore? Maybe the administrators had finally won their battle to keep the area off limits.

They emerged from the brush into a small clearing. "How much farther?" Roberts asked.

"Maybe five minutes to Lookout Point. If we hurry, maybe we can—"

Two sharp whistles cut through the air.

Roberts inhaled sharply and jerked. He fell to his knees and then tumbled to the ground.

"Roberts!" Kendra gasped.

"Down—" His eyes were fixed on Kendra. His flashlight dropped from his hand. "Get—down." He rolled over onto his back, his breath catching in a tortured rasping sound.

The beam from his flashlight pierced the darkness where he lay, and then she saw the blood.

Blood everywhere. On his hands, his neck, and spreading across his crisp white shirt...

God, no.

"Hands where I can see them, Kendra."

She froze. She recognized Dietrich's British accent immediately. She slowly raised her hands, still not facing him.

"Hand me his gun. And yours."

She didn't move, trying to think. Her hand tightened on the flashlight in her hand. "Okay." Then she shrugged off her jacket and balled it up.

"What the hell are you doing?" Dietrich asked harshly.

"Trying to give him a chance, you son of a bitch. You can see I'm not trying to go for a weapon."

"Waste of time. He's a dead man anyway. The guns. Carefully."

She unsnapped Roberts's shoulder holster and pulled out his automatic with her thumb and forefinger. The agent desperately shook his head no.

"I have to." She tossed the gun behind her, then reached into her jacket for her own weapon and tossed it.

"Very good," Dietrich said. "Now slowly turn around."

"In a minute."

"Don't be stupid, Kendra."

"In a minute," she repeated as she knelt beside Roberts. "You're not going to kill me until you absolutely have to or you would have done it already." She pressed her balled-up jacket over the agent's bleeding torso. "Hold this against the wound, Roberts."

Roberts did as she ordered, a move that caused him to grimace in pain.

But as he did it, he revealed a switchblade knife that he'd managed to take out of his pocket when he'd been writhing on the ground the moment before.

Kendra inhaled sharply, quickly slipping the knife into her sleeve as she tucked the jacket more closely on the wound.

Then she turned to face Dietrich. He had just kicked their guns into the brush, and he held his own firearm leveled at her chest. He was too far away from her for her to use that knife, she realized immediately. The minute she made a movement toward him, he'd pull that trigger. He *wanted* to pull it. She could see the anticipation in his expression. But he hadn't pulled it. Why? The beam of her flashlight picked up the highlights in his hair and eyebrows, giving him an almost ethereal appearance. His nose had been recently broken, and his cheeks were still bruised from his encounter with Jessie. But now she could also see that besides the anticipation, there was excitement. He was enjoying this.

"What a pleasant surprise," he said. "This is scheduled to be a very busy night and I was afraid I'd have to make a special trip back to take care of you." His lips curled. "You were going somewhere in a hurry. Should I guess where?"

"Nowhere special. Just up the hill to meet half of the local FBI field office. And about twenty of San Diego's finest. Care to join me?"

"You may be remarkable at many things, Kendra, but lying isn't one of them. I know there are only a few FBI personnel left here. I have more than enough support to take them out."

"For your scheme to smuggle Delgado out of Mexico and into Russia? This was just going to be the way station, wasn't it?"

Dietrich was trying to be cool but she could see her knowledge rattled him. A slight intake of breath, shifting in place, darting of his eyes...

Push him a little more. "We all know what you're doing here," she continued. "And we found out about the old tunnel. You think you're the only one who knows about that?"

He was silent. "Not now evidently. But it must be a fairly recent discovery or this place would be crawling with FBI. I believe I'm safe. It doesn't matter what you know now."

"But you relied on no one knowing before. Or at least you hoped. That needed to stay a secret for any of this to work. *Something* made you murder Mr. Kim and Elaine." She added bitterly, "You didn't expect that you'd run across two people who cared so much about this place and the children here that they wouldn't give up until they knew it was safe. They were onto you, weren't they? It's logical that you'd have to have a drill or some special equipment to break the seal on the tunnel. What Elaine must have seen was you moving it from the shore to take it to Big Rock. When you found out that they knew, you couldn't afford to let them live."

He shrugged. "Collateral damage. Believe me, it's nothing I planned or even wanted to do. Everything was going wrong. I was trying to keep from killing that bitch to avoid attracting attention. Even her damn dog was a problem. Once he heard me in the trees on the cliff and went crazy after me, I just barely got away. Then I had to worry about whether shooting him would cause more of a problem than just trying to avoid him and had to do even more research." He shrugged. "But by then it was too late to matter. I knew she'd have to be taken out anyway. But I was cursing her, because her death made my job much more difficult."

"Your job," she repeated. "Raul Delgado. A man like that with a ten-million-dollar bounty on his head. He must be willing to pay several times that for a fail-safe path into a new life."

"Not just for him. His family, his money, and his product. Quite a large undertaking," he said smugly. "One only I could succeed in providing him."

Kendra stared at him. The asshole was bragging. He was proud of himself. Disgusting, but not unusual for this brand of scumbag. He was getting off on letting her see what a big man he was.

Use it. Keep him talking. It might be the only way to keep Roberts and her alive until Lynch had a chance to find them. Or she could find a way to get close enough to him to use that switchblade.

"But why Elaine's ex-husband, Kit Randolph? What threat could he possibly have been to you?"

"He was still close to his ex-wife, so after we suspected she'd seen something, we monitored her communications. We were smart to do it because after Kim's death, she reached out to Randolph and was trying to set up a meeting. We thought we'd taken care of the bitch before she could tell him anything, but then we found out he was nosing around her apartment and even took her camera and keys." He shrugged. "I couldn't take a chance with him."

"Another senseless murder."

"If you knew anything about me, you'd know I don't do anything that doesn't make sense. This was too gigantic a deal not to take out insurance if necessary." He gestured to Roberts lying on the ground. "And you're the one who caused this man's death."

She looked down at Roberts. His eyes were closed, but he was conscious, still pressing her jacket against his wound. *Live, Roberts. You gave us both a chance. Now stay with me.*

And where are you, Lynch? She knew that only a few minutes had passed, but it seemed forever. Stall. Keep Dietrich talking. Probably the only reason she was still alive was that he wanted to show her how clever he was and how he had outsmarted her.

"And it made sense for you to kill your partners?" She turned back to him. "No honor among thieves?"

"What are you talking about?"

"It all started to unravel after I discovered you and Hayes on the rooftop of that building, right after you killed Kit Randolph. You knew we'd identified Hayes. You couldn't risk him getting caught and spilling your whole scheme. So you killed him in that hotel. Was that your local staging area? A fleabag hotel with no security cameras, where no one notices anyone coming or going?"

Dietrich smiled. "You've given this some thought."

"As did you. You were taunting me with that fake bomb in my car in the manner of some serial killers I've faced off against. You were still desperately hoping that might keep the law from thinking those killings were anything more than the work of a random psychopath."

"Isn't that what you thought?"

"For a nanosecond, maybe. Pro tip: Serial killers almost always work alone, and they don't deal with hired thugs to carry out their plans."

"Very good, Kendra."

"It's like a prism. When the last lens clicks into place, suddenly everything becomes very clear. Like why Cardona had that sticky oil on the bottom of his shoes. I didn't recognize it at the time, but now I guess it was some kind of industrial oil that could be used to run rock drills or jackhammers. He was helping you reopen the tunnel. He wasn't running drugs through the campus at all, was he?"

Dietrich smiled. "Excellent. You've exceeded my every expectation."

"You killed him, but it couldn't have been planned ahead of time. Another dead body on campus and more attention was the last thing you wanted. So you were hoping we would follow the drug angle, since that's how Cardona made his living."

Dietrich shrugged. "It was him or me. It certainly wasn't going to be me, since I was the driving force behind the extraction. He started putting pressure on me for a bigger share when he realized how much money was going to be made on this operation. He shouldn't have been so greedy."

"I think you would have killed him anyway. You would have just waited for the timing to be more convenient."

He chuckled. "You're probably quite right. That prism of yours is working at top form. Too bad that last lens didn't click in for you a bit earlier. When you could have actually done something about it."

"Who says it didn't?"

"Because you're out here alone in the dark and soon I'm going to be on my way to a place where no one will be able to touch me, with millions in my bank account."

Her phone rang.

"Maybe not quite alone," Dietrich said softly. "Lynch is going to be disappointed when you don't answer."

And she was frantically disappointed she couldn't answer Lynch, but she couldn't let Dietrich see it. "He won't be disappointed he's missing all this bull-shit you're giving me. You sound very self-satisfied about your future prospects." She paused. "That's probably because you're going to go with Delgado to Russia." She was putting it all together. "At first, I thought you'd bought the Moscow residence for him, but you decided that after extracting him it might be a good idea for you to retire to a place that couldn't extradite you. It was going to be very hot for you after you pulled this job. That's why you didn't give a damn if you incriminated yourself when you phoned me."

"How could I resist indulging myself when you were so sure you'd beaten me?" he asked mock-ingly. "Delgado will have a much more luxurious palace, but I'll have my own place in his hierarchy. So far he's admired my ingenuity. I'll seal the deal tonight."

"Because you set up a scheme to hoodwink any law-enforcement agency or drug cartel that was after Delgado by staging a departure out of Juarez?"

"Exactly. It obviously fooled you, didn't it? Or you wouldn't be strolling out here on the grounds thinking I was in Juarez and you'd be safe from me."

" 'Stroll' isn't exactly the word. I had a purpose. Tell me, did Delgado give you permission to use the CIA to kill off his men in that hangar to make it look authentic when they rushed it?"

He laughed. "Delgado realizes some sacrifices have to be made for the greater good. He had to be selective, so he brought only his most talented people with him here to make sure that he'd be well protected on his journey. At the moment, there are several exceptionally lethal enforcers moving around here ready to take care of any agents Metcalf left on guard." He was still smiling. "As well as your friend Lynch. Are you waiting for him to come and rescue you? He won't be here. I gave Delgado's men his photo and told them how pleased their boss will be if they take him out."

Chill iced through her at his words. *Don't believe it.* Lynch was too smart, too good. Dietrich was just trying to frighten her. So stop thinking about rescue and try to find a way to take him down herself. "Delgado is clearly as much a dirtbag as you. And where is this great man?" she asked. "Still cowering down in that tunnel?"

"No, we're done with the tunnel. I brought Delgado and his men through the tunnel to Big Rock almost an hour ago. He's waiting back there on the cliff." He nodded toward the trees. "My decision. I'm in control of everything from now on. He has to be kept safe."

There was a hint of impatience in his voice that she'd asked that question. He was not going to let her stall for much longer. He'd almost had enough of stoking his own ego. She had to make a move.

But to do it she had to get closer.

Or get him to come closer.

Kendra let Roberts's knife fall from her sleeve into her cupped hand. Dietrich was still at least seven feet from her, out of range for a quick lunge with the blade.

"Waiting?" she repeated scornfully. "For Delgado's goons to clear his path through those campus exits? They're blocked by FBI agents who are trained experts in what they do, Dietrich. If Delgado's guys screw up, how do you think you're going to get Delgado away from here?"

He smiled and glanced upward. "Why don't you tell me, Kendra? You have such excellent hearing. I'm sure it's close and I insisted it be right on time."

She stiffened. She *did* hear it. The hum of a distant rotor.

Kendra tilted her head. It appeared to be coming from the east. "A helicopter."

"Just the first leg of our journey tonight. Trust me, no one will be able to track us after we lift off."

"More innovative than I thought. I was told you were unpredictable. Everyone would assume you'd use the sea as an escape route since it's so convenient. Was Delgado pleased with you when you suggested the helicopter?"

"Of course." Dietrich's voice was smug again. "But then he's clever enough to realize he's hired the very best."

"Really? Clever? Then I believe I have to see this paragon." She swiftly swung the beam of her flashlight toward the man standing in the shadows of the trees on the hill. She only caught a glimpse of a man with dark hair and dark eyes who straightened with savage anger as the light illuminated his features before Dietrich leaped toward her and knocked the flashlight from her hand.

"Bitch!" And then his hand lashed out and struck her brutally across her cheek, knocking her down. "What are you trying to do?"

"See your lord and master." She sat up and then got to her knees. He was standing over her and was definitely close enough now. "I was not impressed."

"Delgado doesn't like surprises. I'll hear about this." He raised his gun. "Perhaps this will impress you. I believe it's time to put an end—"

Kendra leaped up from her knees as far as she could reach and plunged the knife into Dietrich's hip. He yelled out, cursing, as he backed away from her. She scrambled to her feet desperately trying to strike another blow.

But he hadn't dropped his gun and he was aiming it at her.

Harley burst from the bushes and sank his teeth deep into Dietrich's arm!

Dietrich screamed and tried to pull free. His arm was spurting blood, the skin ripping under the force of Harley's strong teeth. The dog was now thrashing his arm back and forth, causing the gun to wave crazily in the air.

The gun went off twice, muffled by its silencer.

Kendra lunged forward and her knife stabbed down into the back of Dietrich's hand. He screamed again and dropped the gun. But as Kendra dove for it, Dietrich slid out of his jacket—and Harley's grip—and bolted into the brush.

Harley thrashed the jacket a moment longer, then looked up at Kendra with those big, brown-blue eyes as if asking for approval.

She picked up Dietrich's gun and knelt down beside Harley. "Wow," she said breathlessly. "*Good *boy* doesn't seem like enough." Kendra rubbed the soft skin behind Harley's ears. "Just in the nick of time. I think you learned a lot more about K-9 tactics than anyone thought."

But Harley was jumping to his feet and running over to where Roberts was lying. He sat down beside him and turned back to Kendra as if demanding something of her.

"I'm coming. I'm right behind you." She fell to her knees beside Roberts and gently removed the jacket pad. He was conscious, and she saw to her relief that the wound didn't seem as bad as she'd first thought. "I think the bleeding's stopped, Roberts." She took out her phone. "Hang in there. We're going to get you help right away. As you can see, my friend Harley is nagging me to get it done."

"Some dog you got there," Roberts whispered as Harley nestled his head comfortingly on his hand.

The helicopter rotors grew louder. Time was running out, Kendra realized. Dietrich had to be taking Delgado down to meet it by now. Damn!

She quickly voice-dialed Lynch.

He answered immediately. "Where in the hell are you? I've been calling you. You said you'd be here."

"Couldn't answer you. Change of plan. We don't have to check Big Rock for a tunnel. Dietrich is here. So is Delgado. They used it to get here."

"What? Where?"

"Do you hear the helicopter?"

He paused. "Holy shit."

"Yeah. Follow it. They're making their break."

She could see the blue lights of the helicopter. "And send for a paramedic unit right now. Roberts has been shot. I don't think it's too bad, but we can't take a chance."

"What?" Lynch's voice was suddenly harsh. "Are you okay?"

"Yes, I'll tell you about it later. The helicopter. We have to stop the helicopter. I just have to figure out where he'll land so I can tell you."

Roberts reached out and touched the phone. "You're not going to do that sitting here holding my hand. Go help Metcalf and Lynch. Get that son of a bitch who put this bullet in me. What are you waiting for? You just told Lynch you thought I'd be okay."

She looked at him uncertainly.

He smiled faintly. "I'd never live it down if this job was botched because of me. Get out of here!"

Kendra spun around and ran down the overgrown path. Harley was at her heels. "Lynch, I'm on my way. Have the paramedics ping Roberts's phone for an exact location."

"Right. On your way where?"

She thought for a moment, trying to imagine a likely path for a southbound tunnel. "Go to the athletic field. Near where Ronald Kim's body was found."

"Are you sure?"

"No. It's just what makes the most sense to me right now. If they take off in that helicopter, we may never find them. Be careful. From what Dietrich said they'll probably have half a dozen thugs with guns."

"We have our own thugs with guns. I'd bet on ours. And we'll send for backup."

"And I have my own backup. Harley's with me."

"I'd rather rely on the backup Metcalf will send," Lynch said dryly.

"I wouldn't." Kendra looked down at Harley, who was now half a stride ahead, looking protective and alert, the perfect, all-business guide dog. She remembered his fierceness, which had transformed in seconds to gentleness when his task was over and he'd run back to watch over the wounded Roberts. "Do I have a tale for you..."

The helicopter grew louder. Trees and bushes swayed as it roared overhead.

"Lynch, I'm almost there. They're definitely headed for the athletic field."

"We're a minute behind you. Don't do anything until we get there. Do you hear me?"

"I'll meet you on the east side of the field, close to the fence."

"Do you understand me, Kendra? Do *not* engage."

She cut the connection and crouched low on the hill overlooking the athletic field. The helicopter, which Kendra could now see was a large military-style transport vehicle, was hovering over the covered pool house. A large searchlight mounted to its underside played over the surrounding area.

But where in the hell was Dietrich and his cargo?

She'd like to believe the bastard was under a bush bleeding out from the wounds Harley had given him, but that was too much to hope for.

No, she was sure he was headed this way.

Suddenly four men emerged from the trees and ran onto the athletic field.

Dietrich? Kendra squinted. Not yet. It had to be Delgado's goons, the ones Dietrich had told her about. They were carrying automatic weapons. Lightweight Uzis, or something similar. The men surrounded the helicopter, facing out and holding their weapons in front of them.

Kendra ducked and pulled Harley down next to her. She was still holding Dietrich's handgun, but she knew one shot would only bring a barrage of bullets from those high-capacity magazines. And unless the FBI agents happened to be carrying assault rifles, they wouldn't fare any better.

The helicopter slowly descended and touched down on the concrete pad next to the pool house. The rotors were deafening.

Dietrich emerged from the trees with Delgado, sheltering him with his body, keeping their heads low as they sprinted across the athletic field.

The moment Harley saw Dietrich, he gave a menacing growl.

"Quiet, Harley," Kendra muttered, although there was little chance anyone would hear him over the helicopter engine.

The helicopter's searchlight suddenly swung around to the hillside behind Kendra.

What in the hell—?

Kendra turned. Lynch, Metcalf, and two of the other FBI agents were caught in the beam.

No!

Dietrich's men opened fire, riddling the hillside with their artillery.

One of the FBI agents went down as the other scrambled for cover behind the bushes.

She watched as Lynch popped up and squeezed off two quick shots.

BLAM! BLAM!

Two of Delgado's men dropped to the ground.

Dietrich and Delgado crossed behind the helicopter, shielded from Lynch and the FBI agents. The remaining two gunmen retreated toward the copter's side hatch.

Lynch ran down the hill and joined Kendra. "Are you all right?"

She was still watching the helicopter. Her fists clenched. "They're getting away!"

"Metcalf's already called it in. They won't get far."

"They won't need to. Dietrich's already planned for that."

"What are you talking about?"

"He's planned for everything. You told me he's a damn extractor."

Kendra looked down at the helicopter, the athletic field, the pool house...

"But maybe..." she murmured. "I might have an idea."

Lynch ejected his ammo cartridge and popped it back in. "I'm not going to like this, am I?"

"Cover me."

"Where in the hell are you going?"

She held Harley's head in her hands. "Harley, stay."

Harley sat and whimpered.

She turned back to Lynch. "There isn't much time. Draw their fire if you have to."

"Kendra..."

"It will be okay...I think." She crouched and moved down the hill toward the athletic field. She jumped the chain-link fence and rolled onto the ground.

They hadn't seen her.

BLAM! BLAM! BLAM!

They were firing at the hillside again.

The rotor's pitch increased. Everyone was aboard and they were about to take off.

Shit!

Kendra ran for the control panel box she'd seen used just a few days before at the aquatic center. She pulled on the metal lid. Locked.

She squinted to filter the dirt flying from the helicopter's rotors. Her hair flew up, over and around her face.

She pointed Dietrich's gun at the control panel lock and pulled the trigger.

BLAM!

She pulled on the lid. Still locked.

She kicked the panel once, twice, three times...

Success! The lid flew open.

She peered inside, gripped the bright red lever, and pulled. The ground vibrated beneath her feet.

It was working!

She turned to see that the hydraulic pool house cover was swiveling away from the pool.

And directly toward the helicopter.

She bolted back toward the hillside.

The copter rotors throttled even higher and she could hear shouted curses inside the open compartment. They'd seen the pool shell heading toward them.

The helicopter lurched upward, but it was too late. The structure hit the tail rotor.

Sparks flew, and the helicopter's tail swung crazily.
BLAM! BLAM!

Two more shots from the hill, probably from
Lynch's gun.

Another gunman tumbled from the open helicopter hatch.

Definitely Lynch's work, she thought.

The copter spun wildly as the pilot tried to gain
altitude. But it suddenly veered sharply to the left.

BOOM!

The helicopter struck the hillside with a force
that seemed to shake the night. It caught fire and
rolled back down onto the athletic field.

Kendra ran down to the field to join Lynch,
Harley, and the FBI agents who were watching the
helicopter consumed by the fire.

"Interesting solution," Lynch murmured.

Kendra couldn't take her gaze from the burning
helicopter. She could hear *screams*. The flames were
devouring Delgado and all those people... "It was
all I could think to do..."

Lynch and the FBI agents suddenly raised their
weapons toward the helicopter.

A figure was upright and walking through the blaze.

Dietrich, Kendra realized. He was on fire, stumbling forward, one foot at a time. He emerged from
the inferno and stopped, almost as if regarding them
in bewilderment for one long, last moment.

He fell face-forward onto the lawn, burning blue with engine fuel.

Kendra made a sound deep in her throat and then was turning, running across the field. She didn't stop until she was halfway to the gates. Then she dropped down on the grass, holding her knees and rocking back and forth.

"Kendra." Lynch sat down beside her. "They were monsters."

"Do you think I don't know that? They murdered Elaine and Mr. Kim and heaven knows how many other good people. But it doesn't make any difference, I'm the one who killed those particular monsters. I did it with my 'interesting solution.' And death is always terrible."

"Yes, it is." He was pulling her gently into his arms. "Are you going to be all right?"

"Yes." She buried her head in his shoulder for an instant. "I just had to take a minute. Thanks for putting up with me." She pushed him away and got to her feet. The vision of that moment before the helicopter had blown might stay with her for the rest of her life. She forced herself to lift her head to look back at the burning inferno that was still shooting flames into the sky. "They're all ... dead?"

He nodded. "There wasn't a chance of getting anyone out." He smiled faintly. "And no one but you would have made the attempt anyway. Every one of those guys would have put a bullet in you if they'd gotten the opportunity." His smile vanished. "Maybe they did try to do that. How do I know? I don't like working blind. I still don't know what happened to you out there earlier tonight. Tell me."

"Nothing good except the ending and I'm not sure about that." She was hearing sirens. "Oh, great, that must be the fire department. They need to put out that fire before it spreads to the buildings here."

And she was suddenly aware that Harley was standing a few yards away and barking at her. "I hear you, Harley. Just a minute." She saw several FBI vehicles streaming through the gates. "Griffin. You'll need to talk to him, Lynch. We can catch up later."

"Now," he said, through set teeth.

"I can't." She broke away from him and was running across the field after Harley. "Because Harley's right, we've got to go check on Roberts..."

CHAPTER
18

Kendra saw Olivia the minute she turned away as the ambulance with Agent Roberts pulled out of the driveway. "What are you doing here?" Then she saw her expression. "It's okay, Olivia. Everything's all right. Dietrich's dead, and they say that Agent Roberts is going to be okay."

"What am I doing here? It didn't occur to you that I might be worried about someone besides Agent Roberts?"

Kendra smiled teasingly. "And Harley is okay, too. He was a hero. You would have been proud."

"I'm always proud of him, except when I'm not." She walked over to Kendra and went into her arms. "You should have let me stay." Her voice was muffled against Kendra's shoulder. "It was a mistake. I could have talked some sense into you."

"I didn't know it was a mistake at the time. And it turned out all right, except for Roberts." She held her close. "And I always let you run too many risks for me anyway. When I get a chance to not do it, I grab at it."

"It could have been a disaster."

"But it wasn't." Kendra pushed her away and smiled at her. "And now we've put the bad guys down and saved the school we both love. It's all good, Olivia."

"Is it? We'll see." She grimaced. "At least, you did one thing right. You didn't let them hurt my dog."

"I can't take the credit. He was phenomenal. *Your* dog helped save the day." She tilted her head. "And do you realize these days you always refer to him as your dog?"

"Of course I do." She bent down and caressed Harley's head. "But it's not because you conned me into accepting him as a service dog. I'd get along just fine without him. It's just that I realized no one else is capable of training and taking care of him. He's an extraordinary dog and it takes an extraordinary person to bring out his fine points. So we'll hang out together unless he runs into someone else who can do it better than I can."

"That sounds like a great idea," Kendra said solemnly. "Does that mean I don't have to take care of him at night any longer?"

"You didn't do a great job anyway. He was beginning to have a discipline problem."

"I won't even address that charge." She moved toward her car. "But in gratitude for sparing me, I'll take the two of you back to your condo and let you bad-mouth me to Jessie." She gazed at the burning embers of the helicopter lighting Lynch's face as he talked to Griffin while they walked toward the administration building. Listening. Intent. Absorbed. She paused for a moment, feeling a little lonely that she wasn't there with him after all they'd gone through together. What foolishness. She opened the driver's door. "It's all good," she repeated. "But now I'm very tired and all I want is sleep. Everything else can wait until tomorrow. I'm just glad it's all over . . ."

———◆———

ALLISON'S OFFICE
NEXT DAY

"I came to return your books." Kendra handed Allison the four volumes she'd borrowed. "They came in very handy, as you've probably heard."

"Everyone on the planet has heard," Allison said dryly. "The story's been blasting from every TV in the civilized world." She added sourly, "Unfortunately."

"I agree. The reporters have been all over the property and there wasn't anyone here to stop them but the FBI." Kendra made a face. "And they even tried to take their photos, too. I'm glad you're back to take control."

"I'm not," Allison said curtly. "I'm just here to pack up my belongings and bring the accountants up here to settle any wage disputes the employees might have for their termination."

"Termination?" Kendra's eyes widened. "You're closing down? But Dietrich's been killed. That tunnel will be sealed again. Everything can go back to normal now."

"I'm not closing it. Maxine Rydell has withdrawn her support and that means she's closing it. We won't be able to pay the bills after the next thirty days."

"Then talk her out of it," Kendra said desperately. "Persuade her how wrong that would be for the kids."

"I tried, but she wouldn't listen."

"Then go out and get other supporters."

"That all sounds so easy," Allison said wearily. "We're dealing in charity here, Kendra. You can't be that naive. Or maybe you can, you've always been too idealistic." She leaned back in her chair. "I can't really blame her for withdrawing her support. Donors always want their dollars to be spent on crystal-clean projects of which they can be proud. There have been murders and thefts and even hints of drug use here at Woodward during the last weeks. And last night was pure chaos. Any money contributed here would be considered tainted. It would be a joke to expect anyone to contribute." She added bitterly, "And we would be the joke if we asked them."

"It's no joke," Kendra said fiercely. "How can you say that? It's no joke to those kids. No one knows better than you how much they were given and how much would be taken away if we let them be cheated like this. That son of a bitch, Dietrich, would win if we let that happen."

"Do you think I want it to happen?" Allison asked. "I just don't know how to stop it. I'll try and keep on trying, but it's not going to do any good."

"Yes, it will. Don't say that. We just have to figure out how to do it. Just give me a little time and I'll..." She had to stop a moment as her voice broke. "You just stall and don't close Woodward down yet. Will you do that for me?"

Allison nodded and said gently, "But it's not going to do any good. You'll have to face reality soon, Kendra."

"No, I won't. Because that reality hurts too much for too many people, We'll just have to change the reality." She turned and almost ran into Lynch at the door. "Did you hear that?" Her voice was shaking. "They're shutting it down and it will probably be permanently if they can't get the damn money."

"I heard," he said gently as he drew her out of the office. He dabbed at the tears running down her cheeks. "I know it hurts. I probably have enough cash to keep the place going for a little while until you think of something permanent."

"Allison thinks I won't be able to do that," she said jerkily.

"Then Allison doesn't know you." He kissed her cheek. "Just calm down and let the pain go away and then it will come to you." He nudged her toward his Lamborghini in the driveway. "Come on, we'll go for a drive."

"You might have to give up this Lamborghini if I take you up on that offer to fund the school for a while," she said unevenly as he closed her passenger door.

"That would hurt very much, but I'd survive. But please start thinking hard and fast to save me."

She wiped her eyes. "It was a splendid offer, but we really need steady funding in the billionaire category."

"Ah, rejected again. Then just lean back and close your eyes and dream of billionaires..."

———◆———

It was only twenty minutes later that Kendra sat up straight in the seat and said, "You can take me back to the academy now. I've got to apologize to Allison for falling apart on her. I was just hoping so much that everything would go well for the kids that I convinced myself it was going to happen." She added passionately, "And it *will* happen, but I shouldn't have gotten so emotional about it with Allison."

"I like you emotional." He reached out and covered her hand with his own. "I just don't like you hurting. So I'd appreciate it if you'd find a way to save the day without you going through the trauma."

"Allison said I can't save the day, that I'm too idealistic, and I don't think about donors or charities the way most people do."

"She's right, you don't think of anything the way most people do. Every one of your senses is more alive and you see and hear everything more sharply and intensely, and it translates to those emotions that you're going to apologize to Allison for having. But that's not bad. It would be nice if we could all see and experience everything the way you do."

"Don't be ridiculous. I've always said that anyone can do what I do if they'd just concentrate and pay attention. But they have to make the effort, I can't lead them down the path, dammit." They were driving back through the gates of Woodward Academy, and she gestured to the magnificent scenery surrounding them. "And who wouldn't want to do it, to see everything, to feel everything with every ounce of the senses God gave them. Just look at what—" She broke off as she saw another TV van parked in front of the administration office. "Another vulture zeroing in on Allison," she said bitterly. "I shouldn't have run out and left her to—" She stopped and inhaled sharply. "Vulture."

"What?" Lynch asked.

"That's all wrong." She gestured to the administration building "Park. Get me inside. I have to talk to Allison."

His eyes were on her face, and he suddenly smiled. "I believe you do." The next moment he'd drawn up in front of the building, jumped out, and was shouldering the reporters aside to get her to the front door.

Allison unlocked and threw open the door as soon as they reached it. "You should have waited until the TV trucks left."

"No, I shouldn't," Kendra said. "I should never have left." She was pulling the blinds down to allow them a modicum of privacy. "There's too much to do."

"What are you talking about?"

Lynch dropped down in a chair. "Yes, what are you talking about, Kendra?"

"Vultures," Kendra said. "I've never liked the media because they always got in my way and seemed to go for the most sensational stories no matter how ugly they are. Oh, I know they're only doing their jobs and trying to earn a living. They're probably just obeying orders and giving their editors what they want. But what I've been seeing here is that they've been taking the ugliness and spreading it because they think that's what people want to see." She leaned toward Allison. "And you told me that's exactly what any donor would *not* want to see. They'd be afraid they'd be associated with all the ugliness Dietrich brought here."

"I'm glad you realized that I'm right."

"No, it just made me realize that we have to change the narrative." She grimaced. "And we need the media to do it. They can't be the vultures, they have to be the white knights. They have to help us make everyone think about the victims and not about Dietrich and the drugs. The heroes and not the horror."

"Victims. You mean Elaine and Mr. Kim?"

"Yes, but we've got to make everyone know that

all those children are also the victims. We've got to show them in the classrooms, tell their individual stories, tell the story of Woodward through the years. Show them the beauty and the peace that Dietrich tried to steal." She was frowning, trying to see farther down the road. "Make people want to swoop down and rescue them. But we'd have to keep the school in the forefront of media attention until that way of thinking became ingrained whenever the name was mentioned. Sort of like St. Jude Hospital or Shriners ... Guest lecturers, celebrities coming to visit—Jessie has lots of Hollywood contacts because of her stunt work. And I could increase my lectures to once a week and so would Olivia."

"No billionaires?" Lynch asked.

"Of course." She grinned at him. "But we'd have to spend time to find just the right billionaire. We don't want anyone who hits and runs."

"I remember you said steady."

"You're mad," Allison said flatly. "Nice pipe dream, Kendra."

"And one you'd like to share. One you *can* share." She leaned her hands on the desk and leaned forward to meet her eyes. "You love this place. It's home to you. It was home to me, too. We can make this happen. It will be difficult as hell and there will be times when I'll scream at you and ask why you ever let me do it."

"I'd like to be there to see that," Lynch said.

"Be quiet or I'll make you volunteer to give lectures on how to bring down a crime family. That should bring in a crowd."

Allison was silent. "Persuade the media black is white? That would be a king-size headache. How would you do it?"

"Start at the top and hope the rest will follow. Give them a chance to tell a story that will make them feel good about themselves as well as the kids." She paused. "But we have to strike fast while the world is paying attention. I thought I'd call *60 Minutes* and see if they'd like to interview me here on the grounds. They've asked me for interviews twice before. But you'd have to get the children and teachers back in class right away. I want the story to be about them, not me. Do you think you could persuade their parents to do it?"

"Perhaps." She thought about it. "Yes."

"Then do it," she said softly. "Don't let all that love and care and hope vanish because Dietrich thought all the world should be dirty like him and tried to make it that way."

"I'm a realist, Kendra. It's been a long time since I believed in fairy tales. This idea is doomed to failure."

"Do it."

Allison looked at her for a moment and shook

her head. Then she suddenly straightened in her chair. "What the hell? You get that interview with *60 Minutes* and I'll do my part. But you'd better not make me go down with this sinking ship, Kendra."

"I won't. 'Cause that would mean all those kids would go down, too. We've just got to keep the faith." She whirled away from her. "You start making your calls in here and I'll go to the library and try to contact *60 Minutes*." She motioned to Lynch to follow her. "It may take a while for me to get through to them." She made a face. "And convince them they still want me."

"They'll still want you." Lynch watched her sit down at a library table and reach for her phone. "Who wouldn't want you? You're incredible."

"No, I'm scared to death. I thought up to the last minute that Allison would kick me out of her office." She met his eyes. "Or that you would chime in and tell me that I'm as crazy as she thought I was. Where's all that cool intellect, Lynch?"

"Doesn't exist around you. We've been together too long, and I know what you can do. Who you are." He smiled. "If this doesn't work, we'll try something else. But I think you're going to actually pull it off."

"I've *got* to pull it off," she said intensely. "Remember when I said that anyone could see what I saw if they concentrated? But I told you they had to do it themselves and I couldn't lead them. Then I realized that I didn't have a choice in this. I have to lead them if they're going to see what I want them to see here. You understand?"

"Of course I understand. But you're going to hate doing this."

"Every minute. But I won't hate the result." She had a sudden thought. "But it's going to take a lot of time. I should probably move the music therapy classes with my students from town to a studio up here for six or eight months. What do you think?"

"I think whatever you do will be magnificent, and I'm just sorry I might not be here to see every second of it." He paused, and then said quietly, "You'll probably be staying late here tonight and you'll have to take a Lyft back to the condo. I have to catch a flight to Paris this afternoon."

She froze, her gaze flying to his face. "Paris?"

"I told you there was always payback, Kendra. I squeezed Laurent very hard and now he wants his pound of flesh."

"I don't like that phrase." She tried to keep her voice steady. "Particularly when it comes from someone in the CIA. A mission? Can't you just trade him information or something?"

"Not this time. He didn't get credit for Delgado

and he's pissed off. Besides, he says I'm special. Of course he's right, but it does have certain drawbacks." He leaned forward and kissed her gently. "It will be fine. You'll be so busy you'll hardly know I'm gone."

Only every minute. Her mind was running wildly as panic set in. "Where? You told me you'd gone to meet with the CIA in Tangi Valley the day before you left Afghanistan."

"You have Afghanistan on the brain. I told you that operation is on hold." He smiled at her from the door. "Try to miss me. Though you'll probably be too busy. After *60 Minutes*, can *48 Hours* be far behind?"

He was gone.

She wanted to run after him, stop him.

But there was never any stopping Lynch.

Damn him and he hadn't actually said that Tangi Valley wasn't the mission.

She drew a deep breath. He would be fine. Lynch was always fine. She had to believe that.

Forget Tangi Valley.

Concentrate.

She had to call *60 Minutes*.

EPILOGUE

Did you find your billionaire?"

Kendra stiffened and forgot to breathe. "You're back." She turned to face Lynch, who was standing in the doorway of her classroom. He was smiling at her, and she wanted to slap him. No, that's not what she wanted to do. That was only the first impulse you felt to punish someone you loved who had deliberately put themselves in danger. Her second impulse was to dive toward him and hold him with all her strength and make sure he was still alive and hadn't gotten any new scars while he'd been gone. "Three months and you just come waltzing back in here as if you'd never left. Yes, I found my billionaire. Zed Nasbeth, Silicon Valley, toughest businessman on the West Coast, but who wants to adopt every kid he runs into on the property. You'd know that if you'd texted me where I could reach you. Would you like to tell me where you've been?"

"No, not possible. You know how the CIA is about their missions. They don't trust anyone, even themselves. Truly paranoid."

"I don't know because I don't hobnob with half the secret agencies and foreign governments in the world." She shrugged. "But I do know I shouldn't have asked you anything about where you were. It just slipped out from pure shock." She paused. "Am I allowed to inquire if it was successful?"

"Yes, it was. I'm back in good standing with Laurent whenever you ask me for any other favors. Can we stop talking about it now? It's done, not important, and a complete waste of time as far as I'm concerned." He was coming toward her. "All I want to do is look at you. There's a flush on your cheeks and a glitter in your eyes, and I think you might have missed me or you wouldn't have made that slip." He gently touched her cheek. "You're much too smart and wary to make any mistakes around me." His fingers moved across her cheekbone. "Because you persist in thinking of me as the enemy."

"Don't be ridiculous." Her cheek was tingling, and she was a little breathless. "You're my friend and my partner. How could you be my enemy? Look at what you did to help me catch Dietrich. And you probably risked your stupid neck on that mission to do payback for those favors from the CIA. We just disagree on—"

He was kissing her.

Yes.

This was what she'd wanted since he'd walked in that door. Her hands slid around his neck and she was pulling him closer. She was kissing him again and again and again.

"You did miss me," he murmured, his hands moving down to her breasts. "Maybe that CIA job wasn't such a waste of time after all."

"Of course I did." She kissed him again. "But it doesn't change anything. It just means I might have moments of weakness when I know you're somewhere risking that stupid neck."

"That's the second time you called my neck stupid. Not kind. I happen to be very fond of it." He was plucking teasingly at her nipples. "Could we go back to your condo and discuss it? I think you'd get all uptight if we went...in-depth...on the subject here at the school."

"You bet I would." She was backing away from him. "Because you're not listening again. It doesn't really change anything, Lynch."

"Except you have moments of weakness. I'll

definitely take that, Kendra. Moments can escalate into hours and days and then I can go for the big time."

"No, you can't."

"Sure I can." He smiled. "All I'll have to do is risk my stupid neck on some worthwhile project and you'd fall right into line."

Her hands clenched into fists at her sides. "Don't you dare."

His smile vanished. "No, I wouldn't. You'd never have to worry about that with me. I'll find another way." He cocked his head. "Come to think of it, Griffin called me when I was flying back from Paris and was telling me about a terrorist case that had been thrown at him by the director. Four scientists killed and technology compromised. He thought you might be interested, but you hadn't called him back."

"Lynch."

"I didn't promise him anything. But wouldn't you like to save the world?"

"I'd like to teach my students and help save Woodward Academy."

"Well, that would be included in saving the world." He stood there grinning at her. "Tell you what, I'll come to your condo tonight and we'll have dinner and discuss it." He added softly, "Partner-to-partner, friend-to-friend, and anything else of a temporary nature that you decide to give. Doesn't that sound good?"

It sounded too good. She could feel the heat and the sexual tension tingling through her. It was probably a mistake. Just looking at him, she was aware of all that charisma and intelligence and humor that had drawn her to him since the moment they met. She didn't know if she could handle the kind of delicate balance he was offering. She had an idea it could erupt into the passion of those first days when they'd come together.

But if these last three months had taught her anything, it was that she wasn't going to be able to handle the anemic relationship that she'd been demanding. He would always be somewhere in danger and she'd always feel as if they were being cheated. Well, work it out. They were both worth it.

"It sounds like you're manipulating me." She met his eyes. "And I only let you do that if it suits me. It suits me tonight. You'll have to find out what else suits me after we have this 'discussion.'" She made a shooing motion. "Run along. I have work to do. You could start dinner since I might have to worry about saving the world. It seems only fair."

"It does, doesn't it?" He threw back his head and laughed. "By all means, anything you want, Kendra." He winked back at her as he went out the door. "All you have to do is ask . . ."

ABOUT THE AUTHORS

IRIS JOHANSEN is the #1 *New York Times* bestselling author of more than 30 consecutive best sellers. Her series featuring forensic sculptor Eve Duncan has sold over 20 million copies and counting, and was the subject of the acclaimed Lifetime movie *The Killing Game*. Johansen lives near Atlanta, Georgia.

ROY JOHANSEN is an Edgar Award–winning author and the son of Iris Johansen. He has written many acclaimed mysteries, including *Deadly Visions*, *Beyond Belief*, and *The Answer Man*.

Iris Johansen and Roy Johansen have together written *Double Blind*, *Look Behind You*, *Night Watch*, *The Naked Eye*, *Sight Unseen*, *Close Your Eyes*, *Shadow Zone*, *Storm Cycle*, and *Silent Thunder*.